'You fancy sp[...]
a prison camp?'[...]

Gooch was silent. He'd heard the same broadcasts Tully had heard. 'How long will the war last?' he asked eventually.

'The last one went on for four years.'

The thought of four years' imprisonment obviously didn't appeal much. Gooch stared at the end of his cigarette for a while, then he looked at Harkaway.

'What you getting at, Squire?' he asked. 'You're obviously getting at something.'

Harkaway shrugged. 'Why destroy the dump?' he said. 'There's everything we want there. Weapons. Food. Water. Petrol. Why don't we go there, *then* decide what to do?'

'Such as what?'

Harkaway thought for a while. 'Well, we've got more than enough explosive to blow in the front of the cave,' he said. 'Why don't we use some of it to blow up the road to the Tug Argan?'

There was a long silence.

'What for?' Tully asked.

'Stop the Italians.'

Also in Arrow by John Harris

John Harris

HARKAWAY'S SIXTH COLUMN

ARROW BOOKS

Arrow Books Limited
17-21 Conway Street, London W1P 6JD

An imprint of the Hutchinson Publishing Group

London Melbourne Sydney Auckland
Johannesburg and agencies throughout
the world

First published by Hutchinson 1983
Arrow edition 1984

Printed and bound in Great Britain by
Anchor Brendon Ltd, Tiptree, Essex

ISBN 0 09 932960 3

Contents

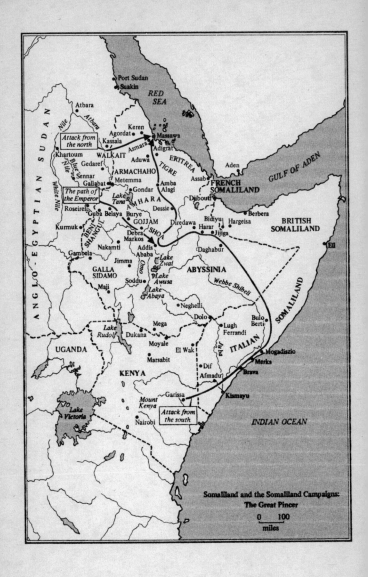

Somaliland and the Somaliland Campaigns:
The Great Pincer

0   100
miles

Author's Note

When Mussolini declared war on Britain and France on 10 June 1940, he thought he was on to a good thing. With the British Expeditionary Force evacuated from France at Dunkirk, and France reeling back before the onslaught of Hitler's armies, victory must have seemed not very far away. He not only expected to lay hold of Nice, Corsica, Savoy and a few other places he claimed belonged to him, but also to pick up from British Somaliland and the Sudan a substantial slice of empire for Italy.

Ever since the conquest of Abyssinia and the dethronement of the Emperor Haile Selassie in 1935–6, he had been piling up in Italian East Africa – which consisted of Italian Somaliland, Eritrea and Abyssinia – troops by the thousand: crack regulars and blackshirts as well as battalions of colonial infantry, and raggle-taggle groups of native guerrilla fighters called bandas. Victory there must have looked easy, especially when, under the terms of the armistice with France, French Somaliland was ceded.

This meant that British Somaliland was cut off and surrounded. To the west lay the great mass of Abyssinia, to the north Italian Eritrea, to the south Italian Somaliland. The only link with the outside world that remained was by sea but, with Italian submarines locking up the Straits of Perim where the Red Sea narrows almost to nothing, and the British hanging on by their teeth in Egypt, there was not much hope of help. South of the Red Sea there was little that could be sent north. Kenya, the Rhodesias and South Africa had entered the war but their forces were ill-equipped and thin on the ground, while Aden, fourteen hours away, had little to spare.

In any case, there wasn't much sense in trying to hang on to British Somaliland. It was tiny, virtually empty and consisted chiefly of desert and mountain. Berbera, its capital, was a huddle of buildings on a blistered shore where the thermometer could climb to 115 degrees Fahrenheit. Besides, while Italy had been piling up weapons and men to the north, south and west, all there was to hang on to the place was a skeleton force, mostly consisting of the King's African Rifles – native troops with white officers and sergeants. And though the Italians had been storing petrol for the possibility of an invasion in British Somaliland, the British had barely enough to get what troops there were to the coast.

Finally, odd as some of the events in the story might seem, many of them actually happened.

Allah created the Arabs, then all
the other peoples of the world,
then he created the Somalis.
Then he laughed.

Arab saying

PART ONE

The Free British

1

'What with their ice cream, their "Oh Soul Mio" and that,' Tully said, 'I reckon the Italians are a right set of twits.'

Gooch studied him, bouncing up and down in unison as the Bedford lorry they were travelling in shook and shuddered on the uneven road. 'Typical of 'em to stab the French in the back,' he agreed.

'Always were untrustworthy buggers with knives,' Tully went on. 'I remember Jimmy Dillon getting involved with one once in Aden. Sailor, I think. Jimmy sent him back where he came from with a few missing teeth.'

Tully smiled reminiscently. He was a small shrivelled man with wide-open innocent eyes that had misled many a girl and many a young officer, a leprechaun face adorned with a thin-nostrilled nose, and a shock of black hair that stood upright on his skull like a yard brush.

'He was a right boy, was Jimmy Dillon,' he went on. 'He was stripped, you know. In front of everybody.'

'Drunk in charge of the guard, wasn't he?'

Tully nodded. 'CO came along and found him. Sergeant tried to save him by backing him up against the wall of the guard 'ouse with a man either side of him and his bayonet jammed in the woodwork. It stopped him swaying, but it didn't hold him up. They shoved him in the cells. I was one of his guards.'

The lorry hit another stretch of ruts and clanked and clattered so much Tully had to remain silent and hang on, bouncing about in the back until it reached level road again.

Gooch looked up. 'Who was the officer, Paddy? When they stripped him.' Gooch leaned forward to offer a ciga-

15

rette, a big man with shoulders that seemed to be bursting out of his shirt, squarely built with hands like shovels and mad dangerous eyes. 'Who was it?'

Tully grinned. 'Fiddleface Patey. You know the one. Long head with hollow cheeks and a big chin.' He looked at the third man in the back of the truck. 'You ever come across Patey, Corp?'

Corporal Harkaway didn't appear to hear. He was a tall good-looking man with well-cut features, pale amber eyes and red hair, and at that moment his mind seemed to be on something beyond the ken of his companions. Tully looked at Gooch and shrugged.

'Go on about Dillon,' Gooch said. 'It isn't everybody gets to see a man stripped in front of the whole battalion.'

Tully obliged willingly enough. 'They forgot to work on his stripes beforehand so they'd come off easy, and Fiddle-face's knife wasn't very sharp. Dillon lent him his. He even helped pull 'em off. He was always polite. He'd still have been serving his sentence but for the war. They sent him out here. I expect they thought that with ten armoured cars, eight old tanks and about four thousand fellers to look after the place, British Somaliland needed every man. Especially Dillon. He knew more about soldiering than everybody else put together, Fiddleface included. They gave him back his stripes and when the Italians came into the war they made him sergeant.'

'Somaliland's different from England,' Gooch agreed.

'A good job, too. One of these days I hope to go home and I hope to Christ it won't be the same as this bloody place.'

There was something in what Tully said. They were travelling across a hot hazy land towards the hills. Small scar-like dongas, or gullies, seamed the scorched thirsty plain which seemed to stretch ahead of them to infinity, incredibly empty, the light brown sand glistening with mica, even the few thorn bushes, grey and brittle with their skeletal branches, seeming to have only a precarious hold on life. There was no green anywhere, not a leaf or a blade of grass, the termite mounds rising like grotesque towers from the wind-flattened, bone-white earth.

As they rattled on, they passed a solitary herdsman by a waterhole with a few goats and hairy fat-tailed sheep and a line of faltering camels, their humps shrivelled and flabby on their bony backs. Over the waterhole, vultures swung in the sky, and nearby were the graves of people who had died trying to reach it, grey acacia branches and brushwood piled on top to protect the bodies from hyenas. Despite the speed at which it was travelling, in the heat of the sun the back of the lorry was stifling.

'It'll be worse now the Eyeties have come into the war,' Gooch said.

Tully nodded. British Somaliland had always been a lost little colony on the shores of the Red Sea. There had never been much contact with the outside world and now, with Hitler rampaging across Europe and France knocked out of the war, it was virtually cut off.

Gooch put his head out, squinting at the empty plain. Vast stretches of it were soft red sand too hot to walk across, others consisted of rough lava boulders which no truck could travel over without rattling itself to pieces. Small dust devils danced among the anthills and, apart from the single macadam strip they were on, the roads were merely motorable camel tracks, traditional paths trodden by Somali or Arab traders, the only arteries of commerce in the whole country away from the highway or the sea coast. It was a land fit only for nomads and fearsome for mechanized transport, and even the best of travellers were brought down by the heat, the dust, diseases such as dysentery and malaria, or stomach disorders caused by the heavily mineralized water.

Gooch seemed to be still preoccupied with the thought of the Italians. "Think they'll come here?' he asked.

'The buggers are on the border already,' Tully pointed out. 'I've heard there are a few Germans with 'em, too. Liaison officers. To stir 'em up.'

'If they'd been coming,' Gooch said, 'wouldn't they have come in June? After they declared war? Or else when they got French Somaliland in the armistice terms?'

Harkaway smiled and spoke for the first time. 'They're coming all right,' he said. 'Why do you think they're bombing Berbera?'

'In answer to *our* raids, p'raps,' Gooch said. 'We've been laying 'em on all over the shop: Diredawa, Gura, Macaca, Asmara, Assab, Kismayu. Besides, it's August now and the South Africans aren't going to sit back and do nothing. That bastard up front who's driving's wondering if he ought to go home and join up. Grobelaar.' He listened to the sound. 'Who'd have a name like that?'

'He would,' Harkaway said. He seemed to have progressed from his brooding mood to an aggressive one. 'He's from the Orange Free State.'

'They're Dutch there, aren't they?'

'*He* doesn't seem to think so. He says they're South African.'

Gooch thought for a moment. 'What's he doing driving a British army truck, anyway?'

'He's a Public Works Department foreman and runs the garage in Berbera for the official cars and, because everybody's getting ready for the Italians whom you say aren't coming, there was nobody else who knew the way. Only Grobelaar, Willie up front and one or two others. Sergeant Conyers, who was there last time, went with everybody else to the Tug Argan to stop the Eyeties.'

'Grobelaar's a civvy.' It seemed to worry Gooch. 'With a glass eye,' he added.

Harkaway gave him a cold look. 'If the Italians come,' he said, 'there won't be any such thing as a civilian. Not even Grobelaar.'

There was a long pause, because what Harkaway said was true. There were so few Europeans in British Somaliland they'd all be in it.

'Italians,' Gooch announced with ponderous wisdom, 'are treacherous bastards. What did Willie think of it?'

Willie – Lieutenant William Watson – riding in the cab with Grobelaar, the driver, his eyes everywhere, knew a little more than the three in the back and was well aware that the moment of crisis had already arrived. If Mussolini decided to launch an onslaught south from Abyssinia, there wasn't much to stop it. The British East African countries had nothing, and the South African Air Force planes were largely old passenger transports – and German ones at that! The Brigade Intelligence Officer, in fact, had bet him the Italians would invade before August and when August had come had offered double or quits for another week, but wouldn't go beyond that.

Restlessly, Gooch stuck his head out of the vehicle again. Not far away a range of razor-sharp hills rose in ridges, first blue, then purple, then misty grey. Up there in a cave was a hidden dump the British had set up against the possibility of invasion and when Lieutenant Watson had been given the job of destroying it he had picked Harkaway, Gooch and Tully because they were all specialists – Gooch an armourer, Tully a radio operator and Harkaway an engineer. Between them, they would make sure the job was done properly. There had to be no mistake because the Royal Navy had already prepared plans for an evacuation.

Gooch was scowling. 'Why did they put the bloody dump so far out, anyway?' he asked. 'It's right on the border.'

'I expect the idea was to stop them before they left Abyssinia,' Harkaway said. 'But that was when we had French Somaliland with us. When French Somaliland was ceded to the Italians, a lot of people changed their minds.'

Tully looked at Gooch. Harkaway always seemed to know the answer to any military problem. They assumed it was because he had a friend in the officers' mess – his educated accent seemed to suggest he might have – but in fact there was more to it than that.

'We'll be lucky to find it,' Gooch grumbled.

'I know where it is,' Tully said. 'I went once. You turn off into the hills when you get to Eil Dif. You ever been to Eil Dif? Used to be a trading station or something. Usual wog town with a few bigger houses where Europeans used to live. Willie said they were built by the slavers and abandoned when the ivory and ostrich feather trade fell off. The local wogs won't live in 'em. They say they're haunted by djinns. There's a camel track goes up into the hills. The

Habr Odessi used it to hide their animals when the Hararis came raiding.'

'*And* the Yunis, the Dolbahantas, the Abos and the Wadigallas,' Harkaway said.

'Yeh. Them too.'

'Well –' Gooch shrugged ' – it's nice to know *somebody* knows his way about. Suppose we got up there and Willie fell out of the lorry and broke his neck or something. How'd we know how to get back?'

'Grobelaar knows,' Tully said. 'He's been up.'

They became silent, wondering about the future. British Somaliland was never a place for comfort and now it was totally isolated. At the best of times there wasn't much to recommend it; now, there was even less, because the only link with the outside world was by a small weekly steamer to Aden that carried camels – and stank of them, too! – or by a small ship built for the bitter Baltic trade and not intended for the tropics. A hell-hole at any time; to get a cool bath in Berbera, you ran the taps in the evening and took your dip the following morning.

The discussion in the back of the lorry stopped as they roared through a small town coiled round the rocks at the foot of the hills, a mere collection of mud huts, their roofs of straw as dry as tinder. A few Somalis, lean men with arrogant, cruel faces, studied them as they passed, their women behind them, tall and slender, their native skirts tight over their hips, watching with black liquid eyes, their children beside them, sifting sand through their fingers on the ground. An old man sat in front of the huts, picking at one of his feet, his face blank. Behind the native dwellings there were a few taller European buildings, crumbling ruins with crazy balconies, broken shutters, peeling paint and plaster, their windows empty, their roofs fallen in.

'Eil Dif,' Tully said.

The lorry began to grind its way uphill. It was an old vehicle and its gears were noisy. They were winding now between the stony pinnacles and towers that fringed the road away from the plain which stretched below them in a never-ending brown sheet to the south. As they climbed higher, the discussion started again and they were so busy talking, none of them was aware of the danger that was approaching. The truck was jolting over a patch of stony road and everything was rattling like a set of tin cans, the box containing Tully's radio banging against the steel floor, the tailgate – which was an indifferent fit – providing a metallic accompaniment.

'One Englishman's equal to two Germans, three Frenchmen and any number of Eyeties,' Tully was saying.

'That's rubbish.'

'It isn't rubbish.'

'It is, you know.'

'It isn't, you know.'

The argument was just rising in a crescendo when the truck stopped dead, sending Tully's box sliding to the front with Tully, Gooch and Harkaway after it. It was only as the clattering stopped that they heard the howl of an aeroplane engine.

'Christ!' Tully scrambled to his feet and dived for the tailgate. Somewhere in front, Lieutenant Watson was yelling for them to take cover.

As Tully, Gooch, Harkaway and Grobelaar, the driver, bolted for a patch of thorn bush on the offside of the lorry, Lieutenant Watson was running as fast as his legs could carry him from the nearside for a clump of rocks. There were two aeroplanes, both biplanes, the sun catching their varnished wings, and as they turned towards them, they saw the stub noses round the radial engines, the wheel spats of the fixed undercarriages and the W-shape of the interplane struts. The white cross on the rudders was centred by the arms of the House of Savoy and on the wings was the emblem of the fasces.

'They're Eyeties,' Tully yelled above the howling of the engines. 'You can see the firewood and chopper.'

The aeroplanes, Fiat CR42s, were heading towards them now in a shallow dive, coming nearer and nearer until they could see the brown and green speckled camouflage. Even as they saw the flash of the guns over the engine cowling, they were aware of the little row of dust spurts flung up on the left side of the lorry. As they caught up with him, Watson seemed to do a double somersault and went rolling over and over like a shot rabbit among the rocks. Tully, Gooch, Harkaway and the South African cowered in the bush as the bullets sent small cascades of dry earth trickling down the hillside on to them.

As the aeroplanes lifted into the sky, turned on their wingtips and raced away north, Harkaway raised his head and stared towards the lorry. The canvas cover showed small rents where it had been torn but otherwise it seemed unharmed. But, beyond it, Lieutenant Watson lay among the rocks in a crumpled heap, a silent dusty figure, the blood red and shining on his shirt in the sun.

2

Watson was huddled in what seemed an impossible posture. His head was under his shoulder and his right leg was twisted up under his humped body. There were two holes in his back, both leaking blood.

Harkaway was turning him over as the others reached him. His eyes were open, though there was dust on them, as if there hadn't been enough strength left to close the eyelids. His jaw moved as he tried to say something, then his head fell back and his body became limp. Harkaway laid him down and straightened up, wiping the blood off his hands on his shorts.

'The bastards,' Tully said. 'The lying, treacherous bastards!'

'We *are* supposed to be at war,' Harkaway pointed out calmly.

There was a long silence. Gooch stared at the sky as if half-expecting the aeroplanes to return. 'What happens now?' he asked. 'We'd better get back to base, hadn't we?'

'Why?' Harkaway asked.

'Because the officer's dead.'

'We all know what he was up to. So why not go on and do it?'

'It's not our bloody place to do things.'

'Why not?' Harkaway snapped. 'We've got brains. We don't have to have a bloody officer standing over us, saying "Do this" and "Do that" for it to be done. We've come to blow up a dump. Why don't we?'

Gooch sneered. 'Listen to the gentleman ranker who knows everything,' he said.

Harkaway's face went stiff. Everybody knew he'd joined the army because of some private disgrace he never spoke of. He was well-educated, intelligent and, from the things he said occasionally, had once been used to money. It rankled sometimes, but it never made any difference when there was anything to be done. A few of them thought the stripes he wore on his arm were there because he had influence among the officers, perhaps even because someone had known him in the old days, at least because he spoke better than the others. The truth was that Harkaway was a natural leader, and all too often they did things merely because he said they should. As they were doing now.

Gooch frowned, unwilling to concede anything. 'You know how to blow it up?'

'Of course I do. I helped Willie more than once.'

'You have to get it right.'

'I'll get it right.'

Tully looked from one to the other but nobody had any better idea and he shuffled his boots in the sand awkwardly and looked at Watson's body. Grobelaar picked up the dead man's cap and placed it over his face. He was a quiet man, not old but with a deeply lined face and a cheap glass eye that stared unblinkingly at you like the glass eye of a doll.

'I suppose we'd better bury the poor bastard,' Tully said.

Gooch unstrapped the spade from the side of the truck and began to dig. The ground was stony and difficult and the hole they scooped out was shallow.

'It'll have to do,' Harkaway said.

They laid Watson in the hole, but only after Harkaway had removed his binoculars, identity discs and watch, and been through his pockets and stripped him of anything that might be of value. There wasn't much – a few cigarettes, a little money, a letter from a girl in Nairobi. They also removed his boots and khaki peaked cap because they thought they might be useful and it seemed silly to put them under the soil.

As they threw the sandy earth over him, Tully looked at Harkaway. 'Do we say a prayer?'

'Know one?'

'No.'

'Then we'll not bother. I don't suppose he'll mind.'

'He wasn't a bad bastard,' Gooch offered as an epitaph.

Harkaway threw the boots and the cap in the back of the lorry, and shared the cigarettes and money among them. Tully offered his share of cigarettes round at once and they lit up and stood drawing at them for a while, all of them deep in thought.

So far Grobelaar had said nothing. Now he spoke. '*Kom, kerels,*' he said. '*Kom*. Let's go.'

They were just heading for the lorry again when Harkaway stopped. He was staring at the plain, his eyes narrowed against the sun's glare, a handsome rangy figure with yellow foxy eyes, holding the cigarette in his fingers, the smoke dribbling from his nostrils, and as the others joined him, he gestured. Below them, heading north-east, they could see small specks trailing feathers of dust. Nobody spoke, merely watching as the specks drew closer and they could identify them as lorries. There was a long column of them, led by armoured cars.

'Eyeties,' Harkaway said flatly. 'Heading for Hargeisa. From Jijiga in Abyssinia.'

By now the vehicles on the plain were passing through Eil Dif along the road they'd been travelling on themselves before they'd turned into the hills. As they watched, another CR42 flew past, just to the south, roaring along in a wide curve to reconnoitre the land ahead. They watched it as it turned and headed north-east. Soon afterwards they heard several dull thuds.

'Bombs,' Tully said.

The sound seemed to bring a realization of their plight. They were a hundred miles from the coast with a whole enemy army between them and safety. Not long before they'd been deriding the Italians, but it didn't require much imagination to realize, no matter how indifferent they might be as soldiers, that there were more than enough of them to stop any attempt at escape. The future suddenly looked very bleak.

Harkaway lifted the binoculars they'd taken from Watson's body. With them he could see the passing lorries were full of men and bristled with weapons.

'They'll be making for Berbera,' he said.

'They're welcome to it,' Tully said bitterly.

'What do we do now?' Gooch asked. 'Give ourselves up?' He sounded shocked.

'Isn't much alternative, is there?' Tully said gloomily, only too well aware of what being a prisoner of war meant because the Italian radio had been full of the thousands captured at Dunkirk.

'They might *not* get to Berbera,' Harkaway pointed out calmly. 'There are road blocks and demolitions, and they're waiting for 'em at the Tug Argan gap.'

'They'll never stop 'em,' Gooch said. 'Watson reckoned they had twenty-five thousand men for Somaliland. We've got the King's African Rifles, the Black Watch and a few odds and ends. They'll be in Hargeisa by tomorrow and in Berbera in a week. Only one thing to do.'

'You fancy spending the rest of the war in a prison camp?' Harkaway asked.

Gooch was silent. He'd heard the same broadcasts Tully had heard. 'How long will the war last?' he asked eventually.

'The last one went on for four years.'

The thought of four years' imprisonment obviously didn't appeal much. Gooch stared at the end of his cigarette for a while, then he looked at Harkaway.

'What you getting at, Squire?' he asked. 'You're obviously getting at something.'

Harkaway shrugged. 'Why destroy the dump?' he said. 'There's everything we want there. Weapons. Food. Water. Petrol. Why don't we go there, *then* decide what to do?'

'Such as what?'

Harkaway thought for a while. 'Well, we've got more than enough explosive to blow in the front of the cave,' he said. 'Why don't we use some of it to blow up the road to the Tug Argan?'

There was a long silence.

'What for?' Tully asked.

'Stop the Italians.'

'You want to win the VC or something?'

Harkaway smiled. 'There's that bit they call the Wirir Gorge,' he said. 'A nice big bang there and the Italians in front will be cut off.'

'Not for long, I'll bet.'

'No,' Harkaway agreed. 'But it might help.'

It seemed to make sense and didn't seem too dangerous.

'We can always chuck our hand in later if there's no alternative,' Harkaway went on. 'We might even think of a way of getting down to Kenya.'

The dump was at a place called Shimber Addi, a natural stronghold in the Bur Yi range which rose a thousand feet from the plain. On the peak of the hill was an old fortress built of stone, complete with firing slits and machicolations, which had been used at the beginning of the century by Mohammed bin Abdullah Hassan, the Mad Mullah, in his campaigns against the British. The place was intersected by deep ravines covered everywhere with boulders and thick scrub. Up here the desert gave way to a greener land with giant cedars and flowers, and the ravine sides were honeycombed with caves capable of sheltering large numbers of men and animals. During the days when Abdullah Hassan had been defying the might of the British Empire the bush round the fort had been cleared to provide a field of fire but it was growing back now and the fort had been destroyed both by bombing and by the pick-axes and crowbars of British soldiers when the Mullah's power had crumbled.

The dump was in one of the largest caves, and the narrow entrance was between two tall pillars of stone. They shifted the rocks that had been piled in the entrance and stood staring into a large cool vault with numerous passages running off to a series of smaller caves.

Harkaway shone a torch. Among the piles of crates and cases along the walls of the caves were a few animals' skulls as if the place had been inhabited at some point by a leopard, but they found they were better off than they had thought.

'Stew,' Tully said, peering at labels. 'Tinned carrots.

Tinned peas. Tinned potatoes. Christ, we've got everything we need here! There's even some canned beer. And – Jesus! – whisky!'

'That'll be for the officers.'

'Petrol. Fags. Toilet powder. Blacking. Blanco.' Tully's head turned. 'Typical of the army. Make sure you're healthy and don't get heat sores, but make sure also you've got the means to shine your boots and whiten your webbing.'

Their spirits were beginning to lift. Suddenly the prospect of being marooned behind the whole of the Italian army didn't seem too bad. Shimber Addi was pretty inaccessible – as the Mad Mullah had decided thirty years before – it wasn't desert, and there was food.

'What else is there?' Harkaway asked.

'Grease,' Gooch said. 'Gun oil. To make sure your bundook works proper. Water down at Eil Dif.'

Harkaway was studying the crates. 'Two Brens,' he said. 'Two water-cooled Vickers. Four Lewises. They must have been in a hurry to get to the Tug Argan to leave this lot here. You reckon they're all right, Gooch?'

'They look it.' Gooch was bending over the crates, a crowbar in his hand. 'They'll need cleaning – they're covered with grease – but they seem all right. There must be a couple of hundred rifles here.'

'Good ones?'

'Depends what you call good. Most of 'em seem to be single-shot Martinis. Old as God. Recoil like a kick in the face. Big bore. Soft-nosed bullet. Used to use 'em on the North-west Frontier for native levies.'

'I expect that's what they're doing here,' Harkaway said. 'In case they raised native troops who never aim properly anyway.' He bent over the boxes. 'Plenty of ammunition,' he went on. 'All types.'

'They made it good and secret,' Tully said, staring about him. 'Nobody's been here.'

'If they had, we'd have been out long since stopping a massacre.' Harkaway was peering about him, his eyes alert and interested. 'This country's full of warriors and they'd as soon kill as look at each other.'

It didn't take them long to get a fire going. There were four large primus stoves but Harkaway suggested that, since they had no idea how long they were likely to be there, it might be a good idea to conserve their supply of paraffin for the hurricane lamps, and there were plenty of dried thorn bushes about. With the aid of twigs, they soon had a billy can of water boiling. They were even beginning to feel cheerful and, since it was their first day and Watson's unexpected death had shocked them a little, it didn't seem amiss to have a can of beer each.

'It's hot enough for *two*,' Gooch pointed out.

'One,' Harkaway insisted. 'We might be here a long time.'

As they prepared the meal they were all busy with their thoughts. Harkaway sat by the fire, staring at the flames, and Grobelaar perched on a rock overlooking the plain, playing a nostalgic Afrikaner tune on a harmonica. Gooch, the armourer, was quietly rubbing at his rifle with a cloth while Tully crouched over the radio. He had discovered that a bullet had struck the transmitter so that, while they could hear what was happening, they couldn't tell anyone where they were or what had happened. There seemed to be a lot of radio traffic and it was clear there was a lot of panic on the road towards Berbera.

By the following day, the suggestion Harkaway had made of harassing the Italians seemed to have lost its point because most of the twenty-five thousand Italians heading for Berbera were already between them and the British, anyway.

'We could still blow up the road,' Harkaway said.

Nobody argued. Three of them were regular soldiers, two of them nearing the end of their career when the war had broken out and, though Harkaway was the youngest, he was also the natural leader of the group, with a brisk no-nonsense manner that nobody ever questioned. Even Grobelaar knew the facts as well as any of them. He had arrived in Berbera from Cape Town donkey's years before and had worked with the army since the war had started the previous year, a good mechanic who knew his job, stoop-shouldered from bending over engines but with an anxious look always on his face as if he constantly expected to be let down. The few officials in Berbera he'd dealt with had always been urging him on with 'Come on, Piet, you can do it,' when they wanted him to repair their vehicles out of turn, but they'd never invited him to eat with them, had never offered him anything more than an occasional beer, and his worried expression seemed to suggest that if he'd ever realized how difficult his job would be, he'd never have taken it on.

Two days later they were still there, still trying to decide what to do. By this time they had learned from the radio that Hargeisa had fallen and that the Italians were heading for the Tug Argan Gap while the Royal Navy was preparing for the evacuation to Aden. Abyssinians, Arabs, Indians, even some Somalis, with their wives and families, had gone rather than accept Italian rule. Civilians and administrative officials had also left and the base personnel were now aboard the ships to make room for the troops who would be arriving from the last-ditch defences that had been constructed in the hills.

Since there was nothing they could do, they made themselves comfortable. It wasn't all that difficult because even in Berbera there had never been either fresh milk or butter and most things had come out of cans, and in the hills the thirsty climate of the plain and the sea-coast gave way to one that was equable, even invigorating. There was grass here instead of sand, box trees, acacias, a variety of flowering aloes with crimson and yellow blossoms, gum, myrrh and frankincense. In some sheltered spots there were junipers or wild fig trees, and in a few of the gorges even maidenhair, while everywhere there were euphorbias lending an artificial stage-like effect with their candelabra branches and dark creased trunks.

'All we need is a few girls,' Tully pointed out cheerfully. 'They're not bad, these Somalis. Slim. Nice hips and taut little tits.'

'Just try and take one,' Harkaway said quietly, 'and their brothers'll have your balls off quick as light.'

'Yeh – well –' Tully considered this. 'Of course, you could do it proper. They'd sell you one.'

'Twelve camels is about the going rate, I believe.'

Gooch was silent for a moment. 'Or a rifle,' he said slowly. 'We've got plenty of them.'

Ten days later they had still made no effort to move because there seemed to be even less point than there had been earlier. At the Tug Argan a desperate battle was being fought and they could hear the thump of bombs and the thud of artillery. Occasionally, they saw Italian aircraft looking for targets, and the main road below the hills was swarming with Italian troops. The native bandas were constantly moving up and down it, wild strong-looking woolly-headed men in white robes criss-crossed by cartridge belts, more than willing to fight, and it seemed better not to try their patience too much. The conquest of Somaliland seemed assured now and perhaps it would be easier to stay put until the dust had settled.

The chief problem was boredom. They hadn't much to say to each other. They were all too different and Harkaway was distinctly unforthcoming. But he always *had* been unforthcoming and they put it down, as everybody did, to his past. Harkaway's past had been mentioned in whispers in the bars and canteens in Berbera but never to Harkaway. Again and again, it slipped out, in references to people he knew, to hunt balls, to taxis when everybody else rode in buses, and for the most part his friends had exchanged glances and said nothing. Now he was brooding over something. Though the others didn't know it, he was becoming ambitious. He could see no future in merely hiding from the Italians, and was itching to do someone some damage. In his lumpish, awkward, aggressive way, Gooch resented Harkaway's aloofness but there was nothing he could do about it. If Harkaway chose to ignore them, then that was exactly what he did.

'He's all right,' Tully said in answer to Gooch's grumbles. 'He just gets things on his mind. What do you think about the situation, Kom-Kom?'

Grobelaar shrugged and gave a shadowy, cobwebby smile. '*Alles sal regt kom*,' he said.

'What's that mean, you Dutch bastard?'

'It means everything will work out.'

The fight at the Tug Argan went on. Every day the Italians surged forward to break the British grip, so their mechanized columns could burst through to the coast, and since there were just too many of them, positions were being encircled and the British were slowly having to withdraw, first from one hill, then from another.

But the troop embarkation in Berbera had already begun and, as men withdrew from their positions and headed for the coast they were taken on board ship while the Italians were still licking their wounds in the hills. The town was full of burning vehicles and by 17 August, less than a fortnight from the beginning of the Italian advance, the men on the hills above Eil Dif learned that the convoys were finally at sea and heading for Aden. Somaliland was lost.

'What now?' Gooch asked heavily. Automatically, his eyes turned to Harkaway. The idea of blowing up the road seemed entirely pointless now and what was in his mind was merely a means of getting south to Kenya.

Tully wasn't listening. He was staring about him. 'You know,' he observed unexpectedly, 'it's worth a bit, this lot.'

'What lot?' Gooch asked.

'This lot here. Two Vickers water-cooled, two Brens, four Lewises, fifty-four Enfield rifles, a bit out of date but still working, one hundred and fifty Martinis, *very* out of date but also still working, four mortars, two pack guns, a few land mines, several boxes of grenades, and Christ alone knows how much small arms ammo. Seems a pity to blow it all up. Think what it'd be worth if we could sell it.'

Gooch frowned. 'Who'd buy it?'

'The wogs.' Tully gestured. 'For hunting. They'd jump at it. There's game around. Especially up here. Dik-dik and gerenuk. I've seen 'em. Perhaps bigger stuff even. All we have to do is show 'em how to use 'em.'

There was a long silence. 'It belongs to the army,' Grobelaar ventured.

'Not now, mate,' Tully said. 'They abandoned it.'

'How do they pay?' Gooch asked. 'I haven't much use for bloody camels. There's no call for 'em in Islington, where I come from.'

Tully smiled. 'There's silver, old son. Silver bangles. Silver anklets. Silver necklaces. You've seen 'em. They'd give silver for a rifle.'

Gooch looked about him uncertainly and Tully went on eagerly. 'We could make a fortune,' he said. 'Make our pile, head for Djibouti with a camel or two and use some of it to hire a boat to get to Aden. We could head for Khartoum. Live there in luxury. Nice house. A few birds. Perhaps we could even get down to Portuguese East Africa. They're neutral there and I bet there are a few skulking there already to avoid the war. We could live like lords.'

3

In the town of Bidiyu, General Ettore Guidotti was in the process of settling in. Bidiyu lay astride one of the roads that ran from Jijiga in Abyssinia across the border of British Somaliland to Berbera, and his job and that of the 7th Savoia Battalion, supported by the 49th Colonial Infantry, was to make sure it remained open.

There was little to fear now from the British, because they'd all disappeared, and Italian troops had even pushed across the borders of Italian Somaliland and Abyssinia into Kenya and the Anglo-Egyptian Sudan. There was little to do, in fact, except bring Roman culture and the dignity of the Duce's empire to the conquered country and wait until Graziani pushed through Egypt from Libya to join them.

Bidiyu was a collection of white buildings surrounded by feathery pepper trees and flat-topped acacias, with here and there a few staunch zinnias thrusting upwards in muted pinks and muddy yellows. It never looked at its best in the hard glare of the sun, when you seemed to see only the shrivelled old men and women gossiping under the thorn trees of the marketplace. Camels plodded by and men from the interior stacked up the piles of dried sheepskins they had brought for sale. Somali labourers, still staggered by the change of ownership but sensible enough to realize it meant little difference as long as they were willing to work for the new authority, sang a high-pitched song as they toiled on the road out of town. A disgruntled Indian merchant who had not bothered to leave with the British sipped spiced tea in the shade of a coffee house, and Somali girls, lean and beautiful, moved past with a grace that would have been the envy of Roman society, enticing in their gaily-coloured robes.

Guidotti had taken over the biggest house in the town, the old British Residence, a place of stone blocks of brownish coral colour with a wooden verandah running the whole way round the second floor. Once it had been luxurious after the Victorian fashion but, between the departure of the British and the arrival of the Italians, Somali looters had rampaged through the place. However, the furniture, carpets, curtains and beds remained, though here and there scattered papers still blew about the corners of the gardens, and on the walls surrounding the house, a few muscular slogans had been painted: *Credere, Obbedire, Combattere* and *Vivere Pericolosamente*. Believe, Obey, Fight and Live Dangerously were good fascist creeds, Guidotti felt. He would have preferred them to have been painted somewhere else, but there were many young men anxious to show their strength and their courage and, if nothing else, the slogans showed their eagerness.

The house was pleasant enough. Its previous occupant had lived well in a country that had little to recommend it, and there was French wine in the cellar to add to the chianti Guidotti had brought with him. The garden was overgrown but there were a few trees and a few bougainvillaeas to give shade to the wide verandah, while the view of the purple hills that surrounded the town was magnificent.

Among the things Guidotti was expected to do was to erect a column with the date of the capture, topped by a bust of the Duce to show who was in charge, and a few kilometre posts of the type that studded the road which ran through Italian Somaliland from Mogadiscio. In Italian Somaliland they were tall and square and made of concrete, gave the distances to the Abyssinian towns of Addis Ababa, Jijiga and Harar, and announced the existence of the Strada Imperiale, or the Via Graziani, as the first governor of the new colony had chosen to call the road. Guidotti's road was to be the Strada Del Duce and he intended to immortalize himself by calling the stretch for which he was responsible the Via Guidotti. There might be objections later, but once it was set in concrete with a fascist eagle or two, complete with laurel wreaths, fasces and the letters SPQR, in the manner of the old Roman legions, it might well remain there for a thousand years.

It would require a parade, of course, with the troops drawn up in lines, the priest and his acolytes in their robes, fascist hymns, and Guidotti in full dress of white jacket, gold-braided lanyard and sword. It was a splendid sword and Guidotti always enjoyed wearing it. He was well aware that it had no purpose whatsoever except as decoration and he was intelligent enough to realize it made him look a little over-dressed, even a little pompous. But he was proud of it. It had been presented to him by General Franco after the war in Spain, and was of finest Toledo steel with a chased blade, a hand-grip of gold wire and a gold-cord swordknot to bind it to his hand if he should ever need to use it, which was most unlikely.

'Not too many wreaths for the dead,' he instructed Colonel Piccio, his chief of staff. 'We wouldn't wish to be too ostentatious.'

He walked to the table and, pouring two glasses of the recently departed Englishman's cool Muscadet, handed one to Piccio.

'To the Duce,' Piccio said loyally.

Guidotti smiled. 'And to *us*, Piccio. You, me, Di Sanctis and the rest of us. After all, the Duce spends *his* time in Rome in considerable comfort. We're the ones who do the work.'

Piccio clicked his heels. 'To *us*, Excellency,' he agreed. 'I think we have this place well under control with little likelihood of trouble.'

'Who could cause it?' Guidotti asked. 'There is no one.'

Well, almost no one.

By this time, the men in the cave above Eil Dif had almost forgotten the war.

The plan to hit at the Italians had finally been abandoned. There was no longer the thump of bombs, the thud of artillery or the flickering light of gunfire in the sky at night.

They had seen lorries approaching from the north-east that were full of British prisoners, and Italian vehicles were now moving freely backwards and forwards along the long straight road with the slow trains of camels while, overhead, aeroplanes droned in safety across the brassy sky.

The Italians were in control. The war was over in that part of the world.

Undisturbed except for the wild cackle of a hyena or the scuffle as an occasional dik-dik or gerenuk slipped among the rocks, they were quite unconcerned. Once they smelled leopard and heard its throaty roar in the night but they saw no sign of anything but troops of baboons that sat among the rocks watching them.

'Bloody things,' Tully said. 'Once when we were out on an exercise near Sheikh the bastards attacked us.'

'What did you do?' Gooch leaned back lazily, a cigarette in his mouth.

'We chucked rocks at 'em.'

'Stop 'em?'

'No. The bastards chucked 'em back.'

During the afternoon, they took the Bedford down to Eil Dif, the back full of empty petrol cans.

The people occupying Eil Dif were Habr Odessi, a clan of the great northern tribe of Aidegalla, and they found the chief in the coffee house in the marketplace, an emaciated old man with a shock of greying hair and one leg crippled from a sword slash thirty years before when the Mad Mullah was terrorizing the country. He stood leaning on his staff listening politely as Harkaway explained in barrakee hausa what they had to offer for the privilege of using the tribe's waterhole, then he gestured at one of the waiting Somalis who vanished and returned with a tall smiling villain of a man with a limp. He wore a long robe, an embroidered cap like a tarboosh and an over-large pair of western boots devoid of laces.

'Hello, Chief,' he said in English. '*Salaam aleikum. Ma nabad ba*? Is it peace?'

'*Wa aleikum, salaam*,' Harkaway replied. '*Wa nabad*. It is peace. You speak English?'

'Yes, effendi. We have palaver?'

'We wish to replenish our water,' Harkaway said. 'We also wish to barter for fresh meat.'

'We have meat to sell, effendi. How much do you offer?'

Harkaway produced several tins of boot polish. 'Very good,' he explained. 'You polish your sandals. Like this.'

He pushed forward the toe of his boot, carefully rubbed up for the occasion. 'Very good,' he said again. 'Your women like it.'

The limping man smiled and shook his head. 'Effendi, I am Yussuf abu Jibril. But I am known to the English sailors as Shovel Joe. I stoker in ships from Aden. My mother Arab. My father Abyssinian. I speak English good. I go many times Cape Town. Once London. All white people have boots like that. I see it. It is worth nothing.'

Harkaway studied the Somali silently. It was not uncommon for a Somali to go to sea, returning after several years with a suit, a stiff collar and a valise full of money and trinkets bought in Cape Town or Alexandria, and then to abandon them all for the nomad life of his ancestors, complete with camels and a herd of sheep and goats and wearing the tobe, the traditional dress of the country, which was nothing more than fifteen feet of Manchester cotton cloth worn like a toga.

'We're up against a business tycoon here,' he muttered to the others. Turning to the Somali he asked, 'How much do you want then, Joe?'

Yussuf shrugged. 'What have you got, effendi? We are a poor people. All Somalis are poor people. It is the will of Allah, though I sometimes wonder why, if Allah is so merciful, he created Somaliland so empty. I leave the sea because too hard work and I hurt my foot. Perhaps I become chief when Italians come to Eil Dif. Chief Abduruman already much old, and I speak also Italian, you see. Many times into Massawa and Mogadiscio.'

Harkaway glanced at the others. Yussuf abu Jibril might well be a useful ally. He thrust the tins of boot polish at him. 'Might as well keep them,' he said. 'Give 'em to your wives. Polish their navels.'

Yussuf smiled but offered nothing in return, and, glancing again at the others, Harkaway went on briskly.

'Tell your chief we have guns to sell,' he said.

Gooch and Tully glanced at each other. Harkaway was a private sort of person and they never knew what he was thinking – usually because he was way ahead of them – but this was unexpected.

'Life's hard,' Harkaway went on. 'Not much meat. Goats and sheep hard to come by.' His arm swept the desert. 'Buck out there. Dik-dik and gerenuk. Even some kudu in the hills. Good eating but hard to catch. Run fast. Faster than a man can run. Further than he can throw spear. Gun stop them. Gun powerful.'

Yussuf smiled. 'Where are these guns? You take us to them?'

'No.' Harkaway smiled back. 'We bring them to you.'

Harkaway didn't bother to explain his impulsive offer and no one attempted to ask him. It had always been assumed that Harkaway was the brains of the group and it was an indication of his potential that they didn't argue.

The following day, when they headed down to Eil Dif, hidden beneath the water skins in the back of the lorry were three of the ancient Martinis.

'We show you.' Harkaway gestured at Tully as the tribesmen appeared, watching warily. 'Set up a target, Paddy.'

Tully walked away from the village and placed a bully beef tin they had brought with them on a small boulder. Harkaway lay down on the sand and took aim. As the crack of the shot echoed in the ruins of the old houses behind them the can jumped into the air to land on the earth with a puff of dust.

'Your people throw a spear that far?' he asked.

The men behind him were silent, leaning forward on their spears, covetously watching the rifle, their eyes glinting with menace.

'You show?' Yussuf indicated the young men.

'Sure.' Harkaway picked a tall young Somali with a lean, intelligent face and handed him the rifle. The Somali backed away but between them Harkaway and Yussuf got him on the ground with the rifle to his shoulder.

The can was set up again, the sights were explained and the Somali fired. The can remained where it was.

'He yanked at the trigger,' Gooch said. 'He didn't squeeze.'

Harkaway took the young tribesman to one side. 'What him name him?' he asked Yussuf.

'He Abdillahi. He speak small-small English. He fireman one-time, like me. One year. Me many.'

'Right. You tell Abdillahi.' Harkaway took the rifle and demonstrated. 'Butt well into the shoulder and up against the cheek. Left hand well down the barrel. Right hand holding the narrow part of the stock. Then you squeeze the trigger. Once for the first pressure. Then again for the second. Tell him to try it again.'

Yussuf explained carefully, his thin black hands fluttering over the rifle as the young Somali held it. This time, though the can didn't jump, the bullet threw up a puff of dust only a few feet to the right.

'Better,' Harkaway said. 'Go over it again.'

The Somali's third shot came within a foot of the can.

'Near enough to bring down a buck. And he could do better if he were closer.' Harkaway went to great lengths to explain the use of the sights. 'You'll need some ammunition to practise with, of course. Nobody can shoot without practice.' He held out a sack containing cartridges. 'Much as you like. Fire a few off. Two days from now you'll be bringing buck down like clay pipes at a fair.'

Yussuf went into a huddle with the old chief and several of the young men. Behind them the women of the village stood in a small group, chattering in shrill voices. Then the ex-fireman turned round.

'How many women you want in exchange, effendi?'

Tully licked his lips but Harkaway shook his head.

'Not women. Money.'

'No have money, effendi.'

'Gold? They have gold in Abyssinia. Don't tell me none

ever found its way down here. Or silver. You've got silver. I've seen your women wearing bangles and anklets.'

'Effendi –' Yussuf smiled his sly smile – 'when the English retreated to the sea, they left arms and equipment at the Tug Argan. I hear of a young boy in Hargeisa with three rifles he find.' His face wrinkled. 'Besides, effendi, what is to stop our young men following you and taking them for ourselves?'

There was a long silence then Grobelaar bent, his hand over his face. When he straightened up again he held up his hand. Between his fingers he held his glass eye. A chorus of 'oohs' and 'aahs' broke from the young men and women and Grobelaar smiled, his face oddly lopsided with its empty eye-socket.

'Fine fetish,' he pointed out. 'You can tell your young men I shall always leave my eye behind me so that I can see if anyone comes.'

They haggled for another ten minutes, then a price was agreed, less than they'd expected but enough. The ex-fireman disappeared and returned soon afterwards with a leather bag full of silver bangles and necklets. The rifles changed hands.

'Now you want women?' Yussuf asked, smiling. 'Perhaps they earn their bangles back.'

Tully looked at Gooch; Gooch looked at Grobelaar, who looked faintly embarrassed.

'Leave me out, man,' he said.

Yussuf indicated a group of girls. They were all slim, their robes tight over their hips and breasts, their dark head-cloths shading exquisitely moulded faces and black spaniel eyes.

'Somali woman always obey her man,' he said. 'Make good wife.'

They drove back up the hill, all of them satisfied with the morning's work.

'That was a good idea about the eye, Kom-Kom,' Harkaway said.

'I've done it before,' Grobelaar explained. 'It always

works. They know there's a trick somewhere but they're never prepared to chance it.'

Gooch was eyeing the leather bag full of trinkets. 'Them bracelets'll fetch a bit in Mombasa,' he commented.

'If you sell 'em in Mombasa,' Harkaway said, 'you'll be a damn fool. They'd bring only beer money there. Save 'em and sell them in London when you go home. The society girls will go for that sort of thing in a big way.'

'How do you know?'

Harkaway gave him a cold look. 'I haven't always been a bloody soldier.'

'Gentleman ranker out on the spree.' Gooch grinned. 'Damned from here to eternity.'

Three days later, a party of Habr Odessi herders from Eil Dif came on a party of Illas, a clan belonging to the Harari Kibal group, using the waterhole at Daraba they called El Wak, the Wells of God, which they considered belonged to the Habr Odessi. They were well aware that the previous year when the rains were slow to come and the country was drying up into a drought, the Harari had been *selling* their water. Which was fine for the Harari but, when there was no money, hard for the Habr Odessi whose herds died. Stumbling on the Illas, therefore, the Habr Odessi from Eil Dif were in no mood to be forgiving. They had been seeking game and were hungry, and across the back of one of their camels a dead gerenuk was slung, its head swaying to the camel's movement. Like all Somalis, the herdsmen were avaricious and saw no reason to share the facilities they considered their own with anyone else, least of all the Harari. They were armed with spears and were quite ready to use them, and the discovery of Harari at their waterhole was a challenge to them. There were more of the Harari than there were of the Habr Odessi, but the Habr Odessi were highly-strung, stoic over pain, treacherous when necessary and, with a contempt for death, were cunning and patient, with fierce eyes that burned like fires with the suggestion of unrest.

For a while they talked quietly together then they meekly offered salaams and went on their way. The next morning, however, they returned with ten others, appearing out of the greyness of the early morning. With them was Abdillahi, the young man Harkaway had taught to use the ancient Martini. While the others watched, he moved quietly away with his camel. The rest waited, while the Illas eyed them warily, expecting a rush.

No rush came. The young man lay down on the sand in the eye of the appearing sun, as he had learned when stalking a foe. He was difficult to see and the Illas could not make out what he was up to. Then his rifle cracked and one of the Illas standing by his camel fell backwards, a glittering red fountain pulsing from his chest as the heavy lead bullet from the Martini struck him. Immediately, two more rifles fired. One of the bullets went winging over the desert but the other struck one of the Illas in the leg, smashing the bone and bringing him down. Immediately, the other Habr Odessi rushed forward, wielding their spears. When they had finished, there were two more dead Illas, one of them a boy of thirteen.

The surviving Illas, who had scattered into the surrounding desert, came together as the sun lifted higher to cast its glittering white light over everything, and swore vengeance. They had no need to find the Habr Odessi at one of their waterholes. Illa men had been killed and Illa women had been left to die, and that was sufficient excuse. The Harari tribe, of which they were a sept, were as vain, cruel and vengeful as the Habr Odessi and they had not failed to hear of the white men who were selling rifles.

A fortnight later, near the Tug Wirir, Gooch and Tully, scouting unwillingly towards the road to watch the Italian lorries, were stopped by an old man who indicated that he wished to talk business.

Suspicious like all old soldiers, they put him off but arranged to meet again. Two days later, armed with Lee Enfield rifles, they stared down from the slopes. The old man was waiting on his own. Leaving Tully and Gooch to cover him, Harkaway went to meet the old man. For a long time they talked. When he returned he was smiling.

'He wants to buy rifles,' he said.

'How much?'

'Same as last time. I think we're in business.'

4

'I make it –' Tully peered into the leather bag where he stored the silver trinkets he had acquired '– seventy-three more shopping days to Christmas.' He grinned. 'That is, of course, taking out Sundays and half-days.'

They were lounging outside the cave at Shimber Addi, each holding a can of beer, enjoying the cool of the evening. Below them the desert of greys and browns was fading into blues, with fierce bronze scarves of fire lighting the sky. A hot wind was still blowing across the hills, rattling the scrub and thorn bushes and lifting into little whorls the shale that lay between the rocks. The land had come alive after the day's heat, all pinks and purples and exuding a soft warmth.

As usual, Grobelaar was sitting alone staring over the plain, playing his mouth organ. It was a quiet, slow tune they'd heard him play before and it made them feel lonely. The life they were living was crude but not spartan, and they spent their time now between the cave on the Bur Yi Hills and the old buildings in Eil Dif which the villagers claimed were haunted by shaitans. They had taken up residence in a tumbledown mausoleum of a house round which stood other crumbled brown-yellow houses long since desecrated by wildlife. Blue flowers and ancient trees grew among the rubbish, and geckos, tiny and transparent as gelatine, clutched the ceiling, displaying their palpitating innards and staring with cold eyes on the human beings who had begun to inhabit the long-empty rooms. It was a bat-infested ruin which had been built by a British official for his Somali mistress during the war against the Mad Mullah, and the doors, white as old bones, creaked horribly when the wind blew, while there was always the rustle of small unseen creatures on the verandahs.

One of the Habr Odessi women from Eil Dif cooked for them and occasionally girls came for Gooch and Tully. But they would never stay after dark and, every now and then, when the relentless heat defeated them, they were glad to go back up to Shimber Addi.

They were not short of food and they used the truck to fetch water. Being cut off was no great hardship because at some time or another they had all served in out-of-the-way spots, sitting over a gun or a radio, or standing guard on a bridge as one of a party of three or four under a sergeant. This wasn't a lot different and even Grobelaar, born and brought up on a farm in the Karroo Desert in South Africa, was used to emptiness and the absence of people. The only thing that bothered them was that there seemed little prospect of relief, little opportunity of regaining the company of their fellows. Gregarious like all soldiers, Gooch and Tully at least missed the noise of the barrack room.

But the war now seemed to have entered a sort of stalemate when both sides were poised for the next swing at each other. They were well aware that it hadn't finished, however, because they had heard through Yussuf in Eil Dif, who picked up the information from God alone knew where, that the RAF and the South African Air Force were raiding Italian targets, which didn't seem to indicate that they considered themselves defeated.

By this time, they also knew something about the opposition. Their immediate enemy was a general called Ettore Guidotti, based on Bidiyu, the man who was repairing the road to Berbera and setting up concrete kilometre markers along the route. His immediate superior was a General Barracca, who had his headquarters just outside Berbera, where a naval officer by the name of Scaroni held sway, and they were both of them under the command of a General Forsci in Jijiga. Some of the information had come from Yussuf and some had been brought in by traders moving between Eil Dif, Bidiyu, Hargeisa and Burao. Guidotti, they knew, was a small man with small feet who liked

shining top boots. 'Twinkletoes himself,' Harkaway said and
the name had stuck. He was, they learned, a straightfor-
ward, honest man who permitted no corruption and was
popular with the people of Bidiyu.

But this was parochial stuff and they were desperate for
news from further afield. With the damaged radio, Tully
picked up a dance band from Nairobi, even a station in
India with high-pitched nervous music, and once the thud-
ding drums of Morocco and snatches of simple flute phrases
from the north. Then they learned that the Battle of Britain
had been won, and Britain, though not now in danger of
invasion, was nevertheless under siege, its cities bombed
day and night; and that the Italians had advanced into Egypt
and invaded Greece. There was little to cheer them up –
save news of bombing raids on the Italian cities of Massawa,
Zeila, Diredawa, Agordat, Neghelli and Asmara – until
they heard the exhilarating reports of the battle of Taranto
and the smashing of the Italian fleet in its own harbour by
aircraft of the Royal Navy.

'It shows they haven't thrown their hand in at home,'
Gooch observed.

It was a warming, welcome item of news but it was barely
enough. In their small oasis in the vast desert of Italian
possessions they felt lonely and a little afraid, and totally
cut off, especially in the evenings when the desert cooled,
the sky went into a riot of crazy colours and everything
became silent.

'My old lady's in Liverpool,' Tully pointed out. 'And
they're bombing it.'

'Mine's in London,' Gooch said. 'Where's yours, Squire?'

Harkaway shrugged. It would have offended them to
know his mother lived in a bloody great house in the Derby-
shire dales, safely away from bombs, with a farm to draw
on for food when everybody else was being rationed, even
a horse and trap for when petrol was rationed. He even
wondered if they could imagine it.

When Harkaway didn't answer, they turned to Grobelaar.
'Where's your home, Kom-Kom?'

Grobelaar shrugged. With his glass eye standing guard

for them, he had taken to wearing an eyepatch he'd made from a scrap of soft leather. It ought to have given him a piratical look but somehow it only enhanced his defeated appearance.

'Anywhere, *jong,*' he said. 'Anywhere I happen to be.'

'No folks?' Tully said.

'Not now. They're dead, I reckon.' Grobelaar smiled his tired shadowy smile. 'I ran away to sea. Jumped ship in Durban and stayed there. Went to the mines in Jo'burg. Then down to the Cape. Then Rhodesia. Then Sierra Leone. Then Kenya. Just drifting, man. Ended up here with the Public Works Department. Not much to boast about.'

Tully, who had been about to commiserate, looked at Gooch and finally said nothing. For a long time, he brooded, then he stirred restlessly.

'With the Italians in Greece, Libya and Cyrenaica,' he said uneasily, 'we get cut off a bit more every day.'

'I'm glad I wasn't at the Tug Argan,' Gooch pointed out.

'You'd have been in Aden now if you had been.'

'He might have been dead,' Harkaway reminded them bluntly. 'A few are.'

There was silence as they thought this one over. 'Well,' Gooch said, 'we're safe enough here until we decide to move. Plenty of food. Even booze. And we're making money. The country's so empty, the Eyeties'll never think of this place.' He looked at Harkaway. 'What do *you* think, Squire?'

Harkaway said nothing. His mind was busy. Possessing more intelligence than either of the other two, he was well aware that the war could last for two or three more years and that by that time the stores in the cave would long have disappeared and they would have to give themselves up. He didn't relish being a prisoner of war. Being a ranker in the army was bad enough, especially when you'd been used to going the pace in Civvy Street.

He shifted restlessly, wondering why he hadn't bought himself out while he'd had the chance, because there'd be no buying himself out now the war was on. Then he gave a grim little smile to himself. Perhaps it was all for the best, though, because, if he *had* bought himself out in 1939, as he'd thought of doing, he'd have wasted his money, because by now he'd have been back in again as a reservist.

When they went down to Eil Dif two days later, they found Chief Abduruman coldly angry.

'Our young men have been killed by the Harari,' Yussuf explained, his crippled foot shifting uneasily in the dust. 'They had guns.'

'Oh?' The first thing that crossed Harkaway's mind was that somebody else had acquired a supply from the Tug Argan and was stealing their business. 'Who're the Harari?'

'They are our enemies,' Yussuf said. 'Our young men disturbed Illas at our waterhole at El Wak. There was a fight. Abdillahi killed one. With the gun you sold. Later the Harari came and killed one of our young men. To be killed for Illas!' Yussuf sounded full of contempt. 'All men know Illas are sorcerers and can call up djinns and shaitans. Like the Yibirs, they make clay figures and stick pins in them. No one has ever seen the grave of an Illa. They don't die. They vanish.'

Harkaway pulled a face. 'I can see you've got a problem,' he admitted. 'Where did the Harari get the guns?'

'From you, effendi.'

Harkaway's eyebrows shot up. 'Who says that?'

Yussuf stared accusingly at him. 'They talked. They said they acquired them from you in the Wirir Gorge.'

'Were *they* Harari?' Gooch said. 'We thought they were just black fellers like you.'

'They are the sons of whores, effendi. Their mothers are camels crossed with djinns. They murdered our young men. *With your guns.*'

There was a hint of danger in the air. The dark eyes which watched them from the circle of lean robed figures smouldered with anger. Gooch glanced at them sideways then turned on Yussuf.

'You're not one of them,' he accused. 'You're a bloody Abyssinian-Arab. What's it to you?'

Yussuf's face didn't change. 'I married an Odessi woman, effendi.'

Harkaway spoke quietly. 'Your young men killed first,' he pointed out. 'I didn't sell you those rifles to kill men. That wasn't why I taught Abdillahi.'

Yussuf sneered. 'If you put a rifle in the hands of an Odessi and he finds a Harari at his waterhole, he will shoot the Harari.'

'Can't you share them?'

'Odessi and Harari have never shared. There has been a blood feud for many generations. Fifty ramazans have passed since I was born. There was always a blood feud.'

There was a deep feeling of anxiety about the white men as they headed out of Eil Dif.

'We could start a war,' Harkaway said, his brows down in a worried frown.

'They're only wogs,' Gooch said.

Harkaway wasn't satisfied. 'I was in that patrol that went out to the waterhole at Gudubi. That time the Dolbahanta set about the Bura. Same sort of quarrel. They caught a bunch of Bura at their waterhole and chopped 'em up into little bits. There were legs and arms all over the shop, a few dead camels and goats, and the dried-up bodies of a few old women they hadn't bothered to carry off.'

'They're only wogs,' Gooch said again.

Harkaway turned angrily. 'Is that the only thing you can say, you bloody oaf? he snapped. 'Use your brains! This sort of thing's dangerous. In this country every male over sixteen's a warrior and if it spreads it'll involve the Italians and they'll start trying to find out where they're getting all their guns.' He stared round at the others, his eyes hot. 'And that,' he ended, 'will be bloody marvellous won't it, if they discover they're coming from us?'

5

Their biggest headache had always been water and now, with the Odessi watching them coldly as they lowered the waterskins into their well, it began to seem a good idea to find another waterhole.

Using the lorry, they began to go to the well at Dubi. But the water was bitter and the men there were Harari and there was more muttering as they appeared. It was clear the Harari considered them as guilty of the death of their young warrior as the Odessi did of theirs, and it seemed wiser to find a waterhole belonging to neither tribe. Unfortunately, the next nearest was a long way away at Boram, and Grobelaar began to worry about their petrol supply.

Harkaway was thoughtful for a while then he spoke with an air of cheerful confidence. 'Why,' he asked unexpectedly, 'don't we ambush an Italian lorry? They're going past all the time, carrying petrol from Jijiga to the coast.'

There was a long silence before Tully spoke. 'Petrol lorries are well guarded,' he warned. 'And there are only four of us. One a civvy.'

Grobelaar jeered. 'I was brought up on a farm on the edge of the Karroo, man. I can shoot as well as you can.'

'You've got a dud eye.'

' *'S macht nicht.* It's the left one. I don't have to shut it when I aim.'

Three days later, in Eil Dif to buy a sheep for meat, they were met by Yussuf. He looked angry.

'The Harari are raiding again,' he said. 'We need more of your guns.'

'You're welcome to buy them.'

51

'Perhaps we come and take what we want. I'm not a savage, effendi. I know that when the white men lose their eyes, they replace them with glass ones. I can persuade our young men.'

Harkaway studied the ex-stoker for a moment before he spoke. 'You try it,' he threatened, 'and we'll come down here with machine guns. You know machine guns?'

'I know machine guns, effendi.'

'Much dying. You understand? If you want guns, you pay for 'em. Remember, we're better at war than you are.'

Yussuf's face was expressionless. 'You are not better than the Italians, I think, effendi,' he said calmly. 'Your people are gone and *they* have come.'

'It seems to me,' Harkaway said slowly, 'that from now on things are going to become difficult if we don't do something about it.'

'What for instance?' Tully asked.

'Well, these bloody Odessi seem to think we're licked and that means they'll probably inform on us to the Eyeties. If *that* happens we might have to move on a bit sharpish.'

The others looked at him, aware that as usual Harkaway had thought of something that had never occurred to them. Gooch was cleaning one of the old Martinis ready for sale and he put it down quietly and looked up. 'So what do we do?' he asked.

'The first thing that occurs to me,' Harkaway said, 'is that all we know about the Eyeties has to come from Yussuf or some of his tribesmen. And that's bad. I think the time's come for us to see 'em ourselves in their natural habitat.'

Gooch, at least, wasn't sure what he meant by 'natural habitat' and Harkaway hastened to explain.

'Bidiyu,' he said.

They looked at each other. The idea of thumbing their noses at the Italians appealed. Especially since they were so smugly sure of themselves, and there appeared to be little danger. They looked at Harkaway. His eyes were suddenly far away.

'It also occurs to me,' he went on, 'that while we're at it

we might even do some damage. Take the smiles off their
dials. It won't be hard. The buggers are so cocksure they
won't be expecting anything and it'll give us face. And face
is important anywhere east of Suez.'

'What you got in mind, Squire?' Tully asked.

Harkaway smiled. 'I could make 'em up a nice little bomb.
Just to show they still have friends around.'

It was easier than they'd thought. Dressed in robes, turbans
and sandals acquired in Eil Dif, Harkaway with a curved
Omani dagger at his waist as if he were a chief, they stuck
to the hills all the way to the town because the boot-blacking
they'd applied to their skins had produced a strange dark
shade that was more grey than brown and looked distinctly
odd in daylight.

The shadows of the pepper trees and acacias hid the
jaundiced mud walls of the tea-shops and the leprous white-
wash of the mosque that thrust up its curved dome among
the foliage. In the milky moonlight, the place looked good,
the Somali huts like silver beehives among trees that were
wreathed with drifting woodsmoke from the cooking fires.

They had acquired camels to give them a reason for being
in Bidiyu and had loaded them with bales of hides exchanged like the camels and the robes in Eil Dif for guns,
and, with their eyes shaded by ragged turbans and their
grubby yellow-brown robes hitched well up to their faces,
they passed easily enough for traders from the troublesome
borderlands. In the darkness the doubtful boot-blacking
gave them the ripe purple-brown colour of a Sudanese or
an Abyssinian, and no one looked twice at them.

There seemed to be plenty of vehicles about in the square
with Italian and native levies lounging about, and red, white
and green fascist flags were hanging from all the larger
buildings. The tea-shops were open, Somalis squatting at
the low tables drinking spiced tea or eating dried dates or
mutton and steamed rice moistened with ghee. There were
also three cafés for the Italians, one for the officers, one for
the NCOs and one for the men. In the officers' café a

gramophone was grinding out 'Santa Lucia' from a worn record.

'Nice to see the lights,' Tully observed nostalgically. 'It's been a long time.'

A soldier in one of the cafés started to sing. It was a song none of them knew but it was a European song, with a European melody instead of one of the strange African tunes they'd had to listen to in Eil Dif, full of half-notes and phrases that never quite seemed to reach where they were going.

The Italians had erected a flagstaff in the marketplace and despite the late hour the tricolour floated there, a light, organized by Colonel Piccio, directed on to it to give a spot of brilliant colour against the night sky. Against the wall of an old house opposite, as if to indicate who was now in command and placed where it could be clearly seen, a column had been erected. It was a standard column that the Italians put up quickly, and it had been only a day's job for Guidotti's men to pour wet cement into a cast to produce a concrete fixture announcing that the fascist forces of Italy had entered the southern hemisphere to bring the light of the civilized world to the dark places of Africa.

It was brand new in white shining concrete, its edges sharp and clear. On top was a bust of Mussolini – all chin, helmet and Roman determination, and opposite, near the flagpole, all strapped and buckled authority, was a sentry.

Standing by the three camels under the eucalyptus trees, Harkaway studied it for a while.

'You know,' he said quietly, 'that's what we should go for.'

Leading them away from the lights in the centre of the town, Harkaway headed for the dark areas under the trees. The plot of land behind the wall where the column stood was full of date palms, gum trees and bougainvillaeas.

'We could tackle it from the back,' he said. 'We could get into that garden and lay the charge from the other side of the wall. It should be enough to knock Mussolini's hat off.'

Leaving Grobelaar as lookout with the camels, the other

three moved quietly into the garden between the trees. The old house was silent, the windows shuttered, the verandah dark. Reaching the wall, Harkaway dug at the mud bricks with his jack-knife until he had made a sizeable hole. Across the marketplace, the Italian gramophone was still grinding away at 'Santa Lucia' and the Italian soldier was still singing in opposition in a high tenor voice. Every now and again lorries ground past and once there was the harsher machine-gun sound of an army motorcycle.

'It's a good job this wall was never expected to keep out invaders,' Harkaway muttered. 'It's falling out on its own.'

Scrabbling with his fingers, he pulled away the rubble and dug again with the knife until the illumination in the market-place showed as a small speck of light at the base.

'We're through,' he murmured.

Gooch's eyes were flickering about him as Tully took over. Enlarging the hole, he lay flat on his face and finally pushed his head and shoulders through. As he withdrew, they heard Italian voices on the other side and Harkaway gave a wolfish grin in the darkness. Clearly, the hole couldn't be seen from the other side of the column.

Digging beneath the plinth, he scooped out the soil then began to feel with his fingers along the back of the column itself. Cast in three parts which had then been cemented together, the column consisted of a base and a narrower top half in the shape of a fasces on which the inscription was inset, with the head of Mussolini resting on top. Similar columns were being raised all over the new East African possessions.

Finding the crack between the bottom half and the top half, Harkaway scraped at it and, finding the cement of poor quality, managed to make a hole. Pushing his explosive through, he jammed it hard into the gap he'd made and plastered it up with mud which Tully made by the simple method of urinating. A second charge was stuffed into the hole beneath the plinth where he used the stones and dirt he'd dug from the wall to tamp it down in a hard wad. Finally, he laid a third small charge just behind Mussolini's head at the top of the column, and led the cordtex fuses through the hole in the wall and away into the shadows.

'Ready?' he asked.

Gooch nodded, and Harkaway gave his cold smile then, lighting a cigarette, sucked it into a glow and applied it to the fuse. There was a faint crackle and a fizz and he watched it for a second moving along the base of the wall.

'Time we left,' he said quietly, and they slunk away through the shadows to the road.

There was no sign of Grobelaar but they eventually saw him walking towards them on the other side of the road. As they hurried towards him, Harkaway gestured and, as he turned to face in the opposite direction, they joined him and headed away from the marketplace.

The part of town where they were now was shadowed by trees and from inside the houses of whitewashed mud and flattened paraffin tins, they could see rooms lit by the yellow light of lanterns where men smoked and drank tea, while the women squatted outside chattering in their high-pitched voices. A scrawny, tubercular-looking Arab lounged on a cart as it rattled past, half-heartedly beating the tiny donkey between the shafts, and a youth rode by on a bicycle, importantly sounding the bell at a misshapen beggar with only stumps for hands and feet. The air was pungent with wood-smoke and a few children were still running about despite the hour. Here and there groups of camels stood, gaunt and ugly in the faint light, their jaws working, or knelt in the dust like piles of dusty matting. Dogs barked but tall Somalis, robed against the chilly night air in blankets embroidered in stiff-petalled flowers, stalked past without paying any attention. Then an Italian lorry, its horn blaring, thrust through the busy street and, as they moved out of the way to let it pass, it began to edge by, its offside wheel crumbling the lip of the drainage ditch.

It had just passed them when there was a sharp crack from behind them and even at that distance they felt the disturbance of the air. Immediately, two more followed. The driver of the lorry yelled something in Italian and as he gestured at his companion the lorry dropped its front wheel

into the ditch. As it canted over, its nose down, they turned
and saw blue smoke rising against the lights of the marketplace and heard voices yelling. The Somalis, always eager
for excitement, began to hurry. Children began to run and
the women rose to their feet and set off after them with
their stately gait to see what had happened.

The driver of the lorry and his mate were standing in the
road, gesturing and shouting at each other in a rage. No
one took the slightest notice of them and in the end they
gave up and hurried after the crowd to see what was going
on. Immediately dark figures swarmed over the lorry from
the trees to remove anything that wasn't screwed down.

Harkaway looked at the other two and smiled under the
boot-blacking. 'Let's join the crowds,' he said. 'This I would
like to see.'

The marketplace was filling with robed and turbaned figures, and Italian policemen, aided by fezzed native levies,
were pushing them back, yelling wildly. A car, its horn
blaring, forced its way through and an officer in a green
tunic resplendent with buttons climbed out.

'*Cosa successo?*' he demanded. 'What's happened?'

'*La colonna,*' one of the policemen yelled at him. '*E
coventrizzata!*'

The officer stared across the square where a wisp of blue
smoke was still drifting across the beam of the light that had
been rigged up to shine on the flag. The ramshackle mud
wall of the old house had disappeared for about thirty yards.
Its condition had not been up to the assault on it and, as
the explosion had carried away a good ten feet of it, the rest
had given up the ghost and collapsed. It was now possible
to see into the garden where the dry grass was still smould-
ering. The column announcing the bringing of light to Cen-
tral Africa by Mussolini's fascist forces was cracked across
the middle so that it had a drunken look, the fasces at the
top leaning forward at an angle of forty-five degrees, while
Mussolini's head had performed a neat parabola through
the air, just missing one of the Italian policemen, to land at
the feet of a sergeant who had just paused to stare up at the
flag.

'*Dov'è il generale?*' the officer in the green tunic snapped.

The policeman gestured and, pushing at the curious Somalis, the officer set off at a half-run towards the Residency, where it was possible to see several figures in white on the balcony, trying to discover what had happened.

Standing among the crowd of chattering people, Harkaway smiled. He nodded at Gooch and Tully and Grobelaar, then at a tall man alongside with fuzzy hair who looked like an Ethiopian. The Ethiopian grinned back at him, pointed to the listing concrete column and laughed. Turning round, he indicated the column to another man and they began to laugh together, the laughter high and infectious. In no time it was running through the crowd with the high ululations of surprise from the women. In seconds half the marketplace was laughing, while the Italian police pushed them furiously back.

At the other side of the square, there were shouts of '*Aprire la strada per il Generale Guidotti,*' and, as the crowd opened, several officers appeared in a group. They crossed the square to examine the broken concrete, the one in the middle talking quietly to the man behind him.

'So that's Twinkletoes, is it?' Harkaway murmured. 'He doesn't look much to write home about.'

'Who did it?' Guidotti demanded.

'It's impossible to say, Excellency,' Piccio said.

'The British?'

Piccio shrugged. 'It might have been British explosive, but that doesn't mean a thing. A lot was left behind after their demolitions.'

'Patriots? Bandits. Shifta, as we had in Abyssinia?'

'It could have been, Excellency. It could even have been Somalis. A few of them are clever enough. It's a land of warriors, Excellency. They're brave, cruel men. In the sixteenth century, a Somali king conquered the whole of Ethiopia. And Mohammed bin Abdullah Hassan, the man they called the Mad Mullah, fought the British for twenty years, wiping out more than one expedition that was sent against him. He was only defeated when they brought in aeroplanes and destroyed his forts with bombs.'

Guidotti looked at Piccio, startled; he hadn't expected such erudition.

'I read it, Excellency,' Piccio explained, faintly embarrassed. 'When we were informed we were to be part of the invading force. I obtained a book.'

'And did your book inform you how to deal with such atrocities?' Guidotti walked up and down, his hands behind his back. 'The column's only been up a matter of a few days,' he snapped. 'Why was no guard placed on it?'

'Excellency, there was a sentry at the flagstaff directly opposite and only a few yards away.'

'Then why did he see nothing?'

'They placed the charge from the garden of the old house behind. They dug a hole in the wall and, since the column is two metres wide at the bottom, the sentry could see nothing.'

'This house? What was it originally?'

'It belonged to a British merchant, Excellency. It's not occupied because orders were given that it had to be kept exclusively for the use of General Forsci if he should visit us from Jijiga.'

Guidotti muttered something about General Forsci never being likely to leave the luxurious quarters he'd made for himself in Jijiga for a town like Bidiyu, and certainly not until the occupation of British Somaliland was more advanced and there was a greater degree of good Roman comfort.

'This is bad,' he said. 'It indicates carelessness and it's my wish that Italian troops should not show carelessness. You heard what the British said when we entered the war. They said they would provide us with more of the ruins for which Italy was famous. They regard us with contempt, Piccio.'

'Excellency.'

'Italian soldiers can fight as well as any other soldiers.' Guidotti was working up to a fine show of bad temper. 'This is the sort of thing that gives the English opportunity to laugh at us. There must be no more of it! Inform all commanders to be alert. *Everybody* must be alert, down to the merest local levy. What if the British should hear of it?'

As it happened, the British heard of it within days.

The Horn of Africa was full of Somali spies for both sides and news travelled swiftly across country by the grapevine. They knew in Mogadiscio what had happened the following day and two days later it was over the Kenya border.

The British forces there, making probes in their armoured cars to worry the victorious but still very nervous Italians, had plenty to keep them occupied, and there wasn't a great deal of comfort. Enduring the shortages of medical supplies, cigarettes and mail, they had sat in their damp patches of borderland throughout the winter as the rain came down like stair rods, outnumbered, but – as Guidotti was well aware – utterly contemptuous of their enemy, and the information that a triumphal column put up one day had been blown down the next sent the dirty, shabby men guarding the frontier into gales of laughter.

'Split it into three,' they shouted.

'Brought down a hundred yards of wall.'

'Mussolini's head almost brained the sentry guarding the flag.'

The British general in command looked up from his papers at the man who brought the news to his headquarters.

'Who did it, Charlie?' he asked with a smile.

Colonel Edward Charlton smiled back. He was a Rhodesian lawyer who had found himself in the army because of his services in the last war and his knowledge of the country, and his chief function was to be dogsbody for the general. With his placid nature and his washtub of a stomach he was not a fighting soldier and didn't pretend to be.

'That's one thing we haven't found out yet, sir,' he said. 'I expect we will eventually.'

'What exactly happened?'

Charlton described as much as he knew, and the general laughed.

'Well,' he said, 'it's nice to know we'll have friends when we go back.'

'Will we go back, sir?' Charlton asked.

'You bet your life we will, Charlie. But this is very much a sideshow – a bow and arrow war compared with the Western Desert. David against Goliath, if you like. All the same –' the general frowned '– I wish we could get just enough elastic to make a sling, and anything that indicates we have support is welcome. Any chance of raising the locals?'

Charlton shrugged. 'Doubt it, sir. Our information suggests that they've taken to the Italians quite happily.'

'Hm.' The general frowned. 'They always were a treacherous lot. They kept us busy for twenty years up to and after the last war. Mad Mullah. Heard of him?'

'Yes, sir,' Charlton said. 'I have. I get the impression that the warlike spirit's dissipated a little since then, though.'

The general waved a hand. 'I'm not so sure. Still it'll be up to you to find out. Do what you can if you get the chance. The more the merrier. We haven't all that many men.'

6

Guidotti was inclined to consider the bombing of the victory column as an attempt by some disaffected Somali still loyal to the British to show his disapproval of the new regime. Since obviously a bomb would have had to be prepared by someone of intelligence from Berbera, however, he contacted Captain Scaroni, of the navy, in command there, and got him to set up a search. But, since the Somali intelligentsia had left almost to a man with the British in August, all that remained were the shopkeepers and traders who were perfectly happy under Italian rule, just as they would have been under any rule so long as trade continued.

Guards were doubled, officers and NCOs were warned to be on the *qui vive* in case of further attempts to undermine Italian rule, but when nothing happened it was assumed that it was an isolated incident and gradually they began to relax.

Unfortunately, just when Guidotti had decided he had everything under control again, the feud between the Habr Odessi and the Harari erupted once more, and quite by chance Colonel Piccio drove smack through the middle of a skirmish across the Strada del Duce that holed one or two lorries and caused their crews to duck hurriedly.

Guidotti listened to Piccio's account with a frown. The Somalis, he had soon discovered, weren't very fussy about who was running their country and most of them had gathered from the Eritreans and the Somalis from Italian Somaliland that the Italians were easier to work with than the British. They brought trade in mutton, milk, grain, hides, cloth and incense, which they used in the churches they built; they were not against sitting down with a chief for a cup of tea; and they laughed, sang and were honest about their need for women. The British were cold, proud, detached and hard; they never enthused about anything; and they maintained their frozen faces whatever happened, unmoved by the excitement or the laughter of the Somalis, whom it was known they despised.

Nevertheless, scuffles such as Piccio was now describing seemed to have been few and far between under their administration in recent years, and Guidotti's job was concerned with law and order along the Strada del Duce from Jijiga to his headquarters in Bidiyu, so that groups of Somalis shooting at each other could not only create a danger to Italian troops but could also cause trouble for General Guidotti.

He had no wish for trouble. He was young and he was ambitious. One day perhaps he could become a marshal like Graziani or Balbo, perhaps a governor of one of Italy's new colonies. He had a beautiful wife in Rome and two small daughters he adored, and it was only the thought of eventually having them with him, of living in comfort, that enabled him to be away from them so often and for so long. It was over a year since he'd seen them and he itched to prove himself so that he could be rewarded. If by nothing else, he thought wistfully, then perhaps by home leave, though, after Taranto, only God knew how he was going to get across the Mediterranean.

'Tell me again,' he said to Piccio.

'We ran into crossfire across the Strada del Duce,' Piccio said. 'Nobody was hurt but we had to set up a machine gun and pepper the slopes. We found one dead Somali, a lot of spent cartridges – and *this*.'

He indicated an ancient Martini rifle which lay on Guidotti's desk.

'British,' Guidotti observed.

'Undoubtedly, Excellency. The British army mark is on the butt. And the cartridge cases we found were of British manufacture.'

'There can be no mistake? In its day, the Italian army has also used Martinis.'

'Only our native levies, Excellency.'

'What's to stop native levies deserting and selling their weapons?'

'Sir, we were in a crossfire. They weren't shooting at us, though we were in danger of being hit. We decided, Di Sanctis and I, that there were around a dozen rifles firing across the road. We would surely know if a dozen men had deserted.'

Guidotti frowned. 'Then if not from deserters, where *did* they get them?'

'Could it be that the British set up a dump somewhere in this area to supply native troops and that the local tribesmen have found it?'

'Twelve rifles is hardly a dump,' Guidotti said. 'Perhaps it's nothing. Perhaps just a tribal quarrel. If it *is* some Englishman, then we'll catch him. He'll be begging for mercy before we've done with him.

Piccio was unconvinced. 'In the meantime, Excellency, shouldn't we double the guards on the convoys passing along the road to Berbera?'

'The arms convoys passing along the road to Berbera are already under heavy guard.'

'There's petrol, Excellency.'

'The Somalis don't steal petrol,' Guidotti pointed out. 'It can't be used with camels and so far I've seen no other form of transport away from the coast.' He frowned. 'In any case, petrol lorries also carry an armed guard. On the orders of General Forsci at Jijiga. And since they travel in groups of ten, that means ten armed men with them, under the command of a sergeant.'

'Sir —' Piccio gestured '— that's the petrol for the coast. But every evening we have one lorry which brings petrol for our personal use here in Bidiyu. That's guarded by one armed man only.'

'The driver also has a weapon in the cab.'

'Two then, sir. But if a serious attempt were made on it, two men would hardly be enough.'

Guidotti frowned. 'Very well then,' he conceded. 'Let's have it accompanied by a second vehicle. Or have Jijiga send the lorry through every two days so they can travel in twos.'

'Sir, General Forsci claims he hasn't sufficient transport for that. I've already discussed it with his transport officer. It's one lorry or nothing. It makes the journey here in the evening, unloads during darkness and returns in the early morning so that General Forsci has its use during the day.'

'General Forsci is a narrow-minded –' Guidotti stopped and smiled, remembering General Forsci was his superior in rank. 'Very well,' he said. 'Then we'd better send something to Jijiga in the late afternoon which can return with the lorry in the evening and be available for our use during the following day. If General Forsci can do this, so can we!'

'Sir, we have only one spare vehicle. A car. A Lancia. And at the moment that has a broken spring.'

Guidotti was growing angry. 'Very well, then,' he snapped. 'As soon as the spring is repaired, send it to General Forsci to accompany our lorryload of petrol. Until then, we shall just have to take a chance. Perhaps this skirmish that worries you so much was nothing, anyway. We've seen no sign of enmity from the natives. The war's over. The land's at peace. There's no more resistance.'

In that, however, he was dead wrong.

The need for petrol was growing urgent. Without it, they couldn't move and they'd been prodigal in its use since they'd arrived at Shimber Addi. Nobody liked walking in the heat and they'd used the truck to collect water and meat, even for Tully and Gooch to visit the girls Yussuf had found for them. With Yussuf still hostile, they needed it more than ever.

Something had to be done and, since they'd already discovered that petrol went regularly from Jijiga to Bidiyu, they decided to find out exactly when. It was a risk they had to take if they were to survive.

Driving Tully and Harkaway to a spot near the main road before first light, Grobelaar dropped them and headed back to Eil Dif.

'We'll be here a week from now, Kom-Kom,' Harkaway

said as the lorry started to move. 'And keep an eye on that stupid bastard, Gooch.'

As the lorry rattled off, they began to climb into the hills that overlooked Guidotti's Strada del Duce. By afternoon, they were staring down at the Wirir Gorge, a slit in the red rocks where the road started to drop down to Bidiyu. Italian working parties had cleared the fallen rocks that had always plagued the road, a neat stone edge had been built and a concrete marker post had been erected.

'Make a nice job of 'em, don't they?' Tully said. 'Roman eagle and the usual firewood and chopper.'

They found a niche in the rocks and erected a tarpaulin. It was cold enough at night to make them shiver as they huddled together to sleep, but there were stunted trees with which to make fires. They were always glad to see the sun next morning, however – just as they were glad to see it disappear after a whole day of its blazing heat watching the road.

Occasional camel trains plodded through the gorge, the cries of the drivers – 'Ei! Ei! Huh-hu-hu-hu!' – drifting up to the watching men like the barking of the baboons they occasionally saw. For the most part, the Italian lorries from Jijiga or Berbera travelled in small convoys, guarded by soldiers, and once they saw a car roar past containing four men in different uniforms.

'Germans,' Tully said. 'One of the buggers is wearing an iron cross.'

Harkaway nodded. 'Watson said there were a few liaison officers with 'em,' he agreed.

The week dragged. His face coated with the dust which stuck to the sweat, Harkaway frowned as an Italian convoy roared past.

'We can't tackle that many,' he said.

Then they noticed that each evening just before dark a single lorry passed. It went by every night at speed, but only when, on the fourth day, it roared by with its tarpaulin flapping loose did it dawn on them that it was carrying cans of petrol.

'Two men,' Harkaway breathed. 'Just two men! We could fix *two* of the bastards.'

Two days later the same camel train that had visited Bidiyu moved slowly from Eil Dif south through the foothills of the Bur Yi to Guidotti's Strada del Duce. Guidotti's lorries passed them without their drivers even noticing them, because there were plenty of other camel trains on the road, moving towards Berbera.

As the vehicles roared past, the flying grit they lifted settled on the dusty hides of the camels, in the folds of the travellers' clothing, and in the wrinkles of their skin. The perspiration made it stick so that they were masked like mummies, a layer of moist dust like mud on their faces. After their fashion, the camels grunted and belched and farted as they plodded slowly along the road. On their backs they carried the same bundles of hides that had been to Bidiyu.

As they halted to drink from a water skin, the tallest of the drivers looked round. 'This is the place,' he said.

He gestured with his head at the entrance to the Wirir Gorge whose sides towered over the road. The fierce white light of the sun reflected dazzlingly from the rocks and made the place look clinical and sterile.

'A charge under that rock there,' he said, pointing, 'and it'll bring the lot down.'

He looked up as a car approached, trailing its cloud of dust. As it passed, he lifted his hand and waved – in the Italian manner the Somalis had been quick to learn, with the back of his hand to the recipient, the fingers moving slowly.

There was a small recess at the side of the road where the hills lay back and where convoys had been in the habit of halting. Its surface was covered with powdery dust criss-crossed with the marks of tyres. At one end, where the camels of nomad tribesmen stopped, the surface was composed of trodden dung and the heavy smell of the animals hung in the air. With a stick, Harkaway prodded the camels forward and persuaded them to kneel. Then they squatted down by the rocks, waiting, watching the traffic. There were no guns and few troops. *They* had passed through long since. Now it was only lorries bringing up supplies, or an occasional car containing an officer.

'You sure them explosives are safe?' Tully asked.

'Perfectly.'

Tully eyed the sack on the nearest camel. 'It's bloody near,' he said. 'Suppose it fell of?'

'Do no harm,' Harkaway assured him. 'You could burn it and it'd only fizz. It has to be put in a hole and tamped down, with a fuse attached.'

'You sure?'

Harkaway smiled in the quiet way of his that irritated the other two so much, then as a car approached, heading at full speed through the pass, he stiffened and did his Italian wave again.

As dusk came, the reds and greys around them died into blues and purples and the sky was full of wild vermilion fires. The traffic stopped and a hot wind came through the pass from the plain, blowing the dried dust of ancient camel dung and lifting the surface of hard fine shale from the earth until little ridges appeared like bones in the reddish sand.

'We'd better get on with it,' Harkaway said. 'Get the crowbar.'

Tully began to unfasten the heavy iron bar they'd found in the cave at Shimber Addi.

'That ought to make a hole big enough,' Harkaway said. 'We'll find a crack and work on that. Get up the slope, Paddy, and keep a look out. Give us a whistle when the petrol lorry comes. If we're ready first we'll whistle to you to come down.'

As Tully began to scramble up the rocky slopes, Harkaway began to jab with the crowbar at a crack in the rock beneath one of the huge pillars that held back the cliff.

'Christ,' Gooch said disgustedly. 'Gimme that! You're poking about like a tart with a knitting needle.' His great shoulders working, he jabbed at the rock with the heavy iron bar. 'How deep do you want it?'

Harkaway held up one of the packets of explosive. 'Big enough and deep enough to get one of these in,' he said.

'How much fuse?'

'Enough to give us time to run.'

There was only one alarm. A soft whistle stopped them as they worked and, tossing the crowbar behind the rocks, they squatted down alongside the camels.

'These buggers niff a bit, don't they?' Gooch said. 'You ever smelt their breath? I had one belch straight in my face once.'

A car rushed past at speed. The men in the rear seat didn't even turn their heads to look at the two men with the camels. As the car disappeared, Gooch got to work again.

'It's big enough now,' he said. 'Shove it in.'

Harkaway stuffed in the explosive. 'Better give it an extra one to make sure,' he said.

Gooch grinned. 'Why not an extra two,' he said. 'Make no mistake.'

Stuffing in the last of the explosive, Harkaway attached the fuse. Packing earth round it, he looked up.

'Better shift the camels,' he said. 'I wouldn't want the poor sods to go sailing over the hill there.'

Leading the disgruntled animals down the road, they manoeuvred them into the recess among the rocks.

'Okay?'

As Harkaway nodded, Gooch put two fingers in his mouth and gave an ear-splitting whistle.

'Could never do that,' Harkaway commented. 'Always envied chaps who could. So bloody useful when you want a taxi in London.'

Almost on top of the whistle there was an answering signal from the dusk and they heard the clatter of stones as Tully began to scramble down the slope towards them. Walking back to where they had planted the explosive, Harkaway paused until he saw the figure of Tully appear, then he lit a cigarette, took a couple of puffs and applied the end to the fuse. Immediately, it began to burn, moving swiftly in short jerky runs.

Tully was coming towards him, waving his arms.

'Run,' Harkaway shouted.

As he set off towards Gooch, he was aware of Tully yelling but he ignored him and they ran together towards the bend in the road. As they fell into the recess where Gooch waited, Tully was fighting for his breath. 'There's a –'

'Keep moving,' Harkaway snapped.

Gooch picked up the heavy iron crowbar and Harkaway the sack of explosives and they began to scramble among the rocks.

'Listen –' Tully panted, struggling along behind them.

'Save your breath,' Harkaway said.

They scrambled part-way up the slope, the stones and shale slipping beneath their sandalled feet.

'Listen –'

'For Christ's sake, man,' Harkaway snarled. 'Dry up!'

Reaching a ridge, they threw themselves over the other side.

'We'll be all right here,' Harkaway panted.

'Listen –' Tully was still fighting for breath.

'What the hell's the matter with you?'

'Somebody's coming up the pass.'

'What?'

'I whistled. Didn't you hear me?'

'I thought that was to indicate you'd heard *our* signal.'

'I saw 'em just as you whistled. They'll be coming round the corner any minute.'

'I hope they're not too bloody quick,' Harkaway said, frowning. 'I wouldn't want the petrol to go up with the gorge. That'd be a waste of time and effort.'

'It isn't the petrol lorry,' Tully gasped. 'And it isn't an Italian. It's somebody on a camel.'

Gooch and Harkaway exchanged glances then they stared at Tully.

'A Somali?'

'I've never seen a Somali wearing a topee.'

For a moment they were silent again, then they stared down into the pass. Just as Tully had warned, a solitary camel was just rounding the bend and on its back was a figure wearing a topee, a Somali blanket decorated with flowers wrapped round its shoulders.

'It *might* be an Italian,' Gooch said.

'Here?' Harkaway said. 'Alone? At this time of night? Not on your bloody life!'

'Well, if it's not an Eyetie, who is it?'

'A civvy. Trying to get to the coast. You've got to stop that bang!'

'How, you bloody fool?' Harkaway snapped. 'It's just about there now. I'm not going near it!'

'Well, we'd better warn him.'

Together, they started to scramble down the slope, yelling. The rider looked up. The face was shadowed in the grey dusk by the brim of the topee but they caught the glint as the last of the light touched the lenses of a pair of round spectacles. Clearly the rider thought their approach was an attack and they saw a hand fish under the blanket then there was a crack and they heard the whine of a bullet sailing over their heads. Automatically, they flung themselves down. The rider spurred the camel into a lope and it began to approach the spot where the pass narrowed.

'Oh, Jesus!'

As Gooch spoke, there was a tremendous roar and a flash that lit up the pass. They saw the camel smash down, legs asprawl, then the pass was full of clouds of dust and billowing brown smoke.

For a moment they stared, then they became aware of soft plops and clicks around them and realized that they were being bombarded by falling stones thrown up by the explosion. Flattening themselves against the ground, their arms over their heads, they waited until it had subsided, then they rose, covered with dust, and began to scramble down the slope again.

The camel was on its side, blood coming from its nostrils. The rider was huddled by its side.

'The bugger's dead,' Gooch said.

But the rider stirred. A shaking hand pushed a pair of steel-rimmed, dust-covered spectacles straight, then the figure was on its feet, its face contorted with rage. Immediately

71

their jaws dropped. The topee and the blanket had been snatched away by the blast and the shirt beneath had been blown open to the waist. And what they could see underneath clearly didn't belong to a man. It was a woman, tall, slender as a sapling, her skin covered with sandy dust, her dark hair, blown into a mop by the blast, looking as if it had had an electric shock.

'Who in the name of Christ,' Harkaway said, 'are you?'

7

The woman was tempestuously angry, unable to get her words out in her fury.

'Those wretched Italians,' she managed at last. 'Catholics every one of them! Slaves to the credo of Rome! Speaking peace even as they make war!'

Clearly she regarded them not as her attackers but as her saviours and was venting her spleen on the invaders as the sole cause of her disaster and discomfort.

'My camel's dead,' she raged on, her hands busy wiping the lenses of her glasses. 'And everything's ruined! I hadn't much, Heaven knows! And look at me! Look what they've done to me!'

She was still dazed and seemed unaware of what had happened to her clothes and they were indeed looking at her, and, now that it was clear she wasn't much harmed, were thoroughly enjoying the sight.

'Look, ma'am,' Tully said, 'what in the name of Christ are you doing here? There's a war on, didn't you know?'

She became aware at last of their stares and that her blouse was flapping open. Hurriedly she drew it together and stood with her hands across her breasts holding it in place. Her hair, covered with dust, still stood out like a mophead round her face.

She gazed at them for a moment as it suddenly dawned on her that there was something a little odd about meeting three English-speaking men dressed as Arabs in the middle of Italian-occupied territory.

'Who are –?'

Harkaway waved her to silence. His mind was still occupied with the reason for their being there. He had been standing with his head cocked as they talked and now he gestured abruptly. 'Listen!'

They stopped arguing at once and immediately became aware of the grind of gears as a heavy vehicle slogged slowly up the slope in the dusk towards them. There were only two men in it, an African askari driver with an Italian soldier as guard and they were both eager to be in Bidiyu. Like many of the Italian vehicles, their lorry was past its best. It had been among those which had been driven into Abyssinia in 1936 and since then four hundred thousand kilometres had appeared on its clock. Because they were cut off from home by Egypt, however, there had been little chance since war had been declared of its being replaced and since Taranto there was none at all, and it was held together by wire while the Italian mechanics in Jijiga daily performed miracles on its ancient engine to keep it going. When it had failed to start, they had left behind schedule, the last vehicle on the road, and the corporal was anxious to be where it was safe before darkness.

As it approached, Harkaway grabbed at the woman and began to drag her among the rocks. Imagining he was about to assault her, she began to scream. Harkaway clutched her close to him and as he forced her down out of sight, clapped a heavy hand over her mouth, so tight it made her cheeks bulge.

The approaching lorry had its headlights on and they could see the light playing on the stony verges as it swung round the corners.

The woman in Harkaway's arms was still struggling. 'Listen,' he said. 'Will you be quiet if I let you go?'

She nodded and he took his hand from her mouth.

'Who are you?' she said.

'Never mind who we are.'

She made no attempt to move and Harkaway realized he was still clutching her to him. In her state of semi-nudity, it was far from unpleasant and he made no attempt to release her.

'Who's in that lorry?' she whispered.

'Italians.'

'How many?'

'Two, we hope.'

The lorry was drawing near now and as it laboured round the last corner, Harkaway became aware that there was a second vehicle behind it, its headlights throwing it into silhouette.

His voice was touched with alarm. 'There are *two* of the buggers!'

They raised their heads a fraction.

'It must be Kom-Kom,' Tully said. 'Come to pick up the loot.'

'He's not *that* daft,' Harkaway snapped. 'He'd never follow that close behind. It must be one of theirs.'

'The one behind's a car,' Gooch pointed out.

'With two swaddies in it,' Tully said. 'One of 'em's got what looks like a Tommy gun.'

'We can't tackle four of 'em!' Gooch sounded alarmed. 'There are only three of us.'

'Four,' the woman said.

'Kom-Kom's a mile away.'

'I don't mean this Kom-Kom, whoever he is. I mean me.'

They turned to look at her. Then Harkaway shook his head. 'We've only got three rifles.'

'I have a pistol,' she reminded him. 'If you recall, I used it to shoot at you. It's not very big but it works.'

They stared at her for a moment, then back down the slope. The lorry and the following car were drawing closer.

'Can you use it?'

'Of course I can.'

'You didn't hit any of us.'

'That's because the camel was moving.'

'*Would* you use it?'

'I once shot an Abyssinian in the leg when he tried to rape me.'

Harkaway studied her for a second. 'Okay,' he said briskly. 'Tully, you and Thingy here take the car. Gooch and I'll take the lorry.' He glanced at the woman. 'Stick your pistol up the driver's nostril, and tell him not to move. That's all you have to do.'

The lorry was almost on top of them now and as its headlights fell on the mass of rocks and earth blocking the road ahead, they heard the squeak of brakes as it slowed to a stop. The Italian soldier alongside the driver opened the door of the cab and stood with his foot on the step, studying the rocks.

'*Una frana,*' he said.

'What's he say?' Tully whispered anxiously.

'He says it's a landslide,' the woman said.

Harkaway's head turned. 'Can you speak Italian?' he asked.

'I've had to live with them.'

As they waited, the car drew up behind the lorry.

'*Che chosa videte?*'

'What's that?'

'He asking him what he can see.'

The corporal in the car made no attempt to climb out, and there was a little shouting back and forth between the two men. After a while the corporal decided to investigate himself and began to open the car door. It was time to move.

Harkaway looked at the woman. 'You sure we can rely on you?' he asked.

'Of course I'm sure.'

'Right. Here we go.'

As the Italian from the lorry moved towards the pile of rock and shale, Gooch appeared at the driver's open window. As the rifle appeared out of the darkness and jabbed at his throat, the askari turned his head, saw the pale face in the moonlight and froze, his eyes rolling. The corporal had got one leg out of the car when he felt the cold muzzle of Tully's rifle on his temple.

'One move, you Eyetie bastard,' Tully said, 'and I'll blow your sodding head off.'

The Italian didn't speak English but he fully understood what was being said. He rolled his eyes to see whether the driver could help, but he was already raising his hands from the wheel and the corporal saw a white-clad figure beyond him at the other side of the car, holding a pistol at the driver's temple.

Unaware of what was going on, the Italian from the lorry was studying the rock-face. He was still studying it as Harkaway appeared behind him and jabbed him in the ribs with his rifle. '*Mani in alto*,' he said.

The Italian stiffened, then slowly lifted his hands. Harkaway took away his rifle and gestured to him to march back to the lorry.

As he did so, he said something in Italian and Harkaway turned to the woman. 'What's he say?'

'He says you've bitten off more than you can chew,' she explained. 'Because he can see another of their lorries coming up behind us.'

Harkaway smiled. 'Tell him that's what he thinks. It's one of ours. It's Kom-Kom with the Bedford to collect the petrol.'

As the truck appeared, Grobelaar beat a hearty tattoo on the horn, then climbed out, grinning. As he did so, he saw the woman in the headlights and stopped dead.

'Who's this?' he demanded.

'We've just bumped into her.'

'How?'

'We blew her up,' Harkaway said quietly.

The woman turned. 'Who's this?' she asked in return.

'Grobelaar. Piet Grobelaar. South African. Known as Kom-Kom.' Harkaway gestured at the Italians and the African driver. 'Look, we haven't got all bloody night to get introduced. We've got to transfer this petrol to our lorry.'

'Why don't we just take the lorry, *jong*?' Grobelaar suggested.

Harkaway smiled. 'Makes sense,' he agreed.

'Why not take the car as well?' Tully said. 'We've got enough petrol now to last us months.'

'Who's going to drive it?' Harkaway asked.

Tully looked at Gooch and Gooch looked at Tully. Neither could drive.

'I can drive,' the woman said.

'An Italian Lancia?'

'We had a Lancia where I worked.'

'Okay,' Harkaway said. 'Get in and turn it round.'

By reversing into the space where they'd left the camels, they faced the vehicles in the other direction. Harkaway beamed at the woman. 'That was nicely done,' he said. 'Who are you, anyway?'

'Bronwen Ortton-Daniells.'

'Mrs?'

'Miss. I was sent out to Africa by LFM.'

'Who's El Effem,' Gooch asked.

'It's not a who,' she snapped. 'It's an it. The London Foreign Mission. They sent me.'

'Why?'

'To preach the word of the Lord Jesus Christ. To teach them Christianity.'

'But all the buggers round here are Moslems!'

'They aren't Moslems in Abyssinia,' she pointed out. 'They're Coptic Christians. That's where I was sent.'

'You a missionary?'

'I'm a mission worker. When the Italians came we moved into British Somaliland, but the British government doesn't like missionaries and in the end we moved into French Somaliland. The French at least go to church.'

'What are you doing here, then?'

'Haven't the French thrown in their lot with the Germans? I couldn't live with cowardice. I set off for British Somaliland. I've been a long time on the way. I had to be careful. I hoped to reach Berbera.'

'Bit late for that, miss,' Tully said. 'Everybody's gone to Aden.'

'How do you know?'

'We've got a wireless.'

'Where?'

Harkaway's arm moved vaguely. 'Up in the hills.'

'Who are you?'

'Soldiers, miss,' Tully said. 'I'm Paddy Tully, Private, Royal Signals. That's Private Gooch, Ordnance Corps. Armourer by trade. That's Corporal Harkaway. Squire Harkaway. Engineers. All on attachment to the King's African Rifles. We got cut off.'

There was a long silence as she studied them. 'What do you intend to do?' she asked. 'Head south for Kenya?'

'Eventually,' Harkaway said.

'But how have you managed to live, surrounded by Italians?'

They looked at each other, wondering how they might explain to someone devoted to the promotion of peace that they'd been selling arms to the natives who, unfortunately, had been using them to shoot each other.

'We managed,' Harkaway said.

'How about food?'

'Bought a bit. Shot a bit. We've got guns.' Harkaway indicated the weapons they'd taken from the Italians. 'Now, it seems we have four more.' His eyes were gleaming. 'And since we're at it,' he went on, 'we might as well have their uniforms, too. They might come in useful. We've been wondering if we couldn't stir up the natives against the Italians a bit.'

Gooch and Tully nodded hurriedly. Trust Harkaway to think of something that sounded honest and patriotic.

For a moment she stood in silence as the embarrassed Italians stripped to their underwear then, as Harkaway threw their uniforms into the back of Grobelaar's truck, she turned to them and flung her arms wide in a dramatic gesture.

'I shall join you!' she said.

Harkaway turned. 'Doing what?'

'Resisting the Italians. The Church was never militant enough against the wicked!'

Gooch and Tully eyed each other. This was an unexpected bonus. Despite her spectacles, Bronwen Ortton-Daniells was a good-looking woman – early thirties, straight back, good before, good behind – and it crossed Tully's mind that even missionaries could probably have a change of heart about things like morals – especially when faced with a fine military presence like that of P. Tully, Esquire.

'What *are* you, miss?' he asked warily.

79

'I'm Methodist,' she informed them proudly. 'What are you?'

A Liverpool Irishman by birth, Tully was Catholic by upbringing, but since he'd joined the army it had never meant much and at the moment it seemed wiser to keep it dark.

'I'm a Baptist,' he said stoutly, hoping his Catholic God wouldn't strike him dead on the spot for his lies.

The woman gestured. 'There's little difference,' she conceded. 'I think we should offer up a prayer of thanks for our safe delivery and for help in our project.'

Gooch and Tully would have let her get on with it but Harkaway, who'd been watching them with his sardonic smile, interrupted. 'Oh, no, you don't!' he said briskly. 'The middle of a bloody battle's no time to be getting down on our knees. Save it till we're well away from here!'

For a moment, she looked at him in the gathering darkness, tall, lean, good-looking with his red hair and foxy face. At first it seemed she was about to protest but in the end she meekly acquiesced.

'Of course,' she said, equally briskly. 'We must get away.'

They found her baggage beside the dead camel and from it, she fished out an old cardigan which she slipped on and buttoned firmly to hold her blouse in place, then she dragged out a comb and started work on the dusty mop round her face.

'I shall need to wash my hair,' she said.

'Not here,' Harkaway pointed out.

'I don't intend to wash it here,' she retorted sharply. 'Merely to comb it.'

'Save it,' he said. 'For all we know, the Italians have already heard what's happened and we ought to be on our way.'

She was on the point of objecting again but, in the end, she stuffed away the comb and was about to pick up her baggage when Tully picked it up for her. Neither he nor Gooch had any intention of riding with Harkaway in the Italians' lorry or with Grobelaar in the Bedford. In fact, Gooch was already sitting in the front of the Lancia alongside the woman and Tully gave him a dirty look, tossed the woman's baggage in the back then climbed aboard himself and put his head close to the woman's.

'Okay, miss,' he said.

As the convoy began to move off, Grobelaar leading, Tully looked back to where the Italians and the askari were still standing disconsolately at the side of the road. He indicated the direction towards the north-west.

'Okay,' he said. 'Hop it, you lot.'

8

The news that the Strada del Duce was blocked arrived at General Guidotti's headquarters in Bidiyu the following morning. He was on the verandah drinking his coffee when a car came tearing into the town, trailing a cloud of dust, and pulled up at the gendarmerie he had set up. A man jumped out and ran inside.

Guidotti sat up, interested, wondering what could have caused such urgency. There had been no sign even of British aeroplanes for several days now. He fingered a signal he'd received from Rome in answer to the one he'd sent informing Mussolini of the naming of the road from Jijiga to Bidiyu in his honour. It offered congratulations and ended with the usual virile fascist greeting. 'The nation's strength comes from its brave men.' It pleased Guidotti and he began to wonder when he might expect promotion.

As he daydreamed, a figure detached itself from the gendarmerie and started to hurry across the sandy square. It was Major Di Sanctis and Guidotti sat more upright, wondering again what had happened. Di Sanctis was a good officer, if inclined to peacock a little. He had an Ethiopian mistress who'd been with him ever since 1938, Guidotti knew, and he'd contrived to bring her to Bidiyu. It was against regulations, he supposed, but since senior officers did it, Guidotti had no intention of stopping Di Sanctis, especially since she was decorative enough to be a pleasure to see.

As he watched, Colonel Piccio appeared from his billet, on his way to take coffee with the general as was his habit. He was spotted at once by the hurrying Di Sanctis and

Guidotti saw them confer. Then Piccio began to hurry towards him, struggling to keep his dignity as he tried hard not to run.

As he stopped in front of Guidotti, his large eyes were angry.

'The road's been blocked,' he said.

'Which road?'

'Our road, Excellency. Your road. Just before last night's petrol lorry got through.'

'An accident?'

'I hardly think so, sir. It was in the Wirir Gorge. The whole cliff's come down on it. It will take days to clear.'

'What is it, Piccio?' Guidotti said stiffly. 'A landslide? Because, if so, spit it out. I haven't all day.'

Di Sanctis stepped forward. 'No, Excellency,' he said. 'Not a landslide. An explosion was heard. Somebody dynamited it. Despite what we thought, there *is* resistance.'

Guidotti was sitting bolt upright now.

'It was obviously carefully selected,' Di Sanctis went on. 'At its narrowest point. At the 200th kilometre sign. You remember we put up one of our markers there. One of the large ones with the eagle and fasces and the laurel wreath. It was our intention to place a bust of the Duce –'

'Get on,' Guidotti snapped.

Di Sanctis stiffened. 'A dead camel was found. There were also three stray camels wandering in the road.'

'Who brought the news?'

'Corporal Brazzi was in command, Excellency. He had with him two privates, one a driver, and an askari who drove the lorry. The askari appeared at the post at Dudub and they telephoned the post at Guldari which sent a car.'

'What about Brazzi?'

'He's still somewhere outside Dudub, suffering, according to the askari, from blisters. He has the two privates with him. The askari ran the whole way after they climbed the pile of rubble the explosion had brought down.'

'Then who –' Guidotti demanded '– is guarding the petrol?'

'Ah!' Di Sanctis frowned. This was the part that had been

bothering him. 'I'm afraid the petrol has been lost, Excellency.'

'Under the rubble?'

'No, Excellency.'

'Spilled?'

'No, sir. It was stolen.'

Guidotti exploded. '*Maria, Madre di Dio!*' he yelled. 'After all this time we have only just got to the crux of the matter! What you're trying to tell me is that we have lost a lorryload of petrol!'

'*And* the lorry,' Di Sanctis said.

'Not only the lorry, Excellency,' Piccio added, 'but also the car. The car we sent to General Forsci to accompany the lorry on its journey here with the petrol.'

Guidotti's face went red. He forced himself to regain control. He knew all the stories about Italians being over-excitable but he came from Rome and couldn't be expected to yell like a Neapolitan. 'Go on.' He spoke quietly, but his hands were trembling.

Di Sanctis cleared his throat. He was not enjoying himself very much. 'Quite clearly a large amount of explosive was used, Excellency. This officer –' he gestured at the man from the car who had appeared just behind him '– says it was planted with great skill, by someone who clearly knew a great deal about it.'

Piccio interrupted again excitedly. 'It will need bulldozers,' he said.

'I haven't got bulldozers,' Guidotti snapped.

'Then we shall have to get them from Berbera, Excellency.'

'If they've got them *there*. Turn out the 49th Colonial Battalion and get them up to the Wirir Gorge. Start clearing it at once. Recruit native labour. They can take the place of the 49th as soon as we have sufficient. We shall probably need explosives ourselves if there are large boulders.'

As Guidotti gave his orders, he remembered General Forsci, in Jijiga, who commanded west of the border and had sent the petrol. 'You'd better inform Jijiga,' he said.

'Warn them to hold up all traffic until we let them know the road's clear.'

As he'd been talking, Guidotti had been putting on his jacket and buttoning it up. His servant handed him his fly whisk and his cap and he was about to head after Piccio when he realized he still wore his bedroom slippers. He took a swing at his servant with his fly whisk and the servant vanished into the house, yelling. A moment later, a soldier appeared with a pair of newly polished riding boots. He was still rubbing at them as Guidotti pulled them on.

An hour and a half later Guidotti was standing on top of the pile of rubble that blocked the Wirir Gorge.

'Mother of God,' he said. 'Who did this?'

'Patriots?' Piccio suggested.

'There are no patriots in Somaliland,' Di Sanctis put in. 'The Somalis don't care who runs the place so long as they're left to herd their camels and goats and sheep.'

'You know this, of course?' Piccio said sarcastically.

'Yes, *Colonello*.' Di Sanctis spoke quietly. 'I know.'

Piccio was about to argue but Guidotti realized that Di Sanctis got his information from his black mistress, who doubtless got it in the market. They always said the best way to learn a language was in bed. Perhaps bed was also the best place to obtain information.

He gestured at Piccio who turned back to the problem of clearing the pass. 'When will native labour arrive?'

'They're on their way, Excellency.'

'Good. Establish an armed post here. Within a day we shall have the road open and in a week back to normal. From now on there'll be lorry patrols of infantry every two hours. They're to stop and investigate anything suspicious. They'll be accompanied by an armoured car. Arrange with Jijiga for refuelling and feeding. Native caravans will be kept off the road. They can go via Mandera. From now on this road will be used only by Italian vehicles.'

To Bronwen Ortton-Daniells, the cave in the Bur Yi Hills looked remarkably uncomfortable.

They were stiff and tired when they arrived at Shimber Addi and Tully was sleeping in the rear of the car, with his head on her baggage. As Grobelaar drew the Bedford to a halt she stopped the Lancia just behind him. As he came towards her, smiling, his eye-patch dark in his tired face, she leaned out of the cab.

'That was a difficult road, Private Grobelaar,' she said.

'*Mister* Grobelaar,' he corrected. 'I'm not a soldier.'

As she climbed out, Harkaway eyed her with interest. She was straight-backed and straight-legged, her head up proudly, her topee top-dead-centre on her hair. The sun was picking up the angles of her face, and despite the spectacles, it was a good face, with strong lines, a good chin, a short upper lip, a straight nose and a high forehead. He put her age at about thirty-two, older than himself but still good-looking, though the heat of East Africa had taken its toll, and there was a tightness about her mouth that suggested there had been some disappointment that had driven her there from England. He wondered what man had let her down.

She was staring round the cave. It was untidy and full of opened boxes. Cigarette ends were scattered on the floor and there were dirty billycans and empty tins lying about, while the ashes of a dead fire smoked in the entrance. Three sets of boxes had been dragged together to make beds. A fourth bed had been made in the native manner with rope by Grobelaar who was older than the others and prized his comfort.

'Is this where you sleep?'

Harkaway threw down the captured Italian uniforms and weapons. 'Sometimes. Sometimes we sleep in an old house in Eil Dif. Not so cold at nights.' As he spoke, he wondered what she would think of the girls who visited Gooch and Tully.

'Sleeping will be a problem,' she commented. 'I don't think I could manage on a hard box. Women have hips.'

'You can have my bed,' Grobelaar offered. 'I'll make another.'

She stared about her through the steel-rimmed spectacles.

'It's very dirty,' she observed. 'We must do something about it. Cleanliness is next to godliness.'

'We've not had much time, Miss – er – er –' Tully stumbled over her name. He could hardly wade through 'Miss Ortton-Daniells' every time he wanted to address her but 'Bronwen' seemed a bit too presumptuous for a mission worker. 'We've got no brushes or anything.'

'Surely you can make one? There are twigs outside. The French make their brooms of twigs.' She looked at Gooch. 'What's your name?'

Gooch looked at her. 'Gooch,' he said.

'I can't call you "Gooch".'

'Everybody else does.'

'Haven't you a Christian name?'

'Yes. It's Harvey. I prefer Gooch.'

'Very well. Gooch it shall be. You can clear the dirty tins. They bring flies.'

As she turned to Harkaway, he smiled coolly. 'I'm an NCO,' he said quickly, 'NCOs don't work. We lead the prayers on church parade.'

She wasn't in the slightest put out by his smile. 'What's your name?' she demanded.

'George. Most people call me "Squire".'

'Why?'

'Better ask 'em.'

'Doubtless because you've had the benefit of a superior education. You've obviously been well-brought-up. You must be in charge, since you're an NCO. But you can still do a little tidying up, surely. Who's the cook?'

'Won't *you* be the cook?' Tully asked.

'I've never been a cook, Paddy,' she said coldly. 'At home in England my family employed a cook. Out here in Africa, we always had an African. Perhaps we can get one from the village down the hill.'

'We don't want them up here,' Harkaway said sharply.

'Why not?'

He gestured at the crates of food and weapons and she was silent for a moment. 'I see,' she said. 'In that case we must take it in turns.'

'Where shall we hang the chintz curtains?' Harkaway asked sarcastically.

Unwillingly they started to tidy the place while Bronwen Ortton-Daniells poked about among the boxes.

'There are primus stoves,' she said. 'And plenty of food.'

'Not enough for a banquet,' Harkaway pointed out. 'There are four of us. Five now. Same with paraffin. It's dark up here at night without a lamp. That's why we use fires instead of primus stoves.'

'I see,' she said again. 'Are there many guns?'

'Two Vickers. Two Brens. Four old Lewises. Two hundred rifles.' He glanced at Gooch and Tully. 'Slightly less now. They're mostly old Martinis intended for native levies with a bullet as big as your finger. Relics of old South African wars, I expect. There are still a lot about. The rest are Lee Enfields.'

'How about water?'

'We get it from Eil Dif.'

'Have we got enough for me to wash my hair and have a bath?'

Tully looked up quickly. Gooch stopped what he was doing and Grobelaar fumbled the twigs he was trying to tie round the end of a pole he had cut from a stunted tree to make a broom.

Harkaway smiled. 'It'll have to be a stand-up affair with a bucket,' he pointed out. 'I expect we can cut the top off one of the petrol cans for you. You'll look like that picture, "Morning" – girl stripped to the buff shoving her toe in a pond.'

She looked round, not in the slightest put out. 'I expect I shall manage,' she said. 'I've had bucket baths before. I think also, for the sake of hygiene and good sense, I'll cut my hair short.'

Grobelaar finished tying the twigs. 'I know how to cut hair,' he said.

She dragged up a box, found a pair of scissors in her baggage and handed them to him. Half an hour later, watched all the time by the others, she emerged with her hair cropped.

'It's all right,' Tully said approvingly. 'I once had a girl in Widnes who had her hair cut like that.'

Even Harkaway was impressed. Bronwen Ortton-Daniells was a good-looking woman with a splendid figure, like the Somali women lean as a gazelle but far from lacking in shape.

She ran her fingers over the stubble on her neck. She was well aware that they were all watching her silently and it was a new experience. The men she'd been used to working with were on the whole men whom, she realized now, she hadn't greatly admired, men who prayed a great deal, talked a lot about Jesus and were largely dull. There had been an Italian doctor who'd arrived with the Italian army whose advances had troubled her, because he was strikingly handsome like so many Italians, but her hatred of them after the butchery of the Ethiopians during the Abyssinian War and the massacre of the Abyssinian intelligentsia following an attempt to assassinate the Governor, Graziani, had been so heartfelt she'd been unable to bring herself to reply when he spoke to her. These men were different. They were British and they were frankly admiring, in a virile, manly way that she found disturbed her.

She turned away abruptly, her face pink.

'I shall now wash it,' she announced.

When Tully rose the following morning, Bronwen Ortton-Daniells, her glasses gleaming in the sunshine, was using a towel on her neck. The bucket they'd made for her was full of dirty water and she was obviously bathed and clean.

Tully looked at her, his eyes full of disappointment. The previous night she had washed her hair with a cake of scented soap she possessed and Tully had hung around for ages in the hope that she'd take a bath. But she'd been as crafty as he was and had bided her time.

'You've had it!' he said indignantly.

'Yes, Paddy,' she said coolly. 'I've had it!'

Tully stared at her sullenly. 'I never saw you disappear,' he said.

'It's one of my skills. Living in Africa where there isn't a great deal of privacy, one learns these things.'

'She's had her bloody bath!' Tully said later to Grobelaar. 'While we were asleep.'

Grobelaar shifted in his blankets. 'Next time you'd better get her to let you scrub her back, man,' he said. 'Then you won't miss it.'

Over breakfast, they studied the three vehicles standing near the cave, all dusty, their wings a little dented, but all in good working order.

'What are we going to do with 'em?' Tully asked.

As they talked desultorily, Bronwen Ortton-Daniells listened to them. It didn't disturb her to be surrounded by men. She'd always lived in a man's world. She had four elder brothers and had spent most of her youth keeping her head above water among them. Men, she considered, had let her down. Her father by going bankrupt and hanging himself just when she'd been thinking of marriage, and the man to whom she'd been engaged by backing away at full speed when her father died. For several years after that she had looked after a sick mother because her brothers, all married with families, had, like her fiancé, backed away from responsibility as fast as they could go. When her mother had died, because she was untrained and could think of nothing else, she had offered her services to the London Foreign Mission.

She had not expected problems. As a child she'd been given the Bible and set the task of learning by heart great chunks of Isaiah, Jeremiah, Judges, Proverbs and Psalms. She'd done it with a dogged willpower, determined to answer her father's fanatic zeal with a zeal of her own. She'd read the Bible to her sick mother, even re-enacting scenes from the Old Testament with her, and in the arid religious household she'd inhabited it was the only fun she remembered.

When she'd reached Abyssinia she'd found it very different from what she'd expected, but by then it was too late and she'd thrown herself into the work. Her mother and father had never spared the rod in bringing up their children and it had given their daughter a courage that took a lot of holding down. She'd often thought of changing her job but she'd started late and, with her life beginning to slip away, it had been too late to think of anything else.

As she sat outside the cave and stared over the dusty plain, she decided it had probably been a dreadful mistake. After six years she'd achieved nothing and, despite her warm heart, the only children she'd had to love had been small black children belonging to other people whom she'd taught in a little school that was pathetic by anybody else's standards but had been accepted with gratitude by the people among whom she'd worked. It had taken all her courage to give it all up and head for Somaliland.

As she sat silently, her Bible on her lap, a lizard stared back at her, motionless, unblinking and statuesque. Somewhere overhead in the brassy sky an aeroplane was droning but she couldn't see it and had no idea whether it was Italian or British from Aden. Unnoticed, the lizard she'd been watching slipped away. Somewhere in the scrub was the strong musty smell of leopard, probably the one which had once inhabited the cave they'd taken over. None of the others seemed to have noticed it and she realized her years in Africa had probably made her more perceptive.

They were still discussing the vehicles they'd acquired.

'We ought to do something with 'em,' Tully said, nagging at the idea.

'Okay,' Gooch said, 'what?'

Bronwen Ortton-Daniells sat up.

'We could always go to war,' she said.

Gooch's head turned. 'We went to war,' he pointed out. 'And we lost it. Here, anyway.'

Tully shrugged. 'It's nothing to do with us now,' he pointed out.

'It was something to do with you when you blew up the road – and me with it.'

They looked at each other. She'd made no further mention of the incident and they'd assumed she'd not known the culprits.

'How did you know it was us?' Harkaway asked quietly.

'I'm not a fool.'

Grobelaar smiled. 'No offence taken?'

'It was in a good cause. It still would be. Why *don't* you fight the Italians?'

'Four of us?' Gooch said.

She looked coldly at him. She knew about guns and had no fear of them. Before her father's bankruptcy, he and her brothers had all shot and she'd often handled guns. And when the Italians had come to Abyssinia, she'd several times been under fire while helping the wounded.

'Five,' she said quietly. 'There are five of us now.'

They were still staring at her when Grobelaar stood up, suddenly alert and peering over the plain below. Harkaway joined him and the two of them moved to where the three vehicles they'd been discussing stood on the edge of the road, overlooking the rocky slope.

'Lorries,' Gobelaar said.

'Here?' At once Gooch and Tully were on their feet and staring with them. As Bronwen Ortton-Daniells joined them, she saw the lorries – four of them, with an armoured car and a scout car – were approaching the white mud-walled flat-roofed houses of Eil Dif.

'They'll find us,' Gooch said.

'No, they won't!' Harkaway gestured briskly at the lorries. 'Kom-Kom, drive 'em higher up the hill! High as you can get 'em! Hide 'em among the rocks, then sweep the road so there are no tracks. You drive the Lancia, Danny.'

Her head jerked up. She'd never like the name Bronwen, associating it somehow with the rigid attitudes of her father. Somehow, also, it could never be shortened so that people had always addressed her by her full title as 'Miss Ortton-Daniells,' which had always seemed too much of a mouthful. 'Danny' seemed so natural she couldn't imagine why she'd never thought of it before, and she hurried to the Lancia, her heart surging with happiness and the feeling that some-how, here, among these rocks, in the company of soldiers, she was finding herself for the first time.

As the engine of the Bedford roared and the gears crashed wildly, Harkaway grabbed the crowbar and led the other two down the hill. They could see the Italian vehicles now pulling into Eil Dif, trailing their feathers of dust.

Half a mile down the slope, there was a gap in the piled rocks. It lay just on the lower side of a group of high boulders that towered above it in silent towers and screes. On the other side of the road, the mountain fell away into tormented rifts and valleys filled with scrub and bare stunted trees. They'd more than once parked the lorry here when they'd been searching for buck and there were plenty of wheel-tracks left in the dust.

'Let's have those rocks down,' Harkaway said, pointing. 'Across the road.'

Struggling with the crowbar, his big muscles bulging, Gooch loosened several of the boulders which crashed down and rolled across the road in a cloud of dust. Tully and Harkaway worked below him and after a while Grobelaar and Danny Ortton-Daniells joined them. Together the five of them sweated and strained until they had a respectable-looking pile of rubble spread across the road as if from a fall of rocks.

'Now,' Harkaway said. 'Get some of that scrub and sweep the tracks beyond them. Make the bastards think we never went higher than this.'

They had almost finished when they heard the grind of gears and, with a last flick at the road, they disappeared into the rocks. A few minutes later, the armoured car appeared, followed by one of the lorries. Reaching the scatter of rocks, the armoured car stopped. A head appeared, then two or three men jumped from the lorry and peered about them. Hands pointed and there was a quick conversation in Italian.

'What are they saying, Danny?' Harkaway whispered.

'They've decided no one could have got a lorry beyond here,' she said.

'Have the wogs in Eil Dif said anything?'

'It doesn't sound like it.'

Two of the men from the lorry had climbed over the scattered rocks and were studying the dusty earth beyond.

'Let's hope they're city dwellers,' Grobelaar whispered, 'and don't know much about tracking.'

'Do you?'

'Sure. Learned it from Wild West films.'

The Italians seemed to examine the track for hours, small dark men with puttees, baggy trousers like plus-fours and wide-brimmed topees. The men with them were all black Eritreans or Italian Somalis dressed in the white robes of a Gruppo Banda, the native guerrilla troops they trained.

'They're going,' Danny said after a while. 'They've decided that a lorry's been up here, but never beyond.'

The Italians climbed back into their vehicles and ground slowly down the steep slope back to Eil Dif. As they vanished from sight, Harkaway grinned and flung his arms round Danny. It was a spontaneous gesture and meant nothing to him but Harkaway was a good-looking young man and it made her blush. As he released her, she pretended to be busy with her shoe, and rose, pushing at her hair, keeping her face away from them until the pink had gone from her cheeks.

From the slopes, they watched the Italians return to Eil Dif and crawl away across the plain. When they were sure they had finally disappeared, they dragged the rocks aside while Grobelaar hurried up the slope to fetch the Lancia. Piling in, they drove down to Eil Dif.

Yussuf met them, his face crafty.

'We told them nothing, effendi,' he said. 'We said we had seen men with guns but that we had none.'

'What did they say?'

'They said they will come back. They said they will keep an eye on the village. Perhaps they don't believe us.'

Back at Shimber Addi, they celebrated with cans of beer. It was cold in the evening and they were glad of the fire which filled the cave with dancing shadows but gave a measure of warmth to their chilled bodies.

'My back's cold,' Gooch complained. 'I need an overcoat.'

'Next time we stop an Italian lorry, we'll get you one.'

'Well, it'd be an idea, wouldn't it?'

They looked at each other, because it *would* be an idea. The lorries they'd seen had often contained men wearing coats for their journey through the hills.

'Get us some music, Paddy,' Gooch said. 'Something to cheer us up.'

Tully crouched over the radio, trying to find his way on to an Italian wavelength to pick up news of what might be happening between Jijiga and Bidiyu. The cave was filled with the clatter of morse then, switching the band, Tully finally found the BBC.

'. . . It is said there are twenty acres of officer prisoners and a hundred acres of men. It has been a classic advance . . .'

Tully switched off the set sourly. 'Looks like they're knocking hell's bells out of us in Egypt,' he said.

Harkaway frowned. 'Switch it on again,' he said sharply. 'It isn't *us* they're talking about. The BBC wouldn't say that if *we* were losing. They'd dress it up a bit.'

'You're a bloody optimist,' Tully said, bending over the set again. 'The Eyeties are in Greece, Cyrenaica, Libya, Abyssinia, Eritrea and Italian, British and French Somaliland. They've got Egypt surrounded.'

'For God's sake –' Harkaway's voice rose abruptly, loud and commanding '– stop yapping and get on with it!'

Tully gave him a sour look and by the time he raised London again, the news had finished, and all he could get was dance music. Working the dials, he managed to pick up Johannesburg and Nairobi but they seemed to have missed the main news and there seemed to be nothing but stories about South African Air Force planes attacking the Italian Regio Aeronautica and destroying their machines on the ground. Harar, Massawa, Mogadiscio, Asmara and Diredawa were all being hammered, it seemed, with considerable losses to the Italians in aircraft and transport. But this wasn't what they were seeking, and Harkaway gestured angrily.

'Try Radio Geneva.'

'It'll be in French.'

'I can understand it.'

Tully gave Harkaway a sidelong look and found Geneva. Once again they managed only to get a fraction of what was being said. 'The British,' they heard, 'are in rear of Nibeiwa . . .'

Grobelaar sat up. 'Nibeiwa's in the Western Desert,' he said excitedly. 'It's where the Eyeties have their line of forts! They run between Nibeiwa and Sofafi. They kept a map in the Public Works Office in Berbera. I saw it.'

Harkaway glared at him. 'Shut up,' he snapped. 'Shut up, all of you. Listen!'

As they became silent the voice of the announcer filled the cave. '. . . The British have now cut the coast road between Buq Buq and Sidi Barrani, which is expected to fall tomorrow. General Wavell estimates that five Italian divisions are likely to be *hors de combat*.'

It was impossible to discover more, but it was enough to put them on edge and Harkaway kept the protesting Tully glued to the set. Eventually late that night, he was able to present them with a picture of what was happening.

'The Eyeties are running like rabbits,' he said in amazement.

Their geography of the North African coast was vague and it was Grobelaar who provided them with the location of the places whose names they'd heard from the map he'd seen.

'Jesus,' Gooch said as the South African drew a rough outline in the sand with a stick, 'we're throwing 'em right out of Libya! If they lose that, this lot here in East Africa are going to be cut off.'

Harkaway's eyes were glinting. 'There's one thing: it means they'll have more on their minds than just us. They'll be conserving petrol, and they'll be worried in case the Abyssinians start on them. They've got no love for them. They only took the place over in 1936 and a lot of 'em disappeared into the hills and formed patriot bands. Shiftas, they call 'em. They didn't like Haile Selassie very much so they've never had much time for the Italians.'

'How do you know?'

'I've read about it!' Harkaway snapped, his eyes contemptuous. 'I don't go about with my eyes shut, my ears shut, and my bloody head shut! I bet they're worried sick. The Abyssinians are bound to have a go at 'em now.'

'Why not us, too?' Danny closed her Bible and turned to them.

They swung round to face her.

'Why not *us*?' Tully asked.

'Yes,' Harkaway agreed briskly. 'Why not us?'

'How do four of us – five then! – how do five of us set about that lot?' Grobelaar asked. 'They've got a hundred thousand men in East Africa, twenty thousand of 'em here. We can't do much against that lot.'

'Let's find a few more then.'

Gooch and Tully were listening speechlessly. Grobelaar was wearing his worried old man's expression. Danny's eyes were shining with enthusiasm.

'Why not?' she said excitedly. 'Before I left French Somaliland I heard of guerrillas in Abyssinia being raised by an English colonel. He'd crossed the border and stirred up enough trouble already to keep four Italian brigades busy.'

'You ought to be in intelligence,' Harkaway said admiringly. 'What else?'

'I heard that another man called Wingate had flown into Gojjam and was passing the news round Abyssinia that the return of the Emperor Haile Selassie was imminent.'

'You sure about this?'

'You know what the Africans are like. The bush telegraph works, even if it isn't connected up with wires to a telephone.'

'That means we must be intending to start an offensive against them. They wouldn't risk it otherwise. They must be coming from the Sudan and Kenya.'

'Christ,' Tully said. 'Listen to the general.'

Harkaway turned on him savagely. 'I've forgotten more about military history,' he snapped, 'than a pinhead like you could learn in a lifetime.'

There was an abrupt silence as there always was when he dropped some hint of his past, and they waited for him to explain. But he went on as if he had no time for their curiosity. 'Where the hell else would they come from?' he demanded. 'Only Aden. Things have changed, can't you see?' He leaned forward, peering at them, willing them to understand. 'Until this thing in the Western Desert, it was British Somaliland that was surrounded. Now, with the Italians pushed back into Libya, it's Italian East Africa that's surrounded. They can expect no help from anywhere. And if we're going to set about Italian East Africa, we'll obviously make for Addis Ababa, the capital. And the quickest way to Addis is from the southern Sudan or up from Kenya.'

'That won't help *us* much,' Gooch said.

'Christ!' Harkaway sounded irritated. 'The navy could set up a landing from Aden like that!' He snapped his fingers.

'Into French Somaliland. Or Berbera. That'd make our friends in Bidiyu think. I'll bet the buggers are running round in circles already, wondering what to do. Why don't we make 'em run faster?'

'What are you going to use for troops?' Gooch asked.

'The Somalis. You can teach 'em to shoot and perform simple manoeuvres. We used to recruit 'em for the Somali Mounted Infantry.'

'They'll fight.' Danny leaned forward eagerly. 'The Somalis are the Irishmen of Africa. Somaliland formed part of the land of Cush mentioned in Genesis.'

'Somaliland's the empire's arse,' Tully said flatly. 'And this place's right up it.'

She ignored him and went on enthusiastically. 'They're greedy, vain, excitable and quarrelsome, and they know that they'll never be wealthy so that victory would mean loot and that would mean riches and wives. And because they're Moslems, the prospect of death doesn't trouble them much.'

Harkaway reached out and touched her hand. It was a sign of approval, nothing more, but it pleased her tremendously.

'The Odessi and the Harari have already shown they can use guns,' he said. 'If only to kill each other. Why not persuade them to kill Italians instead?'

Grobelaar laughed. 'They're not interested in killing Italians,' he said.

'They could be made to be,' Danny said. 'They're brave and indifferent to pain.'

'And they enjoy fighting,' Harkaway added. 'They learn to throw spears while they're still kids. Why not at the Italians? Persuade them there's money to be had. Money that means camel herds and sheep and goats.'

'You can't just turn loose a few hundred uneducated blackies on European-trained soldiers,' Gooch said.

'Then train them to the same standard.'

'Us?'

'We're all soldiers, for God's sake! We all know what to do.'

Gooch and Tully looked at each other, unspeaking.

'We have over two hundred rifles,' Harkaway went on. 'We have eight machine guns, mortars, land mines, grenades. We have three vehicles. Let's teach 'em to drive. Teach 'em to shoot. Teach 'em what to do. Their women will encourage them, especially if they think there's silver to be had, and goats and sheep to feed their children.'

Gooch and Tully looked at each other again.

'They're quick to pick things up,' Danny said, caught by Harkaway's enthusiasm. 'I've taught them skills myself. And they're nomads, indifferent to comfort. Death's part of their everyday life. They'd make good soldiers.'

'The Italians have made them soldiers,' Harkaway went on. 'The British army's made them soldiers. Why can't we? Now's the time, while the Italians are reeling from what's happened in the north.' He glared angrily at them. 'Don't you see, you bloody dimwits? It's changed the whole set-up. Until now, they surrounded the British. Now, the British are surrounding *them*. Now's the time to hit 'em for six, while they're still wondering what to do.'

Tully looked at him indignantly. 'That's been your bloody idea all the time!' he accused.

Harkaway rounded on him. 'Of course it has, you stupid clot,' he said. 'I'm a soldier. You don't think I've been sitting here on my bum all this time like you, thinking of nothing but beer and women, do you?'

'You said we'd go to Kenya! Or Portuguese East!'

'Well, now we're going to hammer the Eyeties instead.' Harkaway paused. 'But, if we're going to recruit the locals we'll need someone who can speak their language.'

'We've got Yussuf,' Grobelaar pointed out.

'I can just imagine a battle with all the orders going through him. "Muchee shootee this side. Very quick run." '

'We can do better than that,' Danny said quietly. 'We *have* someone who can speak their language very well.'

'Who?'

'Me.'

10

The news from the Western Desert had also been heard in Bidiyu.

Rumours had reached them of a disaster in North Africa, and as usual nobody knew where it had come from. Africa was immense but somehow news could travel across its breadth or along its length, passing from one country to another, overcoming frontiers, language barriers, tribal ill-will, and still be the truth. Rome Radio insisted there had been *no* disaster but Guidotti was suspicious and insisted on hearing the news from the BBC.

'They claim Graziani's army's been wiped out,' Piccio said.

'Try to get Switzerland,' Guidotti suggested. 'They're neutral. It'll be the truth from there.'

But Radio Geneva produced exactly the same story: acres of Italian prisoners, and more being rounded up every day.

'Rome still insists there's been no disaster,' Piccio pointed out.

'Propaganda,' Guidotti muttered. '*Troppo propaganda*.'

After all, he thought, when they'd taken Sidi Barrani in 1940, Rome had said they'd got the town back on its feet, even to the extent of opening the night clubs and starting the trams running, when, as Guidotti well knew, there were no night clubs and no trams and Sidi Barrani was only a dusty little Arab town.

And hadn't Rome trumpeted the triumph in British So-maliland as imperishable laurels to be added to Italian arms, when everybody knew it had been a very minor sort of affair. You could hardly call a campaign which had produced less than three hundred enemy casualties a major victory. No matter how much the Duce might offer it as another Polish campaign and compare it with the German triumph in France, Guidotti knew very well it was nothing of the sort.

Piccio, his mind still on the Western Desert, was speaking slowly. 'Marshal Graziani was always a bit of a snail,' he was saying. 'It's a pity Marshal Balbo was killed in that air raid on Tobruk.'

'They say it wasn't the air raid that killed him,' Di Sanctis pointed out. 'They say he was removed because the Duce was jealous of his popularity.'

Guidotti looked at Di Sanctis. '*Who* says?' he asked.

'I've heard it said, Excellency.'

'Then you'd better not listen, my friend.' Guidotti tapped the map. 'Let's think instead of this and its implications for us. How did it happen? Graziani had two hundred and fifty thousand men in Libya. Rome said so. And the Italian navy was well placed to control both the Mediterranean and the Red Sea.'

'Unfortunately, Excellency,' Di Sanctis put in, 'since then there has been Taranto.'

'But the British had no more than seventy-five thousand men for the whole of North and East Africa.' Guidotti frowned. 'Perhaps they just made them seem more. Perhaps too many of our people listened to the Duce's promise that the war would soon be over without fighting and decided it wasn't worth taking risks. Perhaps they hoped that if they did nothing the British would do nothing too.'

'Though we call the Mediterranean *our* sea,' Di Sanctis said slowly, as if he couldn't believe his own words, 'a large part of it has always remained *their* sea.'

Guidotti gestured. 'My brother writes to me from Bardia –' he paused, remembering that Bardia had been swept with Derna and Tobruk and a few other places into the British net and that there would not be very many more letters from there, '– he wrote that they managed to make one man look like a dozen, one tank look like a squadron, one raid look like an advance. In war, you have as many men as you can persuade your enemy you have. I think our country was psychologically unprepared for war.'

'But *Tobruk*!' Piccio's arms flapped in a helpless gesture. 'And now Bardia and Dernia! Excellency, it's not possible. We were a hundred miles into Egypt. Now we're fighting two hundred miles back in Libya.'

Guidotti frowned. Like Harkaway, he had a suspicion that the East African Empire Mussolini had so proudly proclaimed was before long going to be assailed from three sides. Weapons, men, munitions, petrol, transport and aircraft had been stockpiled because of what Mussolini had called a 'total blockade' of British possessions in Africa and the Mediterranean, and the idea was merely to await the relief that would be provided by a breakthrough via Egypt. The idea of cutting the British lines of communication with Egypt now seemed to have sunk with the ships at Taranto, however, and it seemed that the blockade was about to start working the other way. Moreover, never once since they'd crossed the frontier into British territory had the Italian forces been free of air raids. They had never been big but they'd nagged, and the number of Italian aircraft had dwindled with every day they'd appeared overhead. To Guidotti the air raids seemed to point to only one thing: the British intended to return and, now that they'd been relieved of the pressure in the Western Desert, their arrival seemed suddenly imminent.

The idea also seemed to have occurred to the natives. He'd heard revolt was stirring in southern Abyssinia. Circumstances there had always forced the maintenance of garrisons in the centres of populations and, since soldiers couldn't be everywhere at once, the Duce's writ ran only where his troops were massed and there had always been sniping and ambushes. It seemed there were bitter days ahead.

The bitter days Guidotti was expecting were already taking shape.

On the Kenya border, the British general in command was just winding up a staff conference. He'd not long returned from Cairo where he'd been meeting the C-in-C, Middle East, and the commander of the British forces in the Sudan. His men were still struggling to keep his aeroplanes flying against odds that Guidotti never realized. Working in the appalling heat, they were building new landing grounds, tearing down trees, filling up the holes of ant bears, burning the undergrowth, digging away the giant anthills, never with anything more than the miserable huddle of a native town as a headquarters.

As he pushed his papers aside, the general looked up at Colonel Charlton. 'That's it then, Charlie,' he said. 'They stir up rebellion in Abyssinia and retake Massala in February. They've got the 4th and 5th Indian Divisions. It isn't much but the Italians can't be feeling very happy now they've heard what's happening in Libya. Their morale was never the best, anyway. We're going to maintain pressure on Moyale and as soon as the rains are over, we advance on Kismayu and up the River Juba. We have the 1st South African Division and the 11th and 12th African Divisions. That also isn't much, but it's up to us to do the best we can.'

Colonel Charlton nodded, taking it all in quietly. 'I think we shall manage, sir,' he said.

'Yes, I think we shall,' the general agreed. 'All the same, let's not be unprepared. We shall need bearers, mules, and horses, together with drivers. I know it's a mechanized war but you'd better put out feelers just in case. And if we can manage to start a local revolt, so much the better.'

The local revolt the general was hoping for was nearer than he realized.

Because, by a miracle, to the east of Bidiyu, Habr Odessi and Harari tribesmen were standing in lines, mixed together yet not attempting to knock each other's heads in.

It had taken a lot of doing but they'd done it. It had required hours of talking by Danny Ortton-Daniells before Yussuf had been prepared even to put it to Abduruman, his chief. More hours of talking had followed with the promise of much loot before the chief had agreed to meet Chief Daoud of the Harari.

'So far, so good,' Harkaway had said. 'Now we have to persuade Chief Daoud of the advantages of killing Italians instead of Habr Odessi. Can you do it, Danny?'

She studied him, her eyes gentle. 'I can do it,' she said. 'I usually manage what I set out to do.'

He looked questioningly at her and she smiled. 'I was brought up on a regime of porridge, bread and dripping and the sincere milk of the Word. The house was frugal both in food and affection, and I read the Bible under the super-intendence of my father. But there were always fierce shafts of revelation from it to keep us warm and teach us that when we chose a goal we should set out to attain it.'

Harkaway studied her. She tried to meet his eyes but failed.

'Bronwen isn't a name that suits you,' he said. 'Know what it means?'

'No.'

'I had a Welsh aunt who was also called Bronwen. It means "white-breasted".'

He smiled at her and rose, leaving her pink with embarrassment.

'You shouldn't say things like that,' she said.

'Why not? Would your milk-and-water preachers complain that it was lecherous?' He looked at her, smiling. 'Take your glasses off.'

She stared at him for a moment then, as her hand lifted to remove the spectacles, his smile widened.

'I've seen all the films, you know. They always turn out to be beautiful. In fact, it usually makes no difference, but fiction's nice and cosy, isn't it?'

'What about me? What category do I fall into?'

He smiled. 'You look much better.'

'I might look better,' she said. 'But I don't see better.'

Nevertheless, she didn't replace the spectacles. Suddenly, they seemed less important than they had and the extra effort to see things properly more than made up for the fact that Harkaway approved.

*

They started on Chief Daoud as soon as they could get him pinned down.

'There will be loot,' they explained. 'Plenty of loot. There will be gold and silver. The Habr Odessi are not wealthy. They have no gold and silver and not many camels. The Italians are from Europe. They are different and when the Italians are all dead or defeated, the Habr Odessi will be powerful.'

'Why must we fight the Italians?' Daoud asked. 'We have no quarrel with them.'

'One day –' Danny leaned forward '– this country will be yours. There will be nobody here. Neither Italians nor British.' She wasn't sure she was right in offering independence to an obscure chief with little influence outside his own area, but independence and freedom were heady words in anybody's language and, even if the old man were indifferent, the young men who stood around were listening.

The talking went on all day and halfway into the night. It seemed impossible to the Harari that they could stand alongside the Habr Odessi in battle against a common enemy.

'May we not perhaps kill just a *few* Odessi?' Daoud asked.

'Not one! The Italians and their soldiers are your enemies. Chief Abduruman of the Odessi has decided this.'

'Then perhaps we should decide the opposite.'

'Chief Abduruman sees wealth in the future. He sees Italian land becoming Odessi land.'

Daoud looked at his young men and tribal advisers. Someone whispered to him that if Abduruman were allowed to obtain too much of this Italian land it could be dangerous for the Harari.

'Where do we get our guns?' someone asked.

'From the Italians. We have *some* guns already. But not enough. Just enough to kill Italians and take *their* guns. If we use our guns and our machine guns, we could kill fifty, a hundred, Italians. Then we shall have twice as many guns. These can then be turned on other Italians. Until we have many hundred guns.'

Daoud looked at Danny. 'I am an old man,' he said. 'And

I have seen many ramazans. I'm not sure I like this idea.
But my young men see wealth in it for their sons. They see
grazing land and Somalis in Berbera running their own country. I will meet Abduruman.'

The meeting was difficult. The two old chiefs appeared, the
elders of their tribes behind them, tall men wearing robes
of every shade and variety knotted at their waists, on their
heads loose turbans of pink, white and blue. Behind them
were their young men, and behind them in their turn their
young women, lighter-skinned, soft-featured, enormous-
eyed. At first the two chiefs behaved like dogs about to
have a fight, bridling and sidling and dodging, their back
hair on end. But their vanity and their greed finally told.
Neither could bear the thought of the other being stronger
or richer, neither could bear the thought of missing the
spoils that were promised. Even stronger was their wish not
to end up as a secondary tribe to the other. Each was
determined that if anybody was going to benefit, it was not
going to be their old enemies.

'Comes back to what Churchill always used to say,' Harkaway said as they sat back in a break in the talks and drank
native tea spiced with herbs. 'Balance of power. It works
even here.'

The outcome of the talks was the line of Harari and Odessi.
They no longer wore their tobes like togas, but had wrapped
them several times round their waists as loincloths, as they
always did when they wanted their arms and chests free for
work or fighting. Lean black bodies shone in the sun. A few
tried to hold spears or the heavy-headed clubs they used for
beating their enemies senseless, but with Danny's assistance,
Harkaway persuaded then to lay them aside and concentrate
on the old Martini rifles.

They mixed them up well, first a Harari, then a Habr
Odessi, then a Harari, then a Habr Odessi, on the under-
standing that any quarrel would be settled at once between
two men and not be allowed to grow until the whole group

joined in. With the rifles from the dump they managed to arm over two hundred.

'We will learn to use the guns of the white man,' Harkaway told them. 'We will kill the Italians who have brought war to your country. We will take their clothes and their weapons and their vehicles. We will capture their silver and gold.'

'Suppose,' Chief Daoud asked from where he stood watching on the side surrounded by Harari elders, 'suppose we fail?'

'Suppose,' Chief Abduruman asked from where *he* stood in the middle of a group of Habr Odessi elders, 'that instead of us killing them, they kill *us*.'

'They won't,' Harkaway explained, and Danny's hands flew as she clattered into the dialect. 'The art of war, as your warriors will tell you, is surprise. If they don't expect us, they can't win.'

The two chiefs were still doubtful but then, from the group of women who stood watching, arose a contemptuous crying sound. Others joined in and the group started swaying, first the Harari women then the Habr Odessi, slapping the flats of their hands against their mouths until their shrieks became a fierce ululation. The sound excited the young men. One of them leapt into the air and spun like a ballet dancer, his shock of hair flopping over his eyes.

'Are you men or women?' one of the women shrieked.

'We are men!'

More young men started leaping into the air until the whole lot were prancing about, waving their rifles and shouting. It took a good half hour to calm them down.

'I reckon this is going to be a long job,' Tully observed.

'No, it isn't,' Harkaway said. 'It hasn't got to be. We haven't time. Danny, go and tell those bloody women to keep their stupid traps shut. They've done their job and many thanks. Now it's up to us.'

The women were led away and they began to train the troops. Harkaway got the men into a line again and village boys started to set up stones and bottles and cans. None of them were hit but a few of the younger men who were quicker to learn than the others managed, with the aid of Abdillahi, their first successful recruit, to throw up puffs of dust within a foot of their target.

'A few more days, *jong*,' Grobelaar said, 'and they'll be hitting 'em.'

The following day, one of the young Odessi hit the can he was aiming at. At least, they thought it was the can he was aiming at. It might have been the next in line but as the can jumped he threw down his rifle and leapt into the air, while a great shriek of joy came from the watching women.

Harkaway leapt forward. 'Tell him to pick up that bloody rifle!' he roared. 'You don't chuck a rifle down in the dust like that! You look after it! You cherish it! You wrap the breech in your robe! You keep the muzzle clear of dust and grit! Tell him that!'

As Danny spoke the women started wailing, and the young man's proud grin died as he sheepishly picked up the rifle.

'Now tell him to get down there and hit it again. And when he's done it, to stay there quietly.'

The young man lay down again and with his third shot hit the can again, proving that even if the first shot had been a fluke, he was at least getting the hang of it. What was more, he remained where he was. His success even seemed to stir the others to try harder and by the end of the day they had six young men who could hit their target more or less at will.

'Keep 'em at it,' Harkaway said. 'We've not only to get 'em to hit things, we've also got to stop 'em shooting when we tell 'em to. When we've got 'em shooting properly, we'll teach 'em how to fire volleys.'

'Volleys?' Gooch stared. 'Volley firing stopped in the bloody Boer War.'

'Well, it's going to start again,' Harkaway said coolly. 'Leave it to them, and they'll work their way through every scrap of ammunition we possess in half an hour. Volley firing'll preserve ammunition and in volley firing some of the targets always go down, so that every man who's pulled a trigger can claim he was the one who hit it. He often isn't but who's to know? It's good for morale. Besides, it's discipline we want. March 'em up and down a bit. Drill's good for the soul.'

Gooch was soon working at it, with the aid of Yussuf and Danny, marching a squad of young men up and down the dusty marketplace, halting them, about-turning them, making them mark time and stand still. For the active tribesmen, totally unused to discipline, it was difficult. They preferred to express their anger or their pleasure with wild leaps and yells but Gooch was managing to keep them quiet and making them stop and start when he told them to. They were hardly the Guards, and their halts were invariably on the wrong foot but he got them into a squad and marching in threes.

'We'll never get 'em wheeling into line proper,' he pointed out as Harkaway appeared.

'We're not rehearsing the Trooping of the Colour,' Harkaway said. 'They're guerrillas. So long as they can shoot straight. So long as they stay quiet when we tell 'em to. So long as they keep their heads down until we tell 'em to shove 'em up. So long as they hold their fire until we tell 'em to let go, and stop when we tell 'em to stop. That'll be enough.'

By the end of the week, they had a squad of twenty of the keenest and most intelligent men whom they considered they could safely use. They had been careful to pick ten from each tribe so there should be no jealousy and no grumbling, and their ages ranged from sixteen upwards, lean-faced men with skins of different hues and dusty hair, often daubed into ringlets with red mud. Their eyes were bright and their grins were wide and, while their line was never quite straight and they couldn't march in step, they could use a rifle and they did as they were told. There was a lot of grumbling from those who hadn't been chosen but Harkaway got Danny to explain that they'd be chosen when they were good enough, in the hope that it would encourage them to try harder.

By this time, Grobelaar had managed to teach Gooch and Tully to drive. With the British soldier's wariness of being caught for something that wasn't his job, neither of them had been keen.

'Why do we have to?' Tully asked. 'I once tried and it didn't work. I hit a tram.'

'For Christ's sake,' Harkaway fumed. 'There aren't any bloody trams here! There's nothing but desert. Hundreds of miles of it. And we might capture a lorry carrying a load of whisky and need someone to drive it.'

In the end Grobelaar had them both able to handle the Bedford, and, what was more surpising, four of the young tribesmen, too.

Their gear-grinding was enough to make your hair stand on end and the chief problem was to stop them pounding along at full speed. Grobelaar had to explain that the desert floor was uneven, and that driving too fast could break a spring. Gradually it sank in and the day came when Grobelaar, driving the Lancia, led a convoy of two of what the Somalis called 'Iron Camels', at slow speed round Eil Dif, one driven by a Habr Odessi and one by a Harari.

The sight prompted the women to shriek and start dancing, and the young men began to leap and twist in the air in their delight and pride. The two drivers stopped as Grobelaar stopped – jerkily and uncertain, but they stopped – and climbed down to stand at attention alongside their vehicles, looking like a couple of black storks and grinning all over their faces.

'The Boys,' Harkaway said proudly. 'Our Boys.'

11

It seemed to be time to move. In the Western Desert, Bardia was being bombarded and the British were at the gates of Tobruk, while round Eil Dif the Somalis were growing restless and itching to use their new weapons to kill somebody.

Gooch was working over a rifle, cleaning it and wiping it with gun oil so that it had the smell of workshops and lathes. Staring along the sights, he removed the bolt to check the barrel for the patches of rust that showed dark against the shining steel, and put his nose to the barrel and sniffed, like a woman with scent. 'They smell different after they've been fired,' he said. 'Sour. But good.'

Tully was bent over the radio. He had been keeping himself to himself for some time, eyeing Danny sullenly, following her everywhere she went with hungry eyes. As he worked, she sat outside with Grobelaar, watching the sun go down, both of them curiously placid and unwilling to move much.

'BBC,' Tully said and they all swung round as he turned up the volume.

The news still mostly concerned the great victory in the Western Desert. Since it was the only one the British could so far boast, inevitably they were making a lot of it, and the broadcast included an interview with a British officer who had watched.

'The whole of the southern defences have been encompassed,' he said. 'And we're now breaking in from the north. Ten thousand prisoners have been taken and God knows how many more are coming in . . .' It made them itch to be part of it.

It had always been their intention to attack the first reasonable-sized, underguarded convoy that came their way. Convoys of arms were always heavily protected and, since their blowing of the Wirir Gorge, so were petrol lorries. Maize, skins, fruit and other convoys, however, didn't merit such close concentration and the seventeen-vehicle convoy leaving Jijiga at the end of December contained maize, dates and coffee for the troops in Bidiyu, Hargeisa and Berbera.

It was Yussuf who brought news of it. Where he got his information no one knew, but Yussuf felt he had as much right to share in the success of the young Habr Odessi as Chief Abduruman or anybody else. He'd travelled towards Jijiga, and talked at the frontier post at Wajale where they had all the information about convoys. Nobody, least of all a none-too-bright corporal of one of Brigadier Ruggiero Ruffo di Peri's Gruppo Bandas, the locally raised soldiers the Italians used for the dirty little jobs they preferred not to handle themselves, considered Yussuf, with his dusty blanket, limp and greying hair anything but a nosy villager.

'Maize,' he announced on his return to Eil Dif. 'And dates and coffee. Our young men and their families will enjoy the maize. Will there be more rifles?'

'That's up to your young men,' Harkaway said.

Gooch drew a deep breath. 'Think we'll pull it off?' he asked.

Harkaway eyed the excited young Somalis squatting in the dust, holding their ancient rifles between their bent knees. There weren't many of them but they were the brightest and best and they were eager to prove their skill and courage.

'It all depends on that article,' he said.

Danny was talking to them, speaking quietly but forcefully and the Somalis were listening eagerly. They considered her strange because they regarded white women who showed their legs or wore trousers not as women at all, but as miraculous beings who were able to conceive and produce children by some form of magic. Nevertheless, they liked women with shape, especially behind, so that their girls often padded out their clothes like a bustle. Since Danny was well endowed in every department, they were prepared to admire her.

She was lecturing them on the need for absolute obedience.

'Without obedience,' she said, 'many may die. With obedience, you will enrich yourselves, and your wives and children will eat well. We have taken the place of your chiefs. We have not usurped their power. They are still your chiefs but they have given their leadership to us willingly and freely and you must do as we tell you. Your lives depend on it.'

'Think they'll do as they're told?' Harkaway asked as they made their plans.

Danny eyed him worriedly. 'They should, I've stressed that their chiefs have given their power to us. Otherwise –' She shrugged.

Harkaway put his hand on her shoulder and squeezed it. She gave a little shudder and looked up at him unhappily.

'We'll need you, too,' he said, giving her behind a little pat. 'Willing to come?'

'Yes.'

'Not afraid?'

'No.'

'If it goes wrong, the Italians could get you.'

'The Italians are noted for their good manners.'

'But not for their morals. Most of 'em behave like randy ferrets. You might be killed.'

'I had to learn great chunks of Isaiah as a girl and that's enough to put strength into anybody. I have faith.'

Harkaway gave a little frown. 'I sometimes wish I had,' he said.

'Let me give you faith.'

He met her eyes. 'The sort of faith I want,' he said enigmatically, 'has nothing to do with God.'

That night the young men who had been selected for the raid performed the fuqera, the bragging battle dance of the

114

Ethiopians that they'd picked up from across the border, stamping, slapping their thighs and clapping their hands, their voices low and menacing as they moved with weird and grotesque contortions of the body. The other young men joined in, separate but part of the pride, and then the women, their voices raised in high-pitched wails.

There was no need for wheeled transport. The young Somalis could travel almost as fast across the hills on their stork-like legs as the British soldiers could travel in their lorry. Harkaway was in a sweat that they wouldn't turn up. But they did. As the Bedford rolled into a carefully chosen hiding place to the north of Guidotti's Strada del Duce, among the rocks black faces appeared, split by wide white grins.

'I just hope,' Harkaway said quietly, 'that when we hit those Eyeties, the buggers have something worth taking.'

As it happened they were luckier than they knew, probably even than they deserved.

At the last moment, General Forsci in Jijiga, as concerned as Guidotti with the deteriorating situation in the Western Desert and its effect on Africa Orientale, added a petrol lorry to the convoy. Finally, because Somaliland was not self-supporting and the events in North Africa had caused delays in the movement of food down from Abyssinia, among the maize, dates and skins there was also a box containing one thousand Maria Theresa dollars to pay the merchants in Berbera for sheep and goat meat.

Despite the extra value of the convoy, however, Forsci didn't consider, with eighteen lorries, each with an armed guard and the whole lot under the command of a lieutenant of the Bersaglieri of the Savoia Grenadiers, that there was any need to increase the escort. Eighteen native askaries, all Eritreans and all well-trained, an armoured car carrying a machine gun and a crew of four Italians at the front and a sergeant and a machine-gun crew in the rear lorry, he felt, ought to be enough to hold off anybody, especially since there had been no further signs of hostility along the Strada del Duce since the blowing of the Wirir Gorge. Since that event, a new post had been built there, consisting of a wired compound, a small brick-built fort containing a nervous Italian sottotenente and twenty Eritrean askaris, connected by telephone to other posts east and west. The idea was for neighbouring posts to send help in the event of attack, while help moved up to *them* from other posts further along the line, all the way back to Jijiga or Bidiyu in a sort of 'when-father-turns-we-all-turn' manoeuvre, each post supporting the next in line in either direction, no matter which way the danger came.

'Machine guns or anything larger than a rifle need not be feared,' General Forsci insisted. 'The convoy will move at speed and will not stop en route, and the only area where we need worry is between Jijiga and Bidiyu. Bidiyu to the coast can be handled easily by General Barracca. Everything else is well covered.'

While General Forsci was making the final decisions for his convoy, Harkaway had had a good session with a map he'd found in the Lancia they'd captured, and they moved out at dusk and crossed the Jijiga–Bidiyu road to the flatter land beyond, then, swinging in a large arc, they appeared south-east of the road beyond Bidiyu.

'Remember,' Harkaway said. 'We move fast. We don't waste time. We collect all the arms we can and bolt south, into the flat country. Then, with a bit of luck they'll think we came from the direction of Odweina or even over the border. We head for Madoba and take cover among the trees there in case they send aircraft out looking for us. As soon as we can, we head back north-west, cross the road and head for Gumra.'

'Not Eil Dif?'

'No. Harari country this time. They're bound to look for us at Eil Dif so we'll give it a rest for a while. Yussuf can let us know when they've gone.'

They spent the night not far from Hargeisa south of the Strada del Duce on the edge of the desert, silent and unmoving during the heat of the day among the few gum trees and acacias that grew round the waterhole at Duduba. The water was bitter and the heavy smell of the camels and their trodden dung filled their nostrils. Around them was nothing but sand and rock for miles. The wells were being used by a few nomads with their goats and sheep and the camels carrying the frames and mats of their homes. As they stood in a silent half-circle with their wives and children, the Habr Odessi and Harari men eyed them contemptuously, warriors watched by farmers.

A tent was set up for the Europeans among the scrub. Insects clogged the lamp after dark and the stew they cooked was full of tiny corpses and detached pieces of wing.

'You can't tell 'em from the bits of onion,' Grobelaar observed.

The wind that had filled the day with blown sand filled the night with moaning, coating the tea in their mugs with grit. The long shadows of hyenas prowled from bush to bush, with massive shoulders and jaws, their pale-furred throats giving out an eerie groan as their wide nostrils caught the scent of meat. Gooch rose to pelt them with stones.

'They've gone,' Danny said.

'Probably joined the Eyeties,' Grobelaar suggested.

The following morning before daylight they moved quietly up to the road, Harkaway moving ahead in the Lancia to choose a point roughly between Bidiyu and Hargeisa, where there was a gap in the hills. Leaving the lorry and the Lancia hidden, they moved through the gap to the tarmacadamed surface of the road and waited there, surrounded by armed Somalis, some with rifles, some carrying the Brens and the Vickers, one or two gingerly carrying land mines.

As they stood in the silence with only the wind sighing through the gap, there was no sign of Italians and Harkaway looked at Abdillahi, their first recruit.

'Can we do it, Abdillahi?' he asked.

Abdillahi gestured with a thin black hand. '*In sh'Allah, effendi*. If God wills it.'

Harkaway drew a deep breath then gestured to the men carrying the land mines. Digging them into the road in a zigzag pattern so they couldn't be avoided, he scattered sand and gritty earth to hide where he had worked.

With a team of Habr Odessi, Tully set up one of the Brens to cover the road at the point where the halted vehicles would stop. Gooch, with four of the Harari, had placed one of the Vickers further down the road. The rest of the tribesmen, in two groups, were hidden among the rocks at the south side of the road under the command of Harkaway and Grobelaar. They had no idea how long they might have to wait and as they sat in the sun the young men softly started singing a song called 'Mohammed Salih', which Yussuf said was the war song of the Mad Mullah, a hangover from twenty years before. Chief Abduruman had fought with the Mullah and his young men had picked up the song from him.

They seemed to be there for hours before one of the Somalis, posted high on the slopes, waved his rifle and began to slither down the rocky scree to the road. The song stopped abruptly at a sign from Harkaway and the silence that followed seemed immense. A hot wind was blowing from the Haud, the desert area to the east, bringing with it gritty clouds of dust and lifting little whorls like sand-devils from the scree slopes. Harkaway could just see Tully and Gooch and he signed to them to get their heads down. Turning, he saw a dozen pairs of fierce black eyes on him, a dozen sombre expressions. Then one of the young men whispered something to his neighbour and immediately the whole lot of them were grinning in anticipation.

He gestured to Grobelaar further along the road, then turned to Danny who was squatting among the rocks with the Somalis.

'Tell them,' Harkaway said, 'that they must not move until I tell them.'

The young men lifted their hands, pale palm outwards, to acknowledge what she said, and she looked anxiously at Harkaway.

'Be careful, George,' she said, and he flicked her an arrogant glance, sure of her, aware of her growing feelings for him but in no hurry to take advantage of it.

'Now, if you feel like it,' was all he said, 'you can send up one of your prayers. And I hope to Christ He hears you.'

The convoy came into view from the direction of Bidiyu a quarter of an hour later, moving slowly because they had chosen a spot where the road wound round the side of the hill in a series of curves.

It was led by an armoured car. It wasn't a proper armoured car because it had been home-made in Jijiga by attaching sheet steel to the sides, front and rear of a Lancia truck and mounting a machine gun – sufficient, General Forsci thought, to withstand anything the natives could throw at it. Unfortunately, it wasn't constructed to withstand explosives and the land mines blew off the two front wheels, killed the lieutenant in command, together with his corporal, and wounded both the other two members of the crew before they even knew who was their enemy.

The vehicle behind, its driver somnolent and unalert in the heat, ran into the back of the wrecked armoured car, buckling its wing, and the whole convoy concertinaed to a stop. At the rear, the Italian sergeant in command of the machine gun put his head out to find out what had happened just as Gooch opened up with the Vickers. The first burst hit him in the chest, flinging him back into the lorry, and the next, ripping through the canvas cover, killed one of the askari loaders and wounded another. The third decided it was wiser to fling himself flat on the floor, where the maize from the punctured sacks dribbled slowly down on him. The crews of the other lorries jumped out and bolted away from the firing, only to run into a burst from Tully's Bren. Three men fell, one of them dead.

It had been found in the past that, on the whole, the Italian officers were well-trained and courageous, but that when they were killed their forces quickly went to pieces. Now somebody waved a white towel and almost at once more appeared. Gooch gave them an extra burst with the Vickers to convince them and Tully peppered the armoured car with the Bren so that it should give no trouble, then, as an Italian corporal and two Italian privates appeared, their arms in the air, the Eritrean askaris threw down their rifles and lined themselves neatly alongside the road to await events.

Black figures in coloured loincloths began to appear from the rocks on either side of the road. This, Harkaway felt, was the crucial moment. If the Somalis did what their fathers had done under the Mad Mullah in the twenties, they would have a massacre on their hands.

Their new-found obedience almost slipped. One of the young Hararis, overcome with impatience and excitement, stood up, uttered a piercing yell and began to scramble over the rocks alongside Harkaway. Harkaway saw him just in time, stuck out a foot and tripped him up. As he clambered to his feet, indignantly reaching for his weapon, Harkaway swung a big fist and he went down like a log.

'Tell them!' he yelled at Danny. 'Tell them again! If any of them disobeys, he'll be shot.'

The Somalis studied each other with rolling eyes but the prostrate figure of the boy Harkaway had brought down was sufficient example. While keeping their rifles pointed at the new enemies they had found, they kept their eyes on Harkaway for information on how to act.

'Tell 'em not to move,' Harkaway yelled and the information was passed on in a high-pitched soprano voice normally more used to uttering prayer than military commands that made the Italians look round quickly, wondering what they had come up against.

Moving along the line of prisoners, Harkaway checked that they were unarmed, then he gestured to Abdillahi to collect all the weapons he could find and put them in the rear lorry.

What they were doing required quick work and he moved along the trucks, checking their contents.

'Maize,' he announced. 'And dates and coffee. The Boys'll like that. And skins. They can use those. How many rifles?'

Gooch gestured. 'Sixteen,' he said. 'With ammunition. Most of them single-shot that we took off the askaris, but there are several good Italian guns and a Biretta automatic.

There are also two machine guns, one off the armoured car. It's a bit messy because somebody's been bleeding all over it but it'll clean up.'

There was also a box of light percussion grenades of Japanese manufacture. They looked like toys but nobody was anxious to try them. Harkaway took one and tossed it in his hand. 'We'll have these, too,' he said. 'See they're not forgotten.'

'What about the lorries?'

'We take 'em.'

Gooch grinned. 'All of 'em?'

'As many as we can drive. Tell the prisoners to strip. We want their uniforms. We promised the Boys loot. So, okay, they get loot. Gold braid. Pretty hats. They did all right.'

He was still poking about in the lorry as the scared Italians stripped off their clothes.

'What do we do with 'em?' Gooch said.

Harkaway was in the back of the lorry that had run into the armoured car. 'Let 'em go,' he said. 'Without boots, it'll take 'em a while to get to Hargeisa. That'll give us plenty of time. Hello –' he stopped dead '– what's this?'

He was stooping over a metal box with a lock through the hasp. Using the spike of his jack-knife, he broke it easily enough and as he opened the lid, his face split in a smile.

'By God, Goochy,' he said. 'Money!'

'Whose money?' Gooch's head was over the tailboard immediately, his expression eager.

'It *was* theirs,' Harkaway said. 'Now it's ours.' He picked up one of the coins and studied it. 'Maria Theresa dollars.'

'Any good to us?'

'You bet your sweet life they are. They use 'em to pay Africans and Chinese who can't be bothered with pound notes. Useful to bribe tribes to come over on to your side. The Boys'll consider themselves well rewarded if we give them a sack of maize apiece and one of these.'

One by one, Grobelaar and Danny were swinging lorries off the road to the scrub-covered surface of the flatter land. Eventually they had five vehicles lined up alongside their own on the stony soil facing south.

121

Harkaway had chosen them carefully and the petrol lorry was among them. They had thrown into them everything they possibly could from the vehicles they were having to leave behind.

'Hurry,' Harkaway kept saying. 'For God's sake, hurry! We want to be out of sight before they start looking.'

Quickly, Grobelaar backed the other vehicles close together, then he punctured the petrol tanks with a spike so that the petrol flooded into the road beneath them. Shoving the prisoners out of range, Harkaway pulled the pin of the Japanese grenade he had pocketed and tossed it into the pool of petrol. It exploded with a crack that shattered the senses and immediately there was a roar and a blast of air that sent him sprawling.

Danny ran to him but he pushed her aside, grinning at the burning vehicles.

'What a lovely sight,' he said.

The news reached Hargeisa and Bidiyu at roughly the same time, soon after midday. When Di Sanctis appeared, Guidotti and Piccio were studying the map of North Africa and comparing it with the latest news they had received. In the Western Desert, a long line of prisoners was heading eastwards. Bardia was captured now and Tobruk was likely to fall at any time.

Piccio's concern was chiefly with the broken pride of the Italian armies. Guidotti's was more realistically concerned with what it meant to him. There were reports that British forces were building up in the Sudan close to the Eritrean border near Kassala and he knew what that meant. The British were intending to take full advantage of the Italian preoccupation with North Africa to win back some of their losses and, as he well knew, defeat in the desert meant they could expect no help from Rome.

'What is it, Di Sanctis,' Guidotti asked. 'More trouble along the Strada del Duce?'

'Yes, Excellency. General Forsci's convoy's been ambushed.'

Guidotti jerked upright, the Western Desert forgotten.

His question had been light-hearted because, despite the blowing up of the Wirir Gorge and the bomb that had destroyed the Duce's victory column, he hadn't really been expecting trouble. He forced himself not to lose his calm, clenching his fists and straightening his back as he held on to his emotions.

'Forsci's convoy,' he said, 'has already safely passed through the danger area. All the trucks arrived here. I saw them myself.'

'Yes, Excellency, they followed the usual routine and left five of them here, to rejoin the convoy on its way back in two days' time. The rest were going on to Hargeisa and Berbera. They were ambushed on the other side of Bidiyu, halfway to Hargeisa. Five men were killed and the rest disarmed.'

Guidotti fought against the desire to raise his voice. 'The rest?' he asked stiffly. 'How many are the rest, Di Sanctis?'

'Twenty-seven, Excellency. The news has just come in. We've lost the lot.'

'Twelve trucks?'

'Thirteen, Excellency. General Forsci included a lorry-load of petrol without informing us.'

'Who was responsible?'

'It seems they were Somalis, sir. Led by four white men and – a white woman, sir.'

'A white woman?'

'Yes, Excellency. They took the boots, arms and uniforms of our men and made off with five lorries, one of them the petrol lorry. The rest they set on fire. Troops from Hargeisa are on their way there now. The survivors came in just before midday.'

Guidotti looked at Piccio.

'That's not all, sir,' Di Sanctis said. 'This has just arrived.'

Guidotti took the paper nervously, wondering what it contained. He read it carefully.

'Bura has been occupied by the British,' he said.

'That's in Kenya,' Piccio pointed out.

'Indeed it is,' Guidotti agreed. 'But up to yesterday it was occupied by *our* troops. The next move will be across the frontier at Moyale into Africa Orientale. With the British on the march opposite Kassala, it begins to look as if their campaign has started. Within a few weeks' time an ambush on the Strada Del Duce might well appear a trivial matter.'

It took Harkaway's column a fortnight to make their way to Gumra.

They were all stupid with tiredness but, not knowing that the Italians were occupied with other emergencies, were congratulating themselves on getting clean away. Staying in Gumra for several days, they eventually began to head back to Eil Dif, travelling by night and assuming that any searches the Italians might make would be over by this time.

Everybody in Eil Dif turned out to greet them – Harari as well as Habr Odessi – and both chiefs, to say nothing of Yussuf, beaming all over his face, his milky eyes blinking with pleasure, were dressed to kill.

The young men leapt from the lorries and, flourishing their weapons, immediately started doing the fuqera. The old men slapped their thighs and the women started their sing-song wailing while the young men spun and contorted, throwing up the dust in clouds as they whacked their broad flat feet on the dry earth. When they'd finished, and while they were still elated and panting, Harkaway started handing out the bags of maize, sharing them carefully between the two tribes.

'Do you want none, effendi?' Yussuf asked.

'It's all yours,' Harkaway said magnanimously, knowing what Tully and Gooch would have said if he'd offered them mealie pap for lunch.

'Line up the Boys,' he said, and as the young men who had taken part in the fight waited, he went along the line and put into the hand of each startled warrior one Maria Theresa dollar. They stared at them, delighted, then started yelling.

Danny's eyes were on him all the time. His head was up, the sun on his red hair so that he looked like a reincarnation of one of the Elizabethan sea-dogs, bold, brave, dubious perhaps, but wholly admirable. As he caught her eyes on him she hurriedly dropped her gaze.

'Tell them,' he ordered Yussuf, 'that such bounty is only possible if we are lucky enough to capture money. It will buy a great deal. Many goats. Perhaps a wife. But this can't be so every time. Nevertheless, there will be other things. Rifles. Clothes. Blankets. Food. Next time there may not be silver but there will always be treasure of some kind.'

As Yussuf began to talk, Harkaway turned his head to Danny. 'Not bad pay for very little fighting. Did any of them pull a trigger?'

'Not one.' She eyed him admiringly. 'You're a born leader, George. Why is it you're only a corporal?'

Harkaway's face shut down at once. 'Because that's the way I want it,' he said.

With both the Habr Odessi and the Harari delighted with the outcome of the raid and more than willing to do anything for them, they decided to stay at the old house in the ruined area of Eil Dif.

Tully set up his radio, stringing his aerial along the verandah, and almost immediately they were electrified by the news he picked up. Tobruk was on the point of falling and the Italians had evacuated Kassala in the Sudan and were now being pushed from the areas of Kenya they had occupied back into their own territory. The war was coming to them!

Excitedly, Danny dug out the old atlas with which she'd taught her African pupils and, as they stared at it, Harkaway's comment was much the same as General Guidotti's.

'If they're on the move,' he said, 'what we've just done will begin to look like a vicarage tea party.'

Tully was grinning all over his face as he shut down the set. 'We're in good company,' he observed. 'There are South Africans, Rhodesians, British, East Africans, West Africans, Indians and Free French.'

Harkaway's voice was cold. 'They won't any of them do any better than the Free British here in Somaliland,' he said.

PART TWO

The Sixth Column

1

The name stuck. From then on they were the Free British, and Tully's sense of humour persuaded him to have a Union Jack made. The stripes were cock-eyed and of unequal lengths and widths and in the middle of it the Somali women Yussuf had instructed had placed a crescent and a scimitar.

'They'll be calling us the Ethiopian Fifth Column soon,' Tully gloated.

'Not the Fifth,' Harkaway said. 'The Sixth. One better.'

From then on they also referred to themselves as the Sixth Column, and when the news came that the Australians had taken Tobruk with twenty-five thousand prisoners and fifty tanks they were cock-a-hoop.

'They'll be so busy watching their rear,' Harkaway said in his cool calculating way, 'they won't have time to worry about us.'

The following week, they learned that British troops had entered Italian Somaliland.

'Bardia! Tobruk! And now Derna! *Porca miseria!* What a mess!'

Guidotti's face was bleak as he studied the map of northern Africa. The red arrows they had been marking on it seemed to stretch for miles into Italian territory.

Piccio placed a sheet of paper on the table. 'There is more, General,' he said. 'The British have appeared at Beda Fomm!'

'Beda Fomm?' Guidotti's finger moved along the map. 'But that's beyond Benghazi! They can't be there!'

Piccio shrugged. 'Not only are they there, Excellency,

they ran into one of our columns and took five thousand prisoners. They crossed the desert and got in front of them as they retreated.'

Guidotti picked up the sheet of paper and read it carefully. 'Bergonzoli,' he said slowly, 'has surrendered with a hundred and thirty thousand prisoners, three hundred and eighty tanks and eight hundred and forty-five guns.' He drew a deep breath. 'It seems that the badly armed British who had so few guns and tanks now have considerably more.'

Piccio cleared his throat. 'The BBC, sir, announces that they never at any time exceeded two divisions and lost only five hundred killed, one thousand four hundred wounded and fifty-five missing. They sounded very pleased with themselves.'

'They have every right to,' Guidotti said bitterly.

'They have also –' Piccio seemed almost to be enjoying the list of disasters '– crossed the border between the Anglo-Egyptian Sudan and Abyssinia and are advancing on Keren, while the South Africans have crossed the Kenyan border into Jubaland and Italian Somaliland. Africa Orientale is besieged on every side.'

'In the name of God, man,' Guidotti snapped, 'allow me to think! This is clearly going to start the Ethiopian patriots moving. Thank God we have no such patriots in Somaliland – '

'We have now,' Piccio pointed out. 'This lot who destroyed General Forsci's convoy.'

Guidotti waved his hand. 'It may be nothing more than a group of English soldiers who were left behind when we came through from Jijiga to Berbera.'

'They have weapons, Excellency,' Piccio reminded him. 'It's reported there were rifles in the hands of every Somali. There were also machine guns, at least one of them a Bren. I might point out also that they now have two more machine guns – General Forsci's – and several more rifles – Italian rifles.'

Within the day, Guidotti had driven to Jijiga to confer with

General Forsci who was still enraged at the loss of his convoy. 'Leave it to me,' Forsci said. 'They were seen at Gumra. I can draw on southern Abyssinia for troops and I shall consider it my own special task. They will be scattered like chaff.'

Guidotti eyed his superior officer coldly. He had no great liking for General Forsci. He was an ardent supporter of the fascist movement and Guidotti had long suspected that he had got his job through sycophancy rather than for his skill as a soldier.

'There's a suspicion,' he pointed out quietly, 'that Gumra isn't their headquarters, but that they're based somewhere in the Gura–Eil Dif area.'

'Very well!' Forsci was quite certain of his tactics. 'I shall send a column to Gumra and if there's no sign there of them, we shall look around the Gura–Eil Dif area. I shall harry them. I shall learn where they are and give them no rest. Commandante di Brigata Ruffo di Peri can handle it. He has had great experience with this sort of thing against the patriots in Abyssinia. He has a mind full of ideas.'

Guidotti sincerely hoped he had because his own was full only of unhappiness. There was a mood in Bidiyu of general uneasiness after the defeats in Greece and Libya. Too many things seemed to be going wrong and he was conscious of a growing suspicion that the Duce had badly miscalculated by throwing his hand in with Hitler.

At Eil Dif the victory was turning into a tribal occasion with roast lambs and dancing, and Harkaway allowed Abduruman, Daoud and Yussuf a bottle of whisky from their store. He also produced one between the rest of them and carefully hid the rest on the excuse that they had to keep it for emergencies.

Wearing an Italian officer's greatcoat, Gooch nodded solemnly. 'It's an antiseptic,' he agreed. 'If anybody gets hurt, we might need it to sterilize a wound. I've seen 'em do it in cowboy films.'

The decision didn't please Tully. The exhilaration of their success had worked him up to a state of excitement that was difficult to keep in check. He could see Danny opposite him in the flames from the fire. With her hair cut short, she looked no more than a girl, and as she leaned back to reach for her Bible, which she always made a point of reading before going to sleep, he could see the curve of her breast against her shirt.

Harkaway's mind was also busy and he was no fool. On their own, they couldn't do much, however well they trained their tribesmen. A pitched battle, which in effect was what he was beginning to contemplate, was different from the mere planting of explosives. For that, they had to wait until the Allies began seriously to worry the Italians. Deep in thought, he lay quietly in his blankets in the dark. He was never sure how much they could trust the Habr Odessi and the Harari. It was impossible to stop them if they decided to bolt with the rifles, but he'd promoted Abdillahi to sergeant and two other promising youngsters to corporal, even going to the point of marking stripes on their tobes in the hope that their pride in themselves and the influence they had on the others would hold the rest from desertion. It went to Abdillahi's head a little. He had long since fallen for Harkaway's arrogant leadership – what the Abyssinians called being a *Tillik Sau* – and, ignoring Yussuf and even Chief Abduruman, had appointed himself his personal bodyguard. 'I go everywhere with my master,' Danny had heard him saying. 'He is a great man. He does not play football with ordinary people when he is in England. He plays only with King George and the President of the United States.'

But Abdillahi was only one of them and the Somalis were noted for their independence. 'Somalis no good,' Harkaway had once been told by a sturdy Berbera policeman. 'Each man too much his own sultan.' They also suffered from inconstancy, vanity, excitability, greed and fits of the sulks. A mere word could change their devotion, and loyalty was always a chancy business. And if they stayed loyal, if they fought as he hoped they'd fight, even if they won, what if the Italians retaliated? Had he bitten off more than he could chew? Had they only been flexing their muscles to get

Gooch an Italian overcoat for the cold nights? Wouldn't they be wiser to head south, swathed in blankets and daubed with blacking, and make for Italian Somaliland? The Italians had been there ever since the last war and there was a relaxed atmosphere in Mogadiscio, as he knew because, before the war when others had gone to Aden or Mombasa, he had gone there for leave. It wasn't much of a place with its Arab buildings, twisting lanes, crazy balconies and crumbling ruins, but he remembered it as having the secure feeling of being long settled. With luck, they could lose themselves in the back streets there until they could make their way to Kismayu and slip across the border into Kenya.

As he struggled with his thoughts, he heard the scrape of a foot on the sandy floor, a quick yelp of anger, then Grobelaar's voice, harsh and abrupt in Afrikaans.

'*Wie gaan?*'

Grobelaar rarely spoke Afrikaans except when he was angry or excited and, reaching for the torch, Harkaway flicked the switch. In its light, his shadow huge against the wall of the cave, he saw Tully standing in the corner by the entrance to the room where Danny slept. There was no door and Harkaway could see her sitting up in her blankets, her shirt open, the cleft between her breasts visible, her eyes wide, her face angry and afraid. Grobelaar was in the opposite corner, a rifle in his hand, the muzzle pointed at Tully. Harkaway's first thought was that Grobelaar and Tully were quarrelling over the woman and he reacted angrily.

'What the hell's going on?'

'He was after Danny,' Grobelaar said.

'Christ –' Tully was a little drunk ' – she's only a bloody woman.'

'And this is only a rifle, man,' Grobelaar said quietly. 'Go back to your blankets. *Voetsek!* Look slippy, *Mak gou! Ek is haastig!*

Harkaway scrambled to his feet and, as he swung the heavy torch, Tully staggered back.

'You stupid bloody fool,' Harkaway snapped. 'Have you been at the whisky?'

'I gave him mine, too,' Danny admitted.

'Then you're a bloody fool, too,' Harkaway said. He stared at Tully. 'Get back to your place, you oaf! Hasn't it occurred to you we need her? She's the only one among us who speaks the lingo.'

Head up and angry, Harkaway stood between them and Tully finally shuffled away. Gooch was sitting up in his blankets, watching as Grobelaar lowered the rifle.

'I've a good mind to hand you over to the Italians.' Harkaway's voice rose. 'There are only four of us – five with her – and we're surrounded by the buggers. There's only one way we can survive and that's by pulling together. If you'd done what you intended, do you think Gooch wouldn't think he could, too – and Kom-Kom?'

'It never crossed my mind, man,' Grobelaar growled.

'Nor mine,' Gooch said.

Harkaway knew Gooch at least was lying because he'd seen him eyeing Danny when she took off her shirt to wash. He'd known what he'd been thinking because he'd been thinking it himself.

The first sign of Forsci's activities came when Yussuf appeared, grey-haired, limping and evil, on the verandah of the old house.

'The Italians have been asking questions, effendi,' he said.

Harkaway sat up. 'Where?'

'In Guli. And Dorali. They are also searching near Gumra. Effendi, they will soon come here.'

'Right,' Harkaway said. 'Then we'd better move. Send every one of your young men who wishes to stay with us into the hills.'

'What about the weapons?' Gooch asked.

'We take 'em with us. We've now got seven lorries and a car and we stuff everything we can in them and disappear. We'll be all right. With their bloody East African empire attacked on three sides at once, the Eyeties won't want to wander too far from base.'

'What about the spare petrol?' Grobelaar asked. 'We can't afford to lose it.'

'We take it with us. What we can't carry we bury in the desert.'

'Suppose the Italians find it?'

'We'll get Yussuf to park his camels over it. The Italians won't hang around too long looking for it, in case they're cut off. If the South Africans are moving up towards Italian Somaliland, they'll be spending all their time looking over their shoulders.'

However, Yussuf began to see problems. The young men who were expecting loot now considered themselves warriors and digging was beneath them. He suggested instead that they place the petrol in the cellar of the house they were occupying.

'It was built by an Englishman for his Somali mistress,' he said. 'I remember her, effendi. She had hips like a boy and breasts like twin hills. The village women were jealous and stoned her to death when the Englishman went.'

The cellar was a ruin of crumbling walls and tumbled timber covered with the droppings of bats and rats and birds.

'It will be safe, effendi,' Yussuf said. 'And when you have used what you can carry, our old men will bring more on the backs of their camels.'

'I thought we were going to use it to get down to Kenya,' Gooch complained. 'With all the silver we were going to get.'

Harkaway gestured angrily. 'Why go down to Kenya?' he said. 'Let Kenya come to us. They're on their way, aren't they?'

Tully's eyes were shifty. 'What about the woman?' he asked. 'Do we take her with us?'

Harkaway looked at him coldly. 'Were you thinking we should leave her behind?' he asked.

One of the young Odessi was sent off at once to Chief Daoud asking for his young Harari to come, and the young men of the Habr Odessi appeared within minutes to load the lorries with weapons, tinned food and bags of maize.

What they couldn't carry with them they placed under the sandy floor of one of the old houses. By the time they'd finished, the young Harari men had begun to arrive from Guli and Dobalar and a steady stream of petrol cans began to move to the old house like the burdens of a lot of black ants. Old men, young men, women and children all helped, all aware that the precious fluid was connected to their future. The cans balanced on straw rings on their heads, they sent off in a long line, grunting camels and asses among them.

During the afternoon, a youngster came in from Chief Daoud to say the Italians were searching a village near Guli and were expected to move on later to Dobelar, where they were intending to camp the night. There were twelve lorries and many men.

The threat was growing closer and Chief Abduruman sent his women and young boys out of the town with the sheep and goats. Soon afterwards the young Habr Odessi and Harari men who had thrown in their lot with the Free British set off after them.

'They will be waiting for you,' Yussuf explained.

The rest of them left as dusk was falling, followed by groups of children wielding palm branches over the lorry tracks in the dusty road. Seven miles to the north-east a young man with a spear and a rifle and with a panga hanging from his waist, was waiting. As he pointed, the vehicles turned into the hills, one after the other, the car bringing up the rear. The young tribesmen were waiting for them among the rocks while the women and boys had driven the sheep and goats into a narrow valley where coarse grass grew among the acacias and twisted grey thorn trees.

As the lorries appeared, they were moved one after the other into the hills along narrow tracks known to the Odessi shepherds, human muscle helping the grinding gears and spinning wheels. Then the tribesmen moved back down the road and began to trot up and down so that their large flat feet obliterated the tracks.

The next afternoon Commandante Ruffo di Peri's column arrived in Eil Dif. They occupied several of the ruined villas, and a headquarters was set up. The following day, they appeared at the foot of the hills where the Sixth Column was camped. They didn't explore, but moved on to the waterhole at Ruba, where they sat for four whole days, watched from the peaks by the Sixth Column. It seemed wiser to move and, driving the vehicles further into the gullies in the hills, the Sixth Column stacked stones and fallen thorn trees in the entrances to hide them, and travelled on foot to a fresh encampment.

They were only just in time. Two days later, one of the watching Harari boys brought the information that the Italians had found the original encampment lower down the slopes and had halted there. The next day lorries appeared on the other side of the range of hills. It was easy to see them from the crests, small matchbox-like vehicles moving about the flat scrubland. A fresh camp was set up and from it patrols began to push into the hills, so that they had to move higher still where it was colder and more difficult. Because there was no grazing, they had to leave the herd of sheep and goats behind. The girls and children who were looking after it were questioned by the Italians. They gave nothing away but they were ordered at rifle point to drive the herd back to Eil Dif. Watching the little trickle of animals descending the mountains, it was clear life was going to become more difficult.

With the Italians all round them, they were stuck and Harkaway was beginning to grow angry. They even knew now the name of the man who was hunting them.

'The bastard's beginning to annoy me,' Harkaway said.

Two days later they heard that Di Peri had brought in four Germans who had been acting as liaison officers in Berbera. He was clearly determined to catch them and, with half his force on the south side of the Bur Yi range and the other half based on Eil Dif to the north, it was beginning to grow uncomfortable. They could leave no trace of their movements, fires were impossible and they had to leave most of their equipment in the lorries and move constantly from one camp to another.

Then, as they waited, one of the young Harari boys appeared, his face excited, and started to jabber at them.

'Get Danny,' Harkaway snapped.

A moment later, Danny arrived and began to question the boy.

'He says there are four men down the hillside. They are wearing English uniforms and say they are escaped prisoners. They know there are English in the hills and they wish to join them. He didn't believe them and said he knew of the English but would have to find them and told them to wait.'

The following morning, they were watching the four men sitting round their camp fire. They had a single tent and wore shorts and British topees with the flash of the Black Watch, but there was something about them that suggested they were not what they seemed.

After dark they were able to approach near enough to hear them speaking and Danny gestured. 'They're Germans,' she said.

'Di Peri's liaison officers,' Gooch said. 'Do we kill 'em?'

Harkaway smiled. 'I've got a better idea. Tell the boy to go over the hills to the south and fetch the Italians, Danny. Tell him to say he's found the English.'

The Italians appeared the next day, a group of twenty under a sergeant, small dark-haired men with baggy trousers, heavy boots and wide topees. They approached the Germans warily, watched by the gleeful men higher up the slopes, then stepped out, their rifles pointed.

'*Mani in alto!*' the sergeant yelled.

The Germans, bent over the fire in front of their tent, swung round. One of them reached for a rifle that lay across a rock and the Italian sergeant fired. The bullet kicked up stones at the German's feet and he leapt into the air, yelling, and flung down the weapon. The watching group were almost beside themselves.

They could hear angry shouts now, but none of the Italians seemed to speak German and they lined up the Germans and marched them down the mountainside. The Sixth

Column watched them all the way, moving from crest to crest, unwilling to miss the joke. Down on the plain, the Germans were packed into the back of a lorry and a guard set over them.

'Send one of the Boys down to Yussuf,' Harkaway said. 'Tell him to find out what happened.'

The story came back to them the following day. Di Peri's fury had been spectacular and they hugged themselves with glee at the thought of the Germans being arrested by their own side. It seemed they had had enough of Di Peri's attempts to pin down the guerrillas and had taken themselves off to Addis Ababa.

Unfortunately the joke backfired because it made Di Peri twice as determined to find the practical jokers. He moved his headquarters to the town of Gura and from then on his soldiers were always in the hills, so that they had to move even higher for safety. Harkaway was terrified that one of the patrols would stumble on their lorries with their loads of food, arms and ammunition.

They were high enough now to be half-frozen at night and were cut off from their supplies by the bands of Italian native levies so that they could only move in ones and twos after dark. Muttering among the Somalis started. They had no liking for cold and were not equipped for it, and the absence of fires irked them. Gooch and Tully began to complain.

'We ought to have a go at nobbling this bloody Di Peri,' Gooch growled.

Harkaway gave him a cold look. He was more aloof than ever these days, keeping himself to himself, brooding and short in speech and temper. His mind was full of ideas and problems that had never occurred to the others.

'How,' he asked, 'do you propose doing it?'

Gooch had no idea. 'Couldn't we send in some of the Somalis?' he asked feebly.

'The Italians,' Harkaway snapped, 'are a military formation, and more than a match for a few half-trained natives.'

'Why not kidnap him?' Danny suggested.

Harkaway turned to her. She had thought the idea a good one and waited for him to offer her a small measure of praise. He could have done anything with her and she longed for him to give her orders so that she could carry them out. Even more, she longed for a suggestion that he found her intelligent, brave and attractive. It was against all her nature and training but she was unable to push the knowledge aside.

'What do we do with him when we've got him?' he asked with chilly disinterest.

'He'd be a useful hostage. Up here, surrounded by Habr Odessi and Harari, he'd never escape and if we had him with us, they'd never dare bring guns or aircraft against us.'

'It'd be easier to shoot the sod,' Gooch grumbled.

She shook her head. 'Shooting would bring the whole garrison down on us,' she said. 'Kidnapping would be quiet. Especially if we used some of the Italian uniforms we have. We could be miles away before the alarm was raised.'

Grobelaar grinned. 'Think what it would do to the Italians' nervous system, man,' he said. 'Every single one of them would start wondering if his turn was next.'

'We couldn't do it.' Harkaway spoke brusquely. 'We can't hold a prisoner while we're on the run.'

But that night they heard news from Mombasa on Tully's radio that made them feel they might not be on the run for long. There had been a big battle at Agordat a hundred miles inside Eritrea where the Italians had been defeated. They were now retreating into the mountains near Keren, while in the south, the South Africans were across the border and heading at full speed for Mogadiscio in Italian Somaliland.

They stared at each other. It was suddenly beginning to look as though it was time to take the initiative.

'This business of kidnapping Di Peri –' Grobelaar murmured tentatively.

This time Harkaway said nothing and his eyes were suddenly dreamy. Grobelaar looked at Danny and winked, then he turned to Harkaway again.

'How would we go about it?'

Harkaway came abruptly to life. 'When they assassinated Caesar,' he said, 'they watched his movements for days. We shall have to find out what he does and when he does it.' He smiled his aloof smile. 'Let's give it a whirl.'

2

The idea grew.

Gura was a dirty whitewashed town among the palms that pushed through the sandy soil round a group of wells in the foothills of the Bur Yi range just off the Strada del Duce. The original Arab buildings crowded together in a region of twisting lanes, with tall overhanging walls and crumbling ruins. The better part of the town had an air of shabby well-being, with the usual broken shutters, peeling paint and crumbling plaster, the roads cracked and potholed with subsidence, and a few characterless nineteenth-century houses where British officials had once lived, alongside the iron-roofed huts and wood-and-wattle rabbit-hutches of the Somalis.

The place was full of Italians. Ruffo di Peri had set up his headquarters and mess in a house near the marketplace, a large building which had once been the residence of a District Commissioner, while the house where he slept was half a mile away on the slopes in an area of shady gum trees. Yussuf, like Abdillahi completely Harkaway's man since their victory over Forsci's convoy, made a splendid spy with his crippled foot, sitting for hours at a time with a begging bowl, watching the Italians come and go.

Because it was impossible for the Italians to tell which Somalis were actively assisting their enemies and which were not, he was undisturbed and Harkaway was even able to join him. Disguised with a blanket and boot blacking, he sat watching in the dusk with the old man, and when Yussuf waved Harkaway waved with him.

It didn't take long to work out a scheme.

'We've got to ambush him,' Harkaway said. 'He's driven by a chauffeur between his living quarters and the mess, in a Lancia with a flag on the bonnet. Unfortunately, there are two other Lancias in Gura and we've got to make sure we get the right one. Somebody's got to watch the mess and signal when he leaves.'

'I'll watch,' Danny said. 'They'll never suspect a woman.'

Tully eyed her. 'Somali women only wear a tobe,' he said. 'And nothing else.'

'Then I'll wear a tobe and nothing else,' she said spiritedly. 'I'll sell dates or maize. There are always women selling things. I'll join them.'

'It's too bleddy risky.' Grobelaar's voice was concerned.

She turned on him quickly. 'I'm the right shape. Tall and skinny.'

Grobelaar smiled his cobwebby smile. 'Slim,' he corrected.

She shrugged. 'The same shape as Somali women. With a tobe and a headdress, they'd never know.'

Harkaway studied her, his eyes moving up and down her body. She longed for him to say she was brave, even like Grobelaar to admit she was slim. But all he did was nod and say it seemed possible.

That night they had a fillip to their spirits when the South African bombers appeared and began to knock hell out of Hargeisa. From the hills it was possible to watch the flashes beyond the skyline and hear the distant thuds. If nothing else, it convinced them they were right to move to the offensive.

By this time the plan had grown. Yussuf's daughter had been roped in now and was prepared to place her herd of sheep and goats in the way of any attempt to rescue Di Peri after they'd captured him. As Danny, clad in a blanket and darkened with boot-blacking, took up her position with Yussuf near Di Peri's headquarters, Harkaway and Gooch, with Grobelaar, who was the best driver, headed into Eil Dif to try on the Italian uniforms they had hidden.

*

143

It was quite clear that Commandante di Peri was not expecting trouble. Fetchingly under-clothed in her blanket, Danny reported that he spent the day at a desk that had been set up for him in his house, rested during the afternoon, then drove to the mess for dinner, after which he played bridge for two hours before returning to his quarters, which were guarded not only by askaris but by regular Italian soldiers. He usually sat in the front seat of the car alongside the driver and there was a tight security organization that sprang from his sound suspicion that he was in Sixth Column country. Sentries, it appeared, always checked his car before it was allowed to pass.

Where the road from the mess joined the road to Di Peri's house the land began to rise to a steep slope which would slow the car, and Harkaway had worked it out that, because of the trees there, it was always deep in shadow, even if the moon happened to be out. Alongside was a deep drainage ditch. A red lantern had been made by wrapping red cloth round the glass and, dressed as Italian soldiers, Harkaway, Gooch and Grobelaar made their way into the town as darkness fell and took up their positions in the ditch. Among the trees opposite, Tully waited with Abdillahi and the best of their Habr Odessi and Harari warriors to hold back any traffic that turned up unexpectedly, while Yussuf's daughter squatted near her sheep and goats, ready to drive them across the path of any approaching vehicles that came too close.

There were a few false alarms. A car, two lorries and a motorcycle and sidecar passed, but there was no indication from Danny waiting higher up the road that any of them contained Di Peri.

'She's slipped up,' Gooch muttered. 'The bastard's home and in bed by now.'

'Wait!'

Gooch continued to grumble but ten minutes later they saw the quick flash of a torch in the darkness and as they scrambled from the ditch, a dark figure appeared alongside them. It was Yussuf.

'He comes, effendi,' he whispered.

The lights of Di Peri's car appeared, moving down the slope, then, as it paused to turn towards his quarters, Harkaway stepped forward, swinging the red lantern.

'*Alto là!*'

The car slowed to a stop. Harkaway could see two dark figures in the front of the vehicle.

'*E questa la macchina del Commandante di Peri?*' He had got the correct words from Danny and had practised them half the afternoon.

'*Sì.*' The answer came briskly. '*E il Commandante di Peri en persona.*'

Reaching out, Gooch yanked at the handle of the driver's door. Suspecting something was wrong, the chauffeur began to reach for a weapon and Gooch hit him hard at the side of the head with the butt of his pistol. While Di Peri's attention was caught by what was happening at the driver's side, Harkaway yanked the other door open and, grabbing the Italian brigadier by the collar, yanked him back in his seat and placed the muzzle of his revolver against his temple.

'In the back, Goochy,' he snapped.

As Grobelaar dragged the unconscious driver into the ditch, Gooch scrambled into the rear seat to place his pistol at the base of Di Peri's skull while Harkaway snatched the Italian's pistol from his belt and fell into the rear of the car beside him.

'Okay,' he said as Grobelaar slipped into the driver's seat. 'Let's go!'

As the vehicle began to move forward, they saw Tully's group quietly melting away into the shadows.

Not far ahead there was a traffic control point. Coming towards them from the barrier where it had just been halted was a lorry, but it passed without stopping and the man who stepped into the road at the control point shone a torch on to the brigadier's car to pick out the pennant flying on the bonnet. For a second they held their breath as he paused and Gooch jammed the muzzle of the pistol hard against the base of Di Peri's skull. But the man with the torch seemed satisfied and stepped back to wave them on.

'There's another traffic point on the edge of the town,' Harkaway said. 'Keep the bastard quiet, Goochy.'

Di Peri wasn't arguing, however, and sat quietly, his hands in his lap, his mouth tight.

Wondering if the chauffeur would have recovered sufficiently to raise the alarm or whether the control point they'd just passed might have suspected something and telephoned ahead, they approached the second traffic point warily, Harkaway ready to start shooting. But there was no sign of alarm and, after a brief pause, the red lantern which had appeared was whipped away and the car waved on. As they reached the outskirts of the town, Harkaway grinned, his teeth showing in the light from the dashboard.

'Okay, Kom-Kom,' he said. 'Turn up the wick.'

A mile outside the town, Grobelaar swung off the road into the flat scrubland, circling until he reached the road at the other side of the huddle of buildings. Bumping back on to the asphalt, they roared for half an hour towards Eil Dif, seeing nothing but occasional camels or herds of sheep and goats beyond the fringes of the road. Once they saw the glowing eyes of a hyena and once a small dik-dik, green-grey in the light, leaping from a thorn bush to disappear among the scrub.

Eil Dif was silent as they thundered through. They had informed no one there apart from Yussuf and his daughter, not even Chief Abduruman, so they could give nothing away if the Italians appeared. At the turn-off into the hills, a group of young warriors was waiting for them, armed with rifles. As Di Peri was pushed out of the car, they uttered sharp yells of pleasure.

'Away you go, Goochy,' Harkaway said brisky. 'Get him up into the hills. Let him know that if he causes trouble, we'll set the Boys on him.'

'He has no need to,' Di Peri said calmly in English. 'I understand your language perfectly.'

'Well done, *Commandante*,' Harkaway said cheerfully. 'Right, Goochy. Get going, I'll watch your rear.'

As Gooch, the Italian brigadier and the young Somalis vanished into the darkness, Grobelaar drove the car on for another mile then, with his jack-knife, punctured the petrol tank. Taking his handkerchief from his pocket, he saturated it in petrol and, setting fire to it, tossed it into the pool soaking into the sand. The blast as it went up almost removed his eyebrows.

Recovering himself, he set off back down the road, trotting slowly, lathered with perspiration. Just before he reached the spot where he'd left Harkaway, he saw headlights approaching. Glancing back he saw the glow where the Lancia burned and, diving for the side of the road, hid among the rocks. A moment later a lorry-load of men hurtled past. He watched the lights disappear into the darkness then turned off into the hills and began to climb.

Tully arrived at daylight, his group carrying the Bren.

Di Peri was sitting gloomily among the rocks, his breeches ending in stockinged feet because Harkaway had taken his boots for his own use. Tully grinned at Harkaway. 'So we got him,' he said.

'We got him,' Harkaway said. 'And just be careful what you say because he understands English.'

'Probably sold ice cream in the Old Kent Road before the war,' Tully observed. 'It worked like a dream.'

'Not yet,' Harkaway pointed out. 'Danny isn't back yet.'

There was a long anxious wait, but as the sun was setting they saw Danny's angular figure appear on the skyline and they all stood up to wait for her. She had managed to remove some of the blacking from her skin and it showed only in her ears and in the corners of her eyes.

Harkaway grinned and, as she ran down the slope, he flung his arms round her, swung her round, her sandalled feet in the air, and planted a smacking kiss on her lips. She stared at him as he released her and her hand went to her mouth. She was still staring at him as Tully, Gooch and Grobelaar came forward to insist on offering their own salutes.

'Di Peri?' Guidotti said. 'Not Commandante Ruffo di Peri?'

Piccio nodded.

'Are you telling me he's been abducted?'

Piccio nodded again. 'His car was stopped between his headquarters and the house where he lives,' he said. 'By men wearing Italian uniforms.'

So much, Guidotti thought, for Forsci's big talk. Guidotti was a modest man and Forsci's self-importance was always irritating. It almost made up for the bad news they'd received the previous night. South African troops had defeated the Italians on the Juba River well inside Italian Somaliland and were heading now at full speed towards Mogadiscio. With Libya and half Cyrenaica gone and the British probing forward into Eritrea and Ethiopia, Guidotti couldn't see much help coming for Somaliland. Mogadiscio would undoubtedly fall and the South Africans would then turn north across the plain towards Jijiga to cut off everybody in British Somaliland who couldn't slip away into Ethiopia.

Guidotti couldn't see much future for himself and, without doubt, unless he was dead, his brother must also feature among the countless prisoners of war taken in the north.

The fear that it might all lead to reprisals by the natives against the Italians came again and he was determined not to permit atrocities in his area in retaliation. They would all now reap what had been sown by Graziani in Ethiopia. Following an attempt on his life, all the male members of the leading families had been shot or deported and now, according to the reports that reached Bidiyu, the Italians were beginning to fear Abyssinian vengeance. He had no wish for such a state to exist in his own area but he had a feeling it had already started because Di Peri's second-in-command, convinced that the people of Eil Dif had been involved, had managed to find six of them, including the chief, with British-made Martinis and had shot the lot.

'Abduruman?' Harkaway said. 'They shot him?'

'Together,' Yussuf replied, his voice harsh, 'with five of our finest young men.'

'Not your finest,' Harkaway corrected brusquely. '*They*'re in the hills with us.'

'Boys then,' Yussuf conceded. 'But fine boys. On the threshold of manhood. Boys who would become shield carriers within months.'

'What are you trying to tell me,' Harkaway asked. 'That you want your young men back? That you're throwing your hand in?'

Yussuf's old eyes stared milkily at him. 'We are Habr Odessi,' he said. 'We don't retreat from our enemies at the first setback. When Mohammed bin Abdullah Hassan, whom your soldiers called the Mad Mullah, defied your armies in 1915, the Habr Odessi were among his supporters. But we now have no chief. Abduruman was a good man, but he was old and only carried a rifle because he was a chief. He couldn't fight. He could barely walk. But we need leadership.'

'Well, elect yourself a new chief.'

'We have elected one.'

'You?'

'No, effendi. *You!*'

Harkaway stared at Yussuf for a moment, then he gave his cold smile. 'Chiefs have to have a herd of goats and sheep,' he said. 'They have to live here and have wives and children.'

'You have lived here, effendi,' Yussuf pointed out. 'For many moons now. And you are a strong young man. A herd could be bought with the money you have taken from the Italians, and there is one who would be your wife. I know this, and Allah would grant you sons.'

The old man's head inclined slightly towards Danny. Like the others, she had been listening but now she looked, startled, at Harkaway for his reaction. For a long time he was silent then he gave a bark of laughter and turned away.

'You go and elect yourself somebody else, Yussuf,' he said. 'You, for instance. If I remember rightly, you rather fancied the job. But not me. I have things to do.'

Yussuf stared at him for a long time then, with a movement that was like a shrug, he turned away and began to limp back towards Eil Dif. Harkaway's eyes were on Danny.

'Christ,' he said, 'the things they say.'

'Yes.' She stared back at him boldly. 'The things they say. Am I so ugly that the idea's ridiculous?'

Harkaway eyed her for a long time, then he too turned away. 'No,' he said shortly. 'You aren't ugly. And it isn't ridiculous.'

3

The shootings at Eil Dif seemed to stir the Somalis to anger more than anything that had happened so far. Up to that point, everything had been fun, a joyous killing that was more like hunting than war. Now, however, among the Habr Odessi and their associated clans, hatred had entered into the conflict.

A dozen of them slipped away from the camp in the hills to avenge Abduruman. He meant little to them personally and was related to none of them but they were a difficult, quarrelsome people and war was in their blood. They even went so far as to recruit several of the Harari to their cause and, finding a patrol of Italians camped by their lorry in the bush near Gugubi, fell on them and butchered the lot. Most of the Italians were killed in their blankets. The officer, in his pyjamas, emerged from his tent, to find himself face to face wth a tall grave Somali, with a blue-black handsome face who drew back his arm, bared his teeth and lunged with the spear he held. Two Somalis from Hargeisa who had been acting as guides were held down and had their eyes cut out and their arms hacked off before the bodies were slashed and stabbed.

The Italians had not died without taking the lives of four of the tribesmen, however, and when the Somalis reported what had happened Harkaway was livid.

'*Ma'alish*,' the leader said, unconcerned. 'It is the will of Allah. He orders all things and writes each man's fate in the book of life.'

'He doesn't write mine,' Harkaway snapped to Danny as she translated. 'So tell them that from now on they do as they're told. They haven't been trained to get killed in piffling little skirmishes. They've been trained for battle. They're soldiers and soldiers do as they're told.'

'You can't push them too far, George,' Danny protested.

'I can push them as far as I like,' he snapped. 'And it doesn't require a mewling woman with a Bible to tell me so!'

Despite Harkaway's fears, the raid had done less harm than he thought. Down in the south, the news had reached Colonel Charlton and as he appeared in his commanding officer's tent, the general looked up testily. His army was on the move and he had a lot to think about.

They had already run into the scorched summer plains where there wasn't a leaf or a blade of grass, the wind-flattened earth bone-white or a burning red that stung the eyes, the termite mounds like grotesque towers, the thorn trees with their skeletal branches grey and brittle alongside the shrivelled aloes. Outside his headquarters the wind was stirring up dust as fine as face powder, the discouraging landscape almost entirely the same colour, the sun beating down vertically to create distant mirages among the waste of rocks, and plaster the dust into masks on the sweaty faces of the struggling soldiers.

'I'm busy, Charlie,' the general said shortly. 'Is it important?'

Colonel Charlton smiled. 'It might be, sir. It seems I was wrong about the natives of Somaliland.'

'You mean they've turned on the Italians?'

'Hardly that, sir. Not yet. But something's stirring. I got it through the navy in Aden via Berbera. Boats still sneak across.'

The general frowned. He was impatient. British forces had crossed the border of Africa Orientale at five main points – near Mount Belaya, from Kassala in the Sudan, and from Wajit, Bura and Garissa along the Kenyan border.

'Well,' he said. 'What have you heard?'

Charlton's manner was cheerful. 'We've been hearing reports of Italian patrols being butchered and convoys being attacked,' he said. 'Chiefly along what they choose now to call the Strada del Duce – the road from Jijiga to Berbera via Bidiyu and Hargeisa.'

'Well, that's a help,' the general said. 'Who's doing it? The natives?'

'Reports say they're well organized, whoever they are. But there's another curious report. Of an Italian brigadier kidnapped at Gura. Right outside his own headquarters.'

The general began to show more interest. 'Kidnapped? That's a new one.'

'By white men, sir.'

The general put down his pen. 'Renegade Italians? Anti-fascists?'

'That's something we haven't come across in this part of the world, sir. The report's vague but it says they're British.'

'British? Have Cairo been sending people in without informing us? They're forming raiding parties in England. I know. Commandos, they're called. Churchill's idea. Have they sent some out here?'

'Aden knows nothing, sir. Neither does the navy.'

'Could they be a party left behind in the retreat last August?'

'I've been through the returns, sir. No large groups were left behind.'

The general reached out for his pen. 'Handle it, Charlie,' he said shortly. 'Try to find out more about them. If there *is* somebody there operating behind the Italians' lines, it's up to us to get in touch with 'em. We might be able to help. Get the air force to land arms or something. Let me know how it shapes up.'

When Yussuf next appeared, he said that Di Peri's men had left Gura to head back towards Jijiga, and it began to seem important to find out what was happening in the world, because the small group of Somalis they'd gathered round them had suddenly begun to increase.

It was clear the word had gone round and more seemed to be arriving every day. Not only Habr Odessis and Hararis, which were septs of the Aidegallas and Habr Yuris, but also men from other areas — even Rer Ibrahims, who were Ogadens from Abyssinian Somaliland – men of every shade and colour, men from the sub-tribes and restless nomads who had spent their lives scanning the horizon for the rain that rarely came. Inter-tribal fighting and raiding had once constituted the Somalis' national sport and a life devoted to looting seemed irresistible to them. Victory meant riches and wives, death a paradise peopled by houris. They were far from averse to fighting the Italians, especially now the Italians were being defeated.

There were Warsanglis and Dolbehantas, Abr Awals and Habr Toljals from the north-east. With them came men of the sub-tribes, Mahmoud Gerads, Esa Mahmouds, Illas, Illaloes, Hawiyas, Diris, Yahellis, Gadabursis, Issas and Esas. They came in ones and twos and groups, all looking for the chance of killing someone. War had been stamped out in the Somalilands since the death of the Mullah and they had grown weary of peace.

Abdillahi grinned as he watched them arrive, his evil smiling eyes wrinkling. He had the simplicity of a child, a wide-eyed, wicked, handsome child. 'Praise be to Allah,' he said to Harkaway. 'The lord of the world, the compassionate, the merciful. He has given us armies.'

Some of the Habr Yunis from the Tug Argan area had British rifles picked up after the battle there, but for the most part the Somalis had little else but spears, pangas and curved swords, and a few museum pieces kept hidden from the days when the Mullah had rampaged through the country. The rifles they received – though they were only Martinis – made them dance with joy.

They armed all they could. They were remarkably quick on the uptake and, with Gooch to watch over them, became surprisingly skilful in a matter of days. Those who understood the sights explained to those who didn't, while spearmen, noted for their ability to throw, were encouraged to throw stones which they hurled for incredible distances, and these men, though they were not allowed to touch them, had the little Italian grenades explained to them.

Then Gooch assembled the mortars and showed how they

could be packed on the backs of mules or camels. With the assistance of Grobelaar, who over the years had also picked up a smattering of Somali dialects, Danny had to be everywhere at once. Among their recruits they picked up a few who had served with the British along the coast or worked on British ships and they even found an ex-interpreter from the Royal Navy, so that the spreading of the word became easier.

By this time the camp in the hills was a great sprawling area of men, women, children, camels, mules, horses, sheep and goats, because many of the men had brought their families and their flocks with them. Occasionally there were disputes over ownership and a few fights, but on the whole they were settled with little blood being let. Harkaway raged through the camp, swinging his fists and feet to separate the brawlers, and curiously they accepted his word as law. Most of them had brought their own food but, with the great bawling mass of animals and people, eventually it was clear something would have to be done. Either they would have to disperse or set about the Italians.

With Eil Dif emptied of Italians, the Free British thankfully dug out their vehicles again and Tully set up the radio. The news staggered them. The South Africans from Bura in Kenya were advancing at a tremendous speed towards Mogadiscio. A second column from Garissa had joined up with them and, meeting at the Juba River, had defeated the Italians to take Jelib and Margherita. In the north heavy fighting was still going on round Keren.

In British Somaliland, there appeared to be no Italian activity at all beyond obvious preparations to retreat. Yussuf's spies reported that the Italians were burning paper in Bidiyu, and if they were burning documents in Bidiyu, they would certainly be burning them in the more distant Hargeisa and Berbera and other places to the east. And burning documents could only mean that they were preparing to retreat, though for the moment there was no movement, and certainly no aggressive forays into the wilder areas of the countryside. Once more the Duce's writ ran only where his soldiers were gathered in numbers and the Italian commanders were making sure of their safety by sticking to their bases.

Harkaway had become curiously distant from the rest of them. He listened regularly to the radio reports, both from London and from Kenya, Rhodesia and South Africa, and he seemed particularly interested in the news of British air raids.

'Have any of you,' he asked unexpectedly, 'seen any Italian aeroplanes lately?'

They stared at him for a moment, then looked at each other. Nobody appeared to have seen anything of the Regia Aeronautica for some time and it seemed to please Harkaway.

'They've got none,' he said. 'That's why. They've all been destroyed on the ground. If they'd had any, you don't mean to tell me they wouldn't have come looking for us. We're big enough to see now and they know we're here. Yet we've twice hit at them and we've kidnapped one of their senior officers but they've sent nothing after us. I think we can afford to take a few more risks. It's time for the Free British to take the field.'

'I'd rather slip down to Mombasa,' Gooch growled. 'And see the war out there.'

Harkaway studied him for a moment then he shrugged. 'All right,' he said. 'Shove off.'

Gooch growled. 'I can't go on me own.'

'Why not? Kom-Kom's taught you to drive. Take one of the lorries and a rifle and go.'

'What about my share of the silver and the dollars?'

'Take that, too,' Harkaway said offhandedly. 'I hope it lasts a long time. Three months from now you'll have spent it. You're the type. Perhaps it's best. You were never totally reliable.'

'I'm a trained soldier!' Gooch exploded.

'The only thing you were expert at was persuading housewives to provide you with suppers and their daughters to lower their knickers for you.'

'You *said* we were going south!' Gooch persisted.

'For God's sake, man!' Harkaway snapped. 'You wanted

loot, didn't you? What you've got so far's not worth a damn.
But now we've got the whole of Italian East Africa to go
at. Not just native silver. But what the Italians had too!
Good European gold watches. Trinkets. Italian money.'

'Which will be worth nothing in no time,' Danny said
dryly, 'if they're kicked out of the war.'

Harkaway gave her a sharp look but he didn't argue.
'Italian lorries and cars,' he went on. 'Yours for the taking.
Italian silk shirts and suits. Italian wine and brandy. You
can make your fortune.'

Gooch was clearly tempted. He was far from being a
quick-witted man and Danny could see him being manoeuvred in a way that drew her sympathy. Her intelligence
made her want to warn him because she suspected Harkaway was manoeuvring them all in the same way, but her
heart was now entirely Harkaway's and she couldn't bring
herself to protest.

'When do you reckon it'll be over?' Gooch asked.

'Month or two,' Harkaway said. 'No more. After North
Africa, nobody can come to their help. They're as good as
out of the war.'

Gooch nodded. 'All right,' he said. 'I'll stay on.'

As he moved away, Danny edged closer to Harkaway.
'That was cheating,' she said quietly. 'Suppose you're right?
Suppose he *does* pick up loot. He can't sell it here and he
couldn't carry enough south to make a fortune.'

Harkaway's hand touched hers. 'It'll dawn on him eventually,' he said. 'Until then, let's make use of him.'

'Do you make use of everybody, George?'

Harkaway stared at her. He was a tall man but she was
tall, too, slender and angular, especially since their exertions
in the heat had removed some of the flesh. For a long time
his eyes held hers then he moved away without saying
anything.

The following day they learned that Moyale had been captured by the Abyssinians and that the South Africans had
entered Mogadiscio. Bardera, inland on the Juba River, had
also been captured and one wing of the advance was already

heading north, so that the Italians were being swept into a net. Then they learned that, terrified of being cut off, the Italians in British Somaliland were beating a retreat back up the Strada del Duce from Berbera towards Hargeisa. The capital's ancient streets and white houses were being left for the British navy from Aden and they were expected any day.

As Harkaway made his plans, it was noticeable now that he didn't bother to ask the others what they thought.

To their fury, the brightest of the Harari and Odessi men were told to hand over their rifles. Their protests welled up and filled the air.

Harkaway waved his hands and turned to Danny. 'Tell them,' he said, 'that we have better weapons for them.'

As she did so, he turned and pulled the cover from one of the Vickers which he had set up facing a small hill.

'Tell them they will be using *these* weapons,' he said. 'And that they will *see* their bullets killing their enemies.'

He bent over the Vickers and pressed the trigger, swinging the gun on its tripod as he did so. Tracer bullets lifted in brightly coloured arcs that provoked breathless gasps as they tore lumps from the hillside and ricocheted into the air.

'Tell them,' Harkaway went on, and he sounded like a salesman at a fair, 'that they will learn to fire these other guns.'

'You're taking a chance,' Gooch warned. 'Giving machine guns to wogs.'

'They've got to learn to use 'em some time,' Harkaway said in a flat voice. 'We can't leave it all to you. We've now got ten machine guns and you can't fire the lot.'

'What do we want ten machine guns for?' Tully asked.

'Because rifles won't be big enough for what we're going to do.'

As Harkaway turned away, Tully looked at Gooch. Harkaway had always been aloof, keeping himself separate from his companions in a way that suggested they weren't fit companions for a man who'd been well educated.

'What about stoppages?' Gooch called out. 'I can just see these ham-fisted bastards trying to clear a stoppage.'

'They won't have to,' Harkaway said over his shoulder. 'You'll do that. All they'll do is spray what they're told to spray. We now have more ammunition than we know what to do with.'

'That bugger's getting too bloody big for his boots,' Gooch complained to Tully as Harkaway moved out of earshot. 'He's beginning to behave like a sergeant-major or a brand new second-lieutenant. They're both known for having too much lip.'

Nevertheless, what Harkaway wanted was done. With the aid of oaths and cuffs about the head, they managed to persuade the Somalis to fire in short sharp bursts and not to waste ammunition. They picked up the idea surprisingly quickly, though Harkaway allowed none of them to strip a gun.

'That'll come in good time,' he said. 'First, we need camels.'

'What do we need camels for?' Grobelaar demanded.

'Never mind what we need 'em for. Get 'em. Together with donkeys, mules, horses, even women if they can carry loads.'

Harkaway was becoming obsessed with his idea of hammering the Italians and nobody seemed to have the courage to stand up to him. Camels, horses, mules and asses were mustered, paid for by the Maria Theresa dollars they had captured, and they milled round the wells near Eil Dif, bawling and stinking to high heaven, surrounded by the herds of sheep and goats which Harkaway said he wanted as food for his men. Hearing what was in the wind, he was joined by more young men, coming in large numbers now, Rer Alis and Mudus from the south, even a few Mijjerteins and Omar Mahmouds from Italian Somaliland. There were also a few Abyssinians, remnants of patriot bands broken up by skirmishes with the Italians, who even brought their own firearms, and deserters from the battalions of native levies from along the borderlands who were itching to get their own back on the men who had conscripted them into their army. They were an ill-trained, ill-armed, ill-equipped and ill-disciplined rabble whom Harkaway had persuaded to rally round him only by promoting tribal rivalry, inferring one lot were better than the next. As the numbers grew, feeding them became a problem, and Harkaway was well aware that they would have to make a move soon because the Bur Yi Hills had been almost scoured clean.

The others watched him as he worked, puzzled, conscious of his single-mindedness and wondering what was in his mind.

'Your ideas seem to be growing a little,' Danny commented dryly.

Harkaway ignored her. He was a natural leader and nobody questioned his authority, least of all the Somalis. By this time, they had forgotten loot in their delight in their new weapons and were eager for more action. He had even formed a private little group which he called the Imperial Guard, led by Abdillahi; they included the first men they'd taught to use a rifle or drive a lorry, and they would have followed him anywhere.

Meanwhile the little pack guns had been assembled. They were only small weapons but Gooch made them work and the Somalis leapt and danced as he aimed one of them at the old houses on the edge of the town. Mud bricks, timbers and stones flew and a wall collapsed with a roar and a welling cloud of dust.

'Now show *them* how to do it,' Harkaway said.

Danny watched him, a worried look on her face. There was a commanding manner about him now that she'd never noticed before and she saw that the others didn't argue but leapt to do as he bid them. She could only put it down to some inborn quality he possessed, because there was nothing else to make them, beyond a hidden drive that kept him going. It was an inner source of energy that was enough to carry them all along, but in his brooding yellow eyes there was a look that troubled her. She voiced her fears to Grobelaar.

'What's he up to, Kom-Kom?' she asked.

Grobelaar gave her his shadowy smile and touched her hand. 'Better ask him, man,' he said.

Harkaway made no attempt to conceal what was in his mind. 'With the British coming down from the Sudan into Abyssinia and Eritrea,' he said, 'and Kom-Kom's South African friends moving up from Kenya, the Italians are bound to draw in their horns. They're bound to retreat on their centre, and their centre isn't British Somaliland and certainly not Berbera, Hargeisa or Bidiyu. They'll pull back because they haven't a cat in hell's chance of staying where they are. That road from Berbera to Jijiga's going to be busy. That's where the Sixth Column will be.'

He was talking less like a junior NCO and more like a general now. Danny eyed him curiously.

'What's it all for?' she asked.

'To kill Italians, of course.'

'There's no need to kill them, man,' Grobelaar said. 'They're going, anyway.'

'They'll go faster if we encourage them.'

Danny studied him, an anxious expression on her face. 'What are you hoping to get out of this, George?' she asked.

He had been deep in thought and he started and turned to look at her. 'Nothing,' he said.

'Nobody takes the sort of risks you're taking, just for the pleasure of saying you chased off Italians who were going anyway.'

'It's our job to chase them.' His face was grim. 'I'm going to stop up the Strada del Duce. Before they know it, it'll be the Strada degli Inglesi. *Our* road. Just watch me, my white-breasted Bronwen. We have the advantage all the way now. I'm going to stop 'em on the Bidiyu side of the Wirir Gorge.'

'Why there?'

'Because at that point the road's a good ten feet above the surrounding scrubland. They won't pull off it to pass anything that's blocking it, because if they did, they'd never get back on. It's narrow, see, so they can't even turn round. I'm going to split their column so that those in the rear will be concerned only with reaching the front and getting to safety. The rest will be ours. We'll get the lorries off the road into the scrub and disappear.'

'You said you couldn't get off the road there.'

Harkaway's smile was pitying. 'I said they *wouldn't* because they couldn't get back on, which is different. All we have to do is lower them with ropes. There'll be enough of us.' He gestured at Grobelaar standing nearby. 'Kom-Kom's done this sort of thing before, I'm sure.'

She stared at him, her eyes on his face. 'You can't do it,' she said. 'You won't have time. Bidiyu's too close. They'd be bound to radio and Guidotti'll send help.'

'He'll arrive too late,' Harkaway smiled. 'Because I've a few tricks up my sleeve to stop him. There's a gully passes under the road eight miles back for a start, to stop the water coming off the hills when it rains washing the road away. I know it's there because the Engineers laid it in 1939, and I was one of them. At the moment, it's stuffed up with mud and sand and various other kinds of refuse. A touch of explosive there will blow a hole twenty feet wide. *That* should stop Twinkletoes coming from Bidiyu. It'll also stop anybody who manages to get his vehicle turned – assuming that he could or would want to – from returning to Bidiyu.'

'How are you going to get there?' Danny asked. 'You can't move all these men, all these vehicles across the desert. The Italians would spot you at once. And you can't go along the road. They have posts every few kilometres, connected by radio to Bidiyu.'

'I'm not going across the desert. And I'm not going by the road. I'm going over the hills. We did it before.'

'On foot,' Grobelaar pointed out. 'You'll never get this lot over. There aren't any roads. There was talk in the Public Works Department before the war of building one but, because there was no path to work from, they decided not to bother.'

'Shows how little you civil service chaps know,' Harkaway said with tired patience. 'Yussuf says he's taken his sheep and goats along it.'

'Lorries aren't sheep and goats!'

Harkaway seemed weary of the arguing. 'They thought

Stonewall Jackson couldn't get his troops over the hills in the Shenandoah Valley campaign. But he did.'

'How do *you* know about Stonewall Jackson and the Shenandoah Valley campaign?' Danny asked.

'It's prized above rubies at Sandhurst.'

She was staring at him narrow-eyed now. 'How do you know about Sandhurst? Were *you* at Sandhurst.'

He ignored the question. 'Good type, Jackson. Very religious. You and he would have got on well. He smote them hip and thigh until they didn't know where he was coming from next. That's what I'm going to do.'

'You'll never do it.'

'Just watch me.'

Her eyes on his face, she tried to read his mind. 'And what are the camels and the horses and the mules for?'

He grinned at her, a wolfish grin that was frightening. 'To pull the lorries if necessary, my little Jesus waif. That's what for.'

As the days went by, Harkaway grew more morose, like a torpid yellow-eyed eagle, relaxed in broody silence. Yet he never seemed still. He had now started showing the Somalis how to fire a mortar. He wasn't concerned with their accuracy, only that they knew how to feed the bombs into the steel tube and keep out of the way. The accuracy could be provided by himself, by Tully or Gooch, even at a pinch by Grobelaar who had worked with the army long enough to understand them. When he started teaching them to throw the little Japanese grenades, even Tully objected.

'They'll kill their bloody selves,' he protested. 'Probably me, too.'

'No, they won't,' Harkaway insisted. 'Not the way I plan it. Just teach 'em that when you pull the pin it blows up and they have to get rid of it. It won't matter about timing.'

Tully looked at Gooch.

'I dunno what them Italians are expecting,' he said. 'But I bet it ain't what they're going to get.'

By this time, convoys of troops were moving back along the

road from Berbera and they noticed they were beginning to increase in size. The radio informed them that the South Africans had not stayed long in Mogadiscio but, swinging north, had reached Villagio del Duca degli Abruzzi eighty miles inland and were now heading for Bulu Burti, while another column, splitting off at Jelib, was pushing on to Lugh Ferrandi.

It was time to get on the march and the huge, straggling caravan shuffled, gathered its muscles and heaved into movement.

Sitting on a rock at the side of the road by the Lancia, Harkaway watched them go, the camels lurching along under their loads behind the lorries, the stink of their dung heavy in the air.

'They're overloaded, man,' Grobelaar protested. 'You've got around two hundred and fifty pounds on them.'

'Camels can carry two hundred and fifty pounds,' Harkaway said.

'Under ideal conditions. They won't be ideal the way you're going. They need barley to keep their strength up. They'll die.'

'Let 'em,' Harkaway said. 'So long as we get there.'

He turned to Commandante di Peri, who was sitting alongside him, his hands clasped between his knees, a picture of dejection.

'We have to take you with us, *Commandante*,' he explained. 'You realize that? It's for your own safety. There's no one we can leave to guard you. And I wouldn't advise you to bolt. You wouldn't want the Abyssinians coming to fetch you back.'

Di Peri lifted his head. 'As a prisoner of war under the Geneva conventions – '

'Don't bother me with that, *Commandante*!' Harkaway barked. 'We're not fighting the war here under Geneva conventions. In any case, the Geneva conventions state that you should share the conditions of the people who capture you. That's what you're going to do.'

The dusty straggling column began to turn into the hills – lorries, horses, mules, asses and camels, and a long string of lean black men in tobes and turbans carrying rifles. They were unaccustomed to order and had been bored by parades, drilling and instruction, but now, under the harsh glare of the sun, they were facing the real thing and their eyes were hard and excited.

Taking the opportunity to water before they started to climb, men jostled for the greenish bitter stagnant liquid already fouled by the mass of animals. Nobody objected. They were all of them more thirsty than fastidious. As they went higher, they seemed to draw nearer the sun and the fierce white light grew more clinical and sterile. But as the sun disappeared and night came, the winds which had been warm at lower levels suddenly seemed cold and blew through thin robes.

Sitting alone, Grobelaar started to play his mouth organ. In addition to his responsibility for the vehicles, he seemed to have been saddled with the role of camel-master for the simple reason that, with his years in Somaliland, he was the only one apart from the Somali herdsmen who knew much about them. It was a role he disliked because it involved moving up and down the column, first with the lorries, then with the failing animals, yelling them on with Afrikaans cries of '*Voetsek*' and '*Trek ons!*'

It made him lethargic with weariness in the evenings and the tune was slow and nostalgic.

'What's that, Kom-Kom?' Danny asked.

'Old Afrikaner tune,' he said. 'About a Transvaaler a long way from home wanting to get back to his girl.'

'It sounds sad.'

'It *is* sad.' He gave her his vague smile and changed the tune. 'This is 'Brandewyn, Laat My Staan'. Brandy, Leave Me Alone. South Africans sing that one a lot. Brandy's too cheap in the Union.' He rolled his good eye while the glass one remained still and it made him look drunk.

She laughed. 'Do *you* drink much of it?'

'Used to,' he said. 'That's why I look like this. Once saw pink snakes all over the bedroom. Gave it up. Only beer now.'

'Have you got a wife, Kom-Kom?'

He shook his head.

She was silent for a moment. He had always been kind to her, always helpful, and it puzzled her that he seemed so alone.

'Why not, Kom-Kom?'

'Because I'm only a one-eyed motor mechanic.'

She touched his cheek gently beneath the glass eye with the tips of her fingers. 'What happened?'

He shrugged. 'I shot a duiker when I was a kid. That's a small buck the size of a goat. It went into a monkey thorn bush and I went in to get it out. But I was in too big a hurry and I spiked my eye. They rushed me to a doctor but it was no good.' He smiled his shadowy smile. 'That's why nobody ever wanted to marry me. I'm not a good catch and now I'm getting to middle age. Even my name's ugly, and I'll never make any money.'

'That's because you've never had anyone to work for. You could if you wanted to.'

'*Ja*,' he agreed. 'Mebbe.'

'Have you *ever* had a girlfriend?'

He looked at her and grinned, his lined battered face twisted. 'Only you,' he smiled.

The following morning, Harkaway had them moving again as soon as it was light, driving them on at a murderous pace. The first of the camels to fall, a sick mare, came down on the slippery shale on the second day.

'She's had it,' Grobelaar said. 'She's damaged her knees.'

Harkaway was unmoved. 'Light a fire under her,' he said. 'She'll soon realize there's no future in staying down.'

Grobelaar gave Harkaway an angry look but he did as he was told and their nostrils were assailed by the smell of burning hair which eventually changed to burning flesh. The camel stayed put. Harkaway heard what Grobelaar had to say without batting an eyelid.

'Get the load on to the donkeys,' he said.

'Have you seen the size of those bleddy donkeys?' Grobelaar yelled indignantly, even his glass eye looking angry. 'They can carry only a fifth of what a camel can carry.'

Harkaway barely seemed to hear. 'All we want is food, water, petrol and ammunition,' he said. 'Leave what we don't need.'

The road through the hills was steep and treacherous. In some places it looked like a path through the mountains of the moon, the ground bare and smooth like cooled lava, in others it was covered with deceptive cotton grass which the hungry camels tried to eat and just as quickly vomited up. The slopes were smooth chocolate-coloured rock covered with a dust like talcum powder on which the animals slipped and crashed down, bawling in fright and pain.

Riding in one of the lorries, as tired, dust-covered and exhausted as the rest of them, Di Peri objected. 'What in the name of God are you trying to do?' he asked.

Harkaway glared at him, his face black with a muddy paste of dust and sweat. 'That's nothing to do with you,' he snapped. 'You're a prisoner and nothing else. You're here only because of my kindness of heart. I could throw you to the wolves, if I wanted to.'

The problems began to multiply quickly. One of the camels carrying the pack guns began to fall behind.

'It mustn't fall behind,' Harkaway insisted.

'The bleddy thing's sick,' Grobelaar said.

'Then shove the gun on another.'

Grobelaar protested fiercely. 'They weren't built for this sort of territory,' he said. 'We had three go down this morning. Legs broken. Shuffled along on their bleddy knee pads. *Ag, Magtig!* What a sight! And I let 'em, man,' he went on in furious self-disgust. 'Because of what they were carrying.'

'We're not here to be sorry for camels,' Harkaway said coldly.

'I notice *you* keep well away from the bastards,' Grobelaar snarled. 'Have you heard 'em bawling in agony, man?'

'I've got ears.'

'They settle down under a cloud of flies that gets thicker by the minute and wait to die.' Grobelaar looked at Danny, as if he hoped she might support him. 'I never thought much of camels. They're ugly, bad-tempered buggers, but, Jesus, man, they know how to die with dignity. I hope we do, too, when the time comes.'

Harkaway said nothing, watching Grobelaar hurry away along the column, his whole shabby figure angry.

'Do we have to push them so hard, George?' Danny asked.

'Yes we do,' he said. 'It's a military maxim that you can't have an omelette without breaking eggs and anybody running a war has to have enough nerve to accept losses. So far we've only lost camels. We have to be across that road by the time the main bulk of the Italians starts moving back.'

'But why? If they're going, why worry?'

'It's another military maxim that when your enemy's retreating, you hit him twice as hard. That way his retreat becomes a rout.'

'You're full of military maxims,' she snapped. 'Where did you pick them up?'

'I've learned a lot in my time.'

The column limped on, a lurching, winding, bawling string of weary animals and men. On the hills, the mules and horses hauled the lorries upwards and human muscle hauled the staggering camels. The number dwindled all the time. Those which survived, however, still carried ammunition, food and water, but none of the barley they needed and, stubborn to the last, they would eat nothing else. Gawping, creaking and groaning, they struggled on, persisting in dying despite all the exhausted Grobelaar's efforts. From time to time the whole column came to a thankful stop and rested, panting in the heat, while Harkaway and Grobelaar went ahead and removed rocks with crowbars, by blasting, even by the sheer muscle power of their black helps, to widen the path enough for the vehicles to pass along it. The great square ugly vehicles lurched, groaned and protested, jolting and clattering, but still they went on.

Occasionally the baboons came down and watched them, barking like dogs and drilled like armies, the females with the young, the old males long-fanged and wary, watching the outskirts of the tribe, their bare blue backsides catching the sunshine as they hopped and skipped among the rocks. For the most part they left them alone, though they tried raids in the dusk round the cooking fires, and once when they were chased by one of the dozens of half-starved pi-dogs that had attached themselves to the column, they turned round and tore it to pieces.

The baboons were the least of their worries, however. They had a few sick and injured men now who could not be left to fend for themselves, and the radiators of the over-worked, over-driven lorries began to leak. Grobelaar cured them by plugging them with handfuls of dates, but by now the camels were dying like flies and with every foot they climbed the difficulties increased.

'My dove, my rose, my moon, my sweetness without compare!' Abdillahi was coaxing on the donkey that carried Harkaway's personal possessions, determined not to leave them behind. As the animal laid its ears back and started to kick, his tone changed. 'Misbegotten son of a whore! Faithless one! Son of a camel crossed with a djinn!'

As the donkey swung about on the end of the rope, it set one of the camels buck-jumping. The man who held the head-rope dangled, his feet off the floor, yelling his head off as the load was shed.

Di Peri, noticeably leaner and more tired, protested again. 'You're mad,' he said.

Harkaway gave him a cold smile. 'It's the sort of madness,' he said, 'none of *your* generals ever seem to suffer from.'

4

The raggle-taggle force was averaging no more than five or six miles a day from sunup to sundown. Larded with sweat and dust, his beard unshaven, Harkaway's lean figure made him look like an Old Testament prophet.

'Are you trying to kill us all?' Gooch demanded.

'No.'

'How do you know what's on the other side?'

'Maps. I've read 'em.'

'I haven't.'

'It's well-known you've never read anything more intelligent than *Sporting Life* or *Comic Cuts*.'

They were all tired now, Grobelaar's face grey with exhaustion beneath the sunburn. Under the hard glare of the great brass gong above them that never let up for a minute, they struggled on, their ankles turned by the stones, their faces black with dust so that they looked like nigger minstrels. All the way behind them were dead or dying horses, mules, donkeys and camels. You could hear them dying and smell them dead.

'George,' Danny asked as they shivered round the fire in the cold of the darkness, 'what are we trying to do?'

Harkaway's voice was angry as he replied. 'If Napoleon had had to explain everything he did to his bloody generals,' he snapped, 'there'd have been no Wagram, no Jena, no Austerlitz.'

'There'd probably have been no 1812 either,' she retorted sharply. 'Besides, you're not Napoleon. You're not even a general. Not even an officer.'

He gave her such a bitter look she became silent.

They reached the summit at last and the grumbling stopped as they halted among the bare bituminous boulders. Fires were lit and meals were cooked. Grobelaar was the last to sit down, grey-faced and staggering. His shirt was plastered to his body, his lined face was masked with a paste of dust and sweat, and the prickly heat on his body had turned to sores.

As he flung himself down alongside Danny, his jaw hanging, she reached for a mug of tea.

'Here, Kom-Kom,' she said. 'That'll help.'

He fell asleep before he'd finished it, leaning heavily against her. She hadn't the heart to disturb him and left him where he was.

Somewhere in the darkness she heard the low moan of a hyena, then the coughing roar of a leopard. The Somalis laughed. Some of them were high on kât, the stimulant drug they used. They acquired it as raw leaves from a shrub that grew on the high plateau which, when chewed, reduced them to a state of indifference or excitement. One of them started singing a song. They were great poets, talkers and romancers and always enjoyed verses as they halted at the end of the day.

Allah made earth
Allah made water
Deep in the earth
Far down is the water

All the Somali songs were about water, Danny thought. It was inevitable, she supposed, in a land so devoid of it.

Allah made cattle
Grazing he gave them.
Deep in the earth,
Far down is the water.

The chant came over the low murmur of voices, flat, toneless and somehow always missing the notes it seemed to aim at.

They were all suffering from the struggle into the hills

now. A few had even slipped away, but none of the men they trusted, though Danny suspected that if the struggle went on much longer they'd soon begin to notice the desertions. Harkaway seemed unmoved, as if he were confident he could hold his men's loyalty.

As the rest of them prepared for sleep, he was still on his feet, prowling nervously round the camp, and as he reached the spot where Danny sat, he stopped and looked down at her supporting the weight of Grobelaar.

'You'll end up with cramp,' he pointed out, not an atom of sympathy in his voice. 'Put him down!'

She stared at him angrily. 'He's worn out,' she accused. 'You've worn him out.'

She remained where she was as the night grew colder. She was using a blanket but Grobelaar, who had flung himself down straight from working on one of the lorry engines, was wearing only a thin shirt. Moving cautiously, she moved the blanket round them both then, putting her arms round him, letting him sleep against her. When she woke the following morning, as Harkaway had promised, her body was numb and aching. Grobelaar opened his eyes, saw what she had done and moved away quickly.

'You shouldn't have done that, man,' he said.

From now on they began to descend. What Harkaway's herdsmen had told him was correct. The route was growing easier and even Gooch and Tully stopped complaining. But they were all hungry, all tired, and all coated with sweat-caked dust.

'It's a sort of inexpensive mud pack,' Grobelaar said as he watched Danny rubbing it from her cheeks.

As they moved down the twisting goat tracks, any who were sick or injured – and twisted ankles were far from uncommon – were left behind to limp back to their villages as best they could. They had no medical supplies or cigarettes, and no one possessed more than he carried about his person. On one occasion, an unexpected downpour caught them on the face of the slopes, the rain coming down in sheets so that they tramped the next morning through chocolate-coloured mud, the Somalis soaked and shivering under their blankets, Danny in the cab of one of the lorries, flung from side to side as the vehicle lurched and slithered.

No one had ever suggested turning back and now that they were to the east of the hills, spirits began to pick up. They saw the main road at last, a black asphalt ribbon running north-east to south-west. It seemed to represent safety and a degree of comfort they'd almost forgotten, and the column streamed down in a long, winding, straggling line.

By the time Harkaway reached the road, the land on either side was swarming with animals and men, the Somalis yelling and dancing exultantly and jabbing with their spears at the earth in the stance of warriors.

'Shut those bloody idiots up,' he snapped at Danny. 'We don't start celebrating yet! Tully, get this bloody road clear! It only wants one armoured car to appear and the whole bloody operation's sunk!'

To the Somalis, for whom reaching the road had been the limit of their ambition, to have to disperse seemed madness, and they were unwilling and sullen.

'Get 'em into the gullies,' Harkaway stormed. 'I want 'em out of sight! Every bloody one of them. Camels, horses, mules, everything! And make sure they stay out of sight!'

It took time to get the swarm of animals and humans dispersed among the folds of the hills but the Somalis finally accepted Harkaway's word as law. He had given them victory more than once already and they now obediently squatted down in the valleys between the knuckly hills, holding their rifles and spears, wrapped in their robes, waiting for the word what to do next.

Fresh from Bidiyu, Yussuf appeared as order was restored, trotting along on a minute donkey, a bent, shrivelled black figure in an orange robe, his lame foot dangling.

'*Salaams, effendi*,' he said. 'Big convoy comes. General Barracca is withdrawing from the coast to Jijiga.'

'That's what I thought, Yussuf,' Harkaway said. 'When?'

Yussuf lifted several fingers then lowered them one after

the other. 'Two days, perhaps. The marketplace at Bidiyu is filled with lorries and soldiers.'

'Where are they going?'

'Jijiga, effendi. Where else *can* they go? The Ingresi are coming north across the border. And they cannot go into Eritrea because the Ingresi are coming south. The news comes from Berbera itself. I also hear that the Italian general, Guidotti, has sworn to catch you and make you beg for mercy.'

Harkaway's eyes narrowed. 'He has, has he?'

Yussuf chuckled. 'That was some time ago. I think it is now too late. They are defeated, effendi.'

Harkaway was silent a moment, staring back down the black ribbon of asphalt towards Bidiyu.

'Yussuf,' he said, 'how many camp followers have we with us? How many women and young boys and old men?'

Yussuf shrugged and spread his hands. 'Many, effendi.'

Harkaway pointed. 'I want them to roll rocks to the side of the road back there. When Barracca's passed and the gorge's been blown, they're to roll them across the road. The bigger the better. So that Guidotti has to clear them. Every one. Understand?'

Yussuf smiled. 'I understand, effendi.'

That night Grobelaar edged their vehicles off the road and down the slope to the scrubland below. For safety, he attached ropes to their rear springs and teams of Somalis lowered them gingerly because a wrecked lorry would be investigated. When they had them all down, Harkaway directed them into the scrub until they were out of sight beyond the crowding thorn trees and euphorbias. There were protests from the Somali drivers as they realized they were not to take part in the killing that was being planned and it required all Danny's tact to persuade them to remain with their charges.

That night the rest of them took up their positions overlooking the road. Where they had blown the gorge before Christmas there was now a small wired-in post containing a pill-box. Harkaway smiled as he studied it through the binoculars. Defences of that kind helped nobody, he knew. They could only defend their immediate locality and not really even that.

Siting his machine guns where they could be most effective and lining the crests with the Somalis, he stared about him. He had placed some of the weapons at the end of the gorge, the rest a few hundred yards further on. Gooch and Tully were busy, nagging at their black teams and clearing a path along the crests so they could move easily between their weapons.

Di Peri, incongruous in his braided uniform, breeches and Somali sandals, watched what was going on with a weary expression, exhausted as the sun rose on the dead lingering heat of the previous day. Like the rest, he was plastered with a mixture of dust and sweat, his lips cracked, his tongue when he opened his mouth seeming more pink than normal against the uniform greyness of the rest of him.

'What are you planning, Colonel?' he asked Harkaway.

Harkaway turned. 'I'm not a colonel,' he said.

'You have the manner.'

Harkaway's eyes became chilly. 'I have the manner all right,' he agreed. 'But I'm not an officer.'

Di Peri gave a bleak smile. 'As a brigadier, I could claim that I have the right to be escorted by someone of equivalent rank.'

Harkaway's smile in return was equally as bleak. 'You'd be pushed to find a brigadier here,' he said.

Di Peri studied him for a while. 'What are you expecting?' he asked. 'It's clear you're planning a *coup de main*. But then what?'

'Then,' Harkaway said, 'the Italians will be out of East Africa and right back where they should be – selling ice cream up and down the Via Roma in Naples.'

Di Peri looked up. 'You know Naples?'

'I've visited it. Come to that, I've visited Florence, Rome, Capri.'

'You liked Italy?'

Harkaway's eyes were faraway. 'I did then,' he admitted. 'I wasn't old enough to know about Mussolini.'

Di Peri smiled. 'Mussolini has done many things,' he said.
'He made the trains run on time.'

'If he'd stuck to that,' Harkaway said, 'he'd have done
better. Because that empire of his that he said was going to
last forever seems to be falling apart a bloody sight more
quickly than he cobbled it together.'

The road remained empty. The Italians were all too concerned with their future to be aware of the swarm of men
waiting in the hills. Fires were lit and the women who had
accompanied the Somali warriors bent over the cooking
pots. Water was handed out sparingly, but no one quibbled.
Water had always been handed out sparingly in Somaliland.

In the afternoon, Harkaway had the scout car loaded with
explosive and, taking Grobelaar and Danny, he sent off two
of his young Habr Odessis with a donkey and followed them
along the narrow tracks through the hills parallel to the
Strada del Duce until they could rattle and lurch down to
the tarmacadam.

It was dusk as they unloaded the explosives by the gully
under the road. Great drainage pipes had been sunk beneath
the asphalt for when the monsoon came and Harkaway
carefully buried the explosive inside them, then the whole
lot of them began to scoop up sand, stones and rocks to fill
the pipes and tamp it down. Finally, he inserted the detonator and led wires back among the rocks, covering it with
sand as he went. Edging down the slope from the road
towards the scrubland below, he ran it among the bushes
and indicated the scout car.

'Think you can drive that down the slope, Kom-Kom?'
he asked.

Grobelaar put the car in low gear and swung it to the lip
of the slope, then, edging it over slowly, let it grind down
to the scrubland. As he brought it to a standstill, Harkaway
indicated the engine. 'We'll need the battery,' he said.

Watched by Danny and the Odessis, Grobelaar discon-
nected the battery and carried it to Harkaway, who connected one of the wires to it.

'All you have to do now,' he said, 'is touch the other wire to the other terminal.'

'Who has?'

Harkaway smiled. 'Well, it isn't going to be one of the Odessis,' he said. 'I wouldn't trust the inquisitive bastards not to try it beforehand to see if it works. It's going to be you. When you hear the bang of mines going off you do your stuff and up she goes.'

Grobelaar studied the battery. 'When?'

'After the convoy passes.'

'And until then?'

'You camp out.' Harkaway gestured. 'I'll be camping out up there.'

'It's going to be hot.'

'It's going to be hot up there, too. There's going to be a *lot* of sweating done before we've finished, in fact.'

Grobelaar studied the battery again. 'And after it goes up?' he asked.

'We shall have the convoy trapped between the gorge and this spot. They won't be able to move either forward or back.'

'I wasn't thinking of the bleddy convoy, man,' Grobelaar growled. 'I was thinking of me.'

Harkaway gave him his pitying smile. 'You disconnect the battery, wind in the wires, put the battery back in the car, start the engine and drive away.'

'Where to?'

Harkaway pointed south-west into the scrub. 'There. We pick you up when we've finished. You won't miss us. There'll be so much traffic it'll raise a dust cloud a mile high.'

Grobelaar frowned. 'Suppose something goes wrong,' he said. 'I'll be out there – ' his arm lifted, pointing ' – on my own.'

Harkaway gave his cool smile. 'If something goes wrong,' he said, 'you won't be the only one.'

Leaving Grobelaar, Harkaway slung the remaining explosive across the donkey's back, helped Danny up behind and began to head into the hills. When they reached the Sixth Column it was already in position round the Wirir Gorge.

'Machine guns?' he asked.

Gooch gestured. 'There, there, there and there. Two at the other side of the road.'

'Good. Pack guns?'

Gooch gestured again. 'There and there. You can't see 'em. But they're there. The road curves a bit. They'll have a head-on shot.'

Harkaway squinted about him, staring at the high sides of the defile. He was still studying it when Tully appeared.

'Some of the bastards are complaining that they have no weapons.'

'They've got pangas.'

'You can't chop a man down with a panga at a thousand yards. They want guns, long-distance weapons.'

Harkaway frowned then turned to Danny and gestured at the hills. 'Go and tell 'em they've *got* long-distance weapons. Up there. Rocks.' He gestured at the skyline. 'Half those things only need a good shove. There are plenty lying about they can fling down. That'll bring more down. They can put up a barrage that'll stop *anything* if they try. When it's over they'll have all the guns they can carry.'

It was evening when she returned. He smiled.

'We've bottled 'em up behind,' he said. 'Now we'll bottle 'em up in front. It oughtn't to work again because they ought to be looking for them. But they won't, you know. They're such careless sods.'

With the help of Gooch, he laid mines across the road, then stood back, examining his handiwork. 'Now for the real stuff,' he said. 'I'll need a hand.'

He looked about him at the Somalis who loved to see the explosions he made and were always eager to help. He rejected them all and turned to Danny. 'It'll have to be you again.'

She didn't object, wondering why he had kept her by his side all this time, and they began to climb back to the crests, Harkaway carrying a heavy battery in an Italian back-pack, Danny carrying the explosive. It was heavy and he seemed indifferent to her struggling, making no attempt to help her, except once when he turned to reach down and drag her up to him. His pull almost yanked her arm out and brought her close to him, her body against his.

For a moment they stood like that, each aware of the other's shape pressing against their own, then Harkaway smiled, turned and began to walk away. She stood for a second, staring after him, then she hitched at the pack on her shoulders and set off after him. Eventually, he stopped and stared down at the road. In the distance, they could just see the tiny spot of colour made by the Italian flag over the outpost Di Sanctis had erected.

'Poor stupid sods,' he observed cheerfully. 'They're not doing a scrap of good.'

At the other end of the gorge, there was a stark sun-blasted spire of red rock that hung over the road like a fang and Harkaway had had his eye on it for some time. In the heat of the sinking sun, he moved along the crest towards it. From its shelter he stared down on the road, patted the rock and began to work.

Little digging was required and he scraped away at the bottom of the rock until he had made a small deep cleft, into which he placed the explosive. Inserting the detonator, he ran the wire back to a point where he could see both the road beneath and the men lining the crests, then he took the battery from his pack and connected one of the wires.

'Done,' he said, dusting his hands on his shirt.

Danny studied him. 'What now?'

'We stay here. It's too dark to go back. You'd probably break your neck.'

'Would that matter, George?'

He didn't answer and she persisted. 'Why did you bring me up here?' she asked.

He still said nothing, a smile flickering over his lips and she eyed him in the semi-darkness, uncertain what he intended.

'It's not a habit of mine to spend the night on mountains alone with a man,' she said.

'You've been dreaming of it for years,' he said. 'All that

time when you were with those psalm-singing wets at the mission. Isn't that right?'

She said nothing because there was more than an element of truth in what he said. She had dreamed more than once of being carried off by someone more manly and virile than the missionaries with whom she'd been surrounded.

'What's going on between you and Kom-Kom?' he asked unexpectedly.

'Nothing. Why?'

'You seem to be leaning on each other a lot.'

She realized he was jealous and her heart leapt. 'He's a kind man,' she said. 'And he's been driven pretty hard.'

'That all?'

'That's all.'

He nodded. 'I'm not surprised,' he said. 'After all, what is he? A half-educated South African *jaap* with one eye and fingers greasy from poking in the innards of too many lorries.'

The sheer arrogance of the comment irritated her but then, again unexpectedly, he leaned over and kissed her on the lips. 'You've been splendid,' he said. 'You deserve a change.'

He made a small fire in a cleft in the rocks and they sat in front of it.

'It's going to be cold,' Danny said, watching him curiously.

'Better come a bit closer,' he suggested.

'Just what are you hoping to get out of all this?' she asked him warily.

'All what?'

'All this killing?'

He was silent for a long time. 'There are a lot of things I hope to get out of it,' he said.

'Wouldn't you like to tell me?'

'No.'

Already she had an idea. The way he spoke, the way he held himself, the way he behaved, everything about him told her he was trying to prove something to himself and she had long since guessed what it was. Somewhere in his past he had made a mistake and ruined his chances. Somewhere, she suspected, his hope of being an officer in the army had disappeared with something he'd done and this was his way of proving to the authorities what they'd missed.

'Are you hoping they'll commission you?' she asked. 'When we get back to civilization, I mean.'

He was silent a long time. 'They probably will,' he said. 'And that's the best way to get a commission, isn't it? In the field. Without all that bull of going to officers' training school. There wouldn't be much they could teach me, anyway.'

'What happened?'

He looked up. 'What happened?'

'Something happened, didn't it?' she said gently. 'In the past. What was it?'

He looked up and smiled back at her, but made no effort to enlighten her.

'Won't you tell me? It sometimes helps to tell people your troubles.'

'It's not a trouble,' he said.

She told him of her own background and how she felt her life had been wasted.

'I don't now, though,' she admitted. 'I feel I've been part of something at last. Largely thanks to you.'

He touched her hand and kissed her again. Their faces close together, lit by the flames from the dying fire, he raised his other hand to touch her cheek.

'Has anybody ever told you you're beautiful?' he said.

'No,' she said frankly. 'And nobody ever will. Because I'm not, and from now on, at my age, I'll grow progressively less so.'

'Why did you become a missionary?'

'Because I couldn't think of anything else.'

'Not because of a profound belief in religion?'

'No. I was just at a loss.'

'Why didn't you ever marry?'

'Nobody ever asked me.'

'Have you ever been in love?'

'No,' she said. But she didn't add that for some time now she had been entertaining a few hopes.

'Will it be tomorrow?' she asked.

'Probably.'

'I hope you pull it off, George. I hope everything turns out right for you. I hope – ' she paused ' – I hope you achieve your ambition.'

He didn't answer. She caught his eyes on her and returned his gaze without blinking.

'George – !'

She stopped dead, the unspoken words dying in her throat, and slowly he pushed their belongings aside and reached out to her.

For a long time she clung to him, a great warmth flooding over her as she leaned against him, content merely to feel his hands on her, responding eagerly when he kissed her, his fingers in the short cropped hair that made her look like a youth, both of them sinking in the darkness of the passion that overwhelmed them.

After a while, she sat up, shivering as the fire died, holding on to him, touching his features with her fingertips, unable to take her eyes off him, crying occasionally, quietly and ashamedly, as she hadn't cried for years. Her life had taught her not to cry and the sufferings of the black people with whom she'd worked, their sicknesses, their dead babies, their festering illnesses, had toughened her.

'George,' she said. 'What's happening to me? I've not done this since I was a child.'

He pulled her closer, stroking her forehead with the back of his hand.

'Wind up?' he suggested.

'No, it isn't wind up.' She stirred, faintly scared, nevertheless. Chiefly for herself because she had a feeling that she had no need to fear for Harkaway.

'There's nothing to be afraid of,' he said.

'I'm not so sure.'

On her face there was the look of woman throughout the whole of the world's history, loathing conflict, wanting only love and roots deep in the earth, a look to which there was no reply.

'You and I,' she said slowly, 'just happened to fall on the wrong side of life.'

'Not any more,' he said. 'When this lot's over it'll be all right. We'll make it all right. Unless, of course, you're too tied up with your religion.'

She suddenly realized how little her religion really meant to her. She shook her head.

He said nothing, not pushing the idea any further, but it set her thoughts racing along lines she'd not considered for years, wondering if she had enough of her woman's skill left to give him the roots he so obviously needed.

Forgetting her discomfort and the increasing cold, she occupied herself with thoughts she'd never dwelt on before. In her heart of hearts she didn't really believe in them, and, looking round at him, she realized he had moved away from her, restless as ever, to the edge of the rocky ledge and was staring down into the darkness. The moon had risen and they could see the road below like a silver ribbon.

'I hope to Christ none of those silly sods in the post there decides to go for a walk,' he said, his thoughts clearly no longer on her. 'I don't want them setting off the mines before the lorries come.'

5

In Bidiyu General Guidotti was aware of the unpleasant sensation of his world falling apart about his ears. Kismayu was in the hands of the enemy now and in Mogadiscio they were already preparing to surrender the town. It had been Italian a long time and there would be Italian families there, hitherto secure in a colonial way of life. But the colonial way of life in Libya had fallen to pieces already and they would now be expecting it to fall to pieces in East Africa. There would be frightened faces at upper windows and an attempt on the part of the police and the officials to remain calm before the silent Somalis, while the askaris in their scarlet fezzes would be rigid on the steps of the fascist headquarters, though Guidotti had no confidence that they could be trusted in defeat.

In Bidiyu they were already disillusioned. Food was no longer coming through from Jijiga and he was already aware that the askaris were watching him askance, wondering, despite their Italian badges and braid, when it would be safe to disappear. They were already short of petrol and with thousands of gallons in Mogadiscio about to fall into the hands of the enemy, he could see the whole Italian army and air force in the Horn of Africa running to a standstill.

He sighed. As it seemed to have come to a standstill in Libya, he thought. And even Greece. When the Duce had decided to invade Greece from Albania the previous October, he had expected a walk-over victory but the Greeks had proved tougher than expected, and not only had they repelled Italian attacks, they had managed, while the Italian navy was still reeling from Taranto, even to advance into

Italian territory in Albania. The bombast and boasting had come to nothing. Instead of being a conqueror like Hitler, the Duce had turned out to be nothing more than a jackal whining at his master's heels.

Tears started to Guidotti's eyes. That very morning he'd heard that a British army had gone into Greece and he could envisage yet more defeats. And sooner or later, he knew, he would have to leave Bidiyu. Troops were already pouring through from Hargeisa and the coast. A convoy had arrived only that morning, consisting of every kind of vehicle Guidotti could possibly imagine – light tanks, trucks towing guns, petrol bowsers, ambulances, armoured cars, scout cars, staff cars, roaring in one after the other, shaking the town with their noise, setting everything vibrating under the sound of their engines.

General Barracca appeared during the afternoon, worried and anxious-faced.

'It seems to be up to you, Ettore,' he said. 'We are withdrawing through you. Like a sock pulled inside out. You will withdraw through Forsci at Jijiga when the order comes.'

If the order comes, Guidotti thought. If Forsci weren't too busy in other directions. If the road weren't cut.

'If things go wrong,' Barracca went on, 'you will head north towards Djibuti and try to join the Commander-in-Chief, the Duke of Aosta. He's planning to concentrate near Amba Alagi if Keren falls. It'll be your duty to try to reach him.' Barracca finished his drink and lit a cigarette. 'I think Africa Orientale is finished. I think the Duce's pipe-dreams are finished also. Soon they'll be finished in Greece.' He paused. 'Perhaps when we boil it all down, the Duce is finished also.'

Guidotti offered him another brandy then Barracca took a quarter of an hour off to visit the garrison church to light a candle and offer up a prayer to keep him safe to go home to his family. Finally he shook hands with Guidotti, climbed into his car and drove away.

Barracca's first lorry ran over the land mines two hours

later, almost to the minute. There was a tremendous explosion that set off two other mines, and as the lorry rocked back on its springs, one of the front tyres burst and it swung broadside on to the road. The doors of the cabin had sprung open under the blast and from one of them the driver fell out and sprawled in the road. His mate, torn by fragments coming through the floor, remained where he was, moving weakly. The second lorry, slewing sideways to avoid running into the wrecked vehicle, dropped a wheel into the ditch and canted over sharply, its nose within inches of the first vehicle. As the crew scrambled clear there was a puff of smoke as the petrol leaking from the first lorry's punctured tank was ignited by the flames licking the underneath of the vehicle and a 'whoomph' as it went up.

The driver of the second lorry was just struggling to get clear when the first pack gun fired. It was only a sevenpounder of antiquated design which had found its way to Somaliland from the North-west Frontier of India and, because of its age, had been relegated to the reserve and pushed into the dump above Eil Dif. But it still worked and, as the little shell struck, engine covers, wings, pieces of piping, fan, radiator and scraps of metal flew through the air. Just dropping to the ground to run for safety, the driver was hit at the back of the head by a piece of engine casing that shattered his skull and flung him into the ditch.

The Italians were still looking round for this new assailant when Gooch fired the second gun, aiming at the gap between the first and second lorries. Because of its age, this time the shell failed to explode, but it nevertheless removed the rear wing of the second lorry and buried itself in the engine of the third lorry, bringing that to a stop too, so that the whole road was jammed.

Barracca was standing up in his car, halfway along the column, staring ahead. He gestured angrily at one of his aides. 'Get up there,' he ordered. 'Get that road clear!'

It was easier said than done and, from the crest, Harkaway and Danny watched the panic below as lorries tried to back away from the fire. The second lorry's tyres had now also caught fire and a thick pall of black smoke began to rise from the burning rubber.

The Somalis were behaving well and none of them had fired. Harkaway was anxious to spring his trap properly and he was staring backwards with the binoculars down the road to where Grobelaar waited. In the distance, half a mile beyond Barracca's last lorry, they could see small figures swarming down out of the hills and across the road. Yussuf's people were blocking the road as he had ordered. But there was still no sign of the explosion and he began to frown. Without the gully smashed and the surface of the road holed, Barracca could escape.

'Come *on*, Kom-Kom,' he said aloud.

Even as he spoke, he heard a dull thud and saw a smoke ring lifting slowly into the air. Turning, he saw Tully watching him. Down below in the gorge, the Italians were trying to take up positions to protect themselves from something they knew was coming but hadn't yet appeared. Because they didn't know the direction, they were confused. But Barracca was an old soldier and his aides had not been idle. Already, a group of native levies were assembling among the stranded lorries, clutching rifles. They were looking in the direction from which the pack guns had fired and Harkaway could see Gooch and his teams struggling to reload. They seemed to be having difficulty and within seconds they could be overwhelmed.

Harkaway smiled and signed to Danny just below him on the slope with the battery and the loose wire. At his wave she touched the battery terminal.

The faces of the men in the gorge lifted, horrified, as the new explosion came from above their heads. For a while, to Danny it seemed as if nothing had happened and they had failed. Small rocks and stones were arcing into the air and beginning to bounce down the slope through the swelling cloud of brown smoke; and, having moved closer to the point of explosion than she should have done, afraid she might not do correctly what she had to do and terrified that Harkaway would be disappointed in her and scourge her with his tongue, she cowered now as small stones and earth

rained down on her. As the shower stopped, she looked up.
The pinnacle of rock was still standing and she began to
pray, terrified of Harkaway's rage if they failed. Then she
realized that the pinnacle was no longer upright, but was
slowly tilting outwards towards the road.

As it moved further and further, it cracked in the middle
and broke in two, and a tremendous yell went up from the
Somalis lining the crest that was echoed by one of horror
from the men in the valley. It crashed across the slope in a
cloud of dust and a shower of debris and went roaring
downwards, carrying with it a whole landslide of rocks,
stones and scree that thundered down to the road and
crashed into the gorge. The driver of a lorry directly beneath
looked up in horror as he saw it coming and tried to leap
from his cab. But with the door half open, it was struck by
a bounding boulder that slammed it shut, neatly severing
his fingers, then the whole cabin crumpled and bent beneath
the weight of the rocks, stones and earth that piled down
on it.

By this time the whole crest was lined with men who had
begun to set the very slopes rattling down on the men in
the defile. With the sides rearing at an angle of almost ninety
degrees, the Italians had no chance. The men above them
could set virtually the whole hillside moving, and boulders
began to hurtle and bounce into the ravine in blinding clouds
of dust and loose shale, to break bones, bring blood and
send men flying. Sheer terror threw the Italians into confusion as the rocks swept them off their feet, and clanged
against the sides of lorries, smashing wings, buckling wheels
and wrenching at fenders.

Still no one fired from above, though the Italians, hidden
by the rising cloud of dust, were shooting blindly into the
air at their hidden attackers. Gradually, however, the stones
began to stop bouncing and rolling and the dust began to
settle and the running figures below began to appear again.

'Now!' Harkaway roared and, bending over the Bren gun,
Tully fired a long burst into the valley. Immediately, the
whole crest erupted into flame; and the men below, still
wondering which way to face, still staring horrified at the

great landslide of earth and rocks that had cut off the rear half of the column from the front half, began to fall like ninepins. Diving under their vehicles, they began to fire back but, as they did so, mortar bombs began to fall among them. There weren't many and they weren't even well aimed but they were coming regularly and were landing among the scree that bordered the road, flinging fragments of metal and stone to smash windscreens and tear into flesh.

Back in Bidiyu, Guidotti felt cut off.

He had little in the way of orders, except to remain where he was, holding the road open so that the army could pass through him on the way to Jijiga. After Jijiga, he wondered, then what? If the British were coming down from the Sudan, where could he go?

He decided it might be a good idea to light a candle himself. The priest was obviously also preparing to leave and the church had a bare look about it.

'What are we to do, Excellency?' he asked.

'I know as much as you, Father,' Guidotti said. 'However, as soon as General Barracca's safely through and in Jijiga, someone will surely inform us that we can go, too.'

An hour later, however, Di Sanctis telephoned. 'The post at Kilometre 207 reports the sound of firing, General,' he said. 'Between them and the frontier.'

Ten minutes afterwards, Piccio arrived, hot and hurried. 'We've had a radio message from Barracca yelling for help,' he announced excitedly. 'He's bottled up in the Wirir Gorge. There's heavy fighting and he's under fire from machine guns, mortars, grenades, and guns.'

In the pass Barracca's troops were still battling to break out. The engineers were struggling to cut a way through the heap of rock and rubble but only the smallest vehicles could make it and the heavy lorries on the other side would have to be left behind. At the front, the burning truck was filling the gorge with blinding smoke and they were trying to edge the following trucks to one side so that a couple of the light tanks could move forward to nudge it out of the way. But there wasn't much room for manoeuvre and the rearmost lorry had to be moved first, then all the others all the way down the line to the front. And all the time a devastating fire was coming from the slopes, rifle fire in unsteady volleys and a steady clattering of machine guns – among which Barracca recognized Italian weapons – that knocked men over in groups whenever they tried to assemble. Then he heard the thump of mortars again from a position too far up the slopes for his own mortars to reach and he turned to one of his aides.

'Let's have a couple of companies up there,' he said, crouching on the ground alongside his car, well aware that it wasn't particularly safe because the firing was coming from both sides at once. 'They're lining the crest. Find those machine guns and destroy them.'

A company of native infantry set off up the slopes, but they were met by showers of grenades. Some of them were British Mills bombs and some their own Japanese-made grenades, which came rolling down the slope to spray the climbing men with their fragments. There wasn't a lot of skill in the way they were being delivered but they were remarkably effective.

Taking heavy losses, the infantry struggled upwards, one or two of the braver souls attempting to snatch up the bouncing grenades and throw them back, a not very profitable exercise because the bombs mostly bounced back again on to the throwers. With difficulty they struggled to the crest, only to find that the machine guns and the men who had manned them had already vanished.

Swinging round to where they could see other black heads further along the crest, they pushed along the shale slope towards them, firing as they went, only for the guns they had been attacking to reappear behind them. It was like rabbit shooting. Every time a man moved forward across the slope, slipping and scrambling as he went, he was caught by a burst of firing so that he fell forward, rolled over and over until he fetched up against a rock and lay still. Occasionally several men tried to run forward at once but the machine guns and the volley firing sent them tumbling, limp and shapeless, down the slope, and in the end Barracca called off the attack.

The burning truck had finally been nudged off the road, however, and now lay on its side in the catchment ditch, still sending up its thick column of smoke. With the column moving again at last, the road was beginning to clear. But Barracca was well aware that he was going to lose a lot of the heavier vehicles, which would never make it through the blocked pass.

'Tell the crews they must abandon them and rejoin with what they can carry,' he ordered.

But even as the aide turned away, he was hit by a heavy bullet from a Martini wielded by an Odessi youth and crashed down at Barracca's feet. As he was carried away, Barracca gave the message to a sergeant of Savoia Grenadiers, only to be hit in the shoulder himself a moment later.

As the doctor arrived and tried to bandage up the groaning man, he was cursing.

'Where's Guidotti?' he was asking.

The front half of Barracca's column burst free just before dark, but his troops were totally demoralized. Their losses in men had been heavy but their losses in vehicles were disastrous, though Barracca was hoping many would be salvaged by Guidotti when he finally reached them.

As the survivors scrambled on to what lorries remained and broke away to the west, the Somalis came down the mountainside towards the abandoned vehicles, brandishing their rifles and spears. A few fell to the shots of the wounded still in the lorries but the rest came on, leaping like stags over the scree, their high ululating yell enough to strike terror into the stoutest-hearted.

There was bloody scuffling among the abandoned lorries and the spears jabbed and became reddened, then Danny arrived like a fury, knocking up the weapons and pushing the excited youths to one side. One of them, driven to the point of hysteria by the killing, lifted his spear to her and, only just in time, Tully swung a rifle butt and sent him flying.

'Thank you, Paddy,' she said, then she swung round to find Harkaway, his eyes bright, his red hair flying, wielding a revolver.

'Stop them!' she screamed. 'Haven't you done enough?'

Even Harkaway finally accepted that the fighting should stop and he rampaged among the yelling black men, knocking up their weapons and pushing them aside. There seemed to be bodies all over the road, most of them Italian or Italian native levies. On the western side of the road-block they could hear the dwindling sound of engines as the front portion of Barracca's column escaped, but on the eastern side there appeared to be twenty-three abandoned undamaged lorries and a few other vehicles of all types from Lancia trucks to scout cars.

'Prisoners?' he asked.

'About forty,' Danny said, staring round her, sickened by the red splashes on the surface of the road and the crumpled corpses among the rocks. 'But no thanks to you.'

As Guidotti's rescue column roared out of Bidiyu, the first of Barracca's lorries was rocketing down the slope from the road on to the plain. Driven by a nervous askari, with an armed Somali alongside him, it swung over the lip and, tilting crazily, slithered down, to bounce to a halt below, rocking on its springs.

'Now the next,' Harkaway yelled. 'Hurry up! Get a move on!'

Caught by the excitement, the Somalis were yelling and laughing as the second lorry rocked and slithered down the slope to take up a position behind the first. One after the other, they went down, some skilfully, some with a frenzied enthusiasm as the drivers were urged on by the wildly excited Somalis. One of them, slithering sideways, as its driver struggled to keep its nose pointing the right way, swung beam-on to the slope and slowly began to turn over. The Somali jumped clear but the driver was crushed under the cab.

Behind them, Gooch was rapidly taking the mountain guns and mortars apart. Lashing them to the backs of the mules, they were swung off the road and into the hills. Sweating Somalis hurried down the slopes with the machine guns to push them with the captured weapons aboard the vehicles lining up on the scrubby plain below the road.

'Keep going,' Harkaway was yelling, waving his arms. 'Don't stop! Keep going!'

He was moving up and down the road, pushing at the Somalis as they hesitated over the scattered loot. Already strings of camels, mules, horses and asses were beginning to wind away back into the valleys in the hills. Behind them was a line of men, their eyes fierce, their tobes like loincloths round their waists under looted Italian tunics. They carried rifles and swords and bayonets and wore Italian watches and bracelets and Italian sun helmets on their woolly hair. Bringing up the rear were the women and children who had waited in the hills.

Harkaway shoved at one or two last hesitant men still trying to loot the dead Italians then he fired his revolver into the air. As they looked up, he pointed to the hills.

'Go!' he roared. 'If you're caught here you'll be shot! Go!'

They lost one more lorry as it struck a hollow in the slope, tucked its nose down and went down end-over-end. This time, both men escaped, the Somali laughing, the askari driver shuddering with shock.

Harkaway was the last to leave. The whole gorge was down, several vehicles and men under the rubble. Beyond it, there was only wreckage. On his own side there were more dead men, many of them stabbed by Somali spears, and the twisted remains of the two wrecked lorries at the bottom of the slope from the road.

'Mount,' he yelled and everybody who was left began to climb on to the captured lorries. Their own lorries started up as they saw them moving towards them, then the two columns formed together. and began to move south under a spreading cloud of dust.

6

Rushing to Barracca's rescue with what few troops he still had under his command, Guidotti had come to a full stop. Beyond the gaping hole in the road where the gully had been, he could see vultures already circling in the sky.

Standing by his car, he sent his native troops ahead on foot while his engineers struggled to fill the hole in the road. It was a hopeless situation and Guidotti knew that while he was away from Bidiyu, what few troops he had left behind might well be deserting and attacking the women.

Eventually he began to get his lighter vehicles across the gap, with the aid of ropes and a lot of muscle-power, but round the next bend they found the road covered with boulders, scattered over a wide area and obviously placed there deliberately.

His men began to roll them clear, but it was a slow business and his vehicles could edge forward only at the speed at which they were clearing the obstructions. By the time he reached the gorge, he found only a few wrecked lorries, a few dazed survivors and the native troops he had sent ahead.

It was a macabre scene of burned-out vehicles and the dusty, broken-doll shapes that had been flung aside by the tidal wave of earth and stones that had come down. Shocked, he walked through the wreckage among the damaged and abandoned lorries, past the sprawled corpses and the moaning wounded who were calling on Mary, Mother of Jesus, to help them, to the front of what had been Barracca's column. The three smashed lorries which had stopped it dead lay on their side in the catchment ditch, still sending up columns of black smoke between the towering defiles of the gorge.

Indifferent to the possibility of snipers, Guidotti stood still and stared upwards, screwing up his eyes against the light. There was no sign of the attackers and, walking back along the road, assailed by worried aides, he reached his car. There, a group of officers were questioning the survivors. One of them crossed to Guidotti and pointed.

Guidotti lifted his binoculars. Away to the south, he could just make out a dwindling cloud of dust.

Barracca's kidnapped drivers turned up several days later, coming from a totally different direction from that which had been expected, indicating that the stolen lorries had been driven in a vast circle, first south, then west, then north and finally east. Now, Guidotti knew, they were somewhere in the region of Eil Dif.

But now that he knew for certain where they were, there was no longer anything he could do about it. He hadn't the men, time was growing short and the South Africans were drawing nearer every day. One column had reached Ferfer and was heading for Scillave Wells, and the second had reached Dolo. From the speed with which they were travelling, Guidotti expected them in Jijiga around the middle of March and he knew that before then he had to be on his way.

The drivers were distressed and exhausted, haggard with thirst, their clothes covered with dust, but they realized they were lucky to be alive. The stories they brought confirmed everything Guidotti had heard: four white men and a white woman, and Somalis trained to a point to which they had never seen Somalis trained before.

With the Italians in the north already retreating on Addis Ababa, Guidotti was well aware that time was not on his side and that he had to leave Bidiyu. He knew it even more clearly the following day when he heard that Gabredarre had fallen and that the South Africans had reached Daghabur. They would be in Jijiga within a matter of days and then he would be completely cut off.

He called for Piccio and Di Sanctis. He was still awaiting orders from Jijiga and he knew the Duce didn't look kindly on men who moved without them, but he was aware that something had to be done.

'We have no alternative but to withdraw,' he said. 'I've been waiting for orders but Berbera seems entirely concerned with the arrival of the British from Aden, and Addis Ababa is virtually surrounded. We have no alternative but to save ourselves. I shall probably answer for it with my neck if things go wrong – even – ' he paused '– even if they go right, but I wouldn't wish for what happened to Barracca to happen to us. Piccio, you will warn all Italian troops in the town to be prepared to move at once.'

'What about civilians, Excellency?' Piccio asked. 'There are a lot of them. Officials who were sent down from Eritrea and Abyssinia last year. Many of them brought their wives. They thought the war was about to end.'

Guidotti's shoulders moved helplessly. 'I barely have enough vehicles to remove my troops.' The words stuck in his throat.

'Suppose the natives rise, Excellency?'

Guidotti sighed. 'The British are efficient. They're also not unkind. The lot of those who stay might well be better than that of those who go. Inform every man that he will be allowed no more than what he carries on his back. Make sure there's enough food and water and that guns are mounted and ammunition's at hand. And don't rely too much on the native levies. I'm not sure how much longer they'll remain with us. Di Sanctis, I want you to look out a route north. We might have difficulty getting to Harar, but there's a road that goes north via Borama towards French Somaliland.'

'Of course, Excellency.' Di Sanctis paused. 'But then where, sir? Where do we go from there?'

Guidotti was silent for a moment then he shrugged. 'God alone knows, Di Sanctis,' he said. 'I don't. General Barracca told me that the Duke of Aosta's made plans to concentrate his troops near Amba Alagi if Keren falls. From French Somaliland, we ought to be able to reach Assab and from there head inland. If the Duke *is* at Amba Alagi, then we can join up with him. If he's not – ' Guidotti became silent, lifted his hands and let them fall to his sides.

Guidotti wasn't the only one who was bewildered by the turn of events. The British general in the south, moving north behind his troops towards Jijiga and Harar, was puzzled by the reports that were coming out of British Somaliland. It was an empty, God-forsaken country not worth fighting for and certainly not one to plan for. But *someone* was fighting for it and someone was planning for it. And, what was more, appeared to be making a good job of it, with a remarkable amount of energy and considerable military skill.

'This so-called Sixth Column we keep hearing about, Charlie,' he said. 'Where's it come from? Are you sure the navy haven't landed?'

'Not to our knowledge, sir,' Charlton insisted.

'Contact Aden. Perhaps something went wrong somewhere and we've missed a message. Perhaps they landed troops at Assab in Eritrea. I can't see any other alternative.'

But the Royal Navy in Aden, concerned with the forthcoming attack on Berbera, and well aware that their plans were already pointless because there would be no fighting anyway, promptly reported that *they* had been about to ask the general the same question.

The general stared at his maps. This new and obviously very potent force seemed to have sprung to life in the *middle* of British Somaliland and he had received reports of a new and very decisive defeat inflicted on a large group commanded by no less than an Italian general, while the RAF was reporting wreckage near the Wirir Gorge and a distinct sign that the Italians were preparing to move out of Bidiyu.

'Can we contact them by radio?' he asked.

'Sir – ' Charlton coughed apologetically '– that's something that occurred to me. I thought I might even be able to provide you with a *fait accompli*. But Intelligence and Signals insist that they've never even heard them transmitting.'

'But, dammit – ' the general lit a cigarette and slapped the map with the palm of his hand '– their movements are quite clearly conforming to ours!'

'Perhaps they're receiving,' Charlton suggested. 'But can't transmit. If they have an experienced radio op., he could pick up *our* signals.'

'But how the devil do they get about? They were last heard of in the Eil Dif area. Now the RAF says they've seen a great mass of men south of the Jijiga–Berbera road. How the devil did they get there without going over Bur Yi range?'

'That's not possible, sir.'

'Hannibal crossed the Alps,' the general reminded him. 'So did Napoleon.'

'But the reports say they're using trucks, sir.'

'For God's sake, Charlie, other people have got trucks over mountains. Kitchener got an army to Khartoum the wrong way up the rapids of the Nile. What men have they got?'

'So far, sir, our reports mention only four white men and one white woman. Everyone else seems to be Somali, drawn, it seems, mostly from the Odessi and Harari tribes, though I understand that now they're coming from all over Somaliland. Their vehicles are largely Italian but their weapons probably came from a dump left at Shimber Addi in the Bur Yi Hills. It was placed there for a forward stop against the Italians but never used. We were informed it was destroyed by a party under a Lieutenant Watson.'

'Where's this Lieutenant Watson now?'

Charlton gestured. 'I've tried to trace him, sir, but I gather that after he and his party went out to destroy the dump, nothing further was heard from them and it was assumed they ran into the Italians.'

'Do you have the names of the party?'

'Nobody important, sir. Specialists. One radio operator. One engineer. One armourer. All on attachment to the King's African Rifles. There was also a civilian driver from the Public Works Department. None of them had any rank. They couldn't have had much knowledge of what to do.'

The general frowned and took a puff at his cigarette. 'Not that it matters,' he said. 'Since Wavell biffed the Italians out of Libya, nobody notices *us*, anyway.'

In that, however, the general was wrong, because two war correspondents, both of them with famous names, appeared the same day asking questions.

'Asa Wye,' one of them said, '*Globe*. This is Russell, of APA. We're trying to find out something about this bloody Sixth Column. The RAF say there's a great pile of scrap iron in the Wirir Gorge that was once Italian transport and that this Sixth Column did it. Who are they? Why *Sixth* Column? And who's leading it?'

Charlton held up his hands. 'I might as well be honest,' he said. 'I know as much as you.'

'You mean they're guerrillas?'

'We don't know what they are.'

'Well, they've not been idle,' Wye said. 'We've just learned that they hit an Italian motorized column for six and pinched all their transport. To say nothing of kidnapping an Italian colonel some time back.'

'Brigadier, actually,' Charlton said placidly, pleased he knew something the newspapermen didn't know. 'Name of Ruffo di Peri. Commandante di Brigata Ruggiero Ruffo di Peri, if you want his full title. We picked it up from monitored radio messages.'

'*Was* he kidnapped?' Russell asked.

'His chauffeur said he was.' Charlton paused, aware that the military hierarchy had no great fondness for guerrilla forces who hogged the limelight. Since Lawrence of Arabia had been discovered by an American newspaperman and made to appear to have won the war in the Middle East in 1918, they were none too keen on having their thunder stolen, because the fame of guerrilla leaders tended on occasion to be somewhat overblown. 'Those were small operations, of course,' he went on. 'Their big efforts seem to have started only since the Italians have been thrown into disarray by our own advance. It makes good sense, of course. If you hit a chap hard from every angle and all at the same time, he obviously doesn't manage to defend himself quite as well.'

'Okay, Colonel,' Wye said. 'Then where did they come from? Aden?'

'We don't think so. They know nothing of them there.'

'Down from the north? We know a couple of our people were sent in there to stir things up. One of 'em a chap called Wingate.'

Charlton spread his hands. 'That might be the explanation. But our reports are that Wingate's still in Abyssinia.'

Wye scratched his head with a pencil. '*Somebody* must know who they are.'

'Of course they must,' Charlton agreed. 'But they seem to have failed to inform us.'

As the conference ended, the war correspondents went outside to their car. They were a dusty raggle-taggle couple, despite their fame and prestige. They had followed the African war for months now, flying backwards and forwards between Egypt and East Africa, trying in the last few weeks to keep up with the tremendous march of events. They had heard the reports from Egypt and it seemed that splendid stories were going begging up there for the sake of a doubtful and difficult journey across Africa, and they were constantly trying to be in two places at once – at the front or back at headquarters. Either way you got the news, but if you were caught halfway you got nothing and, even if you *had* information, you had no means of sending it.

'We seem to breed these odd characters who raise private armies,' Russell said. 'The South African columns are full of elderly gentlemen who've spent all their life in the bush after big game and relish having a go at something tougher than an elephant. They've all suddenly become majors in command of recce columns.'

'It's not exactly new,' Wye pointed out. 'Half the best regiments in India were raised by types like that.'

He stared northwards. The land ahead was sand and rock for miles and the desert was a sheet of glaring whiteness. The last waterhole they had passed had been fouled by a dead camel and they had found vultures waiting near a beautiful young Somali woman who had held out a can for them to give her water for her baby. She hadn't spoken a word as they had filled it and the baby had remained silent, its head lolling, but she had given all the water to the child, careful not to spill a drop, accepting none for herself. Wye was a hard man with few sparks of conscience but it had filled his heart with misery.

His eyes narrowed as he stared at the grim and blistered horizon. 'It seems to me,' he said, 'that we ought to try to get up there into British Somaliland. If we can get to Jijiga we can surely make contact and it seems there's a hell of a story going begging.'

'It'll be bloody uncomfortable,' Russell commented.

Wye shrugged. 'What's the difference?' he said. 'It's bloody uncomfortable here.

Guidotti's plans for departure took time to mature and it was already growing difficult.

Telephone lines were being cut all over the country. Cut telephone lines were nothing new because the Somalis had always taken them to make bangles and anklets for their womenfolk, but these days it had reached epidemic proportions and it was clear the wire wasn't now being taken merely for decoration.

Its disappearance made it difficult for Guidotti to contact his outposts, and he was concerned for the few Italians and their women who had moved into Bidiyu after its capture the previous year. They were frightened and disgruntled and complaining the war was Mussolini's, not theirs.

Guidotti's honour demanded that he should not abandon them and he knew that somebody would have to stay behind with them. A little clever manoeuvring could delay enemy forces until the rest of them got away and he asked Di Sanctis and Piccio to decide which of them was to take over.

'Honour indicates I should stay myself,' he said. 'Particularly as I speak a little English. Unfortunately, honour and military good sense aren't always compatible and it's never a good idea from the point of view of morale for generals to be captured. I'm afraid, gentlemen, it will have to be one of you.'

There was only a moment's hesitation. Both Piccio and Di Sanctis spoke passable English but it was Di Sanctis who stepped forward and Guidotti suspected he was finding it difficult to put his Somali mistress behind him and was delaying the fatal moment as long as he could.

'At least we can't leave a mere major in command,' he said. 'No one will take any notice of him. You're a colonel, Di Sanctis, as of this moment. You'd better try to find some insignia to put on your uniform. Perhaps you can search Di Peri's kit. It was brought here after he disappeared.'

The following day, dressed in Di Peri's tunic and cap, Di Sanctis listened to his orders. They had just heard that the British navy had landed in Berbera and that it was expected to head for Hargeisa within a very short time.

'When they arrive – ' Guidotti began.

'When *who* arrive, sir?'

'The British, of course.'

'It may not be the British, sir,' Di Sanctis pointed out gently. 'The South Africans are already north of Sassabaneh. It may be *them*. It may also – ' he paused ' – it may also be this Sixth Column which has done us so much damage.'

The same thought had occurred to Guidotti but he let the matter pass and continued to give his instructions.

'You will be responsible for order,' he explained. 'You will go out to meet them. I will leave you two armoured cars. Your job will be to delay. To haggle about terms. To take as long as you can to arrange a formal surrender. Anything that will give us time to get clear. After that, insist on retaining your position as military governor here to keep order. Piccio reports that we're losing native troops every day, but they're still in the town and in the area around, and they'll undoubtedly create trouble. After that – '

Di Sanctis frowned. 'I venture to suggest, sir, that there will be no "after that". *That* will be the end.'

Guidotti frowned and patted the young officer's shoulder.

He tried to say a few words of comfort but was unable to find anything.

He ate a last meal alone and drank a little wine. Because it was unlikely that comfort would be in his programme for some time, he then decided to have a brandy and called in Di Sanctis and Piccio to share it with him. The drink was accepted in silence and swallowed in silence and, because he was at a loss what to say to disperse the gloom, Guidotti decided it was time to break up the party. He rose and extended his hand to Di Sanctis.

They were still clasping hands when the door opened. In the entrance was a young officer of Signals.

'Sir, I regret the interruption, but I felt you ought to know. The British have reached the outskirts of Jijiga.'

'Already?' Guidotti snatched at the signal and studied it. '*Mamma mia*,' he said in a whisper. '*Che disastro!* They've picked up Barracca and most of his men.' He stood still a moment, drawing in a deep breath, then he crossed to the map spread on the table by the brandy bottle.

For a long time he was silent, staring at the map, before he spoke. 'We have no alternative now,' he said. 'With that road denied us, we must go to Djibuti and up to Assab, then inland in the hope of finding the Duke of Aosta.' His hand moved over the map, then it stopped, his finger pointing. 'We must head for Fort San Rafaelo on the border at Djuba. Pavicelli's there with infantry, a squadron of native cavalry and a Gruppa Banda. They can give us support. Piccio – ' the despondency had left him now and his mind was moving briskly ' – inform everybody that the column will be moving off within the hour and that we shall swing north towards Boramo.'

It was Yussuf who brought the news that Bidiyu had been abandoned.

His wrinkled face twisted into a smile as he brought his fingers to his breast in the traditional salute. '*Salaam aleikum!* God be with you, effendi!'

'And with you, Yussuf,' Harkaway said. 'What have you heard?'

'*Wahali* – by God, effendi! Is much trouble. The Italian officers are growing afraid of mutiny.'

'You know what that means, don't you?' Gooch said. 'It means the place's wide open.'

Tully grinned. 'And that means booze and food and beds and women. The Eyeties set up brothels everywhere they go, don't they? All we do is walk in and help ourselves.'

'If you think that,' Harkaway said, 'you don't know much about the Italians. Can you imagine an Italian officer handing over his command to *you*? Look at you.'

Tully looked down at himself. His shorts had ragged fringes, his socks had holes and his boots were falling apart.

'All right, then,' Gooch said. 'Come up with a better one.'

'Let's give 'em full honours. Drums. Bands. The lot. They'll surrender to a lieutenant-colonel and his party of white officers.'

'Us?'

'Of course.'

'Where do we get the pips?'

'We dig up Watson.'

'Dig up Watson?' Gooch stared at Harkaway, aghast. 'You going to wear his clothes?'

'Just his pips. Danny can sew. She can make the crowns.'

Gooch looked at Tully. 'Who gets to wear 'em?' he asked.

Harkaway smiled. 'I do,' he said.

They paused just long enough to make themselves presentable. Dressed in khaki trousers and shirt, shoulders emblazoned with metal stars cut from tins and blackened in the cooking fire, Danny watched Harkaway anxiously. With his 'promotion', he seemed to have acquired a new presence, arrogant, commanding and haughty. With Watson's pips and the crowns she had made, she had to admit, he *looked* like a colonel. Even his entourage looked important. Two of Watson's pips were sewn on Gooch's shirt and, like Danny, Tully wore the fire-darkened tin stars of a captain.

'I'll have to salute the little bastard,' Gooch complained.

Harkaway smiled. 'You'll *all* have to salute me,' he said.

Grobelaar had become a second-lieutenant and the Somali women had washed and pressed their clothes and there had been a great deal of boot polishing. Even Abdillahi had been promoted to sergeant-major by means of a coat of arms cut from a Tate and Lyle Golden Syrup tin and attached to an old watch strap to wear on his wrist. It didn't appeal as much as the stripes he'd worn but Harkaway explained that he was more important now and gave him two of the Maria Theresa dollars to prove it.

'What will you do with them?' he asked.

'Buy camels, effendi.' The Somali smiled. 'I will be a rich man.'

'You could also be killed.'

'Paradise, effendi, has gardens where the faithful recline on divans attended by lovely women. There are many fountains.'

'Sounds all right.'

'It is a desert dweller's heaven, effendi.'

At the first opportunity Danny drew Harkaway to one side. What had happened above the gorge before Barracca's defeat had made her hope for a future but suddenly she felt there could never be one with Harkaway. He was too absorbed in what he was doing and she had a feeling that there was little room for her in his plans.

'After Bidiyu, George?' she asked. 'Then what?'

He touched her hand, then his fingers moved up her arm to squeeze the soft flesh above her elbow.

'For a while, nothing,' he said. 'Rest and recuperate. Get the Boys into shape.'

'I wasn't thinking of the Boys,' she said. 'I was thinking of us. What do *we* get out of it?'

He looked at her. 'Life,' he said. 'There's been too much death lately.'

'There'll be women in Bidiyu.'

He shrugged. 'Most women have minds like frightened mice and think only in terms of homes and children. You've proved yourself bigger than that.'

She wasn't sure she had. Her thoughts seemed to be exactly the same as other women's and only circumstances had moved them from their natural path. But she hadn't the courage to say so, for fear of losing him.

'So what happens?' she asked.

He grinned. 'Champagne, for a start. I'll be surprised if we don't find some. Then the biggest bed we can find. Canopied, the posts silver maidens wearing no more clothing than would make a decent table-napkin.'

She was aware that he was appealing to her physical instincts.

'You'd never find me in the dark,' she said. 'Besides, I'd be scared stiff.'

'Not you,' he said. 'You're more of a woman than you realize. You've heard of the colonel's lady and Rosie O'Grady being sisters under the skin. For years you've been repressed by those milksops at that mission of yours with their bloody prayer meetings. This is Africa, love-making here's conducted with barbaric splendour. I'll have you serenaded with cymbals and drums to bed in a room filled with oriental scents.'

'You make me feel like the sort of woman Paddy Tully's looking for.'

'Tully,' he said, 'is dirt.' He bent and kissed her, his hand roving over the curve of her behind. 'I'll show you what love-making really is.'

So far, she thought, her nerves tingling, her stomach full of butterflies, she had not known love at all. Her fiancé – centuries ago now – had been too stiff and pompous to make more than cautious passes at her, and at the mission there had been only shy glances that had merely bored her. Only the hot-eyed Italian doctor who had noticed her in Abyssinia had roused any feeling in her. She had often regretted rejecting him.

She slapped Harkaway's hand away. 'My backside doesn't provide free roosting for the hands of anybody who chooses to make it so,' she said.

He laughed. 'You love it. You've been starved all your

life of it. Just give me a few hours to sort out the Italians and I'll be with you.'

As she watched him stalk away, his head in the air, his back ramrod-straight, she wondered which he considered more important.

7

Di Sanctis watched the last of the lorries roar through the marketplace of Bidiyu for the west.

The few Italians who remained with him were finishing the last of the coffee in endless small cups to hide their misery. Cigarettes had disappeared and they were using raw leaf from Ethiopia which was so strong some people had to lie down before lighting it.

Di Sanctis frowned. The troops he'd been left were unreliable. Desertion was appalling, and newly recruited askaris wearing thinly disguised Italian tunics were appearing in the fields, while the native bandas, a motley collection at the best of times, had not been seen for days.

Turning on his heel, he re-entered the headquarters building. On Guidotti's desk was a cable which had arrived that morning from Rome. Ironically, just as Bidiyu was about to be given up, the Duce had wired his congratulations on the resistance they were putting up.

Di Sanctis scowled at it and poured himself a stiff brandy. As he replaced the glass on the table, the door opened. In the entrance was a girl. She had a light olive skin with a velvety bloom and an exquisitely moulded face with black liquid eyes. She wore a maroon silk robe with blue and white flowers painted on it, a thin shawl of gauzy silk with gold embroidery, and a gold necklace and earrings.

'They've all gone,' he said.

'*E così la vita.*'

Di Sanctis put the gramophone on, playing the nostalgic '*Un Giorno Ti Diro*'. He was thinking of his native Naples.

The girl touched his hand and he turned and smiled at her. '*Andiamo,*' he said.

Upstairs, they headed for his room but then he decided to use Guidotti's. Previously he had always had to smuggle her in but he was the governor now and should use the governor's apartments. At the last moment, however, he found he hadn't the nerve and headed instead for Piccio's room. Over the bed there was a picture of a smiling Italian soldier, naked except for his steel helmet. He was looking at a woman who was also naked, and the look in their eyes spoke worlds. *Il Taverno degli Dimenticati*, it was called. The Tavern of the Forgotten.

Di Sanctis turned to find the girl quietly unfastening her dress. He stared at her for a moment, suddenly frightened and full of bitterness, and, reaching out to the neck of the dress, he wrenched it from her.

She stood in front of him, naked, her expression half-wild, half-timid, a tribal woman ready to obey her man. Di Sanctis stared at her for a moment, then, as the tears began to stream down his cheeks, she reached out to him, crooning – '*Tesoro, Tesoro,*' words she'd heard him use to her – and pulling him to her, held him closely, her free hand lifting to the buttons of his shirt.

When Di Sanctis woke, the girl was sitting on the hard Arab pillow at the foot of the bed. As he lifted his head she smiled and moved towards him, but he pushed her aside. Today, he knew, he had things to do.

Before midday the urgency of action was impressed on him. Radio messages from Guidotti showed that he'd managed to escape. He and his column had passed through the cleared Wirir Gorge without incident and had turned north to the Abyssinian border. Up there at Djuba, Fort San Rafaelo, mud-walled and white-washed, still flew the red, white and green tricolour of Italy.

So much for the Duce's Africa Orientale! Di Sanctis's eyes prickled as he wondered what he had ever seen in the posturing ass in Rome who liked to parade in a swimming costume on Italian beaches, showing his deep chest and pretending he was as young and virile as he ever was, when everybody knew he was on the verge of sixty. Why hadn't he stopped when he'd had the whole of Italy in his palm?

Dressing carefully, he called on the Mayor to instruct him to have his officials ready on the steps of Guidotti's headquarters when they saw the British approaching.

'When will they arrive?' The Mayor was a small fat man and he was nervous.

'God willing, tomorrow. With luck the day after. With incredible good fortune, two days from now.' Di Sanctis's expression changed. 'However, if they do what I expect they will do, it will be this afternoon. You will have the police in position and there will be order. The band of the 49th Native Infantry will play as they enter. Do you know anything British they could be taught quickly?'

' "God Save the King"! I heard it in the last war.'

'Go and see the bandmaster.'

As the Mayor hurried off, Di Sanctis interviewed the Chief of Police and then his own deputy, Captain – until the previous afternoon when Di Sanctis had promoted him to give himself some sort of strength, Sottotenente – Rudio.

'There will be a guard of honour, Rudio,' he said. 'Pick them from your most reliable men. Let us surrender like soldiers.'

During the afternoon news arrived that a column of vehicles was heading towards the town from the direction of Jijiga. Di Sanctis sighed and called Rudio. 'Have the armoured car brought round,' he said. 'We shall need a white bed-sheet – attached to a long pole, and a man to hold it.'

Putting on his jacket and cap, he went upstairs to where the girl was still waiting. She was still sitting on the hard pillow at the foot of the bed, almost as if she hadn't moved, as if she were made of black ivory.

'I am going,' Di Sanctis said. 'After that, I don't know what will happen.'

She nodded slowly, but made no attempt to say goodbye. Di Sanctis touched her shoulder then turned and left the room. She was still there as he closed the door. She'd been faithful to him for three years now, gentle, kind, affectionate, never disputing his wishes. He wondered what would happen to her.

Accompanied by two staff cars, the armoured car headed slowly out of the city.

They saw the first of the lorries eight miles outside, coming down the slopes in a long line past the kilometre markers the Italians had so laboriously set up. Even at that distance, Di Sanctis could see the lorries were all captured Italian Lancias and he could hardly believe they had so many.

Because Di Sanctis, in the manner of Continentals, was driving on the right side of the road and the oncoming vehicles, in the manner of the barbarian British, were driving on the left, they were approaching each other face-to-face. For a moment Di Sanctis wondered if he should swing to the left and he saw the driver eyeing him for instructions. But changing sides seemed to be humiliating himself unnecessarily.

'Carry on,' he said, but as he spoke there was a burst of firing from the foremost lorry. The driver slammed on the brakes at once and dived for the ditch with the corporal holding the flag. For a second, Di Sanctis tried to maintain a little dignity in the face of his enemies, but the bullets were whack-whacking overhead and he realized he was being stupid and dived after the other two.

The lorries had stopped. Seeing black faces, Di Sanctis realized they were the notorious Sixth Column which had destroyed Barracca and humiliated them again and again on their own ground with their own weapons. For a moment, angrily, he wished he had guns, but he had come unarmed and he saw no alternative to Guidotti's arrangements. He snatched at the white flag and started to wave it violently.

'Get up, Corporal,' he said, and together the two of them scrambled from the ditch.

Trying to retain his dignity, Di Sanctis strode forward, his back straight, his head up, while the Italian corporal who carried the flag hurried along behind him, changing feet as he tried to pick up the step.

A man descended from the first lorry. His shorts and shirt
were faded but clean and pressed, his boots were polished
and his stockings were without a wrinkle. On his shoulders
were the cloth stars and crowns of a lieutenant-colonel, and
on his head he wore a stained British officer's dress cap. On
his belt he wore a webbing holster containing a revolver,
and he held an Italian Biretta sub-machine gun. Behind him
there were two other white men and then Di Sanctis saw
the woman. She wore a uniform of sorts with the shoulder
insignia of an officer and she reminded him achingly of the
girl he'd just left in Bidiyu. She was tall and slender in the
same way, her hair cropped short like a native girl's, and
she carried no arms.

The man with the colonel's badges made a sign and Di
Sanctis saw another man also wearing the stars of an officer
climbing from the driver's seat of the front lorry. The tall
man stepped forward accompanied by an armed Somali with
bushy hair and the face of a god. 'I would like to arrange
terms for the surrender of Bidiyu,' Di Sanctis said. His voice
came out as a squeak and he cleared his throat and started
again.

The tall man frowned. 'We haven't time to arrange terms,'
he said. 'We know there's no one there except police and
a few native troops on the verge of mutiny.'

Di Sanctis began to fence, sensing he was already losing
the battle. 'Perhaps we could arrange for you to arrive in
the middle of tomorrow morning,' he said.

Harkaway laughed.

'There will have to be a reception committee,' Di Sanctis
urged. 'There will have to be a guard of honour.'

The tall man jeered. 'Tomorrow's no good. You will
surrender the city to us at once. If not I shall not be responsible for my men. They have a lot of scores to pay off.'

The woman was looking faintly shamefaced at the bully-
ing, but the man's expression didn't alter. To Di Sanctis he
looked like a young eagle.

'My orders – ' he tried again but the tall man gestured
imperiously.

'To hell with your orders!' he snapped. 'You're in no

position to quote orders at me! You surrender now or I send my men in. I shall also probably shoot you for disagreeing with me.'

Di Sanctis swallowed and tried again, but the English officer drew his revolver and pointed it at his head.

'You have five minutes to make up your mind,' he said.

Di Sanctis was frantic. His instructions covered nothing as barbaric as this. 'Give me one hour,' he begged. 'One hour! That's all! The Mayor waits. There is a band and a guard of honour. If we go back all together, something may go wrong.'

Harkaway smiled. A reception committee and a band was a good idea and it had been his intention all along to agree.

'One hour,' he said. 'Now get back inside that tin can of yours and get cracking. We shall arrive on the dot. And let's have no bloody nonsense, because if there's shooting, I shall turn my Boys on you.' He gestured at the grinning Somali clutching his Italian rifle. 'They don't like you a lot and they won't hesitate to slit a few throats.'

Di Sanctis tried to keep his face stiff before the goading. 'I have given my word,' he said.

'What's that worth?'

'I am an Italian officer,' Di Sanctis snapped. 'And you had better not set your men loose or they might murder the wrong people. There is a prisoner-of-war camp in the town and I would not like accidents to happen.'

As he turned away, Harkaway called him back. Red-faced, Di Sanctis stood to attention in front of him.

'One more thing,' Harkaway said. 'In future, all vehicles will drive on the left of the road. In the British fashion.'

'It might take time for them to get used to it,' Di Sanctis suggested.

'It had better not. You're under British law now. And British laws direct drivers to the left of the road. You will comply. *As of now!*'

The Mayor was waiting on the steps of headquarters when the Sixth Column arrived, together with his officials and the remaining officers. They were glad to see the column arrive because it was felt a massacre was imminent. The askaris had been disarmed but some of them had seized an armoury and, as weapons had been handed out, had started intermittently machine-gunning the town for fun.

In the centre, some of the bolder spirits were pillaging the shops, smashing in the shutters and taking what they wanted. The police were trying ineffectually to keep them at bay with Tommy guns, but already several doors had been blown in with grenades and there had been one or two murders.

They were still at it as the column arrived, men, women and children hurrying to the native quarters, their loot balanced on their heads; and as Grobelaar led the column in a large circle round the centre of the marketplace where the trembling officials waited, trying not to see the looting Africans to their left, the black figures stopped long enough to join the shrill cries of pleasure from the other Somalis.

'*Salaams! Salaams!* Three cheer Brititch Empar! Rooly Britannia! Three cheer Kinky George, Lord of the Seas!'

As the vehicles stopped, Di Sanctis signed to the bandmaster. The native bandsmen were hardly expert at European music, and 'God Save the King' sounded weird, melancholy and Arab. Harkaway stepped from the lorry, cocked his head to one side and, recognizing it, came to the salute.

As the tune finished, without orders the band struck up the old fascist hymn, 'Giovanezza'. Fortunately, Harkaway didn't know it, so he waited patiently until it finished, but as they showed signs of starting another tune, he waved his hand irritably and the sound died away. Di Sanctis stepped forward and saluted smartly with his raised arm.

Harkaway stared back at him. 'You can cut that out,' he said. 'We want no fascist salutes here.'

Di Sanctis hesitated, bewildered, and Harkaway came to attention and brought his arm up in a shuddering military salute.

'That way,' he said. 'That's what we want. Forget the other one. That's finished with.'

'Of course, of course! I apologize!'

As Di Sanctis stepped back, the Mayor approached holding a bunch of wilting flowers. He drew his finger across his throat. 'If you had not come,' he said in English, 'it would have been with us as it was with our army. Pfftt!'

Italian morale had collapsed completely. White flags were everywhere and no one was making any attempt to stop the pillaging. Shouts could still be heard from the shopping area, and the waiting crowd of robed figures began to slip away with their spoil.

Harkaway studied them for a moment. 'Who're they?' he demanded.

'Looters,' Di Sanctis said.

Harkaway frowned, raised his sub-machine gun and fired a burst over the heads of the stream of figures. There was a yell and the loot was dropped as they bolted down the narrow alleys.

Harkaway gestured at the flag that floated at the top of the flagpole. 'Have it down,' he said to Gooch. 'Shove our own up.'

Danny produced the flag Tully had had made and, as the Italian flag was hauled down, up the pole went the crooked Union Jack, crescent, scimitar and all.

Harkaway studied the fluttering red, white and blue for a moment then, stuffing the Italian tricolour under his arm, he looked round calmly.

'Now,' he said, 'we'll get on with organizing this place.'

8

As the old Gladiator circled above them, the column of
vehicles waited, as dust-covered as their crews. They were
South Africans for the most part, clad in shirts with the
distinctive red flash at the shoulder and the brief shorts they
loved so much. In one of the vehicles a man was singing the
song someone had made up to show their contempt for their
Italian enemies, an Italian wail of sorrow for the fortunes
of their North African armies.

> Where do we go from here,
> Now that we've lost Bardia?

Standing by his car, his hand over his eyes, the general
squinted as the Gladiator swung against the sun, then he
turned to Colonel Charlton just behind him, his shirt black
with sweat.

'Seems to be trying to draw our attention to something,
sir,' Charlton said. 'He's doing a lot of waving.'

'Why doesn't he use his radio?'

'Perhaps it doesn't work, sir. Some of these Gladiators
are getting on a bit in years. Like me.'

The general smiled. 'They've also got your figure, Charlie,' he said. 'Broad across the middle. I think he's trying to
drop a message.'

As the Gladiator roared along the column of vehicles, a
small object was seen to fall from it. It hit the ground with
a puff of dust and an NCO of the King's African Rifles ran
to pick it up. He took it to his officer who directed it towards
the general. Charlton accepted it. It was a white handker-

chief in which several copper coins were knotted to give it weight. Wrapped round them was a signal flimsy.

'New form of instant communication,' Charlton said dryly.

'Stop being cynical, Charlie,' the general said. 'What's it say?'

Charlton peered at the message. 'Not much, sir. Just "White flags flying in Bidiyu." '

'What!' The general stared at Charlton. 'Then we'd better get up there and take the place over.' He turned to his Chief of Staff. 'Who can we detach?'

Charlton moved forward. 'Might I suggest, sir, since we have our hands pretty full already, that we direct our friends, the Sixth Column, there.'

'Are we in touch?'

'At last, sir. Somebody among them seems to have fixed up a transmitter and we're receiving messages.'

'Thank God for that! Now we might find out who the hell they are. Ask 'em if they can get Bidiyu.'

Italian troops were still wandering aimlessly about the town, their rifles still on their shoulders, and uniformed and be-ribboned men were everywhere.

Di Sanctis's prisoner-of-war camp had turned out to be merely the exercise yard of the prison and the prisoners were few in number. But they were nearly all soldiers who, like Harkaway, Gooch and Tully, had been cut off and left behind the previous year, and were willing enough to rejoin under Harkaway. He was careful not to let them know his true rank because there were several corporals and a ser-geant among them, and when they appeared he returned their salutes punctiliously. Then, finding them quarters in the Italian barracks, he allowed them a day to enjoy their freedom before ordering them to parade.

They were a mixed bunch, and he stalked up and down in front of them, a walking stick under his arm, Lieutenant Watson's pips and the crowns Danny had made on his shoulders. The stick was a trick he'd learned as a boy, the accent he used was one he'd employed all his life, and its tone was that of his forefathers.

'I'm sorry,' he said briskly, 'that I can't yet send you down to Kenya or Rhodesia to enjoy the leave you properly deserve. But the war's still going on here and I need you. The Italians are almost finished, and when they are the whole of East Africa will be open to us so that we can send troops and munitions direct to the men in Egypt where, it might interest you to know, we are no longer facing just the Italians. German troops have appeared.'

It was an item Tully had picked up on the radio and he made the most of it.

'I don't have to tell you that they'll be different from Mussolini's ice-cream vendors' – there was a polite laugh – 'and to help the chaps up there we've got to clean up the mess the Italians have made here so that the war can go on in safety and I can send you on leave.'

He hadn't the slightest right to send anybody on leave, he knew, but he felt that this too was something he could take care of later.

'Any NCOs?' he asked, and the sergeant and the corporals stepped forward.

'Good, good.' He was laying on the accent a little now, hoping against hope that none of them had ever met him. 'I suppose you have a list of names, Sergeant.'

The sergeant handed over a sheet of paper.

'And your own?'

'Catchpole, sir. There are also three in hospital, sir, and a few cases of the squits. The Italians didn't treat us badly.'

'Any artillerymen?'

'One or two, sir.'

Harkaway almost smiled. Forty-three men, several of them artillerymen. It was more than his cheek deserved.

'What are the numbers?'

'Seven Royal Artillerymen, sir, including me. Six Black Watch, and thirty NCOs and men of the King's African Rifles. All trained soldiers. There are also five civilians formerly employed in government departments or in business.'

'Could you work Italian guns, Sergeant? We've got a few.'

The sergeant grinned. 'Just let me get at 'em, sir!'

Harkaway smiled back. 'Splendid. I'll introduce you to them. I want you to get your men to work in teams. We have two guns with us and I think we shall find a few more here.'

They not only found nine Breda machine guns and one old 75-mm field gun of doubtful ancestry, but also an M 11/39 tank which was immobilized because of engine trouble which the Italians had not had time to cure, and three home-made armoured cars, all mounting 20-mm guns. In addition, there were three scout cars and numerous other vehicles and when they came to disarm the Italians they acquired Biretta pistols and dozens of Breda rifles, even a few Biretta semi-automatics and sub-machine guns.

Harkaway handed them out to anyone he thought capable of handling them and spread his new recruits among the Somalis with instructions to weld them into teams. On Catchpole's advice, he even created a few new NCOs, and informed them that he expected them to drill his Boys. Four of the civilians who'd accompanied the soldiers to prison also volunteered to join as drivers and, since two of them were ex-soldiers from the other war, one of them an ex-quartermaster-sergeant, he swept them up joyfully, giving the ex-quartermaster three stripes and informing him that it was his job to supply and feed his column.

'Christ,' Tully said, faintly awed. 'You've got a bloody nerve! Talking to a sergeant like that. He thought you were a real bloody colonel.'

Harkaway smiled his cool smile. 'I shall be before long,' he said.

As the British prisoners had been released, their gaolers had taken their places and that had seemed to be the end of the prisoner problem. Unfortunately, it turned out there were more in the area than had been apparent and, cut off both from escape and food, these now had no alternative but to give themselves up.

'Look,' Grobelaar complained, bursting into Guidotti's former office, 'I've got two hundred Eyeties outside, crowding round my lorry trying to surrender. I don't know what to do with them.'

'Tell 'em to wait,' Harkaway said calmly. 'Get 'em to come back tomorrow.'

The walls of the city were plastered with maps of security zones and areas forbidden to the Somalis, and Harkaway sent men round with black paint daubing big crosses over them. Inevitably a few of the brighter spirits among the Somalis added their own slogans. 'Fuk Musiloni' appeared almost immediately and the locals seemed to like the sound of it because it soon began to appear everywhere with assorted spellings, and was even chanted by the Somalis as they passed in the street – 'Fuck Mussolini! Three Cheer for Kinky George and Six Column. Brititch army more nice than Italian army. We join Brititch army.' A lot of them did, and before long the marketplace was full of marching squads of men holding Italian rifles and drilled by NCOs of the King's African Rifles.

The strange habits of the Italian army also began to appear as a red lorry was stopped, containing women from a brothel the Italians had set up. They also discovered General Barracca's private caravan parked behind Guidotti's headquarters, the whole ten tons of it, camouflaged and complete with bath and lavatory, together with large stocks of tinned fruit, tomatoes, brandy, wine, pasta, pâté de foie gras, sandbags, batteries, shells and mortar bombs, while in the courtyard of the Bank of Italy it was discovered that two hundred thousand paper lire had been burned.

'Christ,' Gooch mourned, 'what couldn't I have done with that lot!'

Then it was discovered that three trucks which had been standing in the yard since they arrived were carrying twenty thousand Maria Theresa dollars nobody had known anything about, so Harkaway used them to hold a pay parade and solemnly handed one each to his delighted native soldiers.

By this time, the Italians were no longer trying to be

military. There was no longer any drama, no strutting with medals, ribbons and boots. Morale had gone completely with defeat and they were utterly devoid of spirit, still streaming in from the outposts round the town, some brought in by Somalis armed with ancient weapons, some entirely on their own. Harkaway disarmed them all, his Somalis behaving impeccably. They called him *Odei-gi-Rer-ki* – the Old Man of the Tribe – and couldn't do enough for him. Under their supervision, an extra barbed wire cage was hurriedly constructed by the Italians themselves, who then solemnly marched inside and took themselves prisoner.

Harkaway stared at them with contempt. 'If I could only have had a week to train 'em,' he said. 'I could have held this bloody place for a year with sixty baboons!'

The Somalis were no longer using the fascist salute that had been ordered and instead gave the graceful and courteous traditional greeting that was half a bow and half a wave. Harkaway's Boys had long since learned to stick their thumbs up when they were pleased, in the manner of a good old-fashioned British swaddy, and Tully had taught his squads to shout 'Balls to Mussolini!' as they passed each other on the market square, something they did with great glee, wide grins splitting their black faces.

'If you're not careful,' Harkaway said coldly, 'you'll have 'em singing "It's a Long Way to Tipperary".'

It was a challenge, Tully had to admit, and within a few days they were. It was barely recognizable but it *was* 'Tipperary' – just!

Every day now outside headquarters, there were zither-like instruments to greet the Europeans as they arrived, and single-string violins and bamboo flutes moaning out discordant music. The Italian insignia which had graced the town had all gone, all the Roman eagles, all the fasces, all the muscular slogans, all except the broken column Guidotti had set up opposite the flagpole, because in a way that was a trophy of war and an indication of the Italian defeat.

'Pity we can't wear the bloody thing on our drum cloths,' Harkaway said.

It was while he was studying it that Gooch arrived with a message from Tully.

'He's managed to contact Jijiga,' he said. 'He's in touch with the South Africans. They're asking when you can get Bidiyu. He wants to know what to reply.'

Harkaway smiled. 'Tell 'em,' he said, 'that we've already got it.'

9

'For God's sake,' the general growled, 'who is this bloody Sixth Column?'

His staff looked at each other, none of them able to offer anything that was in the slightest bit helpful, and the general threw up his hands in frustration. 'And who's this damn Colonel Harkaway? I've never heard of him. Any of you?'

Nobody had.

'And who are the Free British? Good God! Free British! It sounds a bit spurious to me.'

'There's nothing spurious, sir,' Charlton pointed out, 'about the way he got his men over the mountains to hit Barracca's column.'

The general had to admit the fact. 'Could he be one of these white hunter types?' he asked. 'Some chap who's been put in charge from Aden? There are a few with the South Africans. There's even that renegade Austrian, with the name that sounds like Cami-knickers.' The general smiled. 'When he found a waterhole, the Springboks promptly christened it the Camisole.'

There were still no answers and he went on, bewildered. 'The bloody man only seems to obey orders when it suits him,' he said. 'Are you sure he couldn't have come down from Abyssinia, Charlie? One of Wingate's men. *He*'s an odd character, if ever there was one. Is this chap one of his lieutenants? Harkaway sounds the phoney sort of name they like to give themselves.' The general paused, then made up his mind. 'Charlie, get over to Bidiyu and make contact. For God's sake, let's find out once and for all who they are and what they're up to. And if this chap Harkaway's *not* an officer, for God's sake let's make him one before anyone finds out. It looks so damn bad to have civilians doing the army's job as well as we can do it ourselves.'

As Colonel Charlton prepared his car for the journey he heard someone cough behind him.

The two war correspondents, Wye and Russell, had arrived in Jijiga that morning, their faces plastered with the muddy masks of sweat and dust.

'We've heard that Bidiyu's fallen,' Wye said. 'To this Sixth Column lot.'

'That's right,' Charlton agreed. 'I'm just going along there to make contact.'

'Mind if we come along, too?'

'No trouble at all. Got your own car?'

'We had,' Wye said. 'But the battery's dead and the self-starter's out of action, and we kept having to ask the lorries coming up behind to give us a push start. But then the rear spring gave on these bloody awful roads and the body started slipping sideways.' He grinned. 'We tried to ram it upright with a truck but it didn't work. We'd be glad of a lift.'

Harkaway woke slowly. A warm breeze was coming through the open windows, stirring the netting curtains. Outside he could see palms and a few gum trees and could smell the woodsmoke, the old smell of Africa. No matter where you went – even in the city – you had it with you always.

He turned his head to find Danny staring at him. She didn't return his smile.

'What's up?' he asked cheerfully. 'Got the willies? We're winning, you know. We've licked the Eyeties. The Boys are pleased. I'm here in old Twinkletoes's very own bed. And you're alongside me. What more can you ask?'

She didn't answer at once because she had a feeling he was slipping away from her even before she'd managed to grasp him.

It was hard for her to understand. All her life despite occasional setbacks, she'd been supported by her belief in

224

her Bible and the religious teaching she'd undergone so that she could fight back against despair, but suddenly she felt that this time it wouldn't provide the answer.

'What are you going to do next?' she asked. 'Haven't we finished now?'

'The war's not over,' he said briskly. 'Even if it's stopped in Bidiyu. I'm an Old Testament type myself and I believe in an eye for an eye and a tooth for a tooth. The Italians have sown the wind; they're entitled to reap the whirlwind.'

'Aren't we going to Mombasa? Or South Africa?'

Harkaway gave her his foxy grin. It seemed colder than ever. 'I haven't got Twinkletoes yet,' he said.

'Do you *have* to have him?'

'The bastard said I'd go begging for mercy. I'll just show him it doesn't pay to say things like that about George Harkaway.'

'Don't push your luck too hard, George.'

'You think it's luck?'

'No.' But she hesitated as she replied because, in fact, she did. They *had* been lucky. Things had gone right all along the line.

He was obviously unimpressed by her warning. 'He's nothing but a piddling little Italian ice-cream salesman,' he said. 'My family have been soldiers since Pontius was a pilot.'

'I guessed as much.'

He seemed pleased. 'Does it show?'

There was a long silence, then he went on slowly. 'My family,' he admitted, 'have been army for generations. My father was a general. And he wasn't the first. My grandfather was one too. There were one or two others, too, in the last century. Famous ones.'

'I've never heard the name.'

He laughed. 'You don't think I'd be stupid enough to enlist under my own name, do you? I'd have been spotted at once. I made it up. You ever heard of General MacDonald Tremayne?'

'No.'

'You wouldn't, of course. He wasn't one of the Twelve Apostles.'

It was insulting but she said nothing, beginning to feel a nagging worry for him inside her.

'There've been Tremaynes in the army since the Civil War. It's bred in the bone. What I know I didn't learn at Sandhurst. I imbibed it with my mother's milk. I heard it talked about over the dining table from the day I first started joining the family at meals. It's not a profession with me. It's an instinct.'

'What happened, George?' she asked gently. 'You *were* an officer, weren't you?'

Harkaway hesitated a moment then he nodded. 'Once. They sacked me. I borrowed another chap's car. I took it for a weekend when he was away on a course. He wouldn't have known but I fell in with some friends and got a bit drunk and smashed it up. And unfortunately, he didn't like me, so that "borrowing" became "stealing". The police took a dim view of it, too, because he hadn't intended it to be on the road and it wasn't insured. I didn't know, but it made no difference. I ended up in court. The army showed me the door.'

'For that?'

'Well,' he admitted, 'there was a bit more to it than that. There was a dud cheque, too. It was damn' silly, really, because I could have had the money from my father if I'd asked. But I was young and a bit stupid. People are at that age. I once rode a motorbike down the corridor of the officers' mess. Showing off.' He paused, his mind far away. 'Actually the bookie I gave the cheque to was pretty decent about it. He knew me and didn't want to make an issue of it but when they started making enquiries after the car incident it all came out. I wasn't cashiered. Family name and all that. But I had to leave, all the same. I enlisted again under an assumed name and asked to be posted out here.' He frowned. 'If I'd waited until the war broke out, I could have got a commission as easy as falling off a log in one of the other services. It was a bit of a mess.'

'I'm sorry, George.'

His frown deepened. 'It probably wouldn't have happened if the bastard who owned the car hadn't been a narrow-minded, mealy-mouthed, arsehole-creeper who went to church on Sundays. You can see why I don't like 'em much.'

She touched his arm, gently, affectionately. Despite her doubts, she had ended up in his bed. She had won him and she longed to keep him. 'Don't go, George,' she begged.

'I have to. It isn't over until I've got Twinkletoes.'

Her eyes were tragic. 'Do you even know where he is?'

'He went north into Ethiopia.'

She stared at him for a long time, holding the sheet to her throat to hide her nakedness. 'That's farther away than ever from Mombasa or South Africa. Will Gooch and Paddy Tully go with you?'

'They're like me. They can't stop.'

'You've persuaded them?'

Harkaway shrugged and smiled. 'They don't take a lot of persuading,' he said. 'They're neither of them very bright lights.'

'You're using them. You've used us all.'

'Not you, my white-breasted Bronwen.'

'What am I doing here then?'

She fell silent, realizing how far she'd moved from the moral atmosphere of the life she'd been brought up to live. She was behaving like a loose woman and enjoying it. Suddenly her life had blossomed and she'd come to realize that she needed love. Even her face had changed; the taut, bleak look that had once been there had gone.

She studied Harkaway as he went to the window, naked like herself, strong, muscular and confident. It was Harkaway who had shown her the way, but she had a suspicion that for the future their paths were going to diverge and that she'd have to look elsewhere for affection. Harkaway was too busy, too ambitious – probably, she had to admit, too ruthless – for her to make a life with him.

He swung round from the window. 'Will you come with us?' he asked.

She shook her head. 'I've had enough of living rough. A woman needs a bit of comfort. Her make-up's different.'

'So's her plumbing. And thank God for it.'

He approached the bed and grabbed for her. She pushed him away.

'I'm your warrior lord,' he laughed. 'You're my favourite wife!'

He snatched away the sheet and she screamed. Then he jumped on the bed and did a lopsided dance.

'The magic of the east,' he said. 'I always used to wonder what it was that Rudolph Valentino had that I hadn't got. My sister had pictures of him posted all over the inside of her wardrobe. Always with a bare chest. He was always being photographed only in his pants.' He grinned at her. '*I'm* not even wearing my pants.'

She was unable to avoid laughing at him and he knelt beside her and pushed her back on to the pillows.

'They went for him in a big way,' he said. 'Lots of swooning. Lots of kissing. Like this.' He kissed her fiercely, his hands moving over her body. 'Net curtains just as we have here. A warm breeze. Balmy nights. And a bloody big bed,' he yelled as he dived for her.

For a while she struggled against him, laughing and shrieking, then she stopped suddenly and melted in his arms. He bent over her, kissing her throat and breasts, until her breath came quickly.

'Oh, George!' she begged, her eyes moist with tears. 'Don't go away! Please don't go away!'

But he did.

That afternoon, the Sixth Column lorries, together with a few extra they'd taken from the Italians in Bidiyu, roared out of town. To Harkaway's Boys had now been added a few Ethiopians who until the day before had been wearing the uniform of the Italians.

Danny watched them go, an empty feeling in her breast. For weeks Harkaway had been her sun and her moon. Despite his autocratic manners, he'd come to mean more to her than anyone else in the whole of her life and now he was gone, and she had a feeling life would never be the same again.

Sick at heart, she turned away as the last vehicle, the last marching man, the last straggling woman disappeared from sight. Grobelaar was sitting on the remains of Guidotti's triumphal column, playing his harmonica. As he saw the tears in her eyes, he slapped the spittle from it against the palm of his hand and put it in his pocket. Almost without her realizing it, he stood beside her, lean, faded, and battered-looking with his lined tanned face and glass eye.

'Why did he have to go? she whispered.

Grobelaar shrugged. 'Because he can't stop, man,' he said. 'He'll probably *never* stop.'

She sighed and turned away. He remained where he was and she swung round, looking at him questioningly.

'*Tot siens*, Danny,' he said.

'What's that mean?'

'It's Afrikaans for "So long." '

'Are *you* going away, too?'

Her heart sank. She and Grobelaar had always been curiously close to each other, separate from Gooch and Tully, partly because they were civilians and partly because they'd both suffered more from Harkaway's ambition. When she'd been at her lowest, it had always been Grobelaar with his sad, self-disparaging smile who'd given her the comfort of his own disillusioned self, reassuring because he always seemed in a worse state than she was.

'What are you going to do, Kom-Kom?'

He shrugged and gave her his sad cobwebby smile. 'Go home,' he said. 'After that' – he shrugged – '*Ek weet nie*. I dunno, man.'

'What's it like in South Africa?'

'Like this. Big. But more beautiful. Man, you've never seen such flowers as they grow in the Cape.'

'I've never been to South Africa.'

'You should come.' Grobelaar put his hand on her arm. '*Kom, Kerel*,' he said. 'They've opened the cafés again. I'll buy you a beer.'

*

The column was several miles outside Bidiyu when they saw the car approaching. It stopped in front of them, blocking the road, and Harkaway rose in his seat to yell over the windscreen.

'Get out of the bloody way,' he said. 'We're in a hurry!'

'Hold it, hold it!' A man in a civilian bush jacket was climbing from the car. 'Just hang on a minute! Who are you? You from Berbera? This force that was landed there by the navy? We're trying to contact this outfit that calls itself the Sixth Column.'

Harkaway grinned. 'You've contacted it,' he said. 'This is the Sixth Column.'

The war correspondents eyed each other. Colonel Charlton climbed out.

'You've got a lot more transport than we expected,' he said.

'We helped ourselves to what the Italians left.'

'Artillery, too.'

Harkaway smiled. 'One gun. An Italian 75-millimetre that they forgot to take with them. Three, I suppose, if you count two pack guns. But they only fire toy shells. We've got machine guns, though, and mortars. Old British Stokes and now a few Italian ones.'

The three men were walking forward now, eyeing the long string of lorries, cars and armoured vehicles with wonder. Behind the vehicles was a column of men on foot, Somalis for the most part, many of them carrying spears and accompanied by their families and animals. Suspicious black faces peered at them as they halted in front of Harkaway.

'There are a lot of you,' Charlton said. 'Where did you get your chaps?'

'Recruited 'em.'

'You Colonel Harkaway?'

'Yes.' Harkaway grinned. 'But you won't find me in the army lists. I promoted myself.'

'Bit naughty,' Charlton said. 'The army prefers to do it. Looks better.'

'Thought it would help,' Harkaway explained. 'Knew the

Eyeties liked a bit of dignity so we made our own pips and crowns. Up to this morning we even had an ATS captain. Missionary we picked up.'

'What happened to her?'

'Left her in Bidiyu. She was a bit sick of living rough.' Harkaway gestured at Gooch and Tully. 'Second-lieutenant Gooch and Captain Tully.'

Charlton studied the two figures. 'Are they really officers?'

'Not on your life. But they do the job just as well.'

Charlton fished a notebook from his pocket. 'I'm glad we've bumped into you,' he said. 'The general would like to make it official. He's grateful for what you've done and he's quite prepared to offer you real commissions.'

'I'd rather have medical supplies,' Harkaway said.

'I could arrange for both. Better let me have your names.'

Harkaway gestured. 'That's Patrick Tully,' he said. 'The big chap's Harvey Gooch.'

'How did you come to be left behind the Italian lines?'

'Got cut off when the rush for the coast started,' Harkaway said casually, giving nothing away.

'What about you? Who're you?'

'George Matthew Tremayne Harkaway'.

Charlton looked up. 'Any relation of Mac Tremayne?' he asked. 'He was my commanding officer in the last bunfight.'

Harkaway frowned. Such a coincidence seemed hardly possible in this godforsaken place. 'Relative,' he growled. 'Distant.'

Charlton wrote everything down carefully. 'I doubt if you'll end up a lieutenant-colonel, of course,' he smiled. 'But you never know. Where are you off to?'

'I'm after Guidotti. He's heading north. I'm going to stop the bastard.'

'The RAF reports he's got lorries and guns.'

'*My* people report that he's running out of petrol and that he hasn't much ammunition for his guns. I'd rather take notice of them than the RAF. They're closer to the ground.'

Charlton stepped to one side and peered down the long

raggle-taggle column of men in multi-coloured robes and turbans.

'You really going to have a go at Guidotti with that lot?'

Harkaway glanced back. 'They're not exactly the Guards,' he admitted. 'But they know how to look after themselves.'

As he made to gesture to his driver, Wye stepped forward.

'Hang on, hang on!' he said. 'We'd like a word with you!'

Harkaway stared down his nose at him. 'And who the hell might you be?' he snapped.

'I'm Asa Wye. *Globe*. That's Russell. APA. We've been chasing you all over East Africa. We'd like a photograph.'

Harkaway smiled. He had no wish to have his picture plastered all over the newspapers. That could come when he'd finished and a few people were busy eating their words.

'Sorry,' he said. 'In a hurry. See them in Bidiyu. They know all about me.'

'Who do, for God's sake?' Having found his story, Wye could see it slipping through his fingers unwritten.

'Chap called Grobelaar. Known as Kom-Kom. With us until yesterday. Or there's our own private Bible-thumper. Bronwen Ortton-Daniells. She'll give you a story. She's a good one herself, come to that, and she'd make a good picture, too. Not bad-looking.'

While Wye frantically wrote and Russell scrambled about in the back of Charlton's car for his camera, Harkaway gestured at the Somalis who had climbed down to see better.

'Mount!' he yelled.

'Here, hang on!' Charlton said. 'The general would like to know what you're up to, so he can do a bit of planning. If *you*'re looking after the north, we can go straight on to Addis.'

Harkaway smiled. 'You go straight on to Addis,' he urged. 'I'll look after Guidotti for you. Now, if someone doesn't shift that bloody car, I'll shove it off the road.'

Startled, Charlton scrambled into the car and reversed it hurriedly. As he did so, Harkaway's vehicle pushed past.

As Charlton stood watching the column pass, Wye swore and looked at Russell. 'Get a picture?' he asked.

Russell lowered the camera. 'Three-quarter back view,' he said. 'It'll show he has nice ears.'

'He said *what*?' the General asked.

'He said he hadn't time to come for a conference,' Charlton explained. 'But he said we needn't worry about Guidotti. He could take care of him.'

The general studied him. 'And can he?'

Charlton smiled. 'I'd say he can, sir. He had those Somalis well under control. When he told them to do something, they jumped.'

'Then,' the general said dryly. 'I think we'll let him get on with it. After all, Guidotti can't do much harm to us, and our job's to get to Addis. At least our flank'll be secure, and if he doesn't pull it off – and he might not, of course – then we can always sort it out when we've established ourselves in Addis. What did you say his name was?'

Charlton looked at his notebook. 'George Matthew Tremayne Harkaway.'

The general frowned. 'There was a Tremayne in the Buffs,' he said. 'Made general. Probably his grandson or something. Might explain things a bit. They were damn good soldiers.' His frown deepened. 'I suppose we ought to make him official but if he doesn't pull it off it would make us look a bit silly. Perhaps for the time being, until we see what he makes of it, we'd better keep him out of our reports.'

Charlton cleared his throat. 'I doubt if that will be possible, sir,' he said. 'Wye, of the *Globe*, and Russell, of APA, were there, too. It'll be in every newspaper in England by tomorrow evening.'

The general frowned at his cigarette. 'The bloody press love oddities, don't they?' he murmured. 'Oh, well, I suppose we'll have to do something for him after all. Better make him a major. Temporary, of course. It'll give him the authority to handle those natives of his.'

Charlton frowned. 'He didn't seem to me,' he said, 'to need much in the way of authority, sir.'

10

The countryside was grim, red and blistering, and the strips of murram road were often the only colour in the baked landscape.

Where the scrub died away, the surface was sand fine as face powder, and the sun beat down vertically, making mirages in the brown waste of rocks. Lava boulders as big as footballs that lay everywhere, like hundreds and thousands on a birthday cake, shook the lorries to pieces. As they swerved to avoid one, they invariably hit another so that they were all bone-weary with the shaking.

Harkaway was pressing on hard with the wheeled transport, letting the rest – the camels and the mules carrying the water, the food, the ammunition and the petrol, the marching men, the women and the camp followers with their children – keep up as best they could, so that the column was strung out in a long winding coil, separated here and there like a broken string of beads.

Guidotti wasn't far away, they knew. They'd been following his tracks for some days now, driving in the ruts he'd made, so deep in the surface of the desert it was possible to put the wheels in them then sit back and let the lorry steer itself as if it were on lines. Long-shanked black men, wrapped in blankets and tending their flocks, told them the Italians were just ahead, sheltering in one of the white-washed Beau Geste forts they had thrown up round their borders.

As they drew closer, they kept coming across abandoned trucks, and the remains of the Italians' camps – tins of food and chianti bottles. They even found petrol cans hurriedly tossed aside, the petrol brown and dirty so that it had to be filtered through chamois cloths to avoid clogging the carburettors, but petrol nevertheless, and they knew the Italians were in a bad way, because they would never otherwise abandon the precious liquid that enabled them to keep moving.

They were a long way now from the road that ran between Berbera and Harar, the ancient trade route where slaves, ivory, apes and peacocks had passed since the days of Solomon and Sheba. This was grim, hard country that allowed them to take no chances and nerves were beginning to run a little ragged.

'This isn't what we came for,' Gooch said bitterly as they sat round a flickering fire.

'You didn't object,' Harkaway said, harsh and unrelenting. 'You could have backed out at Bidiyu. But you've been given the King's commission now. You're a full lieutenant, Goochy. "George, by the Grace of God, of the United Kingdom of Great Britain and Ireland, and of the British Dominions beyond the Seas, King, Defender of the Faith, Emperor of India, et cetera, to our trusty and well beloved Harvey Gooch, we, reposing especial trust and confidence in your loyalty, courage and good conduct, do by these presents constitute and appoint you to be an officer . . ."'

Gooch's eyes lifted. 'Is that what they say?' he asked.

'They not only say it. They write it down. They have it printed on parchment with a bloody great red seal in the corner. Temporary gentlemen have 'em framed – to prove to the neighbours they were once better than they seem.'

Gooch looked suspiciously at Harkaway. 'Where've *you* seen one?'

Harkaway gestured airily. 'Oh, I've seen 'em,' he said.

Gooch was silent for a while. 'Will I get one?' he asked.

'Bound to. Eventually. It was confirmed in the radio message Paddy took down. It was quite clear. Harvey Gooch. Patrick Tully.'

'And George Matthew Tremayne Harkaway. Is that your name?'

'Yes.'

'Some bloody name.'

'I could say the same about Harvey Gooch.'

'And they made *you* a bloody major. Paddy and me are only lieutenants.'

Harkaway's face was close to Gooch's. 'Who's running the show?' he demanded. 'Could *you* have done it, Lieutenant Harvey Gooch? Could Paddy?'

Gooch shifted uneasily because he knew he couldn't. 'They'll take it off us again,' he growled. 'When they find out who we really are.'

'No, they won't,' Harkaway said. 'Not now the newspaper boys have got hold of it. They wouldn't dare.'

If they were aware that Guidotti wasn't far ahead, Guidotti was equally aware that *they* weren't very far behind.

He had hoped to escape undetected, but it hadn't taken him long to realize there was a column following them north. He could only imagine it was the Sixth Column, because he guessed rightly that the British army would be less concerned with him than with reaching the Abyssinian capital. The fall of Addis Ababa could not be far away now. Keren in the north had held out for a month but that had gone at last and, almost at the same time, so had Asmara. With Berbera, Hargeisa and Bidiyu gone, too, and now Jijiga, Harar and Diredawa, Addis Ababa couldn't hope to hold out for long. Then his troubles would increase, because as soon as the British had pushed Haile Selassie back on his shabby throne, they'd start seeking out all the lost units of the Italian East African army.

For days as he had crossed the Abyssinian border, he'd been aware of the dust cloud on the horizon that meant they were being pursued, and he was glad to link up with the garrison of Fort San Rafaelo at Djuba. His men were at the end of their tether, but it looked very much as though they were going to have to fight there.

There had been a fortification at Djuba, where a spider's-web of camel tracks came together, since before Christ, because this was border country where slave traders, bandits and nomad families had fought pitched battles for centuries over the wells that pierced the limestone outcrop. King Theodore had built a fort there to guard his southern borders against the hated white men, but the British general, Napier, had destroyed it in 1868, only for the Italians to rebuild it in 1938.

It was a whitewashed square structure now, with twenty-foot walls, except at the back where, because of the shortage of building material, a wall of logs and stones had been scaled down in the belief that the enemy would never get the chance of attacking the place from the rear. It had latticed windows, machicolations, firing slits on its parapet and a high tower at one corner. Inside the fort was a large parade ground with a well which supplied fresh if brackish liquid but unfortunately it was not fitted with a very good pump so that the business of obtaining water was long, hot and arduous. Large barrack rooms and offices were situated round the inside of the walls, their flat roofs forming the walk from which the parapet could be manned but, though attempts had been made by Major Pavicelli, its commander until the arrival of Guidotti, to make it like home, it still remained a bare empty box devoid of comfort, and full – especially at that moment – of nervous anxieties about attack.

Despite its size, Guidotti was well aware that it wasn't big enough for modern warfare. It was surrounded by a zariba of thorn bushes and a barbed wire entanglement, but the barbed wire, like everything else, was in short supply and the low wall at the back worried him. Some former commander had made himself a small garden there, near a group of thorny acacias, so he could sit in the shade in the evening, and a small door had been let into the wall, which was reached by a passage alongside one of the large barrack rooms. Guidotti had had the door barricaded for safety but he recognized it as a danger point; and, in addition, because of the danger of their vehicles being spotted by aircraft and bombed, they had had to disperse them outside the log wall among the trees. Hard up against the walls on this side were sheds for the herd of cattle, sheep and goats which were kept to provide fresh meat.

The approaches to the fort had been cleared to give a field of fire but the scrub had not been pushed back far enough and, beyond the clearing, could hide an army. In addition, just outside the wire was a khor, a sandy river bed edged with tough grass. When the rains came, it carried water but, at the moment, apart from a few large stagnant pools, it was dry, and as Guidotti well knew, could offer protection for anyone about to storm the fort.

As he studied his position, Guidotti didn't fancy his chances. He had had the wooden bridge across the khor hacked down but, while these ridiculous little fortresses were fine against tribesmen with ancient weapons, he well knew that the column coming up from the south was well armed, because it was largely armed with Italian guns.

He stood on the ramparts studying the town and the flat-roofed bazaars where traders bowed on their prayer rugs and gave thanks to Allah that the Italians would soon be gone. Since his arrival he had spent his time putting up extra wire to keep out all the natives except the old women who did the washing and looked after the herd of cattle. There was an Italian arch in the little town bearing a date to show how long the area had been occupied and Guidotti reflected bitterly that it didn't really add up to much.

As the sun sank and the bright brassiness of the heavens faded to jade green and then to lemon yellow, the land outside the fort remained silent, changing with the colour of the sky from gold to salmon pink and then to purples and greys. There were Abyssinians and border Somalis near the waterhole, fine-looking nomads grazing their flocks on the scanty pasturage of the interior, and over the silent air came the faint tinkle of camel bells. Guidotti could see the shadowy shapes passing endlessly through the light cast by the fires, and their smell came to him, bitter and smoky, to pervade the whole interior of the fort.

'Have you finished the wire?' he asked Piccio.

'Yes, Excellency. But there isn't much.'

'Weapons?'

'Set up, sir.'

'How about the troops?'

Piccio shrugged. 'They're nervous. I'm not sure I'd depend on them. The Abyssinians will throw in their hand if they get a chance, and even the Eritreans are not what they were. If rations run short – '

'Rations won't run short!' Guidotti gestured. 'And those people out there are worse off than we are. Besides, we shan't be here long. I propose to stay only until our people are rested, then move further north with Pavicelli towards the Duke of Aosta.'

Piccio frowned. 'We'd better hurry, I think, sir,' he said. 'Fortresses are always dangerous and sieges can become disasters.'

Some time after midnight, on the orders of Piccio, Guidotti was roused by a nervous askari. Dressing hurriedly, he climbed with Piccio to the tower. It stood sixty feet above the ground and it was possible to see for miles.

Piccio pointed. In the distance, a long line of pinpoint lights from fires was strung across the desert in a vast half circle. As Guidotti stared at them, Piccio touched his arm and gestured again. Guidotti stared in the direction of his pointing finger. In the north, too, were lights in another vast semi-circle and it was clear the two semi-circles were endeavouring to join up.

'They've arrived,' Piccio said.

Guidotti didn't have to ask who.

11

The Sixth Column slipped into its place quietly and efficiently. On the right, the town of Djuba lay in a huddle of whitewashed mud buildings, the roads leading to it studded with embarrassed-looking eagles, laurels, and bundles of fasces. There was also an area of iron pickets and rusting barbed wire protecting from jackals and hyenas the neglected sun-baked graves of a dozen Italian soldiers who had fallen when the country had been taken over. Above them rose a headstone chiselled in Italian: 'To the men of Cerutti's column who died in the shadow of the Roman eagles at Djuba in combat with the barbarous foe.'

Staring at the fort, Harkaway hardly saw them.

'Got the bastard,' he said with satisfaction.

Gooch made a growling sound of disagreement. 'If you ask me,' he said heavily, 'you're expecting a lot outa those Boys of yours. The buggers might be able to fire rifles but they aren't trained for attacking a fort.'

'I'm not looking for trained soldiers,' Harkaway said flatly. 'What I want is *untrained* soldiers. The Boys are tough and silent and for the sort of fighting I want they're just the job. They'll carry spears, pangas and anything else that takes their fancy, so long as it's sharp, shines and is likely to put the fear of God into the Italians. To make it better we'll go in after dark.'

Gooch remained unconvinced. 'Night attacks always end in a bloody shambles,' he said.

'This one won't. And once we're inside, I'm going to let the Boys loose. Everything they can get's theirs. That'll make 'em go. They've behaved themselves well up to now and they're itching to have a go in their own way. This time they're going to. When the Eyeties see 'em coming up the stairs and round the corners they'll think it's Adowa all over again.'

'What's Adowa, for God's sake, you toffee-nosed bastard?'

'Adowa's where their army was wiped off the face of the earth by the Abyssinians in 1896. We'll let 'em know we've been joined by several thousand Abyssinians – '

'A hundred's nearer the mark.'

'They don't know that.'

'Suppose the bastards get out of hand?'

Harkaway smiled. 'So much the better,' he said. 'The Eyeties' bloody bandas were given carte blanche to rob and rape, and they'll think it's their turn and won't wait to find out.'

That night, with Piccio behind him, Guidotti stamped briskly round the ramparts of the fort, trying to look more confident than he felt. He was urging the need for constant alertness on the sergeant of the guard, when they heard a whistle. Almost at once there was a crash and a blinding flash just outside the fort that threw up a cloud of dust and stones.

Guidotti looked at Piccio. 'They've got artillery,' he said.

They realized at once that the missile had come from a mountain gun. The weapon was small and of ancient vintage but, firing vertically, was more suited to throw its shells into the fort than guns with a flat trajectory.

Two more shells arrived almost at once, gouging out chunks of the mud-brick wall. As they struggled to fill the gaps with rubble they were expecting more shells, but surprisingly none came and they were just deciding that that was the end of the cannonade when another shell arrived, this time from the east side of the fort.

'They have *two* batteries!' Piccio gasped.

Three more shells fell in quick succession, none of them doing much damage, then there was another long silence.

They were still nervously peering to the east when three shells arrived from the north.

'They have artillery all round us,' Piccio said.

As it happened – as Guidotti immediately suspected – Harkaway had sent a single small gun careering madly round the fort firing from different directions to cause confusion and alarm. As it returned, Sergeant Catchpole jumped from the lorry, grinning.

'That'll puzzle the bastards,' he announced.

The following day, Guidotti stared from the fort, his eyes narrow. There was little he could see, because the besiegers were well hidden in the hollows, the scrub and the dried river bed. But here and there he could see small columns of smoke from cooking fires and once they heard the high-pitched ululation of Somali singing. As dusk fell they waited for the bombardment to start up again but when it came it was different. There was a distant pop and a few seconds later there was a flash in the courtyard and a tremendous nerve-shattering crash.

'Mortar,' Piccio gasped. 'And one of ours, too, by the sound of it.'

The mortars, smooth-bored and of low muzzle velocity, were not very accurate but they could lob their bombs over the walls without difficulty and, with the size of the courtyard, couldn't miss.

Running to the tower, Guidotti peered through one of the firing slits. 'They can't be that close,' he said.

'They could be,' Piccio pointed out, 'if they moved up during last night and lay low all day in the khor.'

Guidotti glanced quickly at him. The idea of lying in the khor through the full heat of the day appalled him. On the other hand he knew the enemy comprised Somalis for the most part and they were well used to the heat. Piccio was trying to make out just where the mortar was concealed when they heard another pop and there was another crash in the courtyard behind them and the shouts of alarmed askaris.

'We'll send out a force to drive them away,' Guidotti said, but Piccio turned worried eyes to him.

'Excellency,' he said, 'if we send native troops, they'll bolt. And we can't afford to risk our Italian grenadiers.'

There was sense in what he said and Guidotti withdrew the suggestion. As they ran down the stone steps to the courtyard, there was another crash. Metal fragments gouged plaster from the walls and Guidotti fell the last few steps to sprawl on his face with Piccio on top of him. As he scrambled to his feet, another bomb fell and he had to fling himself down once more. As he got to his feet again, there was a whistle which he recognized as a shell, and a chunk was knocked off the tower so that the flag he'd insisted should be kept flying day and night canted sharply to one side.

'Gunfire now,' Piccio gasped.

The mortar bombs were coming in a shower when, just as Guidotti was beginning to wonder how many there were, they stopped as suddenly as they'd started.

The inside of the fort was silent as the grave. Lights appeared. Only two men, one a native levy, had been killed, but six had been wounded, three seriously. The damage had not been extensive but the short bombardment had been nerve-racking.

They were just clearing up the debris when the mortar bombardment started again. This time there were only six bombs and they all came together, landing in a salvo in the courtyard to kill another man and wound two others.

Ordering everybody under cover, Guidotti called Piccio into Pavicelli's office to discuss what they could do to counter the mortarings.

'We can't mortar back,' Piccio pointed out. 'We don't know where they are unless they mortar us in daylight.'

Guidotti frowned, almost in tears with despair as he leaned over the plan of the fort spread on the desk. He was still struggling to set his senses in order when he became aware of shouting outside.

'Now what?'

Smelling smoke and hearing the crackle of flames, he

dropped the map and rushed into the courtyard. The stables were alight and the haystore was burning furiously. Pavicelli's native cavalrymen were leading blindfolded horses into the courtyard through the smoke.

'The old women,' Pavicelli panted. 'The old women who look after the cattle! They must have planted some sort of device. We can't get at it. The whole lot's going up!'

While Guidotti was trying to make sense of what was happening, the mortaring started again. Ten bombs fell, one after the other in a long salvo that cracked and rattled inside the courtyard. A horse screamed and shouting started. By dawn, Guidotti's nerves were completely on edge. The inside of the fort was blackened with smoke, the cavalrymen tramping around in a sodden mash of mud, ash and charred straw.

Guidotti was still depressed by the night's events when Piccio appeared, white-faced, to announce that they had lost the small herd on which they relied for fresh meat.

'Those damned old women!' he spluttered. 'They opened the gate of the cowfold while we were fighting the fire and drove the lot out.'

They were still discussing the ration situation when the mortaring started once more and Guidotti ran to the tower to study the land outside the fort. Wisps of smoke were hanging over the dried river bed.

'They're in the khor,' he yelled to Piccio. 'And they're unsupported. Send out Pavicelli. No mercy.'

The native cavalrymen assembled in the courtyard, a mass of kicking, biting, squealing animals still nervous after the fire and the mortaring, their riders uncertain in the confusion what they were about to do. With difficulty, Pavicelli got them into order and they moved forward with a jingling of bits, a proud show of nodding heads, their riders garbed in white robes and armed with swords, rifles and slings of the little Japanese grenades. Guidotti watched from the ramparts as the barbed wire entanglement was dragged aside. As the horsemen bunched, jockeying to shake themselves into line, a gun barked and a shell burst among them. Horses fell, kicking and screaming with pain, one of them, smashed to the ground by the explosion, heaving itself up, its jaws foam-flecked, its eyes bulging, to drag itself along on its stiff forelegs, its hindquarters trailing like those of a dog run over in a Rome street. The rest of the troop were milling about in confusion as they tried to form a line for their charge.

For a moment, Guidotti couldn't make out where the shell had come from, then he realized the gun had been set up among the scrub and thorn bushes. There seemed to be only one – an Italian 75-mm – but then the mountain guns started, backed up by the 20-mm weapons of the armoured cars. Running from the walls, he reached the sergeant-major in command of the two ancient spoke-wheeled 75-mm guns he'd dragged with him from Bidiyu, but even as he gave the order to fire, the sergeant-major gestured in frustration at the cavalry milling about in the line of fire.

Distinctive on his white horse, Pavicelli was circling in front of his squadron, trying to get them back into order, then he raised his sword and, spurring to the front of the line, led them in a loose formation to the right in an attempt to reach the guns from the flank. It was a brave attempt but it didn't have a chance. Through his binoculars, Guidotti saw the men behind the guns lifting their trails and swinging them through a ninety-degree arc to fire into the mass of horsemen.

As men and animals went down, machine guns opened up and Guidotti realized his opponent had thought of everything. As the horsemen swept towards the mortar crews, the guns were firing at point-blank range and Guidotti saw with surprise an unexploded shell bounding along the ground before lifting end-over-end to disappear from sight. Horses were going down in whole bunches and groups of white-robed figures appeared between the guns to pour in old-fashioned volley fire.

The charge ended in a frantic scramble for shelter. Pavicelli was down with both his subalterns and what was left of his squadron was circling back towards the fort. Instead of heading for the gap in the wire, however, they swung to right and left and kept on going, heading north in little groups of twos and threes until they vanished from sight in the scrub.

Watching the last of them disappear, Guidotti turned and stared over the battlefield. Animals lay in heaps, their robed riders alongside them. Over them the dark shadows of the circling vultures moved. A few unhorsed men stumbled back to the fort, a few chargers stood motionless, their heads down, trying to graze, quite indifferent to the butchery, one of them moving in halting steps because its feet were caught up in its own entrails.

He turned as he heard a sound alongside him and saw Piccio standing by his elbow, his eyes wet.

Guidotti swallowed. 'Have the wire closed,' he said. 'We can do no more.'

12

The vultures were feasting on the grisly remains of Pavicelli's action like black-weeded widows arguing at a funeral when Gooch brought a message to where Harkaway was sitting in his headquarters truck.

'A feller with a white flag's come,' he said. 'They want permission to clear away the dead.'

'Tell him nothing doing.'

'The buggers are beginning to smell.'

'They'll smell worse to them than they do to us. They're nearer.'

Gooch went away. He was back a few minutes later. 'He appeals to your Christian instincts,' he said. 'He says it's against all the rules of war.'

'There aren't any rules in war.'

Gooch persisted. 'I think we ought to let 'em.'

'Nobody's asking you,' Harkaway snapped. 'You bloody dimwit, don't you realize everything that adds to their discomfort makes it easier for us when we decide to go in. Those stiffs out there are demoralizing them. They're all sitting behind the bloody walls thinking "I'm next." Tell your Italian friend not to bother bringing any more white flags. I'm not interested. The only thing I'm interested in is unconditional surrender.'

The message was received inside the fort with long faces. Food was beginning to run short and one of the mortar bombs had damaged the well in the courtyard so that water was short, too.

The survivors of Pavicelli's charge who had made their

way back into the fort were exhausted, dehydrated and suffering from wounds not caused by the Sixth Column guns. They had hoped to escape northwards but Abyssinian patriots had fallen on them and cut them up. Only a few had managed to hide in the bush, all of them without horses, and they could think of nowhere else to go but back to Guidotti.

The nightly bombardments of the fort continued – short showers of mortar bombs sending everyone bolting for cover – together with a salvo of small shells every dusk and dawn against the gates. There were never many and they had grown used to them now, so that Guidotti no longer sent his men up to the ramparts in case of attack, but kept them in safety in the rooms below, behind the thick walls.

Hating the static defence that was being forced on him, that night Guidotti sent out a strong patrol with the intention of finding the mortars and snatching back the initiative. But Harkaway was alerted early and, lifting his head to sniff the wind, he gestured briskly.

'Set the bush on fire,' he said.

Men began to run in the dark with brands snatched from the fires and the Italian patrol, moving forward cautiously, saw a line of flames leap up. As their shouts of alarm gave away their position, an old Vickers started sweeping the ground in a slow clack-clacking and the patrol had to fling themselves to the ground. Caught by the wind, the flames moved swiftly among the scrub and dried grass so that they were in danger of being cut off and had to scramble away in the dark, firing at shadows.

From the walls, Guidotti listened to the shooting in an agony of apprehension. When the returning patrol was sighted, he ran to the small back entrance to the fort as they fell inside, a confusion of panting men still raging with excitement and crowding forward to recite the numbers of men they'd killed. The native sergeant claimed that they'd surprised a patrol of Abyssinians creeping forward to plant a mortar and had killed the lot, but Guidotti wondered just how much of it was made up and just whom they really had killed.

He could see the glow of the enemy's fires and his radio operator could even pick up their signals. They were in touch now with British headquarters in Addis Ababa and were replying to all the suggestions that they should be reinforced with the comment that they were not in need of assistance. Guidotti had a feeling they were right.

He couldn't make out why he was being pursued so ardently. He'd heard of the British officer in command of the Sixth Column. A man called Harkaway, he'd discovered, who for some reason seemed to bear malice towards Guidotti.

His eyes narrowed as his thoughts raced. The future looked bleak. Italy's enemies were scenting victory as town after town fell, and the dreaded Abyssinian patriots were coming out of the hills, blowing bridges, passing information, ambushing columns. And, Guidotti had heard, they were now moving down on Fort San Rafaelo.

Harkaway was staring at the bodies of a dozen unarmed herdsmen when Yussuf appeared. Guidotti's frightened patrol had kept well clear of Harkaway's bloodthirsty warriors and when they'd stumbled on the herdsmen they had killed the lot, even some of their flock.

Their mutilated bodies had been found at first light and Harkaway had brought them into camp and made every single man file past. He was fighting a war in the old style of the North-west Frontier, the way his grandfather had described. It wasn't the way civilized European wars were fought, but you could hardly describe as civilization the use of gas on half-naked troops or taking up difficult chiefs in aeroplanes, as Graziani had done, and dropping them out in front of their watching tribesmen. The Italians, among the most civilized and compassionate of races, could also be among the most cruel. You could say, he decided, that he was only using their own methods.

Yussuf's news was of the arrival of one of the Ethiopian chiefs, who came out of the bush looking like Henry VIII, accompanied by a group of his followers led by bagpipes and wearing enough silver bangles to shackle a carthorse.

He was big, fat and bearded, his thick hair standing out round his head like a crown, and he was wearing a captured Italian uniform, gorgeous with gold braid, his chest chandeliered with Italian medals. He said his name was Ras Minelik and he informed them that Eritreans and Abyssinians from Guidotti's garrison were already slipping over the rear wall in the dark, their numbers such that the Italians were growing worried.

A feast of well-spiced mutton and rice was prepared, and the old man stuffed himself with meat and tej and sat back proudly, waiting for them to reward him with arms and money to encourage him to join them. He got neither but the following morning Harkaway noticed he was still around.

'He has decided to join you,' Yussuf explained.

Harkaway gave a grim smile. 'I thought he might,' he said.

That afternoon he called Gooch, Tully, Sergeant Catchpole, Yussuf, Abdillahi and Ras Minelik round his armoured car. On the bonnet he had spread a plan of the fort he'd drawn.

'Tonight,' he announced. 'We've given them long enough for them to scare themselves to death. We bombard the fort as usual, but this time it goes on as long as we have the ammunition. I want the gates smashed down. Are the ladders ready, Gooch?'

'Enough to get over the wall at the back.'

'No prisoners,' Harkaway warned. 'We've nowhere to put 'em.'

'No quarter?' Catchpole looked surprised.

'Do you think the Boys'll give it, Sergeant?' Harkaway said blandly. 'They've seen what that patrol did to those herdsmen.'

'There's just one point, sir.' Catchpole was standing erect. his hands at his side, his heels together, a sergeant addressing his officer.

It pleased Harkaway. He was growing used to command now and hadn't demoted himself when they'd learned he'd been confirmed in the rank of major. 'Go on, Sergeant,' he said. 'What's the trouble?'

'How do we identify them from us?' Catchpole asked. 'They've got Banda men in there who don't wear uniform and half of 'em come from the same tribal areas as our people.'

'Good point,' Harkaway said, ready to dish out a little praise. 'But I've thought of that one. Let every man find a sprig of green and stick it in his hair. There's plenty of it about and they have the sort of hair where it'll stick. Then have 'em paint their faces.'

'War paint?' Tully grinned.

'Two streaks down each cheek. They like painting for battle, so this time they can. It'll act as identification. You got that, Sergeant? You, Yussuf?'

Catchpole grinned uncertainly. 'I reckon it'll scare the Italians out of their breeches, sir,' he observed.

As the sun sank, aware that a battle was coming, the Ethiopians began to dance. The Somalis joined them and the yelling went on for an hour. Among the spears, long curving swords had appeared. No one had seen them arrive, but women had been following the column ever since it had left Bidiyu, and they could only assume that they'd brought the weapons with them.

As darkness fell, Harkaway watched the fort. Alongside him, Abdillahi and Yussuf waited with Gooch, Tully and Sergeant Catchpole.

'There will be many deaths,' Yussuf said slowly. 'The ghelow bird cried all last night.'

Harkaway turned to Catchpole. 'You ready, Sergeant?'

Catchpole stiffened. 'Sir!'

'Okay.' Harkaway gestured. 'Let 'em have it.'

As the first mortar fired, the pop was followed by silence then by a flash and a sharp crack from inside the fort. The men crouching with their weapons in the khor just short of the wire grinned at each other.

As other mortars started the nightly bombardment, from the flanks the two mountain guns started hammering at the gates, supported by the 20-mms on the armoured cars. They were handled well by Sergeant Catchpole, and as Harkaway signed to Gooch and Tully, they moved off with their men into the darkness. Tobes were worn as loincloths and the only sign of the Somalis in the dark were the watermelon grins of white teeth. As they vanished, Harkaway gestured to the main body of his men to move up behind the khor.

Between them, another party moved up with shovels. Twenty feet of the khor were filled in and timber placed over the earth for the armoured cars to cross, then another party slithered forward, flat to the dusty earth, close to the wire. Somewhere in the rear in the darkness, they could hear the women wailing, urging their men on, chanting verses and encouraging them to be brave.

The shower of mortar bombs stopped. The guns stopped. Harkaway walked along the line of his men to where Catchpole waited.

'How's the ammunition?' he asked.

Catchpole stiffened. 'We can't keep it up much longer, sir.'

There was one of the short nervous pauses that worried Guidotti and his men so much, then the guns started again. By this time, Harkaway knew Gooch and Tully must be in position and Gooch's men would be slithering under the wire.

'One last go, Sergeant,' Harkaway said. 'This time knock down the gate.'

As the mortar fire came again, Guidotti watched from the tower. There was no sign of the enemy. He had tried a few mortar bombs against them but his ammunition was low and they had to endure the bombardment without being able to hit back.

As he watched, he saw a flash from where he knew the enemy had sited his 75-mm and, almost immediately, there was a roar below him near the gate. For some time now, the shells of the mountain guns had been knocking chunks out of the walls and Guidotti and his soldiers, sweating to shore up the damage, were growing tired and dispirited.

There was another crash and Guidotti heard the rattle of falling stones and timber.

'I think they're about to attack,' he said to Piccio. 'Bring the reserve up in case they make a rush. Have a machine gun ready to cover the gate.'

Running to the courtyard, Piccio formed up a mixed bag of Italians and Eritreans who waited nervously in the rooms opposite the gate while another squad stood by the machine gun, ready to rush it out and set it up the minute the gate went.

As the shelling continued, Guidotti moved along the ramparts, checking that every man was in his place. He was determined to die like a soldier, to kill the lie the British put out that Italians lacked courage. His men were looking over their shoulders at him, though, and he knew it meant they would probably throw down their arms at the first sign of a reverse.

Descending the stairs, he moved towards the armoury to check that Piccio was in position, but as he turned the corner by his own room, he was startled to find one of his Italian corporals lying by the stairs. He was surprised, because it was impossible that he could have been hit by a splinter from one of the mortar bombs. Then it dawned on him that the man's throat had been cut.

The first thought that came to Guidotti's mind was that his native troops had mutinied. Swinging round, he reached for his sword, that magnificent sword he'd carried ever since the campaign in Spain. He'd never used it, but it was a sign of authority when he wore it and he drew it now, searching the shadowy corners of the corridor.

There was no sign of anyone, and he hurried to where Piccio was waiting. The bombardment had stopped again but the heavy gates were only a tangle of splintered timbers now.

'I think – '

Guidotti had barely started speaking when they heard a swish and saw a streak of smoke going up behind them. It soared into the blackness and burst into a vivid red glow that hung in the sky. Guidotti stared at it, his jaw hanging.

His first idea was that somebody was trying to surrender and he stared round wildly.

Then Piccio pointed. 'They're inside!' he yelled and in the light of the flare, Guidotti saw half-naked black figures running along the ramparts. They held rifles, but they were making no attempt to use them and were slashing instead with curved swords.

'Mother of God!'

Ramming his sword back in the scabbard, Guidotti drew his revolver and fired. One of the black figures stumbled and fell, but others were pouring along the ramparts, hacking at men still peering through the firing slits.

'Watch the gate!' he shouted at Piccio as he tried to gather a few men round him in an attempt to clear the ramparts.

As he rushed up the stairs, he came face to face with a tall, lean black man with bushy hair and wild eyes. He was armed with a rifle and a spear; his face was streaked with yellow and he wore a sprig of foliage in his hair. As he saw Guidotti, he gave a high-pitched yell and flung the spear. It missed Guidotti and went into the throat of the man behind. Guidotti fired and the black man staggered and fell.

Jumping over the squirming body and dashing through the door to the ramparts, Guidotti could see a whole flood of white-robed men on the ramparts now. They were driving slowly forward and, to his horror, he saw his own men beginning to throw down their weapons and run.

He turned and saw an Italian sergeant with a sub-machine gun and pointed. As the gun stammered, the men swarming on to the ramparts seemed to collapse like puppets with broken strings. Then, as he swung round, Guidotti saw a white man, bulky in European uniform, with the stars of a lieutenant on his shoulder, step out of the doorway and, thinking it was his enemy, Harkaway, he fired.

The white man gave him a startled look then, taking a couple of stumbling steps forward, he overbalanced and fell from the rampart to the courtyard.

As the Very light had gone up, Harkaway had blown his whistle, and the dark figures lying on the ground about him had risen to their feet, yelling their war-cries. Slamming in the clutch of the armoured car, the driver revved the engine and moved forward. Behind him the other armoured cars formed a line and, bouncing over the planks laid over the filled-in portion of the khor, thundered towards the fort. A machine gun in a sandbagged position near the gate started to fire but Harkaway ignored it and directed his vehicle towards it. As it drew near, the gunners rose to their feet and all but one of them, who kept the gun firing, began to run.

The armoured car struck the wire, the strands twanging as they snapped and coiled about it. The driver, one of Catchpole's ex-prisoners, gasped and fell forward just as the front wheels hit the sandbags of the gun position, then the heavy vehicle crashed down on top of the gun and the man firing it.

As it came to rest in a cloud of dust, Harkaway banged his head and could feel blood running into his eye. Gathering his senses, he saw that the driver was dead, so he opened the hatch and jumped out as the other armoured cars raced for the gate.

'Get through,' he roared. 'Get through!'

Yelling black men were swarming over and round the splintered gates into the courtyard. A machine gun in the shadows at the opposite side of the fort stuttered and the black wave crumbled. Then the gun stopped, its crew hacked down, and the wave picked up speed again and swept forward. A blast of fire came from the ramparts where Guidotti and Piccio had gathered a group of Savoia Grenadiers round them, and once again the wave crumbled.

His face splashed by the blood of his driver, Harkaway realized he was facing defeat. He had expected Guidotti and the Italians to throw down their weapons at the first rush but they were keeping their heads and fighting back courageously. As another wave, moving against the wall, was swept away by the firing, he leapt forward, brandishing his revolver. 'Keep going!' he was yelling. 'Keep going!'

As the black men poured past him, another blast of fire stopped them dead in their tracks yet again. But the murder of the shepherds had roused the war fury in them and heavy swords hacked and slashed until the Italian native troops began to give way. Surrounded by the remnants of the Savoia Grenadiers and a few loyal Eritreans, the Italian officers had reached the barrack rooms at the rear of the fort and had barricaded themselves in with beds, tables and cupboards, and were firing through the iron-barred windows that gave air to the place in the stifling heat of the summer. Outside the doorway behind which they crouched was a pile of bodies, and the bullets were chipping industriously at the mud walls.

'We can't hold them, Excellency,' Piccio panted. 'We've got to evacuate the place!'

'In God's name, man,' Guidotti snapped. 'How?'

Piccio gestured. 'The lorries are still there under the trees! They haven't touched them!'

Guidotti's head jerked round, a faint gleam of hope in his eyes. 'Are you sure?'

'I've seen them, Excellency. It's worth a try. If we can hold them here, we can hack our way through the wall into the passage that leads to the gate to the garden.'

Guidotti swung round, studying the barrack room with its overturned fitments. The interior walls of the fort, he knew, were largely of mud and could be pierced easily enough.

'Get on with it, Piccio,' he said. 'Take as many men as you need. I'll hold them off. Collect ammunition and any supplies you can lay your hands on. Let me know when you've broken through to the garden and we'll join you. For the love of God, though, hurry!'

As Piccio's party started tearing at the wall of the barrack room with crowbars, bayonets, knives and bare hands, the men outside in the courtyard were pinned down by the fire coming from the barrack-room windows and it was several minutes before it dawned on Harkaway what was happening.

'Tully,' he yelled. 'Where are you?'

A figure appeared alongside him, its hands covered with blood. 'The bastards got Goochy,' Tully said. 'Right between the eyes, poor bastard. He's lying in the courtyard. He's dead.'

Harkaway's pause lasted only a second, then he gestured angrily. 'To hell with Gooch,' he raged. 'They're escaping!'

Outside the gate the women were shrieking shrill encouragement, and black-faced Somali Muslims yelling 'Allah, Allah,' charged forward yet again alongside Christian Ethiopians screaming 'Kill, kill, kill!' They had forgotten their rifles and instead swung the long curved swords and lunged with the broad-bladed spears. A row of water containers made of wicker and mud were smashed to fragments in the frenzy and one of the Italian levies flung himself down with his hands over his head in the debris. A spear thrust killed him at once. Alongside him, an Italian soldier rocked on the sandy earth, holding his knees and yelling for mercy.

Horsemen had arrived now and were galloping about inside the courtyard, shouting that there was no God but God and Allah was his name, while half-grown boys, screaming like hyenas, rampaged along behind them. Some of them carried bows and, as one of the Eritrean levies staggered back with an arrow in his throat, a man with wild eyes and red dust in his hair hacked him to pieces, stabbing and cutting with a frenzy that bordered on insanity.

By this time, the armoured cars were circling the courtyard, looking for something to shoot at, but there was such a crowd of hacking, stabbing men chasing their shrieking victims, it was impossible to take aim.

Italian soldiers began to clamour round the white men, and, terrified of being hacked to pieces, were trying to climb on to the armoured cars, begging to be saved.

'I think it's finished,' Harkaway said, and suddenly the racket faded. The shouting died and they could hear only moans, the triumphant yelling of Harkaway's Boys, the crackle of flames and the dull throbbing of the armoured car's engines.

13

The butchery had been frightful. The heavy curved swords
had slashed the defenders to so much meat, and there were
pools of blood staining the sandy floor of the courtyard. The
walls were splashed with it and almost every room seemed
to contain huddled bodies. Catchpole and his gunners wore
shaken looks and the civilian drivers who had accompanied
them were keeping well clear until the mess had been tidied
up. It wasn't the sort of war they were used to and they
were beginning by this time to regret having anything to do
with Harkaway.

He stared round the courtyard. Two armoured cars stood
together near the well and men outside the fort were trying
to drag the third from the pit where it rested on the smashed
machine gun and the body of the sergeant who had kept it
firing.

Chattering excitedly, blood-splashed Somalis, still wild
with excitement, were dragging away the timbers of the
gate. Others were collecting their injured who were having
their wounds stuffed by their own Somali doctors with pack-
ages of roots and leaves. The bodies were brought out across
the backs of horses, torn, stained sacks, their hands rusty
with dried blood, and given to the women who stood wailing
and beating their foreheads as they waited. The corpses of
the Italians and their native troops were being stacked like
cordwood in another corner of the fort, and Tully, bent
over the body of Gooch, looked up at them, a sick look on
his face.

'Have you seen what that bastard's got,' he said, indicating one of the grinning Ethiopians. 'It's an 'ead!'

They had won, but it had been a costly business and had very nearly been a defeat. After their easy victories of the past, the narrowness of the margin had come as a shock, and the dazed survivors were hardly able to believe their luck. In addition to the black dead, Gooch and three of the white men had died.

The picnic seemed to be over. Harkaway was not deluding himself. Their part in the destruction of the Italian army had been small, and Guidotti had not lost his head. He and his men had fought well and the losses they had inflicted were grievous. Danny had warned him not to push his luck too far and he had treated her suggestion with scorn. But, he realized now, he wasn't as clever as he'd thought he was, his luck had suddenly run out and they'd been saved from defeat only by the ferocity of ill-drilled, ill-armed black men.

'We need help and medical supplies,' he said. 'We've got to contact Addis.'

Tully gave him a sullen look. 'I thought we could do it on our own,' he said.

Harkaway gestured at the Italian and Eritrean prisoners penned in a corner of the courtyard. 'What do we do with that lot?' he demanded, unwilling to offer any other reason. 'We can't guard 'em and we can't shoot the bastards. We've still got a job to do.'

'What job, for Christ's sake,' Tully demanded angrily. 'Haven't we done the bloody job?'

'We haven't got Guidotti.'

'What's so important about this bloody Guidotti?' Tully yelled.

'Don't you realize, you stupid idiot?' Harkaway yelled back. 'With Guidotti in our hands, they'll certainly confirm your bloody commission. Doesn't that mean anything to you? Instead of a couple of bob a day, you'll be earning a fortune.'

'You don't give a monkey's what happens to me!' Tully said bitterly. 'All you want is that they confirm your own bloody rank. If I know you, you'll make sure that you stay a major.'

'What's wrong with that?'

Tully seemed to collapse, as if the spine had gone from him. 'I'll send your message,' he said slowly. 'Then I'm going to attend to old Goochy. Put him away nice. Put a cross up or something. He was a good bloke.'

'He was a stupid bastard,' Harkaway said unforgivingly. 'But for him, we'd have got Twinkletoes. Why in the name of God didn't he immobilize their vehicles? Puncture the tanks? Set 'em on fire? Let the tyres down? The bastards just climbed in and drove away. But for your bloody precious Gooch we'd have been staying here.'

Tully gave him a shocked look. '*Aren*'t we staying here?'

'I'm going after Guidotti.'

'Count me out.'

'I'll need a radio operator.'

Harkaway spoke coolly, quite indifferent to Tully's feelings. Tully glared. He knew he'd go with Harkaway but he said nothing and shuffled off to the radio truck.

'Those bloody people have got Fort San Rafaelo now,' the general said. 'Inside Abyssinia, Charlie. It's a pity we can't turn the buggers loose on the Germans in North Africa.'

Colonel Charlton placed a newspaper in front of him. 'Have you seen this, sir?' he asked. '*Cape Argus*. Flown up by the South African Air Force. Wye's given it the full treatment. I understand it's in all the papers back home, too, to say nothing of the Salisbury, Nairobi and Mombasa rags.'

ITALIAN DEFEATS IN EAST AFRICA, the headline read. ROUTED BY AMATEUR ARMY. WHO IS COLONEL HARKAWAY?

The story pulled no punches. It appeared that the Sixth Column was defeating the Italians on its own. There was a photograph of Harkaway, a snatched one by Russell, showing him with one arm raised, transposed on to a photograph of the Somalis so that he appeared to be giving them orders. There was another picture of a lorry-load of black soldiers armed with rifles and wearing a mixture of robes and British and Italian uniform, and finally one of the column of lean men on foot carrying spears followed by their women and animals.

The general put on his spectacles and began to read aloud.

After a while he lifted his eyes. 'These newspaper chaps certainly know how to put it across, don't they?' he said. He tapped the sheet. 'No mention of our people, I notice.'

It always irritated him when newspapermen picked out the spicy bits and forgot the orthodox soldiers without whose efforts no spare column could even exist.

'Inclined to exaggerate a bit, too, aren't they?' he went on. 'After all, they were hitting troops we'd already demoralized, and they've made no mention of the fact that the Italians had lost all air support because *we'd* destroyed it on the ground.'

'Even so – ' Charlton murmured.

The general looked up, then he nodded. 'Even so,' he agreed.

'There's an interview with a woman, too, sir,' Charlton went on. 'On the inside pages. Missionary by the name of Ortton-Daniells. South African called Grobelaar, too, it seems. The *Cape Argus* is making a lot of him, of course.'

'Could *they* tell us anything about this blasted Harkaway?'

'Thought of that, sir,' Charlton said. 'I got Intelligence to send someone to talk to them. They could tell him no more than appears in the paper.'

The general continued reading. 'I see he's still calling himself "colonel",' he growled.

Charlton smiled. 'Doubtless, when he comes under a proper command, he'll be happy to revert to major. For the moment, he probably considers it best to remain as he is. Question of face perhaps.'

As they talked a sergeant from Signals appeared with a flimsy.

The general scanned the message. 'It's from *him*, Charlie,' he said. 'He's asking our help. Nice of him to acknowledge that we exist. They've lost Guidotti and would like the air force to do a recce. Well, I think we can handle thatsk 'em to drop a few bombs, too, while they're at it. Whatever they can spare. Can we raise anything to send to them?'

'How about the Rajputs, sir? We have a company going spare. We can also manage a company of the Transvaal Scottish.'

'Right. Rustle 'em up. Give 'em a couple of armoured cars, a Signals section and a few Engineers, and send 'em off. Warn the air force not to drop bombs on 'em.' The general frowned. 'Strikes me,' he admitted, 'that it was a good job we gave this damned Harkaway some rank. At least we can now give him a decoration or something. We shall have to, of course. The feller's not only fought battles, he's organized 'em *and* raised his own troops. But we'll play it down. Don't like Irregulars getting all the kudos. After all, they're really only a flea-bite in the end, whether they're Lawrence of Arabia, Orde Wingate or this chap Harkaway. The real fighting's always done by ordinary troops and always was.'

The fort at Djuba was beginning to look tidy at last. The dead had all been buried – Gooch separately and with the benefit of a crude cross – and the bones of the horses killed in Pavicelli's desperate charge had been picked clean by vultures. Harkaway seemed indifferent and spent his time poring over captured maps.

'I want a small column forming, Sergeant,' he told Catchpole. 'We shall need a radio link set up here in the fort to keep contact with Jijiga and we shall be taking the armoured cars, all the lorries we can muster and three companies of the Boys. Can we raise that many?

'Just, sir. It'll not leave many here but, after all' – Catchpole paused, thinking of the slaughter – 'there won't be no trouble here now, will there?'

The column moved off the following day, a line of rolling, lurching trucks followed by the usual raggle-taggle column of men on foot. Everybody possessed a rifle now, however, because their numbers were smaller and they'd picked up large quantities at the fort.

Harkaway led in a scout car. It was a still, sultry day and ahead of them lay the naked plain, beyond it the hills, piling up in pyramids and domes, their hazy crests merging into a single range. Harkaway stared at them narrow-eyed. He had to get to Guidotti before he reached their shelter.

During the afternoon they found the body of an Eritrean soldier which had been hurriedly buried in a shallow grave and dug up again by hyenas, then that of an Italian sergeant who had wandered off into the bush, got lost and been left behind. His shirt and shorts were filled to bursting point and the skin of the tumid body inside was shining as it stretched tighter and tighter.

'Twinkletoes is losing control,' Harkaway observed.

Later, a South African Blenheim passed over them and as it disappeared they heard the thud of bombs ahead.

'They've found Guidotti,' Catchpole said.

They halted for the night at a waterhole. A nomad tribe was there with its flock of goats and sheep and they greeted Harkaway's column with grins and called Harkaway *Tillik Sau*, the Abyssinian words for Chief. He was beginning to feel better now. The near-disaster at Djuba was fading and his confidence was returning with a new certainty of his luck.

He summoned the herdsmen to the car and asked them if they'd seen the Italians. They had. The Italians were not far away, and the herdsmen confirmed Harkaway's suspicion that they were distressed and running out of petrol.

'We've got 'em,' Harkaway said.

'You said that before,' Tully reminded him flatly.

As they squatted by the fire, the radio began to cheep. Tully rose to his feet and crossed to the radio truck. A few minutes later he came back, a startled look on his face, a piece of paper in his hand.

'They've given you the bloody DSO,' he said. 'Immediate.'

Harkaway smiled. 'Now they'll *have* to confirm the commission,' he said. 'Even when they find I'm only a corporal. They commissioned me in the field and decorated me in the field.'

'That's all you bloody wanted, wasn't it?' Tully said bitterly. 'I notice there's nothing for me and Goochy.'

Harkaway smiled. 'I can recommend you,' he said. 'How about an MC? Nice purple and white ribbon on your chest. I'll write out a recommendation at once.'

'Do you know how to?'

'I've seen it done.'

Tully was immediately suspicious. 'Where?'

Harkaway gave one of his cold smiles and said nothing. Taking the message pad, he began to scribble. As he handed it back, Tully stared at it.

'It thanks them for the DSO,' Harkaway said cheerfully, 'claims it's an honour, and very modestly says that I feel that what we've done couldn't have been done without your help and that I would like to recommend you for the Military Cross.'

Tully looked awed and Harkaway smiled.

'I'll now write out the citation. It shouldn't take long.'

The general stared at the message with a frown.

'Good God,' he said, 'this bloody man's got a cheek! He's recommending chaps for gongs now.'

'He's done it correctly, sir,' Charlton pointed out. 'You'll notice that. Regrets the absence of Army Form W 2121 and hopes a signal flimsy will do as well. Everything's above board and as commanding officer he has every right to do it.'

'I suppose he has,' the general admitted. He frowned again. 'I wish we knew a bit more about the bloody man, though. I hope to God he isn't some pansy who was dismissed the service for interfering with boy entrants.'

Charlton smiled. 'At least, sir, he couldn't have been dismissed for cowardice.'

'I still don't like it,' the general mused. 'Even this name of his is too much of a good thing. I bet he's some relation of old Mac Tremayne. That family always had the nerve of the devil. Mac was your boss in the last lot, wasn't he? I suppose we couldn't get in touch with the family and ask 'em if they know anything about this one, could we?'

As they prepared to move off the following morning, Tully picked up the news that the Duke of Aosta, besieged in Amba Alagi, had sent envoys to Diredawa for a parley. It seemed to indicate he was seeking a way of throwing his hand in. Then there was a whole batch of other messages including one gem which announced to the East African army at large that hippopotamus could now be shot in the Atbara, a delight that was countermanded within the hour with 'For "Now" read "Not".'

'Italians can be killed,' Harkaway said dryly. 'But not big game. We're back with the army.'

Messages addressed directly to the Sixth Column indicated that the South African Air Force had spotted Guidotti two days before just to the north and bombed his column. Another informed them that the help and medical supplies they'd asked for were on their way. That didn't please Harkaway too much, because the column was under the command of a major of the Rajputs who would inevitably be senior to him.

His run of luck, he decided, had ended. From now on he'd have to conform. But with a DSO and a major's crown on his shoulder, he felt he could manage that. He might even admit who he was. There'd be a few quiet whistles at the information but there was a war on and people were inclined to overlook errors of behaviour in wartime. The last message confirmed that the recommendation for Tully's gong had been passed to the right quarters.

'If you never do another bloody thing,' Harkaway said, 'you can retire on it to Bognor Regis, with a better pension than you'd have got as a private soldier.'

During the day, the wind got up and filled the air with flying dust and peppered their skin like buckshot. It clung to their sweating skins, caking their lips and sticking to their nostrils and the corners of their eyes, and the vehicles filled with it so that it lay in the folds of their clothes and ended up as usual by giving them all paste-like masks that cracked in the wrinkles round their mouths as they spoke.

The wind held on until the sun went down, then it died suddenly and they camped in a strange calm, exhausted less by driving than by the wind and the flying grit. Making a circle of their vehicles, they built fires and the bully beef came out of the tins in a greasy rush.

Tully packed it away glumly. 'I'm getting bloody sick of this,' he said sullenly.

Harkaway said nothing, staring into the fire with faraway eyes.

'*You're* not, are you?' Tully said.

'No.' Harkaway spoke brusquely.

'You love it, don't you?'

'When it's over, my little friend,' Harkaway said in a harsh dry voice, 'we shall be part of the army again. There'll probably be some feller in charge who's never done anything more than sit at the end of a telephone line. Some little shit in starched shorts and shirt with a paintbox of colour on his chest who's never tasted the sand and the grit we've tasted. He'll tell you what to do and get away with it because, even if he's only that, he's senior to you. Have you thought of that?'

Tully muttered something but he didn't press the point.

Harkaway went on in a dreamy voice. 'I've enjoyed running my own show,' he said. 'They always say you enjoy independent command, even if you're only a lance-corporal. Well, I have and I'm not looking forward to going back to being told what to do. I'll probably join one of these funny outfits they're raising at home. Commandos, aren't they? I reckon I could do it, don't you?'

'Yes, you bastard,' Tully said sourly. 'I expect you could. Bloody well, too. I only hope I'm not with you.'

The following morning, an Ethiopian came in with the news that Guidotti and his little column had come to a stop by a waterhole twenty miles further on. They were almost out of petrol.

Harkaway called Catchpole to the fire.

'I'm going to scout forward, Sergeant,' he announced. 'I'll find out just where they are, then we'll move right round the bastards so they can't run again. There'll be no fight.'

'I hope you're right,' Tully said. 'I'm sick of fighting.'

Catchpole could read morse if it were sent slowly and they arranged for him to listen out for them, and organized a group of simple code words to indicate whether he was to stay where he was or follow in their tracks.

'Right,' Harkaway said. 'Get in, Tully.' He looked round for Abdillahi. 'You want to come too?'

Abdillahi grinned. 'In the name of Allah, the compassionate, the merciful, I am proud to, effendi.'

The wind had disappeared completely as they set off and the land lay dead and still like an exhausted tawny lion. There was a lot of scrub in front of them, cut up by lanes through which they could see the tracks of Italian lorries, and they moved slowly, bumping and rolling over the large stones, the scrub brushing against the sides of the vehicle.

They pushed forward another mile or so, and dropped down to a dried-out river bed. As they clattered across the stones, Harkaway's eyes were all round him. Abdillahi sat clutching his rifle in the rear seat and Tully dozed alongside Harkaway, stupefied by the pounding of the sun.

They were just grinding up the sandy bank at the opposite side, when the firing started. It came in a tremendous blast that wrecked the scout car and flung Abdillahi out of the back to sprawl in the sand, blood pumping from his chest. Flinging himself down, Harkaway crouched under the steering wheel, waiting for the firing to stop. When he lifted his head he saw Tully was still sitting upright in his seat, but his eyes were staring, his jaw had dropped, and the front of his khaki shirt was soaked with blood. He'd never, he thought, live to collect his medal, after all.

14

The men who appeared from the bush were Eritreans and Harkaway recognized them as belonging to a Gruppo Banda. They were dangerous enemies and as likely to murder him as take him prisoner.

An Italian sergeant appeared first, then other men, black men in scraps of uniform with lanyards and tassels of different colours. They came from all sides, their rifles pointed at Harkaway, and he climbed slowly from the car to the dry surface of the river bed, his hands high above his head.

It was only then that he realized he'd been wounded, probably by flying splinters, and blood was trickling down his arm. The men approached him warily as if they thought he'd make a fight of it. Keeping his revolver aimed at his head, the Italian slowly reached out to remove the weapon from his belt then, swinging his arm, crashed the heavy butt against Harkaway's face.

Harkaway knew at once that his nose was broken. Blood poured from his nostrils and over his mouth and he fell to his knees. Immediately, the others were on him, kicking him and hitting him with the butts of their rifles so that he could only crouch on the sand, trying to protect his head. The persistent feet kept coming and he could feel the rifle butts jabbing at his kidneys, but after a while, the Italian spoke and the hammering stopped and he was dragged upright. There was a cut over his eyes and his nose was still pouring blood over his shirt.

The sergeant walked round him slowly, speaking in Italian. Harkaway had no idea what he was saying, but the Italian seemed to think they'd worked him over enough because he drew a handkerchief from his pocket and offered it. Harkaway pointedly ignored it and took out his own, holding it to his forehead to mop the blood that persisted in running into his eye.

The other men were walking round the holed vehicle now, gazing with interest at the corpse of Abdillahi. Harkaway stared at the lean, sprawled black body, its hand still clutching its rifle, the tin coat of arms Grobelaar had cut still proudly on its wrist, and he swallowed hard. He felt more for the Somali, he realized, than he ever had for Tully or Gooch, because Abdillahi had never swerved in his loyalty, had never questioned his intentions.

One of the Eritreans picked up the dead man's rifle and kicked him in the face. Then the Italian walked across to Tully, who was still sitting in his seat, his head fallen forward, his jaw open, his eyes staring at his feet.

'*Capitano*,' the Italian said, touching the blackened tin stars on Tully's shoulders. He walked back to Harkaway and indicated the insignia on the shoulder straps of his shirt.

'*Colonello*?' he asked.

'Yes, you nasty little bastard,' Harkaway said.

The Italian was clearly worrying now that they had beaten up somebody important and Harkaway was signed to lower his hands. His arm was bandaged and another bandage was put round his forehead but his nose persisted in bleeding and his eye was now almost sealed up with the blood that was clotting on his eyelid. Nevertheless the Italian was also clearly concerned that he might escape and his hands were tied behind his back.

'*Avanti!*' Placing himself at the head of his men, the Italian sergeant began to march away, followed by Harkaway, then by his men, pushing Harkaway in front of them. They made no attempt to bury Tully or Abdillahi and no attempt to salvage the wrecked scout car. It was just left there in the glaring sun, with the long body of the Somali sprawled on the ground like a huge black spider, Tully still sitting upright in his seat.

Further in the bush, the Italian had donkeys and he and several of his men climbed aboard them. They made no attempt to offer one to Harkaway and he struggled along at the tail of the last of them, shoved whenever he missed his footing by one of the men marching behind. After an hour, he was sweating profusely and the dust the donkeys stirred up stuck to his skin like paste. He was stumbling now because the ground was rough and, with his hands bound, it was hard to keep his balance. Several times he fell but no one made any attempt to help him rise, merely kicking him until he struggled to his feet, watched by the Italian on the donkey. After three hours of it in the heat, he was weaving from side to side with exhaustion.

Eventually they came to a river. It was narrow and shallow and yellow with mud but, as they stumbled across, he fell on his face and was able to drink. Scrambling to his feet, dripping muddy water, he felt a little better. No one spoke to him and he stumbled on, his clothes drying rapidly in the sun.

He was quite certain now that he was going to be shot. He guessed his captors belonged to Guidotti's group and, considering what he'd done to them, he couldn't make out why they bothered to wait. Colonel bloody Harkaway, he thought bitterly. He was right back where he started, right down to nothing, lower even than that. Nobody cared about the insignia on his shoulder now and the Italian even seemed to enjoy his humiliation. Tully had been right. He'd enjoyed his little bit of power. He'd even pushed it too hard. He might have been wiser to have gone quietly back to the army, find Danny and lie low, doing as he was told, obeying orders, enjoying the kudos that would inevitably come to him as leader of the Sixth Column.

Soon afterwards, he saw the smoke of a fire. Men appeared from the bush and from starved-looking bivouacs that had been made by draping canvas from the sides of lorries. They looked shabby and tired as they came forward, curious to see the prisoner.

An officer with a bandaged hand appeared, studying him with interest, then he turned and shortly afterwards reappeared with another officer with a general's insignia and more than the usual number of buttons and braid on his tunic. Harkaway knew at once that it was Guidotti. At close quarters, he was younger than Harkaway had expected, and good-looking, though his face at that moment was haggard with worry and bleak with the absence of any future.

'*Come si chiamo?*' he asked.

Harkaway shrugged and the Italian spoke again in halting English.

'What is your name?'

For a moment, Harkaway wondered whether to give a false name then he thought, no, be damned to that. He was proud of what he'd done, even if they knocked hell out of him.

'Harkaway,' he said.

The Italian general turned to the officer with the wounded hand and nodded. 'So,' he said. 'Finally, *Colonello* Harkaway, we meet. I am General Guidotti.'

'Thought so,' Harkaway said.

Guidotti gestured to the sergeant and Harkaway's hands were freed.

'You have been wounded?'

'Your bloody soldiers beat me up.'

Guidotti spread his hands. 'I must apologize,' he said. 'They are frightened men these days. You have made them frightened. They are *nervoso* – nervous? Is that the word? I regret I do not speak English good.'

'You're doing all right.'

Guidotti turned to the bandaged officer. 'Piccio, find water. And perhaps there is some brandy left.'

The other officer vanished and returned with water and a bottle of brandy. Harkaway took a swig from the water bottle, then let the brandy run down his throat. It seemed to set him on fire but he felt better at once and they started to talk in a mixture of Italian and English, haltingly at first, then faster and more confidently.

'I thought I was about to become *your* prisoner,' Guidotti said. 'Instead you have become *mine*.'

'Luck of the draw,' Harkaway said.

'*Com'è triste la vita!*'

They talked for a while about what had happened at

Djuba and Guidotti seemed to feel that somehow Harkaway had cheated. But when he explained anything was allowed in love and war, Guidotti agreed and led him to his tent and sent for food. It was only a paste of white beans from a tin but there was an army biscuit with it and a tin mug of wine.

'Chianti,' Guidotti said. 'Italians make sure they have their wine.'

As they talked, Harkaway began to wonder why he had hated this man so much. Guidotti was not a bit like the pompous bullfrog he'd expected, but was quiet-voiced, compassionate and concerned for his hurts. For God's sake, Harkaway thought disgustedly, he was finding he even liked the little bugger.

After he'd eaten, a doctor bathed his injuries, talking softly all the time in Italian. When he left, another man arrived who said he was a padre. 'Father Vaccetti,' he introduced himself. 'I am a Catholic priest, of course, and you will be a Protestant, no doubt.'

'I'm not much of anything,' Harkaway admitted. 'What are they going to do with me?'

Vaccetti shrugged. 'I don't know, my son. There is little they *can* do. Our men have melted away and we are almost at the end of our tether. Until yesterday we seemed to have a chance, but then your planes found us and bombed us. They killed seven and wounded over twenty. Unfortunately, they also hit our petrol lorry and now we are almost out of fuel. We also have many wounded from Djuba and the fighting we have had on the way here. The Abyssinians would not leave us alone.'

During the evening, more Italians straggled in. Several of them were wounded. They had lost touch with the rest of the column and, when their lorry had run out of petrol, had started walking without really knowing which way to go. There was a lot of muttering that was over Harkaway's head, then in the evening the officer Guidotti had addressed as Piccio appeared, and led Harkaway to one of the lorries.

'There are blankets inside,' he said. 'But I'm afraid you will be well guarded, so it's pointless trying to escape.'

When he'd gone, Harkaway loosened the canvas to peer

round him. Banda men were sitting all round the lorry and, having no fancy for another beating up, he crept back to the blankets and tried to decide what to do. But the day had taken its toll and the next thing he knew was that it was daylight and he could hear voices outside.

As he was released, he heard aircraft overhead and the Italians started scattering into the bush. He was about to follow them and take his chance but Piccio appeared with a revolver in his hand and ordered him to accompany him.

The aircraft, three Blenheims, circled overhead before dropping their bombs. The whistle of them coming down sent everybody flat on their faces, then with the crash of the explosions, showers of sand and grit and small stones were thrown up. As they disappeared, they left two of the lorries burning, sending up huge columns of black smoke slanting into the brassy sky. No one appeared to have been hurt but the Italians seemed more depressed than ever. Guidotti was in tears and seemed to be indicating there was little hope left.

'*Sono all' ultimo espediente,*' he was saying. '*A che scopo?*'

While Harkaway watched, Piccio came towards him with the brandy bottle. It was almost empty, he noticed, and he guessed they'd both been at it during the night.

'What's going on?' he asked.

'This is a very sad moment for us,' Piccio said. 'Somehow, today, we must make up our minds. Even if we put all the petrol together there is not enough to take us all into the hills. Once there, we might have been able to reach friends, but now *some* will have to stay behind. It would be pointless taking the wounded. They can do no good. We could leave them here and send a message to your army to pick them up, but they are terrified the Ethiopians will slit their throats. I have suggested that surrender would make sense.'

'Sometimes it does.' Harkaway agreed.

Piccio was looking sideways at him. 'We would need to send a man with a white flag,' he said. 'We would need an emissary.'

The hint was clear and Harkaway's heart leapt. 'What's wrong with me?' he said.

Piccio studied him. 'We have just heard that a second column has joined your men,' he said. 'We expect them to be up with us by tomorrow night or the following morning at the latest. There's little hope for us and it's hard to sacrifice more lives. Do you have any influence with your general?'

'Yes,' Harkaway lied. 'He listens to me a lot.'

'Perhaps I can arrange for you to be sent back to speak for us.'

'I've got a better idea,' Harkaway said. 'Why not let me take you prisoner?'

'Me?'

Harkaway was pushing his luck again, he knew, but the Italians were in a distressed condition, with sick and wounded on their hands, short of food and with no means of transporting themselves to safety.

'Not just you,' he said. 'The lot of you.'

Piccio stared at him for a while, then he turned abruptly on his heel and marched away to Guidotti. Harkaway thought he'd insulted him and that he'd cut the discussion short out of pique, but after a while Guidotti came back with him.

'Colonel Piccio has told me what you said,' he pointed out.

'I can do it.'

'It would be humiliating.'

'It's better than being dead.'

Guidotti nodded thoughtfully and Harkaway went on. 'You'll all be prisoners before long, anyway. Even the Duke of Aosta. He's asking for surrender terms.'

He had no idea what the Duke of Aosta had asked for, but he knew he couldn't be far out in his estimate.

'You have heard this?' Guidotti asked.

'On the radio. The night before your people brought me in.'

Guidotti turned away with Piccio and they spoke in low tones for a while. Eventually they turned back to Harkaway.

'It must be done with honour,' Guidotti said.

'It can be,' Harkaway agreed. 'Your chaps can march out of here with their rifles on their shoulders. Me leading.'

'Aren't you afraid one of us will shoot you in the back?'

Harkaway looked round at the men watching them. They were standing in groups, some without weapons. Their clothes were dirty, stained and torn, and half of them wore bloodstained bandages. Their expressions were bewildered and defeated.

'No,' he said. 'I'm not afraid.'

Guidotti was silent for a while, clapping his hands together in a distracted way. 'I am a general, Colonel Harkaway,' he said eventually. 'Colonel Piccio points out that I'm entitled to an escort of high rank.'

Harkaway almost burst out laughing. The poor little bugger had nothing to recommend his future, yet he was haggling about a guard of honour. Still, it was little enough to ask.

'How high?' he asked.

'Higher than lieutenant-colonel.'

Harkaway considered for a while then he gestured. 'I come from a very distinguished English family,' he pointed out.

Guidotti thought about this for a while then he nodded, satisfied. 'There should also be a guard of honour,' he pointed out.

Harkaway shrugged. 'I expect it could be arranged,' he said. 'We'd have to send a message, though. In clear.'

'It's signed "Harkaway"!' Charlton said.

'Now what's he want?' the general asked.

'I'd better read it: "Have Guidotti. Requests guard of honour. On receipt your confirmation will bring him in." '

The general looked at Charlton, his mouth open. 'Good God,' he said. 'What's he done? Talked him into it?'

Charlton smiled. 'It begins to look like it.' His smile widened. 'You know, sir, I'm beginning to like this Harkaway. Whoever he is, he has a cool cheek that appeals to me. Do we confirm it?'

'Where is he?'

'The Sixth Column's at a waterhole at Upi. But the message came in clear from the Italians, signed by Harkaway and marked for your perusal. He must be in the bush with Guidotti.'

'And where's *he?*'

'The Rajputs say he's about twenty miles ahead of them somewhere.'

'Have the air force spotted them?'

'They have, sir. They want to know if they're to bomb again.'

'Not if Harkaway can bring them in without. Very well, Charlie. Give the bloody man his guard of honour. Tell the Rajputs to provide it.'

'There's a party of Transvaal Scottish there, sir. They want to know if they can play 'em in with the pipes.'

The general's face creased up in a grin. 'By all means. If Harkaway hasn't frightened 'em to death, the agony bags ought to.'

When the message came, it was addressed to Lieutenant-Colonel G. Harkaway, DSO. The general was not inclined to quibble about rank if it brought in another batch of Italians.

Harkaway read it. 'It confirms,' he said, 'that there will be a guard of honour. *And music.*'

Guidotti and Piccio asked to see the message then, holding it in their hands, they conferred in low tones. Eventually Guidotti turned to Harkaway again, his body stiffening.

'I am your prisoner, Colonel,' he said. 'In the words of Pagliacci, *la commedia è finita.* Do you like opera?'

Harkaway stared at him, still not sure whether to laugh or not. The poor little sod was over-acting like mad, yet it was difficult not to be sorry for him.

'Not so's you'd notice,' he admitted.

Guidotti nodded and gave a twisted smile that was full of pain. 'We will follow you into the British lines. I presume your men are in position.'

'Yes,' Harkaway said airily. 'They're in position.'

'There must be many of them.'

Harkaway stiffened. He was getting control of the situation again. 'Oh, yes! Quite a lot!'

'What petrol have we?' Guidotti asked.

Piccio shrugged. 'Barely enough to carry the wounded.'

'Have it siphoned out,' Harkaway said, 'and put into as many vehicles as will be needed for the worst of the wounded. The rest must stay behind to be collected tomorrow. They will be allowed their weapons to protect themselves.'

By the middle of the day they were ready. In his humiliation, Guidotti had tried to break his sword across his knee, but that splendid weapon he had received in the great days of Mussolini was so good he could do no more than bend it and he threw it away into the bush in disgust.

'We shall need a white flag,' Harkaway said, and a sheet was produced and attached to the lopped-off bough of a tree.

The men who were to accompany them waited quietly, their uniforms brushed, their buttons polished, holding their rifles. Harkaway looked about him. He had insisted on shaving with a borrowed razor and somehow, with the last of the water, the Italians had managed to wash and press his shorts and shirt. Of the lot of them he was the only one with any semblance of dignity.

'Well,' he said. 'What about me? I'm not walking.'

'You wish to ride in the truck?' Piccio asked.

Harkaway looked down his nose at him. 'I'm leading,' he said. 'I go on my own.'

Piccio, like Guidotti in full dress uniform, looked puzzled and Harkaway gestured angrily.

'You've got donkeys,' he said.

A donkey was brought forward and Piccio handed Harkaway his webbing belt and revolver which he strapped round his waist without speaking. Then Piccio handed him his cap – Watson's cap – and he placed it on his head over the bandage.

'Right,' he said. 'Let's have your escort in three lines.'

The sergeants got the men into lines, watched by the anguished Guidotti. When they were ready, Harkaway studied them, then slowly strode up and down the lines, staring into the haggard, bearded faces, inspecting them as if he, not Guidotti, were their commanding officer, tugging at a belt here, jerking at a tunic there.

'Right,' he said to Piccio. 'Let's have them at attention.'

Piccio shouted a command and the tired men shuffled to stiffness.

'Not like that!' Harkaway roared, beginning to enjoy himself again. 'Do it again! Make 'em jump to it!'

Piccio flushed and put the men at ease, then repeated his order. This time they were smarter but Harkaway still wasn't satisfied.

'Again! They're going to march out of here like soldiers. Tell them if they've got any pride left, they'll hold their heads up. I have a reputation to keep up and, until it's done properly, we don't move.'

Piccio swallowed, then, standing in front of his men, he made a little speech that Harkaway didn't understand. But the weary men stiffened gradually, and when Piccio shouted they slammed to attention like soldiers.

'That's better,' Harkaway said. 'Tell 'em to slope arms!'

Their rifles on their shoulders, the Italians waited as Harkaway studied them. 'Let's have no slouching,' he said to Piccio. 'They're going to surrender like soldiers. If they don't, I'll do nothing to help.'

Piccio made another little speech and the men listened to him silently, dark haggard eyes on Harkaway.

'Right!' Cocking one leg over the donkey, Harkaway took a final look about him, then he raised his arm and pointed.

'Forward!'

The major commanding the Rajputs and the captain of the Transvaal Scottish were still trying to make up their minds what they were supposed to do when someone shouted. One of the Rajputs was pointing. In the distance they could see a cloud of dust approaching. As they gave orders, the lorries dispersed, then the two officers climbed on to a cabin roof and studied the cloud of dust with binoculars.

'They're coming in, man,' the South African said excitedly. 'Led by a feller on a moke.'

Climbing down, they deployed their men, and for safety magazines were clamped into place on Bren guns. The armoured cars swung round to make a deadly circle, their weapons pointing along the dusty track.

'Where's the guard of honour?'

Rajputs began to double up and fall in, facing the road, blank-faced, stiff as ramrods, heads up, rifles at their sides. At an order, they crashed to attention.

The approaching Italians came forward steadily, left-right, left-right, making no attempt to deploy or get into battle formation.

'The buggers really *are* surrendering,' Catchpole said in an awed voice.

'Pipes!'

With the drone of chanters, the pipers of the Transvaal Scottish hitched at their instruments and the wailing started. The Italians were not used to Highland music and the march became a straggle. Then the man on the donkey at the front, pale, feverish-looking and bandaged, raised his arm and the group halted.

'We'll do without the pipes,' he said.

Guidotti was staring about him. 'Are these your men?' he asked Harkaway.

'Yes.'

'Where are the rest?'

'In position.' Harkaway's hand gestured vaguely.

Guidotti suddenly remembered something he'd said of the British in the Western Desert: despite their small numbers, they had had as many men as they had persuaded their enemies they had. With the memory came an uneasy feeling that he had been fooled, but it was too late now and suddenly he didn't care very much any more.

Harkaway mounted the donkey again. 'Right,' he said. 'Get 'em going, Piccio.'

The Italians set off once more, marching better than the Rajput major had ever seen Italians march before. In front of them, Harkaway rode the small white donkey.

'Guard – !'

As the guard of honour slammed to the 'Present,' the Rajput major climbed down from the lorry and walked forward. As he appeared, Harkaway held up his hand and reined in the donkey. Behind him, Piccio yelled a command and the Italians came to a smart halt and stood swaying with exhaustion, their bearded faces dripping with sweat, their eyes dark pools under the brims of their helmets.

The Rajput major crashed to a halt and saluted. Harkaway solemnly dismounted and returned it. Other officers stepped out of the bush and moved forward, then the NCOs, and finally the men began to appear, all staring at the bunch of ghosts who waited at attention a few yards away.

Harkaway introduced himself and the Rajput major smiled.

'You're supposed to be missing,' he said.

'Well, now I'm not,' Harkaway said. 'I've got your prisoners for you. And there are about three hundred more back there if you can be bothered to collect them.'

15

'I couldn't believe my bloody eyes,' the Rajput major was saying. 'He had the buggers marching towards us, left-right left-right, rifles on their shoulders, picking up their feet and swinging their arms, as if they were about to mount guard at St James'.'

'They didn't need us after all,' he went on. 'He was bringing them in on his own.' He paused, his expression awed. 'One man. On a donkey. I've never seen anything like it: Guidotti, what was left of his staff, and a squad of men marching with their heads up and looking like Guardsmen. No wonder he made something of the Somalis. He had a nerve.'

Yes, he had, Charlton thought. But then the Tremaynes all had nerve. They'd found out at last who Harkaway was and Charlton now understood the force that had driven him on. Signals had flown back and forth and information had finally turned up. Asked to leave the army for pinching a fellow officer's car and driving it without insurance! Police court proceedings. A dud cheque. Family pleas to avoid cashiering. Charlton sighed. Perhaps there had been more to it than that, but perhaps also it had been no more than a boyish prank. Perhaps the owner of the car had disliked him. The Tremaynes were an arrogant bunch and never popular, despite their ability, but there was a suggestion of vindictiveness and envy about it all the same that he didn't like.

While he was still brooding, unaware of what the Rajput major was saying, a commandeered Italian staff car braked to a stop and three or four newspapermen jumped out. Among them were Wye and Russell.

'I hear Harkaway's brought in Twinkletoes,' Wye said.

'That's not how he's known to us,' Charlton said mildly. 'But if you mean General Guidotti, yes, he has.'

'Where is he?'

Charlton gestured. 'You'll find him down the road there. You'll see a horde of black men holding rifles and clutching blankets. I'm sure you'll recognize them as the Sixth Column.'

Wye gestured at the other newspapermen and, as they scrambled back into the car, it hurtled off with a shriek of rubber.

'Can't think why they can never leave without tearing the tyres to shreds,' the Rajput officer said.

Charlton smiled. 'Tradition,' he said. 'You must have seen those James Cagney–Humphrey Bogart pictures.'

Harkaway had been provided with a tent, a table, a waste-paper basket, a camp bed and various other items of equipment. For half of them he couldn't think of a use. So far nobody had told him to take away the pip he wore beneath the crown Danny had embroidered and he had no intention of doing so until he was ordered to.

He was struggling with papers. Some idiot had dumped a whole pile of stores forms on him and he was expected to sort them out and send them back, filled in with requisitions. He stared at them for a moment, then he picked up the whole pile and tossed them into the waste-paper basket. At least he'd discovered what *that* was for.

He was just lighting a cigarette when a shadow fell across the door and a face appeared.

'Wye, Colonel,' the newcomer said. 'You'll remember me from Bidiyu. Russell's here and we've got a couple of other chaps. *Express* and *Daily Mail*. Perhaps we could talk to you for a while.'

Harkaway stared at him coldly. 'Not allowed to,' he said stiffly. 'Back with the real army now. Have to do as

I'm told. Anything you want you'll have to get from the general's press officer.'

Wye frowned. 'We thought it would be all right.'

'Well, it isn't. Nothing I can do about it.' Harkaway wasn't taking any chances. He was doing what he'd wanted all his life to do – command soldiers – what his whole background and his whole nature had designed him to do. The fact that they were black and wore little in the way of uniform didn't matter. People were taking notice of him again and he intended to keep it that way. From now on, he wasn't going to put a foot wrong. From now on, he was only going upwards to where he belonged – at the top.

Russell looked disappointed. 'What about the others, Colonel? Captain Tully and Lieutenant Gooch. Where are they?'

Harkaway looked up. 'Lieutenant Gooch was killed when we took Fort San Rafaelo,' he said shortly. 'Captain Tully, who I might add, had been recommended for the MC, was killed in an ambush near Upi.'

'How did that happen?' Russell asked.

'As I've told you,' Harkaway said. 'He was caught in an ambush.' He had no intention of saying too much. He'd learned from his father and his grandfather the art of letting your great deeds speak for themselves and your mistakes go unrecorded.

Wye tried to pump him but he refused to be drawn and in the end the newspaperman shrugged.

'Oh, well, how about a photograph, Colonel?'

'Have you permission from the press officer?'

'Well, no.'

'Then, sorry.'

Russell lifted his camera. 'Couldn't we just – ?'

'No, you couldn't,' Harkaway snapped. 'And if you use that thing, I'll have my chaps arrest you and destroy your film. So you'd better not. They can be rough.'

Russell lowered the camera and looked at Wye. Wye backed out of the tent.

'Christ, he's changed a bit,' he muttered. 'Talk about the Old Guard. Somebody's stuffed a ramrod up his arse. Or else he's had a rocket from the general.' He paused. He, too, had finally discovered who Harkaway was and he'd also heard the stories going round the camp. Harkaway was obviously expecting to be taken back into the fold – if not forgiven, at least forgotten. But, as Wye knew, the army had a long memory. Having once sacked him, they didn't intend to have him back. He'd keep his rank, but he'd go no higher and when the war was over, he'd be out on his ear. He wasn't surprised. An indifferent polite officer often went further than a good rude one.

He looked at Russell. 'Hang on,' he said. 'There's something else.'

Harkaway looked up as he re-entered the tent.

'I've a message for you, Colonel,' Wye said. 'Almost forgot it. I got it from Miss Ortton-Daniells in Bidiyu.'

Harkaway looked interested for the first time. He'd thought more of Danny than he'd ever dared show. Ambition had had to come first, but he'd never intended to let her slip through his fingers and it was time now to put things right between them.

Wye was leafing through his notebook. 'I wrote it down,' he said. 'She seemed anxious you should get it just as she said it. Ah!' He flicked a page. 'Here it is. "Tell Colonel Harkaway," she said, "that I'm going to South Africa. Tell him that Kom-Kom – " ' Russell looked up. 'Have I got that right, Colonel?'

'Yes. You've got it right.'

' "Tell Colonel Harkaway that I'm going to South Africa. Tell him that Kom-Kom has asked me to marry him and that I'm going to, because Kom-Kom isn't an ambitious man and he knows how to be kind." '

Harkaway was sitting rigidly at the table. His expression had become stiff and bleak. Wye studied him for a moment.

'You got that, Colonel?'

'Yes, I've got it.'

'Make sense?'

'Yes,' Harkaway said. 'It makes sense.'

'Wouldn't be a story in it, would there? Personal story,

for instance. Concerning Miss Ortton-Daniells and this Kom-Kom. Something that has nothing to do with the army.'

Harkaway rose and lit a cigarette. 'No,' he said carefully. 'I shouldn't think so. I shouldn't think it would be worth your while.'

COTTON'S WAR

John Harris

If it hadn't been for the shopkeeper in Heraklion, Cotton might never have been involved . . .

In the spring of 1941 the Nazis were storming their way through Greece. The *Loukia* was crucial to the British cause and the Greek resistance – and her cargo even more so. When the *Loukia* is wrecked in enemy territory, the British gathered together a handful of 'volunteers' for a dangerous mission of retrieval: two RASC men, some sailors, one German-speaking airman and Mihale Andoni Cotonou – otherwise known as Corporal Cotton of the Marines.

A superb story of action and character, *Cotton's War* is one of John Harris's most exciting war novels.

John Harris

John Harris is one of Britain's best known and most prolific writers of war fiction and his following titles are available from Arrow. You can by them from your local bookshop or newsagent, or you can order them direct through the post. Just tick the titles you require and complete the form below.

☐	ARMY OF SHADOWS	£1.50
☐	COTTON'S WAR	£1.60
☐	THE FOX FROM HIS LAIR	£1.50
☐	HARKAWAY'S SIXTH COLUMN	£1.95
☐	LIVE FREE OR DIE	£1.60
☐	NORTH STRIKE	£1.50
☐	RIDE OUT THE STORM	£1.25
☐	SWORDPOINT	£1.50
☐	THE SEA SHALL NOT HAVE THEM	£1.95
☐	TAKE OR DESTROY	£1.50

And as Max Hennessy

☐	BLUNTED LANCE	£1.95

Postage ____

Total ____

ARROW BOOKS, BOOKSERVICE BY POST, PO BOX 29, DOUGLAS, ISLE OF MAN, BRITISH ISLES

Please enclose a cheque or postal order made out to Arrow Books Limited for the amount due including 15p per book for postage and packing for orders both within the UK and overseas.

Please print clearly

NAME ....

ADDRESS ....

....

Whilst every effort is made to keep prices down and to keep popular books in print, Arrow Books cannot guarantee that prices will be the same as those advertised here or that the books will be available.